THE FINAL ADVERSARY

THE FINAL ADVERSARY

GILBERT MORRIS

BETHANY HOUSE PUBLISHERS
MINNEAPOLIS, MINNESOTA 55438

Cover by Brett Longley,
Bethany House Publishers staff artist.

Published by Bethany House Publishers
A Ministry of Bethany Fellowship, Inc.
6820 Auto Club Road, Minneapolis, Minnesota 55438

Printed in the United States of America

Library of Congress Cataloging-in-Publication Data

Morris, Gilbert.
   The final adversary / Gilbert Morris.
       p.   cm. — (The House of Winslow ; bk. 12)
    I. Title. II. Series: Morris, Gilbert. House of Winslow ; bk. 12.
PS3563.08742F55   1992
813'.54—dc20   92–16172
ISBN 1–55661–261–3 (pbk.)   CIP

This book is dedicated
to my son-in-law,
Dr. Ron Smith.
I could not have given
my daughter
to a better man.

GILBERT MORRIS spent ten years as a pastor before becoming Professor of English at Ouachita Baptist University in Arkansas and earning a Ph.D. at the University of Arkansas. During the summers of 1984 and 1985 he did postgraduate work at the University of London and is presently the Chairman of General Education at a Christian college in Louisiana. A prolific writer, he has had over 25 scholarly articles and 200 poems published in various periodicals, and over the past years has had more than 20 novels published. His family includes three grown children, and he and his wife live in Baton Rouge, Louisiana.

CONTENTS

PART FOUR
The Overcomers

THE HOUSE OF WINSLOW

★ ★ ★ ★

THE
HOUSE OF WINSLOW

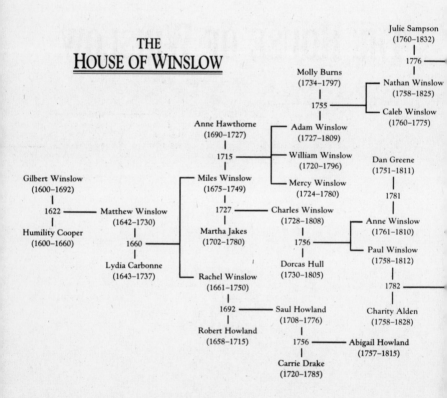

Julie Sampson
(1760–1832)

1776

Nathan Winslow
(1758–1825)

Caleb Winslow
(1760–1775)

Molly Burns
(1734–1797)

1755

Adam Winslow
(1727–1809)

Anne Hawthorne
(1690–1727)

1715

William Winslow
(1720–1796)

Mercy Winslow
(1724–1780)

Dan Greene
(1751–1811)

1781

Anne Winslow
(1761–1810)

Paul Winslow
(1758–1812)

1782

Charity Alden
(1758–1828)

Miles Winslow
(1675–1749)

Gilbert Winslow
(1600–1692)

1622

Humility Cooper
(1600–1660)

Matthew Winslow
(1642–1730)

1660

Lydia Carbonne
(1643–1737)

1727

Charles Winslow
(1728–1808)

1756

Dorcas Hull
(1730–1805)

Martha Jakes
(1702–1780)

Rachel Winslow
(1661–1750)

1692

Robert Howland
(1658–1715)

Saul Howland
(1708–1776)

1756

Carrie Drake
(1720–1785)

Abigail Howland
(1757–1815)

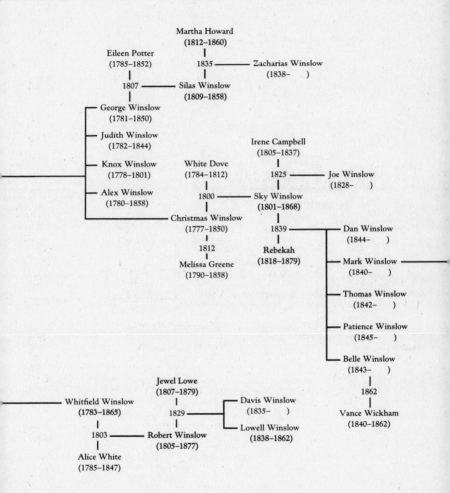

Martha Howard
(1812–1860)
|
1835 ———— Zacharias Winslow
| (1838–   )
Eileen Potter
(1785–1852)
|
1807 ———— Silas Winslow
| (1809–1858)
┌ George Winslow
│ (1781–1850)
│
├ Judith Winslow
│ (1782–1844)
│
├ Knox Winslow
│ (1778–1801)
│
├ Alex Winslow
│ (1780–1858)
│
│   White Dove
│   (1784–1812)
│ |
│   1800 ———— Sky Winslow
│   (1801–1868)
└ Christmas Winslow
  (1777–1850)
  |
  1812
  |
  Melissa Greene
  (1790–1858)

Irene Campbell
(1805–1837)
|
1825 ———— Joe Winslow
| (1828–   )

1839 ————┬ Dan Winslow
| │ (1844–   )
Rebekah │
(1818–1879) ├ Mark Winslow
         │ (1840–   )
         │
         ├ Thomas Winslow
         │ (1842–   )
         │
         ├ Patience Winslow
         │ (1845–   )
         │
         └ Belle Winslow
           (1843–   )
           |
           1862
           |
           Vance Wickham
           (1840–1862)

Jewel Lowe
(1807–1879)
|
1829 ————┬ Davis Winslow
| │ (1835–   )
Robert Winslow │
(1805–1877) └ Lowell Winslow
           (1838–1862)
Whitfield Winslow
(1783–1865)
|
1803 ———— Robert Winslow
|
Alice White
(1785–1847)

THE
HOUSE OF WINSLOW

(continued)

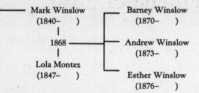

Mark Winslow
(1840–   )

1868 ————

Lola Montez
(1847–   )

Barney Winslow
(1870–   )

Andrew Winslow
(1873–   )

Esther Winslow
(1876–   )

PART ONE

THE PRODIGAL

★ ★ ★ ★

January 1894–September 1896

CHAPTER ONE

A NECESSARY TRIP

★ ★ ★ ★

Two days into the year of 1894, dark, angry clouds gathered over the city of New York. The temperature plummeted, transforming particles of moisture into crystal flakes that stung the eyes of pedestrians scurrying along the streets, seeking shelter from the blizzard they knew would follow. By four in the afternoon large snowflakes began to fall heavily.

"Oh, Tony!" Katie Sullivan exclaimed. "It's like a fairyland!"

Tony Barone shifted his eyes from the paper he was reading to Katie, a smile creasing his face. A handsome man of thirty, with sleek dark hair and lidded black eyes, Tony considered himself an expert in two things: gambling and women. He congratulated himself on his decision to hire the girl. Yes, she was a pleasing sight—tumbling blond hair, sparkling blue eyes, flawless complexion, and shapely figure.

Getting up from the table, he walked over and slid his arm around her. She stiffened at his touch. Amused at her reaction, he thought, *Like a wild rabbit, ready to run for a hole at the first sign of trouble.* Tony dropped his arm and felt her relax. "Yeah, sure is pretty, Katie." He smiled, then lifted her hand, squeezing it gently. "May keep a few of your fans home, though," he laughed. "You're bringing them in, honey—just like I said you would. Ought to make you trust old Tony a little bit more."

Katie's face grew warm at his nearness and the bold look in his eyes. She withdrew her hand and said, "I—I do trust you, Tony."

"That's good. You go over the new number with Nick and the boys?"

"Oh yes! It's kind of a silly song—not too hard. But . . . I think Sally is—"

"Sally's a little jealous?" he asked, catching her hesitation.

She nodded.

"Sure she is, Katie. That's show business. Folks want to see youth, and Sally's been around a long time. I'll have a word with her. Now you—you're going to have to get a little tougher. You're on your way up, and when you have to pass people, some won't like it. I've told you this, remember?"

Katie nodded. "I know, but Sally was so nice to me when I first came. I hate to—to go above her."

Barone stared at her. He had been a denizen of the dog-eat-dog world of show business so long, he had forgotten that gentleness such as Katie Sullivan possessed even existed. Six weeks earlier he had spotted the young woman coming out of a sooty factory, her clothes worn and bulky, yet revealing a nice figure. With a little help, he decided, she could be beautiful.

Getting her to work at his music hall, the Gay Paree, was another matter. Katie was not easily persuaded, in spite of the hard times. It wasn't that Tony had difficulty finding girls; in fact, they came begging for a chance to work—even as a waitress, which soon led to drinking with the customers and then slipping into a lower life. But Katie was different, and her unspoiled beauty sparked Barone's womanizing bent for control.

Katie had refused Tony's first job offer. "I couldn't work in a music hall, Mr. Barone," she said with a smile and left him standing in the street, his eyes wide with astonishment.

"Never got chopped down like that, did you, Tony?" said Studs Ketchel, the huge ex-boxer, who had been with Tony. "Wait'll I tell the guys! Tony Barone—axed by a country girl!" he added, roaring with laughter at the expression on Barone's face.

"I'll get her, Studs," he had retorted. "It's just a matter of knowing how."

Stalking the girl became an obsession with him, and he en-

listed one of his waitresses to ferret out all she could about Katie.
"She's a country girl, Mr. Barone," she reported. "Just come in
from upstate—right off the farm. All she does is work and go
for walks—mostly in Central Park on Sunday afternoons. Don't
have no men friends. One of her girl friends told me her old
man's dead and she sends almost every dime she makes back to
her ma. You want I should find out more?"

That was enough for Tony, and the next Sunday he went for
a walk in the park. There she was. "Why, it's you . . . I've forgotten your name?" he said, joining her.

Two weeks later—after one more Sunday stroll and supper
at a nice cafe—she agreed to go with him to the Gay Paree. Never
having seen the inside of a music hall before, she had been appalled at the girls' scanty costumes and the loose talk among
them. Her shocked reaction amused him. *Better keep her isolated
from the worst*, he had decided, though it had been a relatively
quiet night—no fights or trouble with the customers. But the
next Saturday afternoon, after lunch, he had brought her again.
When she heard the number Nick and the band were practicing,
she said, "Oh, I know *that* one!"

"Sing it, Katie," Tony had urged, and was surprised at the
clear quality of her voice. He had left her with Nick, and two
hours later they were still singing. Nick had commented pri-
vately before the couple left, "Tony, most of the gals you drag in
here screech like a crow. This kid has got a *great* voice. Do yourself a favor and hire her!"

Now as Katie and Tony stood at the window watching the
snow fall, he said, "You've come a long way in a short time,
honey." He smiled and put his hand on her arm lightly. "Remember how scared you were when you first came?"

"I remember."

"You were jumpy as a deer," he mused. "Afraid of your
shadow—and you were absolutely *sure* I was going to make love
to you."

Katie flushed, the rich color of her cheeks glowing under the
yellow light of the lantern. "Yes, I was." She smiled up at him.
"I was wrong, wasn't I?"

Barone moved slightly closer and lowered his voice. "Don't
bet on it, Katie. A beautiful woman like you—a man would have

to be a stone statue not to fall in love with you." Her eyes opened wide and he suddenly bent and kissed her, then stepped back. If she'd been any other woman, he would have pressed his luck, but not with this one. *She's like a ripe fruit, ready to drop*, he thought. *But I've got to be easy—real easy or she'll bolt and run*.

"You're sweet, Katie," he said quietly, not touching her. "I guess I've seen so many hard girls I've forgotten what a real woman could be like." He saw that she was flustered, so quickly changed the subject. "Got a treat for you after the show."

"What is it, Tony?"

"Sally's boyfriend's fighting over at the arena. Studs got two tickets, but he can't make it. We'll go see it, then take Sally and the pug out for a late supper."

"I've never seen a boxing match," Katie hesitated. "Isn't it kind of gruesome?"

"These are professionals. We'll just watch." He smiled, adding, "We'll leave early if you don't like it, honey."

★ ★ ★ ★

Andrew Winslow glanced up from the breakfast table and noted the heavy clouds through the bay window. "Dad, I don't like the looks of that sky. We may be snowed in for a few days when we get to the city."

"All the more reason for staying home." Mark Winslow at the age of fifty-three was only five pounds heavier than he had been twenty years earlier, and just as handsome and fit now as he was then. At that time he had worked under Samuel Reed as his assistant superintendent of construction, but his real job had been trouble—whipping any of the thousands of track hands or gamblers who interfered with the building of the Union Pacific Railroad from Omaha to Promontory, Utah.

Mark Winslow walked to the window and looked out, a frown on his face. "I still don't like the idea, Andy. I know you think it's something we need to do, but it could make things worse."

"Dear, we've been over that," Lola interrupted.

As always, Mark listened carefully when his wife spoke. He was proud of her, and his eyes glowed with the warmth of his love. She was so lovely—even in her plain attire. Unlike the ridiculous fashions of the day, she wore a dark green dress with simple lines. Still, she looked much as she had at eighteen. Her dark hair and smooth olive skin, inherited from her Mexican mother, had changed little. From her Irish father she had the legacy of blue eyes and delicate features.

She continued. "We haven't heard from Barney in two years. What could make things worse than that?"

"Exactly!" Andy nodded. Their twenty-one-year-old son had the rich auburn hair and piercing blue eyes of the Winslow men. He was the same height as his father, six feet, but did not pack the solid muscle of the older man. He jumped up from his chair, his reactions quick and fluid, a phenomenon that had made him one of the finest football players in the nation. With his senior year ahead of him, he was already being sought by all the coaches, for he was equally adept in any position.

"Look, Dad," he said, his voice crackling with unrestrained energy, "for two years we've waited for Barney to write or come home. It's obvious, isn't it, that he's not going to do either? I say it's time we took the initiative. If he won't come to us, we'll go to him! As Mother says, we can't hurt the situation any."

Winslow dropped his head, thinking of his oldest son, Barney, who was completely different from Andy. Barney was slow to speak; Andy, quick. Barney never excelled at anything; Andy did everything well—with a dash that excited everyone's imagination. "I failed somewhere with Barney," Mark said heavily. "I should have been more patient."

"You mustn't say that!" Lola admonished, coming to put her arms around him. "We all misunderstood him, I think—but it's not too late."

He held her, drawing strength from her unshakable faith. In spite of the defeated look on his face, he forced a smile. "I wish I could believe that," he murmured. "Maybe fathers don't have faith the way mothers do." He stepped back and raised his hands in a gesture of surrender. "All right, Andy. We'll do it your way. Let's catch the one-fifteen train."

"I'll be ready!" Lola cried.

"You're not going!" Mark said. "What are you thinking of— a decent woman going to a boxing match!" It had been several years since Gentleman Jim Corbett had defeated John L. Sullivan for the heavyweight championship of the world. Corbett had brought some respectability to the sport, but not much. It was still a brutal event, and only showy women attended.

Lola's eyes glinted. "You won't be upset about my going, Mark, when I tell you the rest of it." She waited, enjoying the juicy morsel, the edges of her lips curved upward impishly. "Esther is going with us."

"You'd take a *child* to a brutal thing like a prizefight? Lola, you're not serious!"

"She's Barney's sister, and she's not a child," Lola replied. "We're his family, and we're all going to see him fight. True, it's not the life we want for him, and God willing, it's not the life he'll have. But for once this family is going to do something for Barney without one critical word or deed. I *mean* it, Mark!"

Painful memories flashed across his mind of those years of rebellion, of struggles to keep his oldest son from a life that was dragging him away from the family. Mark had tried unsuccessfully to bury those images of the past; now he faced her and said slowly, "All right, Lola. I never did anything right with Barney when he was home. We'll try it your way. I'll tell Bates to have the carriage ready."

They left the house at 11:30 and caught the 12:00 train. Scarsdale, the location of the Winslow home, was twenty miles north of the city. Mark Winslow had risen to a directorship on the Union Pacific, and his work kept him traveling. Both he and Lola had agreed to leave the crush of New York City to live in Scarsdale, where they had been since the children were young.

The passenger car was crowded, so Mark and Lola were separated from the children by a few seats. Mark settled back, lost in thought and undisturbed by his wife, who knew his moods well enough to refrain from conversation. Finally he smiled. "Sorry to be such bad company."

"It's all right, dear." She patted his hand. "We must have faith."

"He's so *different!*" Mark sighed.

"Different from whom?" Lola asked gently. "He's not like Andy, you mean. I suppose that's where we went wrong. I've thought about their childhood a lot, Mark. Barney was such a sweet child! Remember when he was small, how he'd wait for you and run to meet you? You two had some great times."

Mark nodded. "Yes. I remember that. I think of it every day. We paid too much attention to Andy, didn't we? Oh, it wasn't intentional. But when your child does something well, you want to praise him for it. And Andy was good at everything. He still is."

Lola twisted her hands together. She was a woman at peace with the world and herself—except in this one area. Here she could not conceal her grief. "I don't know why we didn't recognize it, Mark. We should have found a way to make Barney feel accepted, not rejected. It must have been terrible for him, always losing to Andy!"

She began to cry softly, and he put his arm around her and drew her close. Mark Winslow had been a hard man in his youth. His enemies would say *that* had not changed. Yet toward this woman, he was wholly tender and could not bear to see her weep. They sat quietly, listening to the rumble of the wheels intermingled with their daughter's incessant talking.

"What's a prizefight like, Andy?" Esther asked excitedly as the train approached the station. She had been delighted to get away. Her brown eyes gleamed beneath a shock of black hair, a copy of her mother's.

"Not anything you should be watching," he replied. "I tried to talk Mother out of bringing you along, but you know how she is when she makes up her mind. Might as well argue with a glacier."

Esther, at eighteen, had known little of the world's rough ways, nor had she ever been able to understand her older brother in the least. "I don't think it's right, all of us chasing around after Barney," she pouted. "He's the one who left home and disgraced us all."

"He's our brother," Andy rebuked her. "And it's up to us to do all we can to pull him out of the mess he's in." He gave her a critical look, adding, "You never showed much affection for Barney, Esther."

"Well, neither did you!"

Andy hated to be corrected, but he was also a clear thinker, so he nodded. "That's right, Esther. I was pretty insufferable, I guess. And it's been on my mind for a long time." He looked out the window, then back at her. "Look, I want to be a minister—but how can I reach out to people if I don't care enough about my own brother to try to help him?"

"Andy, he's gone so far down! Drinking and fighting—and who knows what else. We know he was in jail in Kansas for months." Esther shook her head. "I think he'll laugh at us."

"You may be right—but that won't kill us, will it?" He shrugged his shoulders and turned back to the window just as the train station came into view. "Hey, we're almost there. I'll get your bag."

★   ★   ★   ★

"You ain't got no chance boxin' with O'Hara, kid," Benny Meyers, a short, fat Russian Jew, said. "He's a fancy dancer, so I want you should put your head down and go at him like you wuz a mad bull. You got that?"

"Sure, Benny."

"Okay. Now let's go, but remember this fight's important, Barney. O'Hara's outboxed Jake Penny, Little Gans, and some real good ones. If he beats you, he's gonna get a shot at Dutch Wagner. But Carmody says if you beat O'Hara, you'll get the bout. And anybody who beats Wagner gets a shot at the champ. You know what that means?" Meyers' black eyes bored into the boxer's, and he whispered around the short black cigar: "It means the *world*, Barney! All the money you can spend, dames—all you could ever dream of. And everybody will look at you when you come into a hotel, and they'll say, 'There's the light-heavyweight champeen of the whole world!'"

Barney Winslow listened quietly, his deep-set brown eyes half hidden. But at the last words, a gleam appeared. "I'll kill this guy, Benny."

"Now you're talkin'!" Meyers said, leading his fighter out of the dressing room. "He's gonna tag you with a few, kid. He's good—but he ain't got no killer in him like you have. Just let him have his licks—then wipe him out!"

The New York Arena had a name larger than the building deserved. It was no more than a factory that had gone bankrupt under the collapse brought on by President Grant's corrupt administration. For years it had lain fallow until an enterprising young Jewish man named Danny Garfield had bought it on credit and turned it into a sports arena. The high ceiling permitted the construction of bleachers all around the center, with wooden benches radiating out from the ring. Sprinkled throughout were newly developed electric lights, which cast harsh shadows down on the referee and the fighters as they met in the ring.

"Look!" cried Andy. "Over to the side! I think that's Barney."

The four Winslows were seated on the top row of the bleachers. They were lucky to get those at five dollars apiece. As they had pushed their way through the crowd, several men made crude remarks about the women. Once it was almost too much for Mark and he angrily turned to strike the man, but Lola grabbed her husband's arm, murmuring, "It's all right, Mark."

After two five-round bouts, Esther whispered to Andy, "I feel as if someone is going to see me in a place like this. It's *awful!*"

Lola, on the other hand, wasn't as uncomfortable, for she had grown up in a cantina in Mexico years ago and had been part owner of a gambling club in a Union Pacific construction town. The rough talk, the smoke, and the crudity did not shock her; however, the fights did. The barroom scraps she'd seen were nothing compared to the barbaric scene here. It seemed degrading to pay to watch two men maul each other, but she had chosen to come.

Her thoughts were interrupted by the cries of the crowd as the referee introduced the next bout. "Now for our semi-final contest, we have Davy O'Hara, at one hundred eighty-six pounds from San Francisco, facing Battling Barney Winslow, weighing in at one hundred eighty-one pounds from New York City."

He lowered his voice, said a few words, and the two contestants separated to wait for the bell.

Barney had had no contact with his family for two years, and the change took them by surprise. His coarse black hair was cropped short, he'd put on weight, and the muscles in his arms and shoulders rippled as he slapped his gloves together. He turned just as the bell clanged, and Lola thought, *I wouldn't have known him!*

The fighters approached the referee in the center as he held out his hand, the two men touched gloves, and the fight began.

Barney lunged forward, his right hand swinging up in a sweeping motion. O'Hara ducked easily and gave his opponent a sharp blow with his left. It wasn't a hard jab, but it left a red spot on Winslow's cheek. Barney pulled up, turned and moved forward, both hands slightly cocked at shoulder height, and once again maneuvered O'Hara into position, then made another charge. This time his fist caught O'Hara on the shoulder and spun him around. O'Hara twisted his body, took a short step to the left, and shot his left at Barney's forehead.

Mark leaned forward, oblivious to the crowd. He had been in many fights in his youth, and the sight of the two men throwing punches made his nerves tingle. He felt Lola clutch his arm, and heard Andy yell, "Come on, Barney!" Mark was a competitive man and understood Andy's reaction. He, too, stretched forward, pulling for his son to strike O'Hara down.

Lola hated every minute of it, and prayed that God would give her wisdom to deal with her son. She understood Mark's and Andy's response, for she knew men. But she knew as well that they had forgotten her son's predicament—trapped in a world that would destroy him.

When the bell sounded after three rounds, Barney dropped to the stool at the side of the ring and gulped down the water Meyers gave him. "You done good, Barney," his trainer said. "He's gettin' tired. Can't keep that dancin' up all night!"

Barney's face was red and sweaty. The cut over his left eyebrow needed attention and Meyers dabbed at it, saying, "You ain't gonna last for ten like this." He peered down. "You got the nerve to go after him, Barney—I mean dig his grave?"

Barney's eyes glowed. "I'll get him, Benny!"

The bell rang, and Barney sprang like a cougar across the ring. His rushes had slowed down, and though O'Hara had gotten used to the rhythm of them, he was caught off guard. He managed to avoid Barney's first wild blow but caught the second one square in the mouth. It drove him back into the ropes, his eyes glazed. The crowd jumped to its feet, screaming, "Get him, Barney! Get him!"

There was no strategy in Barney's movements. He simply punched wildly, driving home each blow with every ounce of strength, most of the jabs missing. But O'Hara could not avoid the savage attack. He was struck in the face, on the side of the neck, in the body, the last punch sending him to the floor, motionless. The referee waved Barney back and began to count: "One—two—three—"

Slowly O'Hara roused, but his legs wouldn't work. At the count of seven he stumbled to his feet, swaying groggily. The referee stepped back, and Barney rushed O'Hara, hitting the helpless fighter unmercifully.

Lola watched as her son pelted the man in front of him, closing her eyes at last when the bloodied O'Hara fell to the canvas and lay still.

"The winner by a knockout is Bat Winslow!" the referee shouted, and the crowd screamed in response.

Barney felt Benny hugging him, and then the robe was on his shoulders. Men were shouting his name and crowding around to pat his back as Meyers led him through the packed aisles to the dressing room.

Meyers removed Barney's gloves and cleaned him up, chortling with glee at the victory. Just as Barney's shirt was on, the door opened. A pair of soft arms circled his neck and he heard the cry, "You won! You won, Bat!"

Barney felt a kiss on his bruised lips, then Sally said, "Come on! We're going to have a victory celebration and drink champagne—all on Mr. Barone."

Tony stepped forward and smiled. "Bat, I never saw anything like it! No man alive could have stood up to you!"

Barney grinned through puffy lips. "Well, O'Hara did a pretty good job of it."

"But you got him." Tony waved his hands in the air. "Now let's go. All on me—oh, this here is my new star—Katie Sullivan. Katie, meet Battling Barney Winslow."

Katie had been appalled by it all, but there was no threat in the fighter now. He regarded her through eyes almost in slits, then nodded. "Glad to know you, Katie."

At that moment the door opened again, and he saw several people framed in the doorway.

"Hey, we're leaving," Tony said quickly. "No time for talk with your fans."

Barney's eyes were still so swollen he couldn't see clearly. Then he heard "Hello, son."

Dazed, Barney stared. This was worse than any blow he'd taken in the ring. He couldn't seem to move. Suddenly, a cool pair of hands touched his cheeks, and he smelled his mother's scent of lilacs.

He blinked his eyes, trying to focus. Somehow he felt as if he'd stepped back into time. One of those times he'd come home from play, and his mother had met him, held his cheeks, and kissed him, saying what she said just now.

"Hello, Barney."

His mother! It didn't make sense. Then he saw his father watching him with a strained look on his face. Andy! Esther! They were all there!

The roaring in his ears increased. He couldn't think clearly. Finally, he ducked his head and said in a husky whisper, "Hello, Mom."

Then he looked around and blurted out the words he thought were sealed forever: "This—this is my family."

CHAPTER TWO

CAUGHT!

★ ★ ★ ★

Tony Barone perceived immediately that Mark Winslow was an important man, so made the most of it by commandeering two carriages to take them to Antoine's, one of New York's best dinner clubs. There he slipped the head waiter twenty dollars to give them a good table, then arranged the seating, placing himself between Kate and Barney, with the boxer's family across from them.

During the conversation, Tony sensed the tension between the Winslows and Barney and made a mental note to find out why. The six-course dinner, served by a waiter and two assistants, began with oysters on a half shell and ended with delicate servings of ice cream. Between the oysters and the ice cream there were soup, fish, guinea hen and salad, vegetables, and side dishes of salted almonds and celery stuffed with cheese.

"Come on, Katie," Tony coaxed as the waiter brought a French white wine with the first two courses. "Drink up."

"Oh, Tony, I don't know—"

He had already discovered she didn't drink. Her father had been a drunkard, and when Katie left home, she'd promised her mother she wouldn't drink.

"Why, this isn't liquor, Katie," he told her. "It's only *wine*! People in Italy drink it instead of water." He poured her a glass and urged her on. "This is just part of learning to be with people—important people. It's not good manners to sit there while others are drinking. Go on, just a sip."

He noted with satisfaction as the meal progressed that she drank two glasses of white wine; then when champagne was served with the third course, she had two of those as well. "See? It's good for you," he said, giving her arm a squeeze. "That wasn't so bad, was it now?"

Katie had been stimulated by the wine, though she didn't realize it. Her cheeks grew pink and she began to talk more than Tony had ever heard her. By the time the meal was over, she was laughing at Tony's jokes and accepted his invitation to dance.

"I don't know how to do this dance," she giggled as they moved across the floor.

"You're doing fine, Katie—just fine," he said, holding her close for the waltz. "Say, did you notice that something's going on between Bat and his folks? They ain't sayin' much of anything to each other." He was thinking ahead. "But the old man is rich, and it's always good to know rich men, Katie. Maybe he'll back you in a broadway show or something. Be nice to him, kid."

"They seem like a nice family," she said. "But I probably won't see them anymore."

When the music stopped they returned to the table, where Benny Meyers was lauding Barney's accomplishments. "Why, folks, you got to be real proud of this boy! He ain't got much science about him, but he's tough! He'll be champeen inside two years, I tell ya."

"It's a hard way to make a living," Mark countered.

"The way Cleveland has let things go to pot, Winslow," Tony interjected, "a man's got to make a living any way he can. Why, even the Union Pacific's having a hard time keeping afloat, they say. Anything to that?"

He referred to the economic panic that swept the country the previous year. Thousands were out of work, gangs of hobos tramped aimlessly about the country, eating at soup kitchens. In desperation a protest march was organized by a man named Jacob S. Coxey, and the mob headed for Washington, where they sang: "We're coming, Grover Cleveland, 500,000 strong. We're marching into Washington to right the nation's wrong."

Mark Winslow leveled his eyes at Barone. "The Union's had worse times. We'll survive President Cleveland just as we've survived other presidents."

The two men continued to exchange views, with a few comments from the rest of the party—except Barney, who had remained silent the entire evening. The presence of his family disturbed him intensely and he wished he could leave. With relief he accepted Sally's urgent plea to dance.

Sally's attractiveness had long given way to the coarsened life she lived. She was overdressed and her poor speech marked her position clearly. "Say, sweetie," she cooed, "why ain't you never told me you come from a ritzy family? That ring your ma's wearing—ain't it something? Hey, maybe we can go visit 'em—bet they got a fancy place, ain't they, Bat?"

Barney ignored her banal chatter. When he first met her, he had been flattered, but soon tired of her mindless talk and incessant desire for gifts. His mind drifted to his family. *Why did they come to see me fight? They hate my way of life.* As he moved around the floor with Sally's voice humming in his ear, he thought about the heated discussions he and his family had before he left home. It was like another world—both pleasant and terrible.

Dad looks good, he thought, glancing at his father. *I wonder if he ever thinks about the time he took me fishing in Minnesota? That was the best time I ever had—just him and me. Andy got sick and couldn't go, and the two of us camped in an old cabin for two weeks. We fished and hunted, and just talked and talked! He told me all about when he was young and how he fought in the war—I ain't never forgot that!*

The later years, he remembered, were filled with efforts to please his father. Once he'd studied night and day, trying to make all A's, but in spite of that, he'd made mostly C's. *Andy got all A's. Mom tried to say nice things about my grades—but Dad never said a word.* That brought back other memories of trying to fit into the family, but by the time he was twelve years old, he had understood that he'd never be smart enough to please them.

When he went to college, he was convinced he'd never make it. And with that attitude, it was easy to be lured into a group of drinking and disgruntled students. By the middle of his second semester, he'd been dismissed for his behavior. The thought of his father's displeasure still raked across his nerves. *Should have gone on my own then*, he thought. *That job with the Union my dad got me was too much. Everybody expected me to be as smart as Mark Winslow—I was a fool to try it.* The last scene before leaving home flashed into his mind. Standing in front of his parents, pale with anger, he had shouted, "I've never been able to please you—and I never will! You want me to be perfect! Well, you've got Andy—let him be perfect. I'm getting away from here—and I won't ever come back!"

That scene had become a nightmare. All across the country it had awakened him in a cold sweat. He'd gone down fast; and in drunken stupors and in jails, he'd hear himself shouting, "I won't ever come back!" He'd turned to fighting to make big money, so when Benny Meyers had picked him off the street and trained him, it had been like shutting a final door to his past. Prizefighting had brought adulations from both Benny and the crowd that followed him. For the first time he felt accepted, worth something—and it had been pleasant. Even some of the upper crust were drawn to the violence of the ring. Barney himself disliked fighting. It gave him no pleasure to smash another man into a bleeding hulk, and the cries from the crowd made him uneasy, for he knew how fickle they were—cheering just as loudly if he were the one being beaten!

When the music ended, he and Sally joined the rest, where he sat with downcast eyes. Stealing looks at his parents from time to time, he was confused by the contradictory memories rising in his mind. His mother was as beautiful and calm as ever. He remembered when he'd cut his foot, and she had held him in her arms, keeping the gaping wound together with one strong hand while she stroked his head with the other. The sight of blood had terrified him, but he remembered as clearly as if it were yesterday how he had clung to her, and how her hands had soothed his fear. His father looked no different. An overwhelming desire to please his father stirred him again, a desire he had never been able to forget. But he shoved the old impulse down and glanced at Esther and Andy.

Esther, he saw, was uncomfortable, with carefully hidden disgust. She had looked at him all evening as if he were a stranger—and a frightening stranger at that! Barney turned quickly to look at his brother.

Andrew was smiling and talking animatedly to Katie Sullivan. The young woman seemed captivated by Andy's good looks and quick wit. *Guess she's like all the rest,* Barney thought without resentment. Long ago he'd lost hope of being the sort of person his brother was, but suddenly a bitterness hit him. *Why did they have to come down here? They hate it—so why don't they stay in their nice, neat little world and leave me alone?*

Andy was unaware of Barney's stony looks toward him. As always, he was fascinated by any new experience, and the fight had stirred his imagination. "First prizefight I ever saw, Miss Sullivan," he said excitedly. "But you've seen quite a few, I suppose?"

"Oh no!" Katie said quickly. "It was my first one, too."

"Oh?" Andy responded with surprise. He knew the beautiful young woman was a dance-hall girl, though he had no more experience with that type than with boxers. He studied her carefully, taking in the creamy, velvety skin, the glowing eyes and the air of seeming innocence. The other girl, Sally Danton, was the opposite—highly made-up complexion, revealing clothing, and cheap, bold looks. She fit the part. "Miss Sullivan," he said, "you're a singer in Mr. Barone's . . . ah, place?"

Katie noticed his hesitation, and a flush touched her throat. He had been about to say "saloon," she sensed, then had settled for a kinder term. Katie was still sensitive, and merely nodded. But Barone had heard Winslow's remark and leaned forward to say, "You bet she is, Mr. Winslow! But she won't stay long—too good for the place." Barone gave Katie a familiar pat on the shoulder, smiling at her possessively. "She's got talent, and I'm going to see that she goes right to the top." He smiled, his hand tightening on her shoulder. "I'm taking care of this young lady," he said smoothly. "With my help she'll be the toast of New York!"

Despite Barone's flashy good looks and intense masculinity, Lola knew he was a predator. She had learned to recognize the type when she was a girl. Her eyes caught those of her husband, and signaled her desire to leave.

Mark took the cue and said, "Well, it's been good to meet all of you, but we must be going."

Andy looked up with surprise, for he was having a good time, but Esther and her mother nodded assent.

Lola waited for Barney to come to her, but when he didn't, she walked over and put her hand on his arm. "Barney, we've missed you so much." When he made no response, she added, "Your father is being transferred to California. He doesn't know for how long. Why don't you come with us?"

Barney's eyes met hers; then he shook his head. "Don't see how I could do that."

Lola wanted to say more, to coax him, but it was too public. Mark rescued her by saying, "How about next Friday, Barney? Come out for supper."

"Got a fight in Troy," Barney muttered. He offered no more, and an embarrassed silence filtered over the group.

"Well, brother," Andy said quickly, "I'll come down and cheer you on." He was quick-witted and skilled in dealing with awkward situations. He moved to Barney and grabbed his hand. "We haven't seen enough of each other," Andy said, noting Benny's surprise. "But I'll take care of that. You can't hide from me, Barney!" Then he turned and followed the rest of the family out of the restaurant.

"That's a nice family you got, Bat," Meyers said. He rolled his ever-present cigar around between his lips, adding sagely, "Nothin' like a good family, I'm tellin' you!"

Sally was studying the fighter with a new respect. "Didn't know you came from a family of swells, Bat," she grinned. "I'll have to treat you better!"

Barney shrugged. "We don't get on too well," he said, forcing a grin. "Well, Sally, it's early. Let's you and me have a party."

"Sure, Bat!" she said.

Katie watched them leave, then turned to Barone. "I thought they were nice. Especially his mother."

"Yeah, sure," Barone grinned. "But it was the brother you should have been watching. He couldn't take his eyes off you, Katie."

"Oh, I don't care about that!"

"That's the ticket!" Barone laughed. "I'm the man for you!" He put his hand on her arm possessively and guided her out.

As Benny watched them go, he said softly, "Katie, my girl,

if you wuz my daughter, I'd get you away from Tony Barone."
He knew instinctively that Barone would not rest until the innocence of Katie Sullivan had been sacrificed to his desires. It
was an old story Meyers had often seen, and it made his heart
heavy.

★   ★   ★   ★

All the way back to the hotel Mark sat silently in the cab,
paying little heed either to the sights of the city or the argument
between Andy and Esther. Lola took his hand and pressed it.
She herself was subdued. The evening had not gone the way
she had hoped. She had wanted to be alone with Mark, sharing
the grief they felt concerning Barney—a grief neither Andy nor
Esther were aware of.

In the backseat Andy and Esther continued to argue.

"It's no use, Andy. Barney will do just what he wants. He
doesn't care about any of us," she said.

"You're wrong. He's a funny fellow, Barney is. Not too much
'upstairs,' of course, but all the more reason why we've got to
take him in hand. Give him a lift, you know?"

"Barney's not dumb!" Lola broke in sharply.

"Why—I just meant he's slow, Mother."

"I'm not sure about that," Mark said. "Some of the best men
in our company were slow, as you call it, Andy. But they kept at
the job—sometimes after the quicker fellows gave up."

Like many other men of his age, Mark's years in the Confed-
erate Army had been the most traumatic of his life, yet molding
him more than any other experience. He had lived through life-
and-death situations in the army and later when he had fought
to get the Union Pacific built. Hard experiences were good for
men and women, not the easy ones. Now as he studied Andy's
smooth face and clear eyes, he thought, *He's pretty sure of himself—but he's never had a severe test.*

"Well, sure, Dad," Andy agreed quickly. "I didn't mean to
put Barney down. Matter of fact, I've felt pretty guilty about the
way things turned out." A rueful expression scored his lips.
"Looking back, I can see where I could have been more thoughtful of Barney."

His words stirred Mark's feeling of remorse. Seeing Barney

had been more painful than anything he'd known for a long time. "I know what you mean, Andy. I guess it's too late, but I wish I had it all to do over again."

"It's never too late, Mark!" Lola put in quickly. "Nothing is too difficult for God."

"You sound like my father," Mark sighed. "I wish he'd been around. He'd have done a good job with Barney. Not like me. But I guess it will have to be God. Barney's shut the door on all of us."

"Aw, don't worry, Dad," Andy encouraged. "He just needs a little attention. I'll start working on him." Andy's handsome face glowed with confidence. "I'll start by going to the fight in Troy next week. I could see he was glad I said I'd come."

"I wish we weren't moving to the coast, Mark," Lola fretted. "We won't be able to see or encourage him while we're there."

"Don't worry, Mother," Andy nodded, patting her shoulder. "I'll be here for the next few months. Maybe I can talk him into coming out when I do."

"That would be wonderful!" Lola said, her dark eyes filling with hope. She leaned back, thinking, *Andy could do it if he would stick with it.*

★ ★ ★ ★

"Bat! Come out of it! This guy's gonna beat your brains out if you don't wake up!"

Benny had doused Barney with water, trying to bring him to. As the bell rang, he struggled to his feet and moved toward the weaving shape before him. He lunged at Louis Maddox, the tall, lanky fighter, but caught a hard right to his own mouth, driving him back on his heels. Barney tried to clench the man, but Maddox twisted to one side and sent two more blows to Bat's head, then a powerful right to the stomach. Barney grabbed the man's hand and held on, hoping his head would clear.

When the bell sounded, he turned and walked away. As he lowered himself to the stool, he looked over the crowd. Benny began to wipe Barney's face with a sponge, saying angrily, "What's *wrong with* ya, Bat? Why you been lookin' out at the crowd all the time? Maddox ain't there—he's been right in front of you! You gotta concentrate!"

Truthfully, Barney didn't know what was wrong. He'd been unable to shake off Andy's last words: *I'll come down and cheer you on in Troy.* Barney realized it had become important to see his brother and found himself searching the crowd for him. He wanted to prove himself to his family. So when the fight started and Andy didn't appear, Barney had become sullen. Benny was mystified, for the young fighter was usually cheerful and easy to coach.

In the end, Barney lost to Maddox, and it angered Benny. All the way back to New York, Meyers spewed out his bitterness. "You ain't goin' to be no champeen fightin' like you did tonight! You looked like an old woman out there, Bat!"

Barney said nothing, and for the next ten days Meyers nearly went crazy. Barney disappeared for a week, and when the manager finally found him, he was in the drunk tank. Meyers paid his fine and tried to talk to him.

"Look, Bat," he said as the two of them made their way down Twenty-third Street toward Barney's rooming house, "I know you feel bad, but it ain't the end of the world, you know? So you had a bad night. So anybody can lose a fight! John L. Sullivan himself lost a few! Now, what we do is get you cleaned up, and we go have a steak at Tony's place. Then we start in the mornin' with the roadwork. I got you a bout over in Jersey in two weeks. Arlie Flynn. He's a comer, but you can take him."

But the next day Barney didn't show up at the gym. He had full intentions of going but after breakfast was sidetracked by a game of cards, which lasted until noon. During the game he drank freely from the bottle, and left the place broke and half drunk. Unlike most of his friends, he was unable to hold his liquor very well, and it quickly went to his head. He headed down West Thirty-second Street, morose and irritable. The loss of the fight had hurt his pride, and Meyers' outburst hadn't helped.

For two hours he walked the streets, glum and thick-headed from the liquor. He found himself in the Bowery and finally decided to go meet Meyers and take his tongue-lashing. But as he walked down Pearl Street, he heard his name called.

"Hey, Bat, hold on!" It was Studs Ketchel. "Let's have a drink."

"Can't do it, Studs," Barney muttered. "Got to go to the gym. Benny's waitin' for me. He's going to skin me for not showin' up for practice."

Ketchel just laughed and pulled him inside. "Plenty of time for that. Heard you had bad luck in Troy. Well, don't worry. You'll nail that palooka next time!"

Ketchel was a local political boss on a minor scale. He was not intelligent enough to rise high in politics, but he was Dan Carmody's right-hand man. Carmody, the ward boss, used Ketchel when he wanted some roughhousing done. Barney allowed himself a few drinks as Ketchel and the other men patted him on the back and told him what a great fighter he was. That helped restore his bruised pride somewhat.

As the afternoon wore on, he drank more, and by the time it was dark, he was fuzzy and unsteady on his feet. "Got to go, Studs," he mumbled.

"Wait a minute, Bat," Ketchel said. "I got a proposition for you." He took Barney to a back room and studied him carefully. "Got a little something to do tonight, Bat. Nothing big, you understand, but I need one more guy with muscle."

"I'm drunk, Studs," Barney said. "Besides, I don't—"

"You're broke, too, ain't you, Bat?" Ketchel interrupted. "When's your next fight?"

"Two weeks."

"Well, I'll give you a hundred bucks for ten minutes' work."

"A hundred?"

"Sure." Ketchel lowered his voice and laid out the plan. Barney tried to listen, but his brain refused to function, and he caught only snatches of Stud's words. He knew Ketchel hired tough fellows to pressure gamblers who were behind in their payments, and he assumed that was what he was being asked to do. He didn't like the idea, but he was dead broke—couldn't even pay his rent.

Finally Ketchel took some money from his pocket. "Here's half the dough, Bat. Be at the pier by Rossetti's place at ten. Don't be late."

Ketchel left, and Barney tried to pull his thoughts together. He stared at the money in his hand, then at a half-full bottle of whiskey on the table. When he left the saloon an hour later, his head was so muddled he couldn't hear the sound of his footsteps clearly.

Rossetti's Bar was located in one of the worst parts of the city. The street was lined with saloons and gambling houses—all booming with business. He stood under a streetlight, blinking stupidly as he waited. Finally a man emerged from the alley and stood beside him. "Let's go, Bat."

Barney recognized the short, muscular individual as one of the toughs who sometimes came into Tony's place. In his stupor Barney followed blindly. He felt sick, and the man turned, rasping, "You're drunk, Bat!"

"Yeah, I better get out of here." He had difficulty framing the words and was turning to go when the man grabbed him by the sleeve.

"None of that! I got no time to get anybody else. Come on!"

He walked down a series of side streets, stopping finally in the shadows of an alley. "You wait here, Bat. I'm going in. If you hear any trouble, come runnin'—got it?"

Barney nodded and slumped against the brick wall as the man wheeled. He didn't even see the tough use a small bar on the front door of a little shop with a sign ADAM'S JEWELRY and enter silently. Barney's stomach was churning, his brow cold with sweat. He tried to stay upright, but the world was whirling around. He slowly collapsed onto the pavement, unaware of the shots echoing from inside the shop, or the weight of the gun that was tossed into his lap, then clattered to the sidewalk.

The next thing he knew, rough hands were pulling him to his feet and throwing him into a vehicle. He recognized the sound of hooves on the pavement and realized by the swaying that he was in a wagon of some sort. He lay there, trying to ignore the sickness. Then the horses stopped and he was pulled upright and carried roughly into a building and dropped onto a cold, hard floor.

Forcing his eyes open, he blinked until a form swam into focus. The thin, hard face of a policeman peered down at him. He looked around wildly, taking in the bars and the other policeman. "Wha—what am I in for?"

"Why, you've found a new home," the policeman laughed harshly. "But don't get to liking it too much. You won't be here long!"

Barney stared, licked his dry lips, and asked, "Where will I be?"

"You'll be in a castle," the policeman grinned. "Ain't that right, Hank? They call it the Castle on the Hudson." Then he dropped his smile and gave Barney a vicious kick in the side. "You shot a man, fellow. It's Sing Sing for you!"

"I didn't shoot nobody!"

"'Course you didn't," the other guard laughed. "Never have had a guilty man in here. Every one of you birds is innocent as angels." He stepped back, along with the other policeman, and slammed the door shut. "After about twenty or thirty years in Sing Sing, you'll get some manners, I reckon!"

Barney lay still, his cheek against the cold concrete floor. *Sing Sing!* The very words riddled him with fear. He'd heard about the notorious prison. Had known a few who came out of it, mostly shells of men. He got to his feet and gripped the bars with trembling hands. Staring down the gloomy hall, he tried to think, tried to pray—but could do neither. Finally he lay down on the cot, shaking uncontrollably. The ceiling and the walls of the windowless room seemed to close in on him, and he rolled over and buried his face in the stinking mattress to keep from screaming.

CHAPTER THREE

BARNEY'S DAY IN COURT

★ ★ ★ ★

Simon Jolson was the most successful trial lawyer in the state of New York—in the entire country, he might have added. Though his appearance was not impressive, the stocky man made up for it in intellect. He had a razor-sharp mind, and could charm a jury almost like magic, to the detriment of his opponents.

But today Simon Jolson was restless as he sat in Mark Winslow's ornate drawing room, his thighs overflowing the Chippendale chair he occupied. A beautiful Duncan Phyfe sofa and memorabilia of all kinds filled the room. His gaze focused on a tapestry of a hunting scene covering one of the walls. In the middle distance stood a majestic castle, probably owned by a great lord or king of the seventeenth century, surrounded by forests and rich foliage.

Jolson wished he'd lived in the castle, or one like it. Surely the lives of those people weren't plagued by the problems facing Winslow. Simon had been asked to defend Barney.

He concealed his discouragement, forced a smile on his thick lips, and said, "Well, we'll do what we can for the boy."

Mark's eyes clouded. He'd been dealing with men all his life and was a hard one to fool. "That means you can't do much, doesn't it, Simon?"

"The jury hasn't been selected yet, Mark," the lawyer said. "Never bet on a jury, though. They're the most unpredictable thing in the universe. But there's always a chance for Barney."

"Did he say anything you could use when you talked to him yesterday?" Lola asked.

"Not really," Jolson admitted.

"It's plain he's protecting somebody," Mark growled.

"That's what I think," Jolson nodded, a scowl creasing his forehead. "He's got a fool idea about 'honor among thieves,' or something like that. Don't rat on your buddies. Which is non-sense! Most crooks will throw their 'buddies' to the wolves to save their own skin. But I can't get that across to Barney."

"I've got a feeling Barney may have had something to do with the robbery," Mark said slowly, "but not with the shooting."

"Could be. I wish we could get him to admit even that much." Jolson shook his head, adding, "It would be a lesser charge."

Lola asked quietly, "What's going to happen to him, Simon, if he's convicted?"

Jolson removed a cigar from his pocket and stuck it between his teeth, yellowed from smoke. "Depends on the judge. And here again, we've got a bad break. Presson will be on the bench. They call him a hanging judge."

"What's the worst he could give Barney?" Mark asked.

"Forty years."

"Forty years!" Lola gasped. "That can't happen!"

"We'll try to do better," Jolson promised. He pulled a match from his pocket, lit his cigar and sent a cloud of purplish smoke toward the ceiling. "It's all circumstantial. Adams has failed to identify Barney. That's in our favor."

"But he was found outside the store with the gun," Mark said grimly.

"That's right. On the other hand, he was dead drunk. The police know that, but they may *forget* it when they testify."

"Why would that make a difference?" Lola asked.

"Someone so drunk he couldn't stand up would have been obvious to Adams. He's told the police the man who shot him didn't *seem* to be drunk. I'll get that out of him when he's on the stand."

Lola's face was tense as she said, "Andy's convinced that Barney's protecting someone, as you say. He's gone down to the Fourth Ward to try to dig up something about who Barney was friends with."

Alarmed, Jolson warned, "He'd better be careful. There's men in that Ward—even women—who'd slit your throat for a nickel." He stood to his feet, pulled out his watch, adding, "I'll see you in court tomorrow. Come a little early."

★   ★   ★   ★

Andy's feet hurt. He'd spent most of the day moving from saloon to saloon. It wasn't a good plan, perhaps, but he had to find someone who knew Barney, who his friends were.

Unknown to him he had bumped into at least half a dozen men who knew Barney fairly well, but they weren't about to talk to a well-dressed stranger asking loaded questions. Most of them thought he was a policeman; others, a lawyer. And the people who roamed the Lower East Side of New York had little use for either breed.

It was afternoon before Andy got to Tony Barone's place. "I'm looking for a friend of Barney Winslow," he said to the bartender. The men drinking on both sides of him gave him a quick look, then ignored him.

"Don't guess I know him," the bartender answered.

"He's a fighter," Andy insisted. "You must have heard of him."

The bartender shook his head. "I don't go to the fights." He left the bar and headed straight for Barone's office. "Boss, there's a guy out here, says he's looking for a friend of Barney Winslow."

"You know him, Ed?"

"Never seen him, but the word is he's been in every bar in town asking questions. Thought you'd better know."

Barone nodded and followed him into the bar. He recognized Andy immediately from the evening with Barney's family. Feigning surprise he said, "Hey, it's Mr. Winslow, ain't it?"

Andy turned quickly. "I'm Andy Winslow."

"You may not remember me, but we had supper together once. I'm Tony Barone."

"Oh yes, I remember. Maybe you can help me. You heard about Barney's arrest?"

"Sure, it's too bad. He's a good kid."

"Well, I think he's being railroaded! What I want to do is—"

"Let's go where we can talk, okay?" Barone interjected, indicating a table in an angle of the room. "No sense letting everybody know your business. Now, about Barney, you don't think he did it?"

"No, I don't," Andy nodded. "And I met one fellow who told me as much."

"Who was that?" Barone asked quickly.

"He didn't want to talk at first, but finally agreed—if I'd pay for it. I didn't have the money then, but I will when I meet him tonight. He said Barney didn't shoot Adams, and that he knew who did."

"I don't think I'd hand over cash for talk like that," Barone shrugged. "He's probably just after your dough."

"That may be, but I'm checking it out anyway." Andy went on, bent on pursuing every scrap of information. "Who's Studs Ketchel? Someone told me he was mixed up with the shooting."

Alarmed, Barone's mind raced. This man might be dangerous.

"Why, Ketchel wouldn't have anything to do with a small-time job like Barney's mixed up in," he said. "He's Dan Carmody's right-hand man. And you know Carmody—the big boss of the whole city! Even the mayor walks softly around Big Dan!"

"I don't give a continental about Dan Carmody!" Andy exploded. "I'm going to find out what this man Ketchel had to do with Barney!"

"I guess you can do that," Barone replied. *This guy has got to be stopped—but quick!* he thought. "I can give you a phone number, and you can talk to him yourself!"

Andy took the slip of paper and on his way out stopped at a table where Katie Sullivan was playing solitaire.

As soon as Andy left, Barone called, "Turk—come here!"

A thick-shouldered man with a battered face responded immediately.

"Go find Studs," he ordered. "Tell him a guy named Winslow is stirring up trouble. Tell him it's Barney's brother, and he'd better do something about the guy."

"Bury him?" Turk asked bluntly.

"No, just cool him off until after the trial. Just tell Studs. He'll know what to do." Barone dismissed the man and continued to watch Andy and Katie at the table, his eyes cold and thoughtful.

Andy said quietly, "Miss Sullivan, do you remember me?"

Katie looked up. "Why, you're Barney's brother, aren't you?"

"Yes. May I sit down?"

"I guess so." She regarded him carefully, then said, "I'm sorry about Barney."

Andy studied her. She looked different from what she had been at the dinner party. That night he had wondered how such innocence could exist in a saloon entertainer. Now Katie seemed hard, as if she were slipping down hill. It was not that she was less attractive, but the hard light in her eyes had replaced the softness he had seen before. She also had a glass of liquor in front of her. He remembered distinctly her refusal to drink that night, though she had given in after much persuasion.

But he said only, "I'm looking for help. Barney goes to trial tomorrow, and he's going to be sent to prison if something doesn't happen."

Katie shrugged her shoulders. "I don't know anything about it, Mr. Winslow."

"You know Barney. Who were his friends? Somebody was in it with him. Did you hear anything about the shooting—anything at all?"

"No, I didn't," she said.

The flush in her face and her answer had been too quick, Andy noticed. *She knows something,* he thought, and for the next few minutes, he tried to get her to talk.

His questions upset her, and she shot back, "I tell you I don't know *anything*! And even if I did, this is a rough place, Mr. Winslow. People who talk too much have been found in the river with a bullet in their heads. Now, I'm sorry about Barney, but I just can't help. I'll have to go now."

He had failed again. He looked at the number Barone had

given him and left the saloon, unaware of Barone's deadly eyes following him.

★ ★ ★ ★

Simon Jolson searched the courtroom anxiously for the Winslows. It was ten minutes before the time assigned, and he had expected them to show up early. He needed them, for he felt they might have some influence on the jury. *Even a mother's tears never hurt,* he thought.

"Your people are late, Barney," he said testily, turning to face his client, pale and subdued. "Still time for you to tell me whatever it is you're keeping back."

"I've told you all," Barney said stubbornly.

Jolson had expected as much. Then he looked up as the Winslows walked in. "There they are," he said with relief. "I'll go have a word with them."

"What's the matter?" he asked.

"It's Andy," Mark said, bitterness edging his voice. "He was beaten up last night. He's in the hospital. That's where we've been."

"Is he going to be all right?"

"Yes, but he won't be too active for a few weeks," Mark said. "You were right about it, Simon. That's a rough part of town."

"Did he come up with anything?"

"We don't know," Lola said. Her eyes were swollen and her hands unsteady. "He was unconscious all the time we were there. We hated to leave, but the doctor said he might sleep for twenty-four hours. We rushed over to be with Barney."

"All rise!"

"There's the judge!" Jolson left the Winslows and made his way back to his seat beside Barney.

Judge Presson, a tall, lean man with keen, piercing eyes, took his seat, and the trial began.

Simon Jolson was a master at cutting trials short, or stretching them out. But this time he had nothing to work with. There were few witnesses for the prosecution and none for the defense. By midafternoon, the prosecuting attorney said, "Your Honor, the prosecution rests." And at ten the next morning, Jolson had to say, "The defense rests."

Judge Presson instructed the jury, practically giving them an ultimatum to bring in a verdict of guilty; then the jury retired. The judge left, and Jolson walked back to the Winslows. "How's the boy?" he asked.

"Better this morning, thank God!" Mark said. "But he's all confused. He can't remember much about what happened."

"May have had nothing to do with the trial," Jolson shrugged. He talked with them for a time, then was surprised when the bailiff announced, "Court is in session!"

"So quick?" Lola asked. "I thought it would take longer."

"So did I!" Jolson said grimly. "I must get back." It was proverbial that a quick verdict usually was bad news for the accused. He watched with apprehension as the jury filed in.

"Have you reached a verdict?" Judge Presson intoned.

"We have, Judge Presson."

"Prisoner will rise and face the jury."

Barney stood beside the lawyer as the judge asked, "What is the verdict?"

"We find the defendant, Barney Winslow, guilty as charged."

"No!" a woman's cry went up.

The judge continued. "The court thanks the jury. You are now dismissed."

Judge Presson turned to face Barney. He gave a short speech about the rise of crime and his duty to hold it back by putting criminals where they could not harm society, then said, "I sentence you to twenty years at Sing Sing. Court is adjourned."

"I'm sorry, Barney," Jolson said solemnly.

Mark and Lola rushed forward, shocked beyond words. "God will be with you, Barney," Lola said, unable to say more.

Barney's head shot up, and he looked at her with such bitterness she cringed.

"I'll *never* believe in God again—and I'll *never* trust a human being again as long as I live!"

CHAPTER FOUR

CASTLE ON THE HUDSON

★ ★ ★ ★

Barney awoke to a cold icy rain pelting down on the city hall jail. It was the fifth day of March and Barney had been there five days—an eternity to him. He and five prisoners were rousted out of their cells at dawn and led to a room on the first floor of the jail. There the convicts were bound together with chains attached to each right ankle. As the manacle on Barney's ankle snapped shut, the sound sent a sickening lurch to the pit of his stomach. He wanted to run and scream. But there was no place to run.

On their way from the city jail, the prisoner chained to Barney's left, Larry Imboden, a slight man, short of stature, with thin features and a small mustache, filled him in about Sing Sing. "This is the second jolt for me. I already done three years in the Castle."

"The Castle?" one of the prisoners asked. "What's that?"

Imboden laughed. "Well, it ain't like no castle you ever heard of in fairy tales. That's what they call Sing Sing—the Castle on the Hudson. You ain't never heard it called that?"

"Never even heard of Sing Sing," another inmate said. It was dark in the closed carriage, and Barney couldn't see the faces of the men.

"Well, you heard of it now," Imboden snorted. "But you'll

wish you hadn't." The carriage rattled on, and after a silence he said, "It ain't like no other jail, Sing Sing ain't. The guy that built it was named Elam Lynds, and he was the first warden, too. He's the one who made the no-talking rule."

"No-talking rule?" Barney asked. "What's that?"

"What's it sound like?" Imboden snapped. "The rule that no cons can say a word. They can't talk to each other, can't write nothin' to each other, can't look at nobody or even wink! Can't whistle, sing, dance, run or jump or nothin'!" He broke off, and after a moment's silence, added, "Don't know why he made all them rules. Nobody in the Castle's in much of a mood for singin' or dancin' anyway."

"I knew a guy who did time in Sing Sing," a prisoner spoke up. "He never moved his lips when he talked. I thought that was just his way."

"Naw, that's the way you'll get," Imboden said. "I can spot a man who's done time in the Castle anywhere in the world. Shifty eyes, a shuffle when he walks and no movin' his lips—except me." He sighed deeply. "If you got anything to say, you better say it now, 'cause you won't be talkin' much on the inside." Suddenly the carriage jolted to a halt, and he said, "All out. Watch yourselves. These people will give you all the grief you need and then some!"

As Barney stumbled out of the closed carriage, a chain that was attached to his left leg and joined the ankles of five other prisoners caught, and he stumbled, falling against the man in front of him. The man cursed loudly and turned to face Barney, but a surly guard yelled, "No talkin'!" He rapped the prisoner on the head sharply with a nightstick and walked toward the steel gate set in the face of the grim, gray building before them, blocking out the sky.

Sing Sing was located on the edge of the Hudson River about thirty miles north of New York City. It consisted of cell blocks five tiers high with two hundred cells to each tier. The cells were back to back so that one hundred faced out on each tier, with a narrow walkway running alongside. An outer wall was built around this cell block. It was pierced by windows only ten inches wide and twenty-four inches high, mere slits to admit the slender rays of daylight.

The new convicts were taken to a room where their shackles were removed and regulation prison dress—baggy suits with stark horizontal stripes—were issued. As soon as the prisoners were dressed, a stone-faced prison official appeared. "All right, listen to me!" The lower part of his skinny face was covered with a full beard, and a pair of steely sharp eyes, set close together, bored into them. "I'm Captain Nathaniel Dollar." His high-pitched voice reverberated against the walls. "We don't waste time on formalities here. Behave yourself and you'll be all right. Get out of line, and I'll break you down. I expect some of you will try me out. You just fly right at it." He smiled grimly. "It's been tried before. But I'm still here and most of the cons who thought they could beat me are in the lime pit just outside the wall." He walked down the line, staring each man in the eye, then said, "Wallen, give them the rules; then lock them up for the day. They can go on work detail tomorrow."

"Yes, Captain." A short roly-poly guard stepped in front of them as the captain left and began to read the list of regulations, skipping over words that were too difficult for him. He closed the book and grinned. "What all that means is keep your trap shut, do your work, and don't cause no trouble. You make waves, you're gonna get drowned! Now, come on."

He waddled ahead of them, leading the prisoners through a series of steel doors with a guard stationed at each entrance. As they were waiting for one guard to open a door, a small man behind Barney whispered, "Boy, it won't be easy to break out of this place!"

"Hold it!" Wallen shouted. He walked back to the man and barked, "You're Mackey?"

"Y-yes, sir. Tim Mackey." The inmate was more boy than man, no more than seventeen, Barney guessed. About five feet five inches tall, thin as a rail, with watery blue eyes and buck teeth that clamped down on his trembling lip, the timid man shook before the guard.

"You heard the rule, Mackey," Wallen said. "No talking."

"I—I'm sorry!"

"Not as sorry as you *will* be!" Wallen snapped. "McCoy, fetch me a collar!"

A guard emerged from a side room, holding a peculiar item

in his hands. Wallen held it up for all to see. Then he grinned. "This is the iron collar, men. Let me show you how it works."

The collar looked like a barrel-shaped bird cage with an open top and bottom. Two iron bands about an inch and a half wide held each end together. Six narrower iron bands ran like staves from the top to the bottom.

The boy flinched as Wallen unlocked the bottom ring and opened the collar on its hinges. The guard approached him, saying, "Just hold still, Mackey. This won't hurt as bad as the thrashings your pa give you!"

Wallen slipped the contraption over Mackey's head, closed the collar so that it fit snugly around the boy's neck, and turned a key, locking it securely. Then he stepped back. "Now, that's a right pretty bonnet, ain't it?"

The sight of the pale-faced youth with his eyes staring out from the steel affair sickened Barney. It was not painful, but it was denigrating, an insult to a man. In days to come Barney would become so accustomed to the iron collars that he would pay no attention.

"You'll wear that for a couple of days," Wallen told Mackey. "Makes sleeping a little hard, and it ain't so easy to get your grub between them bars, but it'll teach you to keep your mouth shut." He glanced around at the others, adding, "We got a plentiful supply of these little gems. Any time you want one, just open your mouth and I'll accommodate you! Now, come on."

Ten minutes later, after climbing several flights of stairs, Barney stood before a steel door and was shoved inside. When the door clanged shut, Barney surveyed the cell. *Just like a coffin*, he thought—no more than three and a half feet wide, about seven feet high, and seven feet long. A coffin of stone, separated from other coffins by walls a foot thick.

A cot and a bucket stood in the stark coffin. With no plumbing, the bucket accounted for the overwhelming stench in the prison—a thousand buckets that filled and stank.

Sing Sing was built directly on the ground a few inches above the water's edge, so the flagstones were always wet. It was cold and damp now. *What will it be like in the grip of an icy New York winter?* Barney wondered. He turned and looked at the cell, trying to find something to distract his mind from the terror crowding in on him.

There was a ventilator about three inches in diameter, which, he discovered later, led to a small duct between the walls. This, he also learned, helped spread the odors and the dampness. It was a haven for vermin, for each prisoner simply swept the dust out so that it filtered down on the man below him. And no power on earth could rid the fleas and lice and bedbugs from the ventilators.

Barney's eyes moved from the ventilator to a shelf on the wall with a pitcher resting on it. Water! He grabbed it and began gulping the contents down to quench his burning thirst. It was tepid and had a putrid iron taste, but he didn't care.

"Mate! Say, mate!"

The whisper came from his left. He put the pitcher back and leaned his head against the bars. "Yes? Who are you?"

"Keep it quiet, mate! Real nice and quiet!" the voice whispered hoarsely. "Me name's Gardner. Awful Gardner, they calls me. What's yours?"

"Barney Winslow."

"Just come in, eh? First time in the place?"

"Yes."

"Well, better save a bit of that water. It'll have to last you a spell. Bloomin' guards sometimes skip a day, you know. How long you in?"

"Twenty years."

"Oh, my word!" Gardner whispered. "That's a bad 'un!"

"What about you?"

"Me? Oh, I'll be gettin' out in a year. Done me four already. So about Christmas next year, I'll be gettin' back to the world." A silence followed; then Gardner asked, "What you in for, mate?"

"Armed robbery."

"Now, that's a hard 'un. But you just keep your spirits up, boy, and you'll come through it. The Good Lord won't forget you."

At the mention of God, anger and fear boiled over, and Barney slammed his fist against the stone wall. "God? Where is *He* in all this? Twenty years in this rat hole for something I didn't even do? Don't talk to me about God!"

"Just listen, boy—don't be talkin' so wild!"

"I'll talk as I please!"

"Not in this place," Gardner advised. "You'll be havin' your head in an iron collar, and besides, you'll find out that you need God here like never before."

Barney clamped his lips, then forced himself to speak softly. "Your name is 'Awful'?"

"That's not me proper name. Orville, that's it. Orville Gardner."

"Why do they call you 'Awful'?"

"Because, old chap, that's exactly what I was—just *awful!*" A breathy laugh punctuated Gardner's speech. "Nothin' too low for me—a fighter, a thief, a drunk, a whoremonger! But no more, thanks to the Good Lord! I come to this place the chief of sinners, but the Lord Jesus found me, and He saved me by His blood!"

"I don't want no preaching, Gardner. You can keep your God to yourself!"

"As you please. Watch your step in here, you understand? When we go to chow, keep your head down and don't say a word. The guards watch the new blokes real close, so don't give 'em no excuse, Barney."

Gardner ceased talking and Barney lay down on the cot. He was still thirsty, but took Awful's advice. The minutes drained away slowly. Without a watch, there was no way to judge time anyway. Besides, the dim murky twilight made it impossible to see anything. *I'll lie here week after week, year after year, no sun through those slits on the walls. The warmth won't even penetrate this gloomy, damp hole!* The thought sent a cold chill down his spine.

More than once Barney almost moved to put his head to the bars—just to hear a whisper again. The silence and gloom terrified him, though he knew it would pass in time. He forced himself to lie still on the cot, fighting off the wild desire to scream and beat his fists against the stones.

The only diversion that first day was a guard walking down the narrow way outside the cell, sometimes bringing an inmate back to his cell. Even that became an event to be anticipated, something to look at, to hear.

Finally there was a clanging sound, and he leaped to his feet and pressed his face to the bars.

"Chow time," Awful whispered. "Remember—keep it down!"

The guards unlocked the cells and marched the men down the narrow way. Gardner, Barney noted as they fell into line, gave him a wink, but said nothing. He was six feet tall and had a full head of hair and a beard to match. The men lined up a few inches apart in front of a door. Barney flinched when a pair of hands touched his shoulders, but saw down the line that each man had put his hands on the shoulders of the one in front of him. He did the same, and when the line moved, it was a lock step—a shuffle. As they entered the massive mess hall, the serpentine line reminded Barney of a centipede—a human centipede.

A warder, armed with a club, watched every move. No smiles, no winks, no glances, Imboden had said, so Barney kept his face a frozen mask. When his section of the line turned, Barney sat down at a table. Awful Gardner was on Barney's left, he knew, but kept his eyes fixed in front of him. He waited with the rest, eyeing the tin cup and single bowl with a tin plate on top. A rough chunk of bread lay on one side of the bowl, a spoon fork on the other. Each table had a large pitcher.

"Eat!" The sudden command by a warder was followed by a clatter of plates pulled into place. Barney removed his tin plate, looked into the bowl, and almost threw up. It was a stew of some sort, but he'd have to shove it down. He poured the conglomeration into the tin plate and began to eat. It was thick and grimy, with soggy vegetables and bits of rancid meat, from what he could not tell. The meat was very salty, and he knew he'd be thirsty later on, but he ate slowly, not knowing when they'd be fed again. The bread was old and wormy; still, it was better than the stew.

The lack of talk was eerie. He had not known how much talking and eating were joined. It seemed natural to converse with the man eating beside him, but one glance at the dark-skinned prisoner across from him and the others all over the mess hall wearing collars, who were forced to shove their food between strips of steel, stopped him.

The meal finished quickly, and the men were marched back to their places of confinement. As the door to his cell clanged shut, Barney remained where he was, watching as the other prisoners were herded into their stalls. Finally it grew quiet, and he dropped to the cot and held his head in his hands. How long he sat there, he didn't know; then he heard Gardner whisper, "Cheer up, lad! Never fear!"

That was all, but it helped. He lay down on the hard cot, pulled the single blanket over him, and closed his eyes. The time dragged on. Finally he drifted off to a fitful sleep, awaking abruptly when a warder hit his nightstick against the bars as he walked down the hall. The night passed somehow, and when the first murky ray of light came to his cell from the slotted window, he sat up. The stench of the place was just as bad, he knew, but his sense of smell was already becoming immune. *Soon I won't even know the place stinks*, he thought grimly. *After I've been here a few days.*

Breakfast was like supper. The lock-step march to the mess hall, the silent meal, then dumping the plates and flatware into a small barrel as they passed out of the place. Barney was called out by one of the warders and told, "You've been assigned to clean-up detail."

This meant, he discovered, sweeping and mopping the offices and the guards' quarters. It was hard work, but that night in his cell, Awful commented, "Clean-up detail? Coo! Now you see, lad, how the Good Lord is looking after you—just like I said!"

"What's so great about *that*?" Barney whispered.

"Why, a chap gets to move about, don't you see? Just be glad you didn't get in the carpet-weaving shop! My word! Sitting there ten hours a day with a warder breathing down your bloomin' neck, and usually with a hard hand, too! No, dear boy, cleanup is the best there is. They don't usually let a new man have it, so it must be that God is favoring you."

Barney did not respond, for he was still confused by the enormity of his personal tragedy. He slept little that night, or the nights following. He was like a man in a coma, or suffering from shell shock. The dreadful physical conditions of the prison—the food and the confinement in the coffin-like cell—could be adjusted to. But the loss of all freedom and the stripping away of his human dignity could not be accepted by Barney.

As the days passed, then weeks, he learned to shut things and people out as he lay for hours in his cell. At other times, he lived in the past, for, like his mother, he had the same gift of remembering the past vividly. These memories dwelt on his childhood days—fresh and sharp images. He remembered the days at the ocean with his father and mother when he was the only child. At times he could almost feel the sting of the cold brine and hear the roar of the breakers.

One scene came to him over and over—a day he and his father had walked along the beach looking for shells. It had been hot that summer day, and they had strolled for miles on the wet dunes. Finally his father had said, "Let's rest here." Sitting in the elbow of the trunk of a large tree, his father told him of the building of the railroad. Barney could still remember the weight of his father's arm across his small shoulders and the look of his blue eyes in the bright sunshine. Then they had gone back down the beach, and Barney remembered finding the shell, the biggest and best he'd ever found. It was a chambered nautilus, beautifully wrought. His father had said, "God sure knows how to make things, doesn't He, Barney?" Barney had kept that as his prized possession. It was still where he had left it—at his old home, in his room.

Barney became numb to the prison routine—rising at dawn, eating breakfast, going to work, having the evening meal, returning to his cell. He performed his duties mechanically and was shoved along like stock herders prodding cattle, with no particular interest in any one animal.

The one break in the routine was Sunday. That day prisoners were given a choice of going back to their cells from the dining hall with their food and being locked in until the next morning— or attending church. Like most of the inmates, Barney stubbornly refused to attend church, in spite of Gardner's repeated invitations.

These were the long dismal hours when the whispers, sighs, and groans of a thousand men echoed against the blank walls, and the smell of a thousand bodies and a thousand buckets saturated the damp and gloomy air. Barney usually filled the day with dog-eared novels that he could read by holding the book up to the dim light filtering down through the slit from above.

After two months, Barney couldn't face another long day. As they were lining up for the walk to the dining room, he whispered, "Awful, I'm going to church."

"Good–O! It'll be a good 'un, Barney."

The service was held in a long, narrow room with rough benches. At the front of the room was a low platform with a crude pine pulpit and a table holding a pitcher of water. Awful sat beside Barney and handed him a tattered songbook. "Let's 'ere you sing out, lad!"

Two men were seated on the platform, and one of them stood up and began singing. He was not a particularly good singer, and for the most part the inmates were either unskillful or indifferent. Yet as the singing went on, something began to happen to Barney. It was the songs, for many of them were the ones he had sung in the church he had attended all his life with his parents. He could almost hear his mother's clear voice as she sang "The Old Rugged Cross" with great joy. Another, "Alas, and Did My Saviour Bleed," was his father's favorite. As the song filled the room, Barney remembered standing beside his father as a child, holding his hand, and his father had cried as he sang:

Alas, and did my Saviour bleed? And did my Sovereign die?
Would He devote that sacred head for such a worm as I?

Was it for sins that I had done He groaned upon the tree?
Amazing pity! Grace unknown! And love beyond degree!

But drops of grief can ne'er repay the debt of love I owe:
Here, Lord, I give myself to Thee; 'Tis all that I can do.

And then the chorus:

At the cross, at the cross, where I first saw the light,
And the burden of my heart rolled away.
It was there by faith I received my sight—
And now I am happy all the day.

Tears gathered in Barney's eyes, and he choked on the words. Barney heard little of the sermon, but the words of the song rolled over and over in his mind: *It was there by faith I received my sight—and now I am happy all the day.*

After the service he returned to his cell, and that afternoon he allowed Awful Gardner to speak of his love for the Lord Jesus Christ.

From that time on, Barney attended chapel every Sunday. He

said little, but Awful was happy just to have him there. "You'll find it, laddie, never fear!" he would whisper every night.

The months rolled by, and Barney was surprised to discover that he had been in prison for a year. "Time don't work in here like it does on the outside," Gardner said.

"You'll be getting out pretty soon, Awful," Barney said. They were sitting in the chapel where they could speak quietly, waiting for the service to begin.

"Right-O! Only a few more months. And I'm prayin' that you'll get time out for good behavior. I'll be waitin' for you out there, no fear!"

Fortunately, Barney didn't let his mind think of release, for only a month later he got into deep trouble.

Winslow had always been a good self-taught artist. One day he found a tablet and began illustrating sketches of prison life. Most of the simple drawings were of the men in the prison—inmates and guards. He showed them to no one, and it was only by accident they were discovered when Barney and Awful Gardner were sitting side by side in chapel. As Barney was sketching the visiting minister, Awful caught a glimpse and nudged Barney.

"Lem'me see the rest!"

Gardner was delighted as he recognized various individuals. "Look at 'im!" he exclaimed. "It's Captain Dollar down to 'is last hair! And 'ere's Timmy Mackey—the spittin' image!" He handed them back, saying, "Better not let any of the wardens see these. They don't like it when a chap enjoys 'imself!"

Barney had no intention of any prison official seeing them. He continued to sketch, then in his second year he began to draw different aspects of Sing Sing—the grimmer side.

From the first day he was aware of the cruel punishments dealt by the guards. The iron collar was one of the more gentle ones Barney'd seen; but the cat-o'-nine tails, a whip with nine leather thongs embedded with bits of metal in each strap, was common. He had never seen it used, but he had been a witness of the result. Once while cleaning the primitive "hospital" floor, he had been shoved out of the way by two guards who brought an unconscious man through the door and dumped him on one of the cots. "Better give him a pill, Doc," one of them laughed.

"He's got a backache. Got it from talking back to a guard."

Barney had turned to look, and one glance made him sick. Naked to the waist, the man's upper back was a mass of bleeding pulp. He was unconscious, but his body was jerking, crawling like the skin of a horse trying to shake off flies. The flesh was laid back in such terrible furrows that the back of the rib cage was exposed, white bone laid bare in the bloody flesh.

One of the guards had seen Barney's revulsion at the sight. "Better watch yourself, Con. You might get a bit of this yourself."

Barney had been unable to forget the sight, and one of the victim's descriptions had only intensified his vision of what it was like. The man from Tennessee, eyes stark with fear, stared at Winslow. "They chain you to the floor, all stretched out, and then one of them puts on a special white coat and a little flat hat. The rest of them gather around to watch. It's bad at first, like fire! But then you pass out. Look at my back."

His back had been so deeply scarred that it would never heal, and for months afterward Barney had nightmares about the event. He drew a sketch of it, not understanding why.

The other punishment was known as "The Shower." It sounded innocent enough when Barney first heard of it. One of the inmates said that he'd been caught breaking the rules and was going to get "The Shower" that night. Barney had remarked, "Well, that's not so bad, is it?"

"I'd rather have the cat!" he'd said bitterly.

Awful had been subjected to "The Shower" more than once. "They puts you in the regular shower, the one you know, Barney. Big wooden box with the shower head up high. Only they put a chair in there, and it's got a sort of thing like a trough attached to the top, you see? It fits around a bloke's neck, and it's like havin' your 'ead in a big basin. Your hands is strapped to the arms and you can't move a finger, see?" Awful's face contorted. "So when the guard starts the shower, the bowl fills up—and when it fills up to your mouth, you try to drink it to keep it out of your nose. But you can't do it, so under goes your nose. What you do is *drown*. So they let you drown; then they takes you out and pumps you dry. And then—they do it again. Once they done me six times." Gardner's battered face was pale at the memory, and he shook his head. "Rather die than go through it again, I would!"

Barney had drawn a graphic sketch of that scene, unconsciously using Gardner as the victim and Captain Nathaniel Dollar as the executioner. It had been Dollar who had applied the cat to the prisoner Barney had talked to, and the man had become a symbol to Barney of the many guards who were cruel and savage.

If he had thrown away the sketches, he would never have encountered the most harrowing experience of his life. Actually he forgot them, having tucked them in the back of the tablet, continuing to sketch the less terrible aspects of his surroundings. And it was on a Sunday morning that this oversight caught up with him in a burst of fury he had never dreamed could happen.

He had taken his tablet to chapel, and the service ran overtime. When the preacher closed, the guards came running down the aisles, hurrying the prisoners in order to keep to the rigid schedule. Barney had placed the tablet beside him, and in the pressure forgot it. He was outside the chapel before he remembered what he'd done, and stopped abruptly. The sudden movement jostled the man behind Barney, invoking the guard's wrath. "Get on now!" he yelled.

"I left something in chapel—" Barney began, but the guard punched him with his stick, waving him on. Barney was heartsick, but when he told Awful what had happened the other was not worried.

"One of the preachers will probably find it. It'll be there next Sunday."

But an hour later Barney was aroused from a nap by the abrupt sound of his cell door opening. He opened his eyes, but not soon enough, for he was struck in the stomach with a club and dragged out of his cell, gasping in pain.

"What's wrong?" he cried hoarsely when his breath returned.

The two burly guards silently dragged him down the narrow walkway. Fear coursed through him, and he tried to resist, but a sharp crack on the side of his head sent showers of bright lights before his eyes. The next thing he knew he was hauled through a door and shoved so violently that he fell sprawling on the stone floor. Rolling over on his side, he saw Captain Nathaniel Dollar standing rigidly in the center of the room beside the shower. Barney saw at once that a chair was fastened inside with a bowl affixed to it.

"Is this yours?" Dollar demanded. He held out the tablet, and Barney's heart sank. He nodded silently. Dollar stared at him, then slowly nodded. "Quite an artist, aren't you, Winslow? What did you intend to do with these pictures? Sell them to a New York newspaper?"

"No, sir!" Barney said with alarm. "I don't do anything with them."

"Oh, you don't?" Dollar scoffed. "You think I'm a fool? You're a clever one—but we have ways of dealing with smart ones." Anger blazed out of his close-set eyes, and he waved his hand. "Put him in the chair."

There was no use struggling, and Barney tried to get himself mentally prepared for what was coming as the guards strapped him in the chair. He stared straight ahead as they fastened the basin around his face, and then he heard Dollar say, "Let's see if we can't wash a little of that smartness out of you!"

What followed was the most horrendous experience of Barney's life. As the water rose, he began to gag, and he held his breath, but the water filled the bowl so that his nose was under, forcing him to breath. The water surged up his nose and into his mouth. He struggled with all his might. The torture was repeated over and over until he eventually passed out.

When he became conscious, he was still in the chair, and Dollar snarled, "That was just the beginning. Here's some more for you!" Barney tried to cry out, but it was useless. Again he lost consciousness, and again he was revived. How many times this occurred, he could never remember.

Barney was only dimly aware of being hauled by his arms across a floor. Then he felt the cold bite of iron on his wrists and ankles. Gagging from the water, he rolled his head to one side and saw Dollar standing over him with the whip in his hands. A smile curled his thin lips as he said, "Now, Winslow, we'll bleed you a little bit. The old-time doctors always bled their patients, I understand."

Barney shut his eyes and pressed his cheek against the cold stone. The first stroke of the cat ran through him like fire. Again and again the whip struck his back. Barney had one thing on his mind as the punishment went on: *I won't let them make me cry out!*

And he didn't, though it would have been better if he had. His silence enraged Dollar, and he continued until one of the guards said nervously, "Better give it up, Captain. He's had it, I reckon."

Barney did not hear this—nor anything else for a long time. The experience with "The Shower" and the beating taken together put him into a coma. He was taken back to his cell, but when he didn't regain consciousness the next day, he was carried to the hospital. His wounds became infected, and it was many days before he returned to his cell.

Awful Gardner watched as two guards came down the walkway, supporting Winslow's thin body. One glimpse of Barney's face made Gardner cringe at the change he saw. When the guards left, Gardner waited until he heard the cot creak, then whispered gently, "Are you all right, laddie?"

"Yes."

The brief answer was curt, but Gardner went on. "I know 'tis been hard, lad, but you're alive. We'll see you through." He paused, and when there was no reply, added, "I've prayed for you every day, you know."

Again silence. Then Gardner heard Barney Winslow's reply, laced with bitterness and steely anger. "Don't pray for me, you hear? And never mention the name of God to me! I'm through with all that."

Gardner put his cheek against the cold steel bars and shook his head. When he lay down on his cot, he put his hand on the foot-thick stone that separated him from his friend and began to pray.

CHAPTER FIVE

LOLA MAKES A CALL

★ ★ ★ ★

Mark leaned back in his chair and looked across the table, picked up his cup of coffee and sipped slowly. "Are you glad to be back home, Lola?" he asked.

"Yes, I am. Are you?" Lola lifted her eyes to the dining room she had not seen for eighteen months.

"I like the climate better there."

"So do I, but—" She broke off abruptly and dropped her white linen napkin in her lap. Ordinarily a strong and composed woman, Lola could not hide the pain that was wrenching her heart.

"I know," he nodded slowly. "You never were settled on the coast, but you've been more restless than usual." He got up and placed his hand on her shoulder. She held it tightly. He squeezed it hard. "It's Barney, isn't it?"

"Yes."

"I thought so. It's been hard for me, too."

Lola stood up and leaned against him, pressing her face to his chest. He held her trembling body, surprised at the emotion. The past months had been extremely difficult for her. She had lost the sparkle and glow that made her so delightful, and none of the activities he had suggested to entice her in Sacramento had worked. He knew it was because of Barney. He had tried everything to help him, had even hired an expert private detective agency, but they had found nothing that would exonerate him. Finally, Frank Carswell, head of the agency, said, "Mr. Winslow, we can't keep taking your money for nothing. We've exhausted every lead."

Mark and Lola had written Barney, but his rare answers were so empty and meaningless. He never spoke of himself, just thanked them for the gifts and the money they sent. His last reply had been only two lines.

"He's given up on life, I'm afraid," Mark said.

"He can't!" Lola cried, the fiery Spanish blood showing in her eyes as she drew back. She struck Mark on the chest as though he were the prison she so hated. "I won't let him give up!"

The grandfather clock in the foyer struck, the hollow sound reverberating through the house, and Mark said, "We'll talk about it when I get back. We'll go to the prison this week."

"Mark, do you have to go to the meeting?"

"I'm afraid so. You know how I hate political meetings, but this one may be important. The Democrats are going to nominate their candidate for president pretty soon, and I think it may be the young man who's speaking tonight. Name's William Jennings Bryan. I'm meeting with the committee to talk with him afterward." He paused. "I wish you'd come with me. I hate for you to be home alone on our first night back home."

Lola smiled and patted his arm. "I won't be home. Andy and I are going to Moody's meeting."

"Wish I could go with you," Mark said enviously. "I'd rather hear Dwight L. Moody preach than listen to the best political speech ever made! What about Esther?"

"She's spending the night with Louise Fellows." Lola reached up and patted Mark's cheek. "You'd better get ready. Let's have a midnight snack when we get home, just as we used to do."

He grinned and embraced her. "Good thing it's church you're going to. I wouldn't let such a good-looking woman go anywhere else. Some handsome young fellow might run off with you!"

"Don't be silly!"

He kissed her hard. "Now, tell Andy I want him to keep an eye on you—for my protection," he teased.

Lola laughed, but he had succeeded in changing her mood. As she left the room, he grabbed his coat, his mind on his oldest son, not the presidential candidates.

★ ★ ★ ★

Lola was waiting in the foyer when Andy rushed into the house at a quarter of six. "Good! You're ready," he said. "Say, you look great!" He grinned. "Should be a good meeting!"

Lola was wearing a simple suit of light gray wool, a blouse of dark green silk, and a small hat that made her large dark eyes seem even larger. She had no patience with the current fashions that New York women had taken to. The ridiculous bustle made its wearers look as if they were carrying shelves concealed under the backs of their skirts. This horrible style was going out, but the "sheath gown" was coming in. This was simply a tube made of cloth that reached from the hips to the shoe tops. "It looks like a gun barrel!" Lola had told one of her friends. The women who did wear them found they could take steps no more than six inches, which is why they soon were called "hobble skirts."

"We'd better hurry, Andy," she said. "We'll be lucky to get a seat in the auditorium."

"Don't worry about that," Andy responded cheerfully. "I've got a little surprise for you." He refused to elaborate, but she liked his cheery mood. When they arrived at the auditorium, he led her into the expansive building, and as she had anticipated, it was already filled to overflowing.

"I expect we'll have to stand up," she said, glancing over the packed crowd.

"Come along," he grinned. Lola followed him, wondering what he was up to. She gasped when he led her down the long aisles to the front and handed a ticket to an attendant who was standing at the foot of the platform. He looked at the ticket, smiled and said, "This way, please," walking up to the seats on the next to last row of the platform.

"Andy, how did you ever manage such a thing?" Lola demanded.

"Why, I was on the committee that did the groundwork for Mr. Moody's visit," he said. "When I met him, he recognized my name. Wanted to know if I was any relation to Mark Winslow—the one who'd given so liberally to Moody Bible College in Chicago. Well, I lost no time assuring him that I was the son of that illustrious man, and he insisted that I sit on the platform."

"How nice!" Lola said with a pleased smile. "I'm sorry your father couldn't be here, but I think he'll come tomorrow. You know how much he admires Mr. Moody."

After about half an hour Andy exclaimed, "There he is! There's Mr. Moody! Come on!"

"Andy, no!"

"Sure, he said he wanted to meet Dad, but he'll have to be satisfied with you."

Lola had no choice, so she followed Andy until they were directly in front of the famous evangelist. "Good to see you, Mr. Moody," Andy said. "My father was unable to be here, but I'd like you to meet my mother."

Mr. Moody was not an impressive man, Lola noted. Short and thick-set, with a full graying beard, kind brown eyes, alert and clear. His grammar wasn't the best, but there was none of the arrogance sometimes found in famous people.

He smiled at her with a genuine air of pleasure.

"Mrs. Winslow," he said in a pleasant tenor voice, "I have written your husband several times, thanking him for his generous support of our Bible college, and it gives me much pleasure to thank you personally."

"Oh, Mr. Moody," Lola replied, awed by the opportunity to meet him, "it's been little enough, but we pray for you every day."

"Thank you," Moody said, then he gave her a steady look, and after a moment's silence asked, "Is there anything I can pray with you about, Mrs. Winslow?"

Lola dropped her eyes, then raised them, tears ready to spill over. "We have a son who is in prison, Mr. Moody."

Moody considered her, then in a conversational tone began to pray. It was as though he were addressing a close personal friend, with none of the wordy ministerial prayers often heard. "Dear Father, it is your joy to reclaim prodigal sons. This, thy handmaiden, and her companion are your faithful servants. I ask that you bring their son back from the depths of sin and lead him to the cross. Save him, Lord, for we ask this in the name of Jesus Christ, the friend of sinners."

Unable to see Moody clearly through her tears, she whispered, "Thank you, Mr. Moody."

"I believe God has begun His work in your boy. I believe he will soon be set free," the evangelist said.

"Oh, thank you," she said again, then took Andy's arm as they returned to their seats.

"That was wonderful, Mother!"

Lola smiled, her heart rejoicing at the words echoing in her mind: *I believe he will soon be set free.* Though the service was wonderful, she scarcely heard Ira Sankey, the great musician, sing, or Moody's powerful message as the Spirit of God moved in the hearts of people. She could only think of Barney.

On the way home as Andy talked about the sermon, his mother interrupted him. "Andy, tell me again about the night you went to find the man who shot Adams."

Surprised, Andy said, "Why, Mother, I told you about that before." But at her insistence, he recounted the details again. When he finished Lola asked, "About this girl, Katie—you thought she knew something?"

"I thought so at the time, but now I don't know. Those people are suspicious of anyone like us."

"Andy, I'm sure you were on the track of something," Lola said quietly. She sat there thinking hard, and then added, "I think God has brought us back to New York to help your brother."

"Why, Mother, Dad's paid out a fortune to private detectives! They tried everything."

Lola smiled at him. "But Barney's not their son."

That night long after she went to bed, she kept hearing the words: *I believe he will soon be set free.* A voice whispered that

Moody had meant that Barney would be saved—be free from sin. But Lola shook her head fiercely. "No, Lord! Save him *and* deliver him from prison!"

★ ★ ★ ★

Katie came out of her drunken stupor slowly. Someone was shouting at her and slapping her face, but she could not tell who it was. Finally she forced her eyes open, and saw the man standing over her.

"All right . . . Tony," she whispered. "I'm awake."

"You're drunk, that's what you are!" Barone pulled her from the bed to her feet and held her up, or she would have collapsed. Cursing, he reached over with one hand and grabbed a pitcher of water and doused it over her head. "I told you to lay off the booze!"

Gasping and sputtering, Katie wiped her face as she tried to speak, but the raw gin had thickened her tongue. "I—just had a little drink to—help me get ready!"

"Liar!" Barone shoved her back on the bed and picked up an empty bottle from the floor. "You drank the whole quart!" He tossed the bottle at the rumpled figure. She had been the biggest disappointment he'd had with women. Looks, voice, ability—she'd had it all, but in less than a month it had become apparent that she couldn't tolerate alcohol. She'd have one drink, another—then drink until she passed out. "Worse drunk I ever saw!" he'd told his friends. "She'll have to lay off the booze."

But Katie couldn't do that. She lived in a world where liquor was more plentiful than water, and there was always someone ready to buy her a drink, no matter how hard Tony Barone tried to watch her. Now looking down on her, he said, "I've had it with you, Katie. You know who was coming to hear you sing tonight? Lindsey Black, that's who! The biggest producer in this town! I worked on him for weeks. Now he's coming and you can't even stand up!"

"I—I can sing, Tony!" Katie said. She struggled to her feet, swaying. "Just—give me—a few minutes!"

"I'll give you *nothing*, you drunk!" Barone raged. "You're

through singing. You can hustle like the rest of the girls."

"No! I can't do that!" Katie cried. She reached for him. "Tony, you said you loved me, that we'd get married!"

He laughed harshly. "Think I'd marry a drunk like you?"

"You—you gave me my first drink, Tony!"

"Everybody gets their first drink from somebody," he said callously. "Get your stuff together. I don't want you in my apartment. You can have one of the rooms with the other girls."

Katie stared at him in unbelief. "I can't do that!"

"Do it or get out!" Barone said. He stalked away, then stopped. "If you're in here when I get back, you'll wish you were gone!"

The door slammed, and Katie sank down on the bed, shaking. Confused and terrified, she slowly began to dress, for she knew Barone meant what he said. *I'll clean up, go away and sober up for a couple of days*, she thought. *Then Tony'll take me back.*

An hour later she left the saloon, but her plan failed almost at once. A man she knew slightly stopped her on the street. "Well, this is my lucky day! I was going to eat alone, but if you'd join me, Katie, I'd be favored."

She hesitated, then nodded. He took her to an expensive restaurant, and during the meal she drank several glasses of wine. Afterward, they went dancing, and soon she was drunk again. The next morning she woke up in a room she didn't recognize. She dressed and left, passing the room clerk on the way. "Come back soon, dearie," he called after her, smirking.

The sharp autumn wind bit her face as she moved along the gray sidewalk. For hours she walked the streets, and not knowing what else to do, made her way back to Barone's place. His manager, Pete Shuffield, met her as she came through the door. "Tony ain't here, Katie," he said. "But he said to tell you nothin's changed. Either start hustlin' at the bar or clear out. Sorry, but that's the way it is," he shrugged. "I put all your stuff in the room at the end of the hall."

Katie numbly climbed the stairs and stood in front of the door. She knew what it meant—she would be "one of Tony's girls," a common prostitute. Slowly she opened the door and entered, packed her one suitcase, and left. She tried to think back to the day she had come to Tony's place, but the memory was too painful. She found a cheap room in a dilapidated rooming house, and went out to look for work.

Times were hard in the country, the slums of New York stark evidence of the poverty. Many had come from the country seeking work, but there was none. Katie returned to the factory where she had worked before going to Barone, and found it closed and abandoned. She could not hold back the tears as she gazed at the battened-down windows, the sullen ghostly old brick building. She had always thought she could go back to her former job. Now that, too, was gone.

For two weeks she walked the streets seeking work, and every night she ended up getting drunk. At first it was just a few drinks "to go to sleep," she told herself. But as things got more desperate, she began to drink during the day. Finally she was spending most of her time in a stupor. Her money ran out the third week, and it was then she secured a job waiting on tables at a cafe in Brooklyn. The hours were long and the pay low, and she was forced to find a cheaper room—this time over a bar down the street. The small, dark, vermin-infested place was overrun with rats. It was frightening, but Katie had no choice.

She worked from noon until ten, and as soon as she left work, she usually went to her room and began drinking. Men of the lowest sort in the district constantly stalked her, but she managed to elude them. The uncouth owner of the cafe, Clyde Posten, tried to force himself on her, but gave up with a curse when she fought him off. He didn't fire her, because she was cheap reliable help, but he made things as difficult as he could.

She saw a few people from Barone's place, but never Tony. One of the bar girls named Nellie had advised her to return. "It's better than working your arms off here," she had said. But Katie had resisted.

One September night, Katie came out of the cafe, exhausted and discouraged. She stopped at a liquor store and bought a bottle of gin, then went home and began to drink. She was halfway through the bottle when a knock at her door aroused her. "Who is it?" she asked, not getting off the bed. It was not uncommon for one of the men who lived in the neighborhood to come and try to get her to go out with him, and she assumed it was one of these.

But it was a woman's voice. "My name is Winslow. May I talk to you, Miss Sullivan?"

Katie stood to her feet and brushed her hair from her face. She was groggy and her hand was unsteady as she slipped the bolt on her door. "What's that you say?" she asked, her tongue thick from the liquor. She peered out into the dark hallway, unable to see the features of the woman who stood there. "Who are you?"

"We met once, Miss Sullivan. I'm Barney Winslow's mother."

"Barney?" Katie tried to think, and a memory came back to her. "Yes, I remember Barney." She hesitated, then shrugged. "You can come in if you want to." She turned up the low burning light in the lamp on the table, then said, "You want to sit down?"

Lola took the only chair in the room, saying, "Thank you." She showed no sign of the disgust that filled her at the foul-smelling room, for she was actually more shocked at the change in Katie Sullivan.

She had thought of her often, and now to see the girl's dirty face and unkempt, filthy hair shocked her. Katie had changed so greatly that Lola would never have known her.

"I know you're wondering why I've come to see you," she began.

"How'd you find me?"

"I went to Mr. Barone's place. A young woman named Nellie told me where you lived." Lola hesitated, then plunged in. "I need your help, Miss Sullivan. I don't think Barney shot that man, and I'm going to prove it."

"I don't know anything about it," Katie said thickly. She picked up the bottle, took a drink from it, then shook her head. "It was a long time ago."

"My younger son, Andy, came to see you after it happened. Do you remember that?"

"I guess so. But I told him I didn't know anything."

Lola said gently, "So he said. But he told me he felt that you did know *something*. He sensed you were afraid to talk."

"Well, it's not a good idea to squeal on people in this part of town," Katie nodded. She took another drink, then stared at Lola. "People have been shot and thrown in the river for talking too much."

Lola sat there quietly, trying to think of how to approach the girl. Katie Sullivan was at the bottom—that was clear. But all other leads had run out. She breathed a quick prayer, then said, "My dear, I wouldn't have you come to any harm."

The simple words struck against Katie's drink-dulled senses. She stared at the elegant form before her, seeing the kindness in the woman's eyes, and it brought tears to her eyes. "I guess not many people are trying to keep me from harm," she said. "But I'll tell you what little I know."

"I'd be very grateful," Lola said. She reached out and touched Katie's hand. "It would mean a great deal to me."

Katie paused, then said, "Well, I heard Tony talking with Studs Ketchel the day after the shooting. I was in the next room, and I guess Tony forgot I was there. They were talking about the robbery, and Studs was afraid of something. Then Tony said, 'Don't worry, Studs. Nobody knows you hired Barney for the job. It's your word against his.' And then Studs said, 'You're wrong about that. Manti knows.' And then Tony says, 'Legs won't talk, Studs. Young Winslow's takin' the fall for him.' Then somebody came in, so they stopped talking."

"Do you know a man called Legs Manti?" Lola asked.

"He used to come into Tony's place all the time. He'd been in prison, and everybody said he was a dangerous man."

Lola sat there thinking, compassion for the distraught girl welling up. "You've changed since I saw you last." Katie's head dropped, and the older woman added, "I'd like to help you, Katie. You don't have to live like this."

Katie looked up, startled, as a roll of bills was pressed into her hands.

"This is not just for telling me what you know about this case," Lola said. "I'd like to see you get out of the life you're living here. God will help you."

Katie shook her head. "No, God doesn't care about me."

"You're wrong about that, my dear," Lola said, and for some time she tried to convince the unhappy young woman about her condition, but it seemed useless. Realizing she'd done what she could, Lola wrote something on a card and handed it to Katie. "Katie, call me if you ever change your mind. Now, let me ask you one thing. I think the day is coming when the truth is going to come out about the crime Barney's in prison for. Will you tell the truth as you've told it to me—to the authorities, I mean?"

Katie looked down at the roll of bills in her hand. They represented the first kindness anyone had shown her in a long time. "Yes," she replied. "But I don't care what they do to me. I'd be better off in the river, anyway!"

CHAPTER SIX

MR. CARMODY'S VISITOR

★ ★ ★ ★

No man rose to the top of the political structure of New York City in the year of 1896 without being tough, but Daniel Patrick Carmody was more than just hard. He had climbed out of the slums of the Bowery, fighting and defeating every opponent with a thoroughness that shocked observers. He entered the business world and applied the same ruthless technique with such efficiency that in ten years he controlled a huge share of the city's revenues. When he entered politics at the age of thirty, onlookers predicted he would not so easily run roughshod over hardened ward bosses, but they were mistaken. By the time he was thirty-five years of age, he was the boss of New York's political machine.

In the process, Carmody had made quite a few enemies, as any man would be forced to do who climbed so rapidly and so high. But many of them were either dead or ruined, so he gave them little thought. But Carmody's success whetted his appetite for more. Being the boss was a beginning—why not something with more class? Mayor of New York, for example? That could propel him even further—say, senator?

Dan Carmody sat in his office musing over his future. He was not a poetic man, yet he did have a bold and sweeping imagination where his personal goals were concerned. His eyes flicked to a picture on the wall of two men shaking hands—one, William

McKinley, who would in all probability be the next President of the United States; the other, Dan Carmody.

"Mr. Carmody, there's a lady here to see you."

His secretary's abrupt announcement tore Carmody's eyes from the picture. "What lady?" he grunted, irritated.

"A Mrs. Winslow."

"Is she anybody?"

"I don't know, sir," he replied, hesitating. A major part of his job was to decide who should be allowed to see his boss. Finally he shrugged. "I think you better see her. She's top drawer." He glanced at the picture of McKinley and Carmody and winked. "She's a swell, Dan. Might be a heavy contributor to your campaign fund next year."

Carmody's eyes sparked with interest. "Show her in, Patterson."

The woman was top drawer, all right, Carmody noted. Dressed in simple but expensive clothing and wearing little jewelry, except for the diamond that glittered at her throat, she spoke of money. He got up at once and advanced to meet her.

"Mrs. Winslow? Dan Carmody. Won't you have a seat."

"Thank you, Mr. Carmody." Lola sat down gracefully, then said, "I'll get right to the point, Mr. Carmody. My son is in prison for a crime he didn't commit. One of your lieutenants is responsible for it, and I intend to see that he is brought to account. And when that happens, you will, of course, be embarrassed."

Carmody prided himself on his iron will, and was not a man to show emotion. But when the beautiful woman with the enormous black eyes spoke out, he was stunned. He saw that she was aware of his confusion, and it angered him.

"Mrs. Winslow, you're making a mistake," he said. Carmody's first impulse was to strike back. Hit hard and they won't return, he often said. His eyes narrowed and he said in a threatening voice, "You'd better leave."

"Very well," Lola said calmly, rising to her feet. "I thought we might settle this matter quietly, but I can see you're not ready for that. You can expect a call from my husband later in the day."

"And who might he be?"

"Mark Winslow. He's vice-president of the Union Pacific Railroad." She saw his eyes open wide, so plunged the barb a little deeper. "And he's also chairman of the Democratic National Committee."

Carmody cleared his throat, and saw with alarm that the woman was already heading for the door, her back straight as a soldier's!

"Now—just a moment, Mrs. Winslow—!" He jumped up to intercept her at the door. "You've got the best of me." Carmody was a big, fine-looking man who could charm anyone when he chose to do so.

Smiling and shaking his head gently, he said, "You must forgive me, Mrs. Winslow, but you just don't know how many people come into this office with strange ideas. Here, please sit down and let me hear more of this. Believe me, I know nothing about it."

Lola took her seat, saying, "I think that's probably true, Mr. Carmody. A man with your busy schedule has to delegate responsibility. My husband tells me that's the most difficult part of business."

"He's a wise man, Mrs. Winslow!"

"Yes, he is." Lola paused, then said slowly and with great emphasis, "My husband also says that a man who is interested in public office is even more vulnerable. For he may be betrayed by the inefficiency—or the corruption—of his people."

Carmody was fully alarmed now. His mind had been working rapidly, and he recalled that Mark Winslow was indeed a power within the party—the party whose support he *had* to have if he expected to climb to the top. He nodded. "Very true, Mrs. Winslow. It's inevitable that a man will make some mistakes in choosing his lieutenants. Suppose you tell me about your son."

Lola had carefully planned her meeting with Carmody, not even informing Mark of her intent. She was wise enough to know that the evidence she had was pitifully thin, that it was not enough to cause the courts to reconsider their verdict.

But she was also aware of Dan Carmody's keen political ambitions. With that in mind, she had put together the few facts she held in a way that would affect those ambitions. In blunt terms, Mrs. Winslow recounted the story of the robbery. She stressed the fact that Adams, the man who had been shot, could not identify her son as the assailant, but that she had evidence a man named Studs Ketchel had hired Legs Manti to commit the holdup.

"What evidence do you have against Studs Ketchel?"

"That will come out in the trial—if it comes to that, Mr. Carmody," Lola said evenly.

"I'll have to speak to Ketchel—but I don't think he's guilty. Come and see me tomorrow."

"Ketchel is in his office down the hall," Lola said. "Call him in right now. The three of us will have this out." She saw the anger rise in Carmody's face, and added, "When I leave this office, your opportunity to handle this quietly is gone. I will go straight to the newspapers and then to my husband. I don't know if it will get my son out of prison or not, but it will be very hard on you, Mr. Carmody. Fatal, I think, to your political aims."

Carmody had never been so helpless. Anger raced through him, but he knew he had no choice. "Patterson!" he called, and when the secretary appeared, said, "Get Studs in here!"

"Yes, sir."

As the door closed, Carmody went to his chair and sat down. The woman didn't speak, and in the silence, his eyes fell on the picture of himself shaking hands with William McKinley. He shifted his glance toward Lola Winslow, thinking that if things were different, he could have her "taken care of." But he knew that was impossible, so he began sifting through ways to get clear of the problem.

When Ketchel came through the door, Carmody said, "This is Mrs. Winslow. Her husband is vice-president of the Union Pacific Railroad—and chairman of the Democratic National Committee."

Ketchel was a shrewd man. He understood the message at once: *This woman is important!* "I'm glad to meet you, Mrs. Winslow."

"Mrs. Winslow, tell Studs what you just told me."

Studs turned to listen, at a loss as to what the woman could want to tell him; but with her first sentence, his highly developed sense of self-preservation began to function. He had always felt uneasy about the Adams robbery, and now it was rising from its grave.

Lola said briefly, "You hired a man named Legs Manti to hold up the Adams jewelry store, and you hired my son to help him. It was Manti who shot that jeweler, not my son. I intend to see that Manti goes to jail and my son is set free."

Ketchel froze, his jaw slack. "Mrs. Winslow—I—I had nothing to do with it," he stammered.

"You'll have your chance to prove that in court, Ketchel," she said, then rose to her feet, addressing Carmody, "I'm going to step out of the office. I'll give you men five minutes. If you can come up with a plan to get my son out of jail and save yourselves, I'll listen. If not, we will have to go to court."

When the door closed, Ketchel stared at Carmody, saying in a strained voice, "Dan! What's going on?"

"I'll tell *you* what's going on!" Carmody snapped. "I'm going to lose the race for mayor—and *you're* going to Sing Sing!"

"Dan! She can't prove a thing!"

"You guarantee that, Studs?" Carmody demanded sarcastically. "You personally guarantee that the wife of the chairman of the National Democratic Committee can't put the skids under me?"

"Wait a minute!"

"Wait, nothing!" Carmody barked, slamming his hand on the desk. "You made this mess, Studs! I told you to quit fooling with penny-ante stuff! Now you've got five minutes to think of something! That woman means business!"

Suddenly Ketchel exclaimed, "Wait a minute!" He stood there, his crafty face working. Then he smiled, "I got it!"

"It better be good!"

"It is!" Ketchel cried. "I guess you forgot about Legs."

Carmody paused, his mind working rapidly; then he said slowly, "Yeah, I did forget." A smile touched his lips. "He's up for life."

"Sure! No parole for Legs, the judge said."

"So we make sure he confesses to the Adams' job, right?"

"Right!" Ketchel nodded. "I mean, they can't give him more than life, can they? Anyway, he done the job. The Winslow kid never even had a hand in it. He was drunk on the street; never done a thing."

"What makes Legs confess?"

"Why, he's had a change of heart, old Legs has! Can't stand

the thought of poor old Barney suffering in the Castle for something he never done!"

"But how do we make him do it?"

Ketchel shrugged. "Won't be hard, Dan. Guys in Sing Sing need things. Legs don't have no dough. We slip him a few bills— he sings like a canary." Then a brutal gleam flashed in his eyes. "'Course if Legs balks on us, we can get someone to *persuade* him. Not a good idea to get on the bad side of the guards in stir. I found that out. I'll just tell Legs he can look for a few cold showers and a session or two with Captain Dollar and his little toy. But Legs will do it. He ain't got nothin' to lose, and he needs the dough."

"All right, that's it." Carmody walked to the door, opened it, and said, "Mrs. Winslow, will you come in, please?"

When Lola stepped inside, Carmody said, "I'm afraid there's been a terrible miscarriage of justice, Mrs. Winslow. But thank God we can do something about it!"

"I was sure you could, Mr. Carmody," Lola said evenly.

"Studs here was involved, but not as you think," Carmody went on. "He's been angry and upset over the way the case was handled, but we've found a way to get your son out."

"You work very quickly, Mr. Carmody," Lola said mockingly, then added, "I will expect to hear from you." She turned on her heels and walked out of the room without another word.

Carmody stared after her with reluctant admiration. "Now there's a dame for you, Studs! Wish the men that work for me had that kind of nerve."

"She's something," Ketchel admitted. "I'll see Legs today. Better get this thing done."

"Right!"

Ketchel turned to leave, but asked one more question. "You think she'd have gone through with it, Dan?"

Carmody smiled thinly. "I think she'd have skinned the two of us with a dull knife to free that boy. Now, get with it, Studs. And no slip-ups!"

★　★　★　★

"Come on, Winslow!"

Startled, he raised his eyes from the loom in front of him.

Manners, one of the more decent guards, was standing in front of him. "Come along," Manners said when Barney hesitated.

Winslow rose without a word. He had become a changed man since the torturous beating. And after Awful Gardner left, Barney never communicated with any of the men in adjoining cells, nor had he gone back to chapel. All his guards noticed his silence. "Reckon you took the fight out of him, Captain," one of the guards reported to Dollar, and that was accepted as the standard explanation for Winslow's silence.

Now as he followed Manners out of the carpet-weaving area, Barney felt certain that he was in for another punishment—though he could not think of any cause he had given. Manners, however, didn't turn toward the area where punishment was dealt out, but rather toward the section of the prison where the warden and other administrators had their offices.

Barney had cleaned the offices a few times before being placed in the carpet-weaving room, but now as he followed the guard to the first floor, he became wary. He was like an animal that had been mistreated to absolute submission. Unable to see good in a change, he sullenly shuffled along with the guard. Manners stopped before a door marked WARDEN. He opened it and stepped inside, saying, "Step in, Winslow."

Barney entered the room, and a man in a dark suit looked up from a desk against the wall. "All right, Manners, you can go," he said.

Surprised, Manners asked, "Hadn't I better wait to take the prisoner back?"

"No," he said, waving at the door. "Go along now!" When the guard left, he turned to Barney. "Go on in, Winslow—through that door."

Barney approached the door and hesitated. "Go on in!" the warden repeated. The confused prisoner opened the door and found himself in a medium-sized room with two large windows allowing so much light he was dazzled for a moment. As he tried to clear his vision, a man standing by the windows said, "Visitors for you, Winslow."

A movement from the left side of the room caught his eye, and he turned. His parents!

His mother rushed to him, her eyes filled with tears, and

caught him in a hard embrace. He stood as if transfixed, his mind unable to grasp what was happening. Then his father came forward and put his arm on Barney's shoulder.

Warden Sam Muntz watched the scene with interest. Nothing like it had ever happened in his time—or in any other warden's time so far as he knew. He looked at the paper on his desk, thinking how shocked he'd been when he read the governor's personal note, ending with the words: *You may release the prisoner, Barney Winslow, at once, for he has been fully pardoned by my hand.*

Now he said, "Well, this is a private time. I'll leave you three alone."

"Barney! You're free!" Lola cried.

"Free?"

"Yes," Mark said, opening his arms wide. "You've gotten a pardon from the governor."

Barney stood there, unable to comprehend it. Finally he whispered, "How can that be?"

"It's your mother's doing, Barney," Mark said. "She won't even tell me how she did it."

"Barney, I'm so happy for you!" Lola said, tears running down her face as she held him.

Barney looked at them in unbelief. Then Mark said quickly, "Let's get you out of here, son. We can talk later."

It took two hours to get through all the red tape, but at the end of that time Barney walked out of the iron gates with his parents. He was very thin and had said almost nothing. While he had been getting processed, Mark had said to Lola, "He looks bad, doesn't he?"

"Yes—but it'll be all right now," she'd replied.

As they walked to the horse and carriage Mark had driven to the prison, both of them were somewhat subdued—and afraid. The change in their son was heartbreaking. Barney turned and stared at the gray stone walls, his sunken eyes void of expression.

"Come on, Barney," Lola urged. "I can't wait to get you home! I'll make you forget this awful place!"

Barney looked at her, then back at the walls of Sing Sing.

"No. I'll never forget this place," he said quietly. Then he turned and shuffled toward the carriage. Though they rode away, it seemed as if the prison in the background stayed with them.

Mark thought, *We've gotten Barney out of prison—but it might not be so easy to get the prison out of Barney!*

PART TWO

THE MISSION

★ ★ ★ ★

October 1896–December 1897

CHAPTER SEVEN

Homecoming for Barney

★　★　★　★

"He doesn't seem to have any—well, any *life* about him, does he, Mother?"

Andy was sitting across from her, watching the nimble fingers as she sewed. He had come to tell about the last stages of his seminary work, only a few months left. As usual, he had a fine record and was glowing with excitement. He had led his class academically, and had been an assistant pastor for one of the prominent pastors in New York the past year.

But now, Lola saw as she looked at Andy, there was a puzzled frown on his brow. He had spoken with great vigor of how things were going to be different for Barney, now that he was out of prison. "I'll take him in hand," he had said confidentially to his parents. "Barney just needs a little push, to give him confidence, you know?"

His attempts had failed utterly. Barney had not been receptive to any of Andy's attempts to rehabilitate him. He had flatly refused to go to church, which had surprised Andy, for he expected Barney's miraculous release would bring out a surge of gratefulness in his older brother. But that had not happened. Barney had not committed his life to the Lord. In fact, he wanted nothing to do with God—or any part of religion.

How different my two sons are, Lola thought. Aloud she said,

"He needs time, Andy. After all, it was a terrible experience for him, and we have no conception of what he went through. He has said little of his treatment, but seeing his physical and mental state it must have been agonizing."

"Well, sure—but it's been over a *month*." Andrew spoke of that span with all the impatience of youth. He himself had encountered no terrible problems, and lacked understanding of those who had. But he would have been highly insulted if anyone had mentioned this to him, for he considered himself a highly competent counselor, able to deal with any problem.

"You'll just have to be patient," Lola insisted. "God's working in his life."

"I don't see much evidence of it! He won't even come to hear me preach," Andy protested.

Lola smiled. "He's missing great sermons, I'm sure. But sometimes people need more than preaching."

"Like what?" Andy asked aggressively.

"Oh, love, I think."

The answer galled Andy. "That's a simplification, Mother," he protested. "After all, God can do only so much. A fellow has to make an effort, you know!"

Lola took a careful stitch, then looked up at him. *He's so sure he's right*, she thought. *And because he's always been successful, he can't enter into the hearts of those who are down.* It was a serious failing for a minister, and she tried to get her fears across to him. "Andy, you've learned a lot of theology in school, but people aren't *theology*. Most of the people who gave Jesus the most trouble had plenty of doctrine, didn't they?"

He stiffened. "Mother, are you saying that I'm being a Pharisee?"

"No, Andy. I'm saying that you've been in school so long that you haven't had time to experience what people are like, to accept them the way they are—the problems they face, how to cope, how to see God as the answer to their need."

He began to pace around the room, disturbed by her attitude. He was highly sensitive to criticism, and having received little of it, especially from his mother, could not deal with it well. He paused before her, his eyes puzzled. "I only want the best for Barney," he said.

Putting her sewing aside, she walked over and hugged him, then leaned back, smiling. "Don't you think I *know* that? Your father and I are so proud of you! But you have one disadvantage."

"And that is what?"

"You're *young*," she said, and laughed at his expression. "But there's a real cure for that. Next year you'll be a year older, and soon that beautiful red hair of yours will be all gray."

He could never resist her when she smiled at him. "Maybe you're right, Mother," he said. "I'll try to be more patient," adding, "You can sure take the starch out of a fellow, Mother!"

"Why don't you take Barney to a ball game or something? Don't try to preach at him, Andy. He knows the gospel. What he needs is acceptance."

"I'll do it!" Andy grinned. As always he was ready to plunge headlong into a new venture. He left the room, his head popping with new ideas for "being patient" with his brother. He found Barney raking leaves. "Hey, Barney, put that rake down."

Barney looked up as Andy came across the yard. He smiled slightly, for he had a great affection for his younger brother. The month at home, away from prison, had brought the color to his cheeks and filled him out. But he slept little, and nightmares brought him bolt upright in the bed, bathed in cold sweat.

"Somebody has to rake the leaves," he said.

"Let Pat do it," Andy said, speaking of the yardman. "He likes it."

"So do I," Barney remarked. "It feels so good out here."

Andy looked at Barney, thinking, *It's the little things that seem to give him pleasure.* Aloud he said, "It *is* kind of nice. But I thought you might go with me this afternoon. Not to a service," he added quickly. "A baseball game. Let's take it in."

Barney smiled. He loved baseball. "I'd like that. Just let me finish raking these leaves."

"Go ahead. We'll leave after lunch."

Andy ran back into the house to tell his mother. "All right, boss lady, I did what you said. Barney and I are going to the ball game this afternoon." He turned, then stopped and grinned. "*And* I promise not to preach at him!"

★　★　★　★

Andy and Barney enjoyed the game immensely. "That pitcher is something, isn't he, Andy!" Barney said. "Look at the power in his arm. Wow!"

"He's got what it takes," Andy agreed. "Wish I could play like that."

Barney suddenly looked at him. "I've got to talk to you."

"Why, sure," Andy said, hope rising in his heart. It was the first effort Barney had made to break his long silence, and Andy was certain his brother was going to open up, maybe even give his heart to the Lord. "Let's have it, Barney."

"I don't really know where to start. Guess I won't ever be able to say how much it's meant to me—getting me out of prison and letting me come home."

"Why, it's been so good—for us, I mean," Andy said emphatically. "We're all expecting great things of you."

It was the wrong thing to say, a tactless remark that would have made his parents wince.

Barney shook his head. "I don't want to disappoint you all again, so what I want to tell you is, I'm going to be moving out."

"Moving out!" Andy stared at Barney in disbelief. "Why, you can't do that!"

"I can't do anything else," he replied. He clasped his big hands in front of him and tried to think of a way to explain how he felt. He had never been good at addressing sensitive issues, especially to Andy, and sweat broke out on his forehead as he struggled for words.

"Look, Andy, I've caused enough trouble for you all. It was bad when I left home the first time. I know you all hated what I was doing, but I had to get away. It was like I was being—I don't know, *squeezed*."

"It's your home, Barney. We're your family."

"You are, but I'm just different." He looked at his brother, adding quietly, "You're the smartest person I know, Andy, but you've never been able to see that I'm not like you."

After a moment he went on. "I haven't told Mom and Dad. They're going to hate it."

Andy was stunned. "What are you going to do?"

"Same thing. Go back to fighting." He caught the distaste in Andy's eyes and said, "Sure, it's a rotten way to live. But it's the only thing I've ever been good at."

Andy wanted to argue, but he saw that Barney's jaw was stubbornly set. "It'll be hard on the folks."

"I realize that," Barney murmured. "But I've got to do it, Andy. Come on. Let's go home. I may as well get it over with."

★ ★ ★ ★

Benny Meyers couldn't believe what he was hearing. "Barney, you're in no shape to fight. You're thin, don't have the muscles. You'd get killed if you stepped inside a ring."

"Sure, Benny, I know that," Barney said. "But I can get in shape. Just give me a chance. I've got some money, so all I ask is that you train me until you think I'm ready."

Benny chewed on the cigar, debating, then made a quick decision. "Look, Barney, you took it on the chin bad in Sing Sing, I hear. Some don't never come back from that. There's lots of guys in the fighting game walkin' around on their heels, listenin' to things nobody else hears. I wouldn't want that to happen to you."

"Just give me a chance," Barney pleaded.

Benny threw the cigar on the floor and nodded. "I'll give you this: You come to the gym for a few weeks. Do what I tell you. Then we'll see."

"Thanks, Benny!"

"No promises!" Meyers warned. "You don't fight until I say so."

Barney replied eagerly, "You're the boss, Benny!"

With joy in his step, Barney left to buy his gear, convinced that he could fight again.

* * * *

"You gonna take the kid on, Benny?" A man named Maxie Plummer had overheard Barney's request to Meyers.

"Thinkin' about it."

"Better not waste your time," Plummer advised. "A good fighter—he's like a fine watch. One thing goes wrong and it never runs right again. Don't think the kid can come back."

"You may be right, but I'll give him a chance."

* * * *

The next morning Barney arrived early at the gym and began his workout. It didn't take long before both trainer and fighter discovered Barney was not the boxer he had once been.

"Your timing is off, your punches ain't got no snap. You're underweight by at least ten pounds," Benny complained. "If I was you, Barney, I'd find a good job."

"You just give me a month, Benny. You'll see."

Day after day he came in early and stayed late. He worked harder than any fighter Meyers had ever seen, and three weeks later he was getting back his old skills. Meyers commented on it one afternoon. Barney was punching the light bag, making it rattle with a precision that sounded like a drum.

"Better call it a day, kid," Benny said. Then he laughed. "Never thought I'd see the day when I'd have to tell a fighter to stop training. You've done good, Barney."

"Good enough for a fight?"

"Maybe in two weeks or so."

Benny would say no more, so Barney left and decided to celebrate. He had been off liquor since his arrest. That night, though, elated over his progress, he had a few drinks with another fighter—a middle weight named Joe Maddox. They had trained together, and upon meeting went for the bars just like old times. By ten o'clock they were more than a little high.

"I've had enough, Joe," Barney said.

"Aw, we're celebrating, Barney!"

"You can celebrate without me. I'm going home and get some sleep."

He made his way toward the boardinghouse. On both sides

of the streets, the bars and gambling joints were doing a roaring business. He stopped mid-stride when he heard his name called.

"Barney! Barney Winslow!"

A man rushed up and grabbed Barney in a big embrace. He tried to shake him off, not sure what he wanted. Then he heard a voice from the past.

"It's me, dear boy! Awful Gardner!"

Barney couldn't believe his eyes. Sure enough, it was Awful! He looked much the same as he had in prison—tall, thin-faced with gray eyes and a full head of black hair.

"Awful!" Barney cried. "It's you!"

"Indeed, it is!" Gardner slapped him on his shoulders, saying, "How good it is to see you!"

"It's wonderful to see you, Awful," Barney said. Then his smile faded as a memory flashed into his mind. "Better than the last time we met in Sing Sing."

"'Course 'tis better," Gardner insisted. "Now, let's go where we can talk. Me place is right around the corner."

"All right."

"But I can't go for a bit. Got a spot of work to do."

"Work? What sort of work, Awful?"

"Oh, just a bit of my own. Wait right here. Won't take more than a shake of a duck's tail!"

Gardner ran across the street and joined a small group in dark uniforms. Soon the sound of music filled the air. Barney watched as the Salvation Army band played. They had more enthusiasm than skill, he decided, but a crowd soon gathered around them. One song, "Washed in the Blood," brought back memories of the prison chapel where he'd last heard that song.

After a while the music stopped with a resounding boom from the big drum, and Awful Gardner stepped up on a small box and began to preach. His voice rose over the crowd gathering around him. "God loves you all! The Lord Jesus died for your sins—for every sinner. And who's the worst sinner on this bloomin' street? Me! Awful Gardner! Why, I've spilled more liquor than most of you have drunk!"

As Awful continued to preach, Barney listened. He was a

hardened man, not ready to hear any preaching. Yet he had seen Gardner act out his gospel. Here was no high-church preacher, but a con out of Sing Sing, who had been able to keep a sweet spirit in a hell on earth.

Barney had plenty of arguments against religion and the Bible—but none against Awful Gardner. As he listened to the ex-con expound, Barney thought, *He may be wrong about God and the Bible, but he believes it with all his heart!*

Little by little the crowd began to drift away, and Gardner gave them a parting blessing, then came running over to Barney. "Now, dear boy, how about a spot of tea, wot?"

Barney followed Gardner to his room, a small room in a fairly nice boardinghouse. As they talked, or rather, Gardner did, Awful scurried around, heating water, finding the sugar, pouring the tea, providing a little jam for the small biscuits he set on the table.

"I work all day washin' dishes, and spend me evenin's with the Salvation Army preachin' on the street," Gardner said.

"Happy as a clam, I am!" he said when Barney asked if that satisfied him. "The Good Lord is with me, I'm able to move about, and I get to spread the gospel every day." Then he put his hand on Barney's shoulder. "And you, old chap? How goes it with you?"

"Good." Barney nodded. "I'm in training now. Looks like I'll get my first fight in a couple of weeks."

Gardner eyed him doubtfully. "A hard life, fightin'. It done me in, just about."

"It's all I know, Awful."

"Aw, laddie, we will see. If God can get you out of Sing Sing, He can do anything—wonderful things with you!"

Barney shifted around and Gardner saw his visitor's discomfort at any mention of God. "Well, now," Awful said wisely, "I'll come and watch you train, and you can come and drink me tea."

"I'd like that, Awful." He hesitated, then smiled. "I never did tell you what a big help you were to me in prison."

"Ah!" Gardner scoffed, waving his hand. "Not a bit of it!"

"Yes, you were." Barney thought for a moment. "I still have

bad dreams about that hell hole. But nearly always when it starts closing in on me, I remember that you were always there. I could always count on you—calling me 'dear boy' and promising me things would be all right. It—it meant a lot to me, Awful. It really did!"

On that note, Barney left, and true to his word, Gardner was at the gym the next day. Barney, too, kept his promise and had tea and cake in Awful's room.

Three weeks later, on October 14, Barney's first fight was scheduled. But the afternoon before he fought, he was walking along Water Street, when a woman stepped out of a bar. At first he paid no attention. Then she turned.

It was Katie Sullivan! She did not see Barney, and he darted back to watch her. She and the man with her staggered down the street. She still looked as petite as she had the first time he saw her at Antoine's when his family had visited him. But now she had the appearance of a common woman—painted face and droopy mouth. He realized he was not the only one who had changed over the past months.

His mother had told him that Katie's testimony led to his release. Strangely enough, his bitterness at being locked up had fastened on her.

"If she'd spoken up," he'd said to his mother, "I would never have gone to prison."

Lola had tried in vain to explain that Katie had little to offer and had not understood how important it was.

"It was her fault," he told himself. "All she had to do was speak up—but she wouldn't!"

Looking at the retreating figure, he felt hatred rise up, and he wanted to smash her face in. Then he pushed the rage aside. *Can't get into trouble with the police*, he decided.

The night of the fight he boxed poorly. Benny thought it was because Barney wasn't trained properly, but he blamed it on Katie Sullivan. The hatred he felt toward her made him so angry he rushed his opponent, flailing blindly. The other fighter, a skilled boxer, stood away from Barney and left him looking like hamburger.

Barney lost the fight on a decision. The disappointed

trainer said afterward, "Barney, you used to be a good boxer, but now you're just a street fighter. You'll get your brains scrambled if you go on in the ring. Get a job."

That night, instead of going to sleep, Barney got drunk, then crawled to his room at daylight and fell across the bed, his sodden mind raging, *It was her fault—Katie Sullivan! I'll get her sooner or later!*

CHAPTER EIGHT

RESCUE MISSION

★   ★   ★   ★

"Miz Winslow?"

"Yes, Helen, what is it?"

As the maid came into the drawing room where her mistress was reading a book, she said in a perplexed tone, "Ma'am, there's a man come to the door asking to see Mr. Winslow."

"A gentleman to see Mr. Winslow?"

"Well—not to put too fine a point on it, ma'am. He ain't no gentleman. Not no *regular* gentleman, that is."

"Bring him in, then," she said, putting her book down.

That response wasn't enough for Helen. She was proud of the Winslow status and quick to protect it. "He ought to go to the back door, not come up to the front."

"Is he a tradesman?"

"I dunno, Miz Winslow." She shrugged her shoulders. "He just don't fit into no kind of pattern."

"Well, just bring him in," Lola said again, smiling as the maid stalked off. The roly-poly maid's insistence on protocol amused Lola, for she herself was not given to class consciousness. She got up and looked out the window as she waited.

"Here he is, ma'am," Helen sniffed, adding, "and keep your muddy feet off things."

"That will do, Helen," Lola rebuked.

The man was dressed in a dark suit, worn but neat and clean. He was in his mid-thirties, with clear gray eyes and thick black hair.

"Sorry to be a bother," he said. "I'd like to see the mister if he's home." His words rolled off his tongue in a distinct accent.

"My husband is in Chicago. Perhaps I can help you?" she offered. "His office is in the Strand building. You could see him there next Friday, I think."

He hesitated, his bony hands twisting his hat, as though trying to make a decision. "Is it Barney's mum you are?"

"Why, yes," Lola answered. "Barney is my son."

"Well, Miz Winslow, me name is Gardner. If it's not—"

"Why, of course! You must be Awful Gardner!"

"That's me, ma'am," Gardner said, encouraged by her response. "I hate to be bustin' in like this, but I didn't know no way to get a word with you and the mister."

"Do have a seat, Mr. Gardner," Lola offered. She smiled as he eyed the fragile Queen Anne chair, adding, "Go ahead, it won't break."

Gardner sat down carefully, placed his hat in his lap, and clutched it as if it would give him security in the midst of such grandeur. Perspiration dotted his broad forehead, for it had taken considerable courage to come to the Winslow mansion. He felt completely out of place and might have fled except for the kind smile from the beautiful woman seated across from him.

"Barney has told us so much about you, Mr. Gardner," Lola said. "You were a great blessing to him in prison."

"Just call me 'Awful,' ma'am," Gardner nodded. "But it wuzn't much I wuz able to do for the dear boy. Just a kind word now and then."

"It was a great deal to Barney. He's often told me how you kept his spirits up when things were so dark." Her smile dimpled and she added, "I told Barney you were probably an angel in disguise, sent by the Good Lord to encourage him."

"Me? An angel?" Awful shook his head and smiled ruefully. "No fear, Miz Winslow! Just an old con saved by the blood of Jesus."

"Barney's heart is hardened against God right now, Awful," Lola said. "But your witness about Jesus won't be lost."

"I pray not, ma'am, I do indeed," Gardner nodded vigorously. "It's the prayer of me heart that the dear boy will come to 'imself and find the Savior."

"Have you seen him lately?"

"Yes, ma'am, that I have. It's that I've come about," he said, shifting his eyes.

Lola sensed he was having difficulty. "Is Barney in trouble?"

"Well, yes, ma'am, he is. You know he's gone back to fightin', and that's a rum go for any bloke." Gardner shook his head sadly. "I've tried to get him to shake free from it. Used to be a pug myself, Miz Winslow, and it's no life for a man."

"His father and I have tried to get him to do something else, but he refuses our help."

"Right-O! The lad's got a stubborn streak!"

"I'm afraid he comes by it honestly," Lola sighed. "All the Winslow men seem to be that way." She bit her lip, then asked, "What else is it? That's not all you came for, is it?"

"To tell the truth, ma'am, I just felt I had to come." Gardner shifted uncomfortably in his seat, and then looked Lola in the eye. "I been trying to help the lad, but he won't let me do much. The truth is, he's gone on the grog."

"Gone on the grog?"

"He's drinkin', ma'am. Pretty bad."

"He can't do that when he's in training, can he?"

"Lots of them do," Gardner shrugged. "John L. Sullivan was a whiskey soak. I talked to his manager, Benny Meyers, and he tells me that he's warned Barney to stay off the sauce—but Barney won't even pay no mind to Benny."

Lola jumped up and began to pace. She had known things were not going well for Barney. He had not come to the house for days, and Andy had heard that his brother was back to his old ways. She and Mark prayed much for him, and spent endless hours trying to find a way to help their oldest son. The burden had become so great that Lola was never free from it—always finding her mind and heart turned toward Barney.

Gardner sat quietly, his eyes taking in the anguish on the woman's face. He had heard enough from Barney to know how much he loved his parents, how he had broken their hearts. Then when Katie Sullivan told him about Mrs. Winslow's courageous efforts in freeing Barney from prison, Gardner had decided he must come.

Lola stopped before him. "Do you have any idea how we can help Barney, Awful?"

Gardner gave her a startled look. "Coo!" he said with admiration. "If you ain't a sharp one now!" he said, then added, "No offense, ma'am!"

"No offense," Lola assured him. "Tell me what you think we can do."

"Well, I have an idea, though I ain't so sure it's a good one. That is, the idea is good, but I don't know if it'll pull him out of it."

"I'd like to hear about it."

Gardner could not stand the fragile chair, so he got up and walked to the window. A plan had come to him weeks earlier while he was praying. It was as clear as if it had been spoken aloud: *Go tell Barney's parents about this.* Gardner was a simple man and assumed that it was God who was giving him instructions. He had ferreted out the Winslow's address and come directly to the house. All the way from the city he had prepared a speech, but now it didn't seem to be the right one. Finally he turned, spreading his hands in a helpless gesture.

"Miz Winslow, I ain't no good with words, so let me just tell you. You see, the poor people in the Bowery and other bad parts of the city, they won't go to a regular church. I mean the real down-and-outers. The drunks and the common women. They ain't got no fine clothes, and if you give 'em money for such, they'd spend it on booze—and keep on drinkin' till they run out. They got no more idea of the Lord Jesus and His cross than the heathens in Africa!"

As Awful continued describing the terrible conditions in the slums, tears gathered in his eyes. "I tell you, ma'am, it fair breaks me heart to see it! Every day there's some of 'em dead on the street!"

"And you want to help them, Awful?"

"Yes, Miz Winslow, I do. I want to start some kind of place, a mission, where they can come when they're drunk and when they've been beat up. A place where they can have a free meal and a place for the night, you know? Where they feel free no matter *what* they've done."

"I think that's a fine idea," Lola said. "Do you think Barney would come to a service in a place like that?"

"I don't know, ma'am," Gardner said. "But I do know he won't go to no regular church. To be plain with you, I'm afraid Barney's goin' down pretty fast. Sooner or later he'll hit bottom. And I want there to be a place he'll come to, with folks like me who been at the bottom to tell him about the Lord Jesus and His cross."

"Oh, I'm glad you've come to me," Lola said. "My husband will want to help. What can we do?"

"Well—" Gardner was embarrassed now, and ducked his head. "Well, now, not to hurt your feelin's, Miz Winslow, but I don't think right at first, you and your husband ought to be at the mission. It might scare some folks off."

"I suppose you're right. Maybe we can help get it started? You'll have lots of expenses."

"To be plain, ma'am, you can. That's why I come. I want to quit my job washin' dishes. Not that I'm too good for it, but there needs to be somebody at the place all the time. I got a building all picked out, an old store down on Water Street, in the worst part of the district. It's got room upstairs too. It won't cost much to rent, but I got no money at all."

Taking a key from her pocket, Lola walked quickly to the rosewood desk and removed a small metal container from the drawer. "Here," she said, opening the box and pulling out some bills, "will this be enough for the first month's rent?"

Gardner stared at the cash. "Oh, my word! Yes, ma'am, and to get the place all cleaned and buy some furniture as well!" He looked at her and stated, "You don't know me, Miz Winslow."

Lola knew what he was saying. "I think I do, Awful. The spirit of man is the candle of the Lord, and I can see His Spirit burning brightly in you. Would you come back next week when my husband is here? He'll want to know all about this."

"Yes, ma'am, I'll do that." Awful burst out laughing and held the money high. "How do you like that, devil?" he cried, his face wreathed in smiles. He began to praise the Lord so loudly that the maid rushed in.

"What is it, Miz Winslow? Shall I call the police?"

"No, Helen," Lola laughed. "Don't do that. Come and join

us as we give thanks to the Lord."

Helen sniffed, saying under her breath as she left, "Indeed! Church is the place for a thing like that!"

Gardner shoved the money into his pocket. "I won't thank you, ma'am, for I can see you're not the sort to want such things. But I'm prayin' that our dear boy will be one of those who comes to Jesus in this place."

Lola walked with him to the door and waited until he was out of sight. Then she returned to the drawing room and knelt to pray. For the first time in days she felt the presence of the Lord, and with that the assurance of Barney's salvation.

★ ★ ★ ★

Of all men, Awful Gardner better understood the terrible living conditions of the poor of New York City. He knew what it was like to be in the police station lodging room, for he had spent many nights there. It was a room about twenty feet by ten feet. Along the wall was a slightly raised and inclined platform, extending the whole length of the room. On this the men lay themselves down, side by side, without mattress, covering or pillow. Drunk or sober, ragged or not, covered with vermin or clean, it made no difference. The air reeked with offensive odors and vibrated to lewd jests and vulgar oaths.

It was, perhaps, better than the gutter, but not much, and Awful Gardner had a vision of a place where he could keep derelicts overnight. That was in the future, however. Now, armed with cash and boundless energy, he plunged into the first phase of the Rescue Mission. He had no trouble renting the store, for it was bringing in no revenue to the owner. Taking a year's lease by faith, Gardner threw open the door that very afternoon, and worked until the wee hours of the morning, throwing out the rubbish and cleaning with broom and mop to get the place presentable.

Everyone knew Awful, and soon word was out that "the Limey's startin' a church down on Water Street." For the next three days Gardner worked hard, and he encouraged those who stuck their heads in out of curiosity. "Come in, boys!" he would call out. "No proper service until Saturday, but I can give you a sample right now!"

When Saturday arrived, he held the first service, aided by the Salvation Army Band. The audience was sparse, but Awful preached as if he were in a tabernacle seating a thousand. He knew how to preach to the derelicts who came to get out of the cold, the women with bruises on their faces, and the men who were getting over a drunk. Awful would proclaim himself as the worst of sinners, then say, "If Jesus can take a rummy like me and clean 'im up, He can do it for anybody!"

The following Monday, he went back to the Winslows with his report. "Oh, it was glorious!" he said. "Just a beginnin', but you'll see the devil whipped regular at the Rescue Mission!"

"I don't suppose Barney came?" Mark asked.

"No, but we must be patient," Awful nodded. "He'll be around."

But two weeks went by and Barney didn't come. Twice Gardner went by the gym, but Barney was not there. "He's drinking too much," Benny Meyers told Gardner. "He won't be no fighter actin' like that."

Finally Gardner spotted Barney one afternoon walking down Cross Street and hurried after him. "Barney, where have you been hiding?"

"Awful?" Barney turned, then shrugged. "Oh, I've been around."

"Sure, now, you've got to come and see me new place, dear boy," Gardner said. He skillfully led Barney to the Rescue Mission, speaking so rapidly that Barney had no chance to argue.

But when they got to the mission, Barney stared at the sign. "Rescue Mission? What's this, Awful? You trying to trick me into going to church?" he asked suspiciously.

"Not a bit! No regular services yet. Going to take a bit of work to get under way. Just wait, lad, pretty soon we'll have a room for the chaps who are down-and-out and some good food for them as have nothin'! But we can have a bite to eat. I've got a pair of chops, and I wuz just lookin' for a good man to join me!" He pulled Barney into the back of the building where he had made a comfortable room for himself, and soon he was busy cooking the chops, talking all the time.

Barney sat at the table, his face stolid and flushed. He had not been doing well, and was angry at himself. He knew he was ruining his chances for a career in the ring by his drinking and loose living, but he could not seem to stop. He had taken to running with a crowd that never worked. It seemed easier to do that than to train. He had a fight on the next weekend, and had made up his mind that after the fight, he would break off with his companions and train in earnest.

Finally the meal was ready, and Awful bowed his head and prayed a quick blessing, then said, "Well, now, how do you like me new place, laddie?"

"All right, Awful." Barney glanced toward the larger part of the building, asking, "How are you paying the rent on this?"

"Oh, the Lord provides, lad!" Gardner said cheerfully. "And it's just a beginnin'. Next week we'll have the space where we can keep men who are really down. You know, give 'em a good hot meal and a spot to sleep."

"And a sermon to go with it?"

"Oh, that will be available," Awful laughed.

"You'll have every deadbeat on the East Side of New York."

"No fear! The Lord's table is large, dear boy. Didn't He feed five thousand with a few bits of fish and bread?"

Barney shook his head. "It won't work, Awful. You ought to know that."

"Why should I know it? Didn't the Lord change me?"

"You're the exception to the rule. Most of us just go right on the way we have to."

Gardner didn't argue, but for an hour the two talked and sipped their coffee. Barney's misery was obvious, but the older man knew that until the young man hit bottom, he would not hear any sort of counsel.

Finally Barney got up to leave. "Thanks for the supper, Awful. It was real fine."

"We'll do it often, lad," Gardner nodded. "I hear you're fightin' next week."

"Yes." Barney gave Awful a tight smile. "If you want to pray for me, ask God to let me win the fight."

He turned and left, leaving Gardner alone. Awful sat there for a while, saddened by the tragedy of young Winslow. Then he bowed his head. "Lord, I ask you to let the boy lose this fight. Protect his life, but he don't need to be winnin' no bouts. Dear

Lord, I know as how you loves the dear lad better than me, and you knows best. But if you could just cut 'im down to where he don't have no place to look but up—and then give 'im a glimpse of the Lord Jesus, I'd be most grateful."

He kept praying for a long time, and finally got up, saying, "Thank you, Lord. I'll be available when the time comes."

CHAPTER NINE

THE END OF EVERYTHING

★ ★ ★ ★

Reynolds Sports Arena was one of the less ornate of the New York boxing centers. It was actually an old warehouse that had a ring in the center and wooden benches for seats. The dressing rooms had been created by throwing up a rickety wall in one corner of the open structure. There was no shower, and Benny Meyers said as he finished taping Barney's hands, "This is a rat hole if I ever saw one! City ought to condemn the thing!"

Barney nodded absently. He cared little about the surroundings, for his mind was on the fight that was in front of him. "Tell me again about this fellow I'm fighting, Benny," he said.

"Leonard? Well, he's not much of a boxer," Benny said. "Clumsy as a bear—but just about as mean and strong. Nobody's ever knocked him down, so you ain't likely to." He shook his head in wonder, adding, "I don't think he'd go down if you hit him with a railroad tie! Got a head like cement!"

"So I just stay away from him?"

"You'd *better*! If he gets you pinned on the ropes, he'll maul you to pieces. But he's slow, so you ought to be able to stand off and pepper him with a left. Just don't try to slug it out with him, Barney."

A man stuck his head through the door, calling out, "Hey, Benny, get your guy ready. You're next."

"Let's go, Barney," Benny said, leading the way. Barney followed, with another man behind, carrying the bucket to the ring. Thick cigar smoke and noise from the crowd filled the air as they made their way to the center of the arena. Barney climbed through the ropes and went to the center of the ring, where the blunt-featured referee instructed the contestants to keep their punches up and break clean. The boxers touched gloves, then retreated to the side until the call.

Barney turned to face Leonard. The thick-set, beetle-browed opponent outweighed Winslow by ten pounds. Meyers pulled Barney's robe off, reminding him of the way to attack, the jabs and the ropes. A few voices from the crowd called, "Beat his brains out, Bat!" It felt good to hear his name and to know he had some supporters, but *they* wouldn't be up in the ring trying to keep Leonard from scrambling their brains. They could cheer or boo!

The bell rang, and Benny called sharply, "Remember—stay away from him!"

Leonard came roaring out to the center, bringing a right hand up, and it was easy for Barney to step to one side and let the burly fighter sail by. Leonard plunged into the ropes, and as he turned and reared back, Barney jumped in and shot two sharp lefts to Leonard's jaw. But he might as well have been tickling the man with a feather, for all the effect the blows had.

The first round went by quickly, with the pattern always the same. Leonard would come rushing at Barney, who would duck to one side, putting Leonard off balance. Then Barney would send his lefts in, sometimes with a hard right.

When the bell sounded and he went to sit on his stool, he said, "It's like a bull fight, Benny. He just comes charging in, and I dodge him."

"Yes, well, be sure you keep dodging!"

The second round was a repeat, and so was the third. By now the crowd was getting tired of it. Someone called out, "Hey, Winslow, you think this is a waltz? Stand up and fight!" Others took it up, and when he went back to his place at the end of the round, the crowd was openly booing him. Benny said, "Let 'em boo. You're doing fine, Barney."

But in the fourth round Barney discovered that he was getting tired. He was not in good condition, and he was beginning to gasp for breath. His legs were getting rubbery, too, and he knew that sooner or later he'd have to slow Leonard down. He dodged one of the fighter's wild rushes and took a chance. Planting his feet, he swung with his right and caught the surprised Leonard square in the face as he came careening off the ropes. The blow stopped him dead, and Leonard stood there unable to move.

Barney thought, *I've got him!* He moved forward, his right cocked to send the blow that would put the man down—and then he caught a tremendous right hand in his mouth. It was a disaster, beginning in his face and running down to his heels! Reeling backward, he tried to get his hands up, but he had no chance. With a roar, Leonard came charging in, battering Barney's face and body with powerful punches. Barney took a smashing left that knocked him to the canvas, and he lay there trying to think. He heard someone shouting "Stay down, Barney!" but he rolled over and got up.

The referee looked in his eyes, asked, "You all right?" When Barney nodded, he waved the two together and stepped back. Barney tried to dodge Leonard's rush, but his mind was spinning. He got his hands up, but the fists of the raging fighter came smashing through. Barney felt the ropes on his back, and Leonard battered Winslow's side with short, wicked punches, and then drove paralyzing blows at his head. Barney never saw the punch that sent him to the floor. He found himself back in his place, on his stool, and heard Meyers say, "I'm gonna stop it, kid!"

"No!" Barney cried out. "I can do it!"

"He'll kill you, Barney," Meyers said.

"Just give me a chance, Benny!" he gasped. "I'll stay away from him."

Benny shook his head, but the bell rang and Barney came off his stool and moved to the center of the ring. He had his left out, and when Leonard came at him, Barney managed a sharp left jab, but it made no impression. When Leonard charged him, he might as well have tried to avoid a freight train. A wild right struck Barney, sending showers of lights in front of his eyes, followed by a barrage of blows to his head and body that drove him to the floor.

He got up, but went down again, and then Leonard caught him with a roundhouse right that knocked him out. He hit the canvas loosely, and Meyers threw the towel in. It fluttered through the air, and the referee stopped the bout, holding Leonard's hand high.

★　★　★　★

Coming through a long, dark tunnel, Barney tried to figure out where he was. He opened his eyes slowly, painfully.

"Hey, you've come around," Benny said. "I was worried. You all right, kid?"

Barney looked dazed. He tried to sit up, but his head was spinning and his eyes wouldn't focus. He seemed to see two of everything. He fell back, and Meyers said quickly, "Don't try to sit up yet. You took quite a pounding in there."

Barney lay back, and when the room stopped spinning, he looked around. "Where am I? Where is everyone?" he asked.

"You're in the dressing room and you've been out for three hours, Barney. I was just gettin' ready to take you to the hospital."

Barney didn't answer. Feeling was coming back, and it seemed as if every inch of his body screamed with pain. He tried to take a deep breath, and gave a small, involuntary cry.

"What's wrong?" Benny asked.

"My side!"

Meyer touched the spot Barney indicated. "I think you got some ribs cracked—maybe broke. We better get you to the hospital."

It took a long time, for Barney could move only with great care, but they made it to the hospital. The doctor examined him thoroughly. "He's got two broken ribs, a bad concussion," he said to Benny, "and he'll need stitches in that cut over his eyebrow."

The doctor taped Barney's ribs and sewed the cut together, but Barney could not see well.

"Why don't you stay in the hospital for a couple days," Benny suggested.

"No. Just get me home. I'll be all right."

Meyers took him directly to the boardinghouse, helped him

up the stairs to his room, and put him to bed. "I'll check with you tomorrow, Barney," he said.

"I didn't do good, did I?"

Meyers looked at him, then said carefully, "Barney, you got to stop fighting. You're going to be a punch-drunk pug if you don't."

Barney lay there silently, then said, "You mean you won't be my manager?"

"I wouldn't be doing you a favor if I did." Meyers stood beside him. "I've always liked you, Barney. When it looked like you could do it, I was glad. But I been around fighters all my life, and I tell you that you can't make it. Maybe prison took it out of you—I dunno. But whatever done it, you've lost the touch." He put his hand on Barney's shoulder. "It's not the end of the world, kid. You got a good family, rich people. They'll help you."

Meyers saw that Barney was not listening, so he said, "You'll feel better in a few days. It'll be all right." He left the room, closing the door quietly. As he walked down the stairs he said to himself, "The kid is pretty low—but he'll come out of it."

Barney lay on the bed, feeling empty and miserable. His body screamed with pain, every breath giving his rib cage a spasmodic jerk. But the futility of his future, his fragmented relationship with his family, his inability to find his place in the world hurt even worse. Fighting was the only thing he'd ever done well. Maybe he could still do it, find another manager and try again. Yet . . . could Meyers have been right?

Barney dragged his battered body to the dresser, where a bottle of liquor beckoned him—the medication he needed to numb his physical and mental torment. He drank heavily, the soothing liquid flowing freely down his throat. Going back to the bed, he dropped down and waited for the liquor to dull his nerves. Soon he grew dizzy and slumped in a heap, but he held on to the bottle. No one had ever told him that a person with a concussion should never drink, so he continued taking sips from the bottle until he finally passed out.

The next morning, he awakened with a splitting headache. The bottle beside him was empty, and he lurched to his feet. The room spun around and he crashed full length to the floor. Great sheets of pain ran through his sides. Unable to curb the agony, he lay gasping for breath. After about an hour, Barney rolled carefully to one side and managed to struggle to his knees; then hanging on to the wall, he made it back to his bed. He searched his pocket and found some cash. "Gotta get something for my head," he mumbled. He rose slowly to his feet, stumbled to the door, and left the room. His first stop was the closest saloon, where he drank steadily for an hour.

The bartender stared at him, and when Barney looked into the mirror on the wall, he saw why. His face was swollen and covered with purple bruises, his eyes almost slits. The cut over the one eye had bled, leaving the dried blood splashed across his forehead. His lips were puffed like doughnuts, and his hair caked with dirt—*a total mess*, Barney thought.

Gotta go clean up, he decided as he staggered to his feet, too drunk to do more. "Maybe if I walk a bit—clear my mind," he mumbled to himself. He headed for the door and down the street. He hadn't gone far when he felt sick to his stomach, and stepped into the saloon nearby. From that moment on, all was a blur to him. He woke up sometime that night in an alley, struggled to his feet, and made his way back to the boardinghouse. He groped his way up the stairs to his room and headed for the pitcher of tepid water, gulping down all there was.

Falling across the bed, sick again, he tried to think, but his brain was muddled from alcohol. He fell into a stupor, and when he awoke hours later and checked his pockets, he discovered the money was gone. He looked in the dresser and stared at the few dollars left. He began to feel pangs of hunger and decided to get a sandwich at the saloon. But after eating, he spent the rest of the money on whiskey.

When Barney left the saloon in the early afternoon, he wandered aimlessly down the street for hours. Drunken men were no novelty to people, so nobody stopped him or asked if he needed help. As he walked, he tried to think. The more he thought the angrier he became. Life had given him a rotten turn. People had done him in!

Filled with this bitterness, he turned down Pearl Street—just by chance.

It was by chance also that Katie Sullivan was on her way down Pearl Street. She had worked all day at the cafe and was heading home. She didn't even notice the man coming toward her. As usual, she was so exhausted that her mind was fixed on getting to her room and having something to eat.

Barney saw the woman but didn't recognize her at first. Then he stopped, shook his head to clear his blurred eyesight, and felt a dull anger race through him.

Katie! Katie Sullivan! It was her fault! He had been frustrated ever since Sing Sing, trying to figure out *why* he had been imprisoned. Later when he had discovered through his mother that Katie Sullivan had been in possession of the information that might have kept him out of prison, he blamed her. He didn't reason all this out—indeed, he didn't reason at all, but had found someone to fix the blame on for his own errors. His mother had tried to counter his accusations, but he had shut his mind; and now as he stared at the girl, an uncontrollable rage engulfed him.

Without thinking, he followed the blind impulse that seized him. Rushing up to her, he grabbed the startled girl by the arm and shouted, "You little tramp!" Shaking her violently, he ignored her cries, then slapped her across the face.

Katie screamed and begged him to let her go. But by now he was so insane from whiskey and the injustice done him that he was devoid of any mercy. He continued to hit her repeatedly until she fell to the pavement. As though driven by an unseen force, he reached down and pulled her up, still cursing her.

Hearing the commotion, Simon Wintz, a tall, thick-set Polish butcher sweeping in front of his shop half a block down, rushed to the rescue. Unlike most street people, who had learned that it was better if they let assailant and victim—even damsels in distress—fight their own battles, he had to intervene.

"Let that woman go!" Wintz shouted. He was new to the country and had not learned to ignore men's attacks on women.

Barney paid no attention, as though he couldn't hear Wintz. The butcher grabbed the attacker's arm and jerked him away. But Barney turned like one robbed of his prey and struck Wintz, catching him high on the cheek. Wintz immediately drew back his huge fist and sent it crashing into Barney's side—the one with the broken ribs.

With a cry of agony Barney fell, clutching his side.

Wintz ignored him and helped Katie to her feet. "Are you all right, ma'am?" he asked.

"Yes," Katie sobbed. She had not even recognized Barney Winslow in his filthy condition, but now she did. Shocked at the discovery, she thought of Lola Winslow and the hurt this would bring her.

"What's going on?" a voice behind interrupted.

"Mr. McGivern," Wintz said, recognizing the local policeman on the beat, "this drunk was beating up the girl."

"You know the man?" the officer asked Katie.

"N-no, sir," Katie lied. "He just came up and started hitting me."

Ryan McGivern stared down at Barney, who was doubled up with pain. "What's wrong with him?"

"I gave him a hit," Wintz said, "but not that hard."

"Well, I'll take him along to the station. Help me get him up."

It took both men to get Barney to his feet, but he couldn't walk. McGivern shook his head. "He's got something busted. We'll have to have the wagon for him."

They put Barney down, and he lay doubled up until the wagon came. "Better take him to the hospital first," McGivern said. The driver nodded, and when the wagon was gone, the officer turned to Katie. "I'll have to have your name in case something comes of this."

Katie thought fast. "My name is Eileen Smith. I work at the shoe factory on Tenth Street." She wanted nothing to do with the law.

The policeman wrote the information on his note pad, nodded, and said she could go.

Katie wasted no time and in a flash she was gone.

* * * *

Barney groaned with pain as the doctor examined him.

"How'd you break those ribs?" the physician asked.

"In a boxing match," Barney answered.

"You should have better sense than to get into a fight with broken ribs. They're going to give you some real trouble now."

His words were prophetic. The police took him into custody and threw him into a crowded cell, but that night he developed a burning fever. The sergeant in charge consulted the captain, saying, "He don't look good to me, Cap. I think we better let him go. We ain't got enough on him really. The girl didn't press charges."

So it was that Barney found himself on the street an hour later. He had a high fever and the pain was unbearable. Every step was torture as he made his way back to his room.

For two days he lay there, drinking water from the pitcher and eating little. The landlord kept the pitcher filled and brought food twice—until he learned Barney was broke.

"You'll have to move along, Winslow. I'm not running a charity here."

Barney only half understood the man's words, but the next day he left the boardinghouse, pale and sick.

That night he slept under a bridge, delirious and shaking with fever. The next day, one of his fellow derelicts under the bridge shared a bottle with him, but he had nothing to eat.

Darkness fell, and his fever rose. He shook so hard his teeth were clicking audibly. Unable to stand it any longer, he left the shelter of the bridge. The air was biting cold as he staggered down the street, lurching from side to side, barely keeping his balance. The shadows cast by the lights were like ghosts of the past. His mind wandered, and he couldn't discriminate between the shadows and reality.

How he got there, he was never able to tell afterward, but he looked up to see a narrow three-story building in front of him.

Then he heard music, music he'd heard before. A band was playing and someone was singing. He leaned against the lamp-post and listened to the words:

What can wash away my sins?
Nothing but the blood of Jesus;
What can make me whole again?
Nothing but the blood of Jesus.

Oh! Precious is the flow
That makes me white as snow;
No other fount I know,
Nothing but the blood of Jesus.

Then he remembered where he'd heard the words. In his church, growing up as a child—and later in the prison chapel— the men had sung the song.

Something began to happen to Barney as he stood there. He was quaking with a chill, and his mind was not clear, but the words of the song hit him in a way they never had before. All his life he'd heard about the blood of Jesus, but it had been only something the preacher was saying.

Now he suddenly saw the cross of Jesus; it was not a vision, but almost so, for in his mind he could see the bloody form of one stretched out on a cross, dying in agony.

The singing stopped, and Barney walked to the door. When he pushed it open his mouth dropped in surprise. Awful Gardner!

Gardner had just stood up to preach to the small group when he saw the door open. He thought it was just another latecomer—until he saw the battered, filthy form of Barney Winslow, and he knew it was God's timing.

He lifted his hands and cried out, "Come unto me all you that labor and are heavy laden, and I will give you rest!" He quoted verse after verse, and Barney began to weep, tears washing down his face.

"You've sinned, but Jesus is the friend of sinners," Gardner cried out. "You've hit the bottom, but Jesus stands ready to lift you up. Oh, the blood of Jesus! The blood of Jesus! It makes the foulest clean!"

Barney didn't understand what was happening to him. He was weeping and shaking like a leaf. All the misery and unhappiness of his life were like a ton of bricks on his shoulders. At the name of "Jesus" he flinched as though struck—and yet there was something deep within him that longed to hear more. As Gardner spoke of the love of God and the mercy of Jesus Christ, it was water in the desert for Barney.

He took one step forward, not knowing why—and then when Gardner lifted his hands toward him, he staggered down the aisle. Gardner met him, threw his arms around him, crying, "Thank you, Jesus! Thank you, Lord God!"

He drew Barney to his knees and began to pray, tears streaming down his cheeks. When he lifted his head, he said, "Tell the Lord you've sinned, and ask Him to save you for Jesus' sake!"

Choked with emotion, Barney tried, but the words were stuck. Finally he managed to cry out, "Oh, my God! I'm so rotten! Save me for Jesus' sake!"

Over and over, he repeated the phrases until a most wonderful thing happened. The despair and fear that had gripped him began to lighten. He continued to pray, and soon his tears flowed like a river—but now, tears of joy!

"You've got it, dear boy!" Gardner could hardly contain himself.

Barney lifted his face to his friend. It was a battered face, but the eyes were bright, not with fever, but with joy.

He nodded, and the words came out in great sobs. "Jesus! He's come to me, Awful! Oh, the love of Jesus!"

Awful Gardner lifted his voice to the Salvation Army Band.

"Beat your drums! Play those trumpets! The prodigal—he's come home!"

CHAPTER TEN

A NEW BARNEY

★ ★ ★ ★

Mark led the way down Water Street, closely followed by Lola, Andy, and Esther. It was the first of April, and the last feeble rays of the sunset filtered over the rows of buildings, mixing with the yellow gleam of light emanating from the streetlamps. "It's toward the end of the street," he said.

Here and there sallow-complexioned children played in the filthy alleyways. In the gutter, a girl, no more than four or five, was enjoying the antics of a boy in ragged overalls tossing a dead rat around with a stick. The air reeked with old cabbage, liquor, unwashed clothes, and smoke. "It stinks!" Esther said, wrinkling her nose. "I can't believe Barney actually *lives* down here!"

"It's pretty rough," Mark agreed. "But we've seen as bad, haven't we, Lola? Some of those hell-on-wheels towns we lived in when the UP was crossing the country were worse." He glanced at a small sign in front of a three-story house, peered at it, then said, "This is it."

He ushered Lola and the others up the walk, and held the door as they entered. He was surprised at the small room. A simple platform with a table took up a strip in the front, with rows of plain wooden benches filling the rest of the room. Many of the seats were already occupied, Mark noted as he looked for a place to sit.

"Mr. Winslow—and you, Miz Winslow!" Awful Gardner smiled as he spotted them. "What a joy to have you!"

"Hello, Awful," Lola smiled, holding out her hand as he hurried over to greet them. "It's nice to see you again." She and Mark had met with the Australian twice while making plans for the Rescue Mission, but this was their first visit to the place. "You've done a wonderful job," she said.

"Oh, it's Barney who's been doin' most of the work, Miz Winslow," Awful acknowledged. "Since he got saved, I've had to step lively to keep him from runnin' over me!"

"Is Barney here?" Andy asked.

"He's gone to get a poor chap who's too weak to make it alone. But he'll be comin' in soon, no fear. Now, just find yourself a seat, folks, and we'll be gettin' started in no time."

The family sat down on the rough seats, and as the building filled up, Lola and Mark looked around with interest. Both of them had wanted to come, but after talking with Gardner they had wondered if their presence might inhibit the regulars. However, Lola observed that among the obvious drunks and roughly dressed women were several middle-class couples. Mark commented on this. "I see we're not the only new ones here. Awful said a few curiosity seekers have come now and then since the newspapers got wind of Barney's conversion. They printed the story, FIGHTER GETS RELIGION."

"That's not good," Lola said. "As a matter of fact, I feel out of place."

"Doesn't matter, Mother," Andy interjected, thinking of the positive side. "It'll help, the publicity, I mean."

Lola couldn't agree, but didn't voice it. She continued watching the door for Barney.

"There he is, Mark!" she exclaimed.

Barney entered the room pushing a wheelchair. The somber thin-faced man in the chair had only one leg. Barney wheeled him right down to the front and bent over him with a smile. Mark noted the evident happiness on his face.

"He looks good, doesn't he?" Mark whispered to Lola. They had not seen him since he visited them a few days after his conversion. Then he had looked bad, though remarkably changed. It had been a joyous reunion, a time of open sharing of hurts and mistakes on both sides, ending in forgiveness and tears. But now there was a fullness in his face, and the wounds and bruises from the fight were almost gone.

"Yes, very well."

Just then Barney looked up and saw them. His face broke into a smile and he walked quickly to where they sat. After greeting the others he turned to his mother. She couldn't refrain from hugging him and immediately wrapped her arms around his neck, so grateful for God's miracle in her son's life. When he returned the hug, Lola warned, "Don't hurt your ribs, dear!"

"Ribs!" he grinned, his brown eyes warm with welcome. "That's ancient history, Mother!" He looked at his family and waved his arm in a circle. "Isn't it great?"

"Yes, it is," Mark said. "We're all very proud of you."

Seeing the light flush in Barney's face, Mark thought, *Probably the first time I've ever said that to Barney! But it won't be the last!*

"Awful's told me how much you've helped him," Barney said.

"That's nothing compared to what you and Awful have done. You're the ones who are doing the work. Are many getting saved?"

"Every night!"

"What about afterward?" Andy asked. "Do they stay faithful?"

"I haven't been here long enough to tell, but Awful says some of them are doing well, but not all," Barney said. "That's what Awful and I do all day and late at night. They're just like children, you know, and the temptation is hellish. Don't I know! But we never give up! I just keep reminding myself how long it took before I really came to the end and was willing for God to take over. I don't want them to go through what I did."

"You really have changed. What's Awful like as a preacher?" Mark asked, adding, "I doubt if he's as good as your grandfather." He put his arm around Lola. "What would your father think if he could see the work your two sons are doing?"

"He'd be very proud! I think he probably knows."

Barney nodded, then said, "Well, it's about time to start. I'll see you after the service."

"All right, Barney," Lola said. When he walked away, stopping to speak to men as he moved across the room, she said,

"It's a miracle! He's so—so outgoing! He was always so shy."

"I noticed that," Mark nodded. "Thank God for Awful Gardner and the Rescue Mission!"

The service was boring and distasteful to Esther. She sat bolt upright as the singing went on. "Why," she grumbled to herself, "they can't even carry a tune!"

The singing *was* a little rough, but to Mark and Lola, who had spent many hours in services much like this on the UP as it went across the country, there was much more. They loved their own church, but once Mark leaned across and whispered, "I wish our deacons would come down here! They might get a touch of real old-time religion!"

Lola agreed that the fervor of the service was something she had missed, too. The Salvation Army Band performed with zeal, if not with musical excellence, and Awful was a good song leader. It was refreshing to hear the old-time songs again, such as "Rock of Ages" and "There Is a Fountain Filled with Blood." From time to time he urged the congregation to liven up.

"You're like a bunch of Egyptian mummies!" he exhorted once. "Open your mouth, Mick, and let me hear you! Open the door, too! Now, sing so they can hear you clear down to Dover Street and up to James Slip!"

The volume increased, Esther cringed, but Gardner was satisfied. He put down the tattered songbook and said, "Now, we'll hear from the saints, how Jesus saved you. You see that sign? It means what it says!" He pointed to the crude handwritten letters splashed across the front wall: SPEAKERS ARE STRICTLY LIMITED TO ONE MINUTE!

"I want you all to tell what God has done for you," Gardner said. "Be as short as you can. You've heard of the three men with a pot of stew, ain't you? Three chaps had a pot of stew, but only one spoon, and the stew wuz too hot for the hands. One man had to use the spoon, then pass it on to the second, and so on. Now, what would they be thinkin' if one fellow took the spoon and kept it all the time and let the others starve? Well, pass the spoon!"

A small man with a pinched face stood up near the back of the room. "I wuz once a sinner, but now the Lord Jesus Christ is in me heart! Praise the Lord!"

"Short and sweet, dear brother! How about the rest of you!" Gardner urged.

The testimony service continued for ten minutes, and then a lull hovered over them. Gardner's eyes swept the group. "Ain't there one more sinner saved by grace? Come on, let's have it!"

Lola's heart raced, the flush rose in her face, her stomach churned. She tried to resist the impulse, but finally stood up. "When I was a young woman," she said, her voice trembling, "I worked in a saloon. I dealt blackjack in every hell-on-wheels town along the line of track the Union Pacific lay. . . ." As she went on, her words became clear and strong. A reporter in the back shot up in his chair and began writing furiously. Every eye was riveted on the beautiful woman who spoke.

"It is only by God's grace that I am not in the depths of sin right now. I thank Jesus Christ that I am saved—and I thank Him for saving my two boys and my daughter."

She sat down and a murmur ran through the room. Lola's eyes were filled with tears so that she could not see Barney staring at her with love in his eyes, but she felt Mark's hard hand gripping hers and heard him murmur, "Fine! Fine!"

Gardner looked out over the congregation and seemed to have forgotten what to do momentarily, then said, "It's my custom to preach after the testimony service, but tonight I feel the Spirit of God is doin' somethin' different. So, I'll not preach. Instead, we'll have a message from a young chap who's new to the army of the Lord. Most of you have seen him fight in the ring, but I'm tellin' you he's goin' to win greater victories for God outside the ring than he ever did inside it. The fight crowd calls him Battling Winslow, or sometimes just 'Bat.' I calls him a dear brother in the Lord! Come along now, Barney. Let's hear what the Lord Jesus has done in your life!"

Barney sat stock-still. If Gardner had told him to fly out the window, he couldn't have been more stupefied. Then he heard Andy call, "Go to it, Bat! Give the devil a hard knock-down!"

He looked at his family—Andy's hands clasped over his head in the fighter's gesture of victory, his parents beaming encouragement. Slowly he rose and walked to the table. The room grew quiet, and the reporter poised his pencil over his paper. Haltingly, Barney began.

"I'm not a preacher. You'll all find that out soon enough!" He paused as a slight ripple of laughter ran around the room, then continued. "This time last month I was drunk in the gutter. If it wasn't for the power of the gospel, I'd still be there tonight!"

"Amen, dear boy!" Awful boomed out.

Barney saw many of the men he'd been witnessing to lean forward, hungry for the same thing. "I was a fighter," he went on. "And I know what it's like to hear the crowd calling my name. It feels pretty good to have people come up and ask for your autograph, to hear them tell their friends, 'That's Bat Winslow, the contender!' All I wanted was to be a successful fighter." He smiled and raised his voice. "But I'd rather be saved and a servant of Jesus than to be champion of the world!"

Every eye was glued to the speaker. As Barney lost his self-consciousness, he poured his heart out, telling in graphic detail the terrible life he'd led, and then how Jesus had saved him.

"It was in this room," he said, "right here at this altar I found Jesus. All He wants is for you to come to Him! If you'll just ask Him and mean it, you'll leave this building saved and bound for heaven!"

Barney had hardly gotten the last words out when a man rushed to the front. He fell to his knees and cried out, "Oh, God, help me! God, help me!" Another man joined him, then two more. Soon the altar was lined with seekers.

Awful and Barney began going from man to man, praying with them; but there were too many for them to minister to, so Awful appealed to the Winslows. "Come and help us."

Mark and Lola seemed to freeze, but Andy said, "Let's go!" When he made his way to the front, Mark and Lola were right behind him. All three began praying with the men. Only Esther remained in her seat, embarrassed and wishing she could hide.

Two hours later, nearly everyone had left, including the reporter, who rushed out to get his copy ready for the morning edition.

Awful turned to the Winslows, beaming. "Well, now, that wuz a glorious time! We'll have our hands full with a whole flock of new lambs tomorrow, Barney!"

Lola put her arm across Barney's shoulder. "I was so proud of you!"

"So was I!" Andy added. "I didn't know you were such an eloquent speaker. I'll have to look to my laurels."

Barney shook his head. "I'm no preacher. I just told what happened to me."

"That's what the apostle Paul did, didn't he?" Mark said, eyeing his sons with pride. "You are a blessing to your father."

★ ★ ★ ★

The morning edition of the paper carried a long story, relating how Bat Winslow, the fighter, and his aristocratic family had left their mansion and were rubbing elbows with the lowest class in New York City.

"Well, it's all here," Mark said as he read the account at breakfast. "Everybody knows you dealt cards in a saloon. Does that bother you?"

"Of course not," she said calmly. "It says that you were a quick-shooting gunman for the Union Pacific. Does that bother you?"

"No, but it's not the same thing."

"Yes, it is. We both had a hard time when we were young, and we've been saved and forgiven. What difference does it make what people think?"

She had an opportunity to prove that shortly when she was snubbed by several of her acquaintances. Relating the incident to Mark, she laughed. "Let's go to the mission. There's more worth in Awful Gardner than in the whole bunch of phonies!"

They did go to the mission—and so did many others, including a prominent businessman named Sidney Castleton, a member of a large church. He was going to the Rescue Mission, he told his wife on the way there, to encourage Barney and Gardner. But they were both surprised by joy unspeakable as they joined the drunks at the altar and were wonderfully saved. From that day forward, he and his wife Edna were firm supporters of the Rescue Mission.

A month later, on a bright sunny morning in May, Barney and Gardner had spent some time praying together after breakfast. As Gardner rose, Barney said, "Awful, I've got something to talk to you about."

"What is it, laddie?"

Barney dropped his eyes, then raised his head. "It's something terrible I did before I was saved."

"Oh, lad, that's all under the blood!"

"I know it is—as far as God is concerned. But . . . I hurt someone. I can't stop thinking about it."

Gardner paused, then nodded, "Well, laddie, if that's the case, the Lord is tellin' you to make it right with the fellow."

Barney looked miserable. "I . . . I'd rather take a beating from Captain Dollar!" He jumped to his feet. "I've got to do it. Can you spare me for half a day?"

"Right-O! Some of our new converts are growin' fast. Littleton can fill in until you get back. I'll be prayin' for you!"

Barney left the mission and headed for Water Street. He had tried to shut out the scene that had haunted him since his conversion. Again and again he would see the terror-stricken face and hear the screams for help. Finally he'd groaned, "All right, Lord. I'll do it."

The sun poured down a steady stream of light, clean and pure, and he thought as he made his way to Tony Barone's saloon how wonderful it would be if the people on the street were all like that. He arrived at Barone's place and was greeted by the bartender, Larry Pool. "Hey, Bat, didn't expect to see you here! What do you want to drink?"

Barney smiled. He had become accustomed to the ribbing. "Just a glass of water and a little information."

Pool gave him the water, asking, "It is true about you being a preacher, Bat?"

"Well, not much of a preacher, Larry." He drank the water and asked cautiously, "Is Katie Sullivan still here?"

"No. Tony put the skids under her a long time ago, shortly after you were sent up the river." The bartender polished a glass, then asked curiously, "You looking for a girl friend, Bat? I can give you some good ones."

"Nothing like that, Larry. I just need to talk to her."

"Her friend Nellie's still here. It's pretty early for her, but if you come back about noon, she might be able to give you something."

"Thanks, Larry."

Barney left the saloon and spent the morning giving out

tracts, which had become a custom for him. Several times he talked to men about their souls, two of them praying with Barney. At noon he returned to Tony's place and was told he could see Nellie.

As he walked up the stairs, he remembered going up the same steps but with other intentions. "Lord," he prayed, "forgive me for the many I sinned against." He was learning to bring past transgressions before the Lord as he was confronted. Again he found cleansing and freedom from guilt.

When Nellie opened the door, she looked at Barney with distrust as she answered his question. "Katie? No, I won't tell you nothin' about her, Bat. The last time you saw her, you beat her up."

Barney squirmed at her bluntness. "That's why I want to see her, Nellie. To ask her to forgive me—and to help her if I can."

Nellie eyed him suspiciously. She had little reason to trust men, but the open expression on Winslow's face caused her to say, "She's had a pretty rough time. If you give her any more grief, I'll sick one of Tony's roughnecks on you."

"I just want to talk to her."

"All right. She's livin' over Anderson's Grocery store. She works at the Delight Cafe over on Madison Street."

"Thanks, Nellie."

Barney left the saloon, heading toward the cafe, then decided to wait till she got home, where it would be more private. All afternoon he roamed the Lower East Side of the city, enjoying the sunshine and the fine weather. He was happier than he'd ever been in his life.

At seven o'clock he made his way to Anderson's Grocery store, in a rough section of the town, and asked about Katie.

"Yeah, in number six," the clerk replied.

Barney went up the dark narrow stairs and knocked at the door, but got no response. He had no way of knowing what time she got off work, so he went across the street to a cafe, got a cup of coffee, and sat at the window where he could see the doorway to the stairs.

For an hour he waited, eating and drinking coffee. Darkness fell, but by the faint streetlight he could still see the doorway illuminated. No Katie, though. He was just about ready to leave when he saw a woman coming down the walk.

Crossing the street he approached her, noting that she was walking slowly, as if she were drunk. Hoping it was Katie, he waited until he came close, trying to see her face.

"Katie? Is that you?" he said hesitantly.

She stopped and lifted her head. "Who is it?" Her voice was so hollow and hoarse, Barney thought he had made a mistake.

"I'm looking for Katie Sullivan," he said.

"What do you want?" she rasped.

Barney moved closer. It *was* Katie! She looked frightful. Her face was pale and her eyes sunken—like a skull.

"Are you sick?" Barney asked, taking her arm gently as he saw her sway, her eyes closed. "Tell me. What's the matter?" he urged.

Katie opened her eyes, trying to focus. "Who—are you?"

"Barney Winslow, Katie."

She licked her lips and would have fallen if he had not held her upright. "Come back—to beat me up again?" she cried.

"No! I came to help you. What's wrong?"

"Sick—so sick!" she gasped. Then her eyes rolled up and she went limp. He could hear the hoarse, hollow breathing that seemed to tear at her lungs.

"Got to get her to a doctor!" he said in alarm.

He turned toward the grocery store to get help, but it was closed. He had to find a cab! Carrying the unconscious form, he ran three blocks before a cab came rumbling down the street. He stepped in front of it.

The driver jerked the horse to a stop, cursing. "You wanna get killed, huh?"

"This woman is sick," Barney said. "Take us to the hospital."

"You got the fare?"

"Yes. Get moving."

He climbed inside and held Katie's slight form as he would a child's. Except for her ragged breathing, she looked the picture of death.

When the cab stopped, Barney tossed the man some money and rushed into the hospital. A nurse brought him to the doctor immediately.

"She's got double pneumonia," the doctor reported. "Why'd

you wait so long to bring her here?" He nodded his head somberly. "She's not likely to make it. Not much I can do. She's going to need lots of nursing. Be just as well if you took her home."

Alarmed, Barney said, "Tell me what to do, Doctor."

"Not much you or I *can* do. She's probably going to die no matter what."

"God's not going to let her die."

The doctor shrugged and picked up his stethoscope. Barney knew there was no help here, and he prayed desperately, "God, help!" The Rescue Mission flashed into his mind, so he picked Katie up and rushed out and hailed a cab driver just passing.

Barney kept praying as the driver tore down the street toward the mission.

Gardner looked up as Barney walked in.

"It's Katie, Awful! The doctor says she's going to die."

Gardner noted the ashen face. "Well, now, that just goes to show how little some doctors know, don't it now? Let's put her in the room with the big window. That way she can see the sunshine!"

CHAPTER ELEVEN

A VOICE FROM AFRICA

★ ★ ★ ★

The pain flooded her as she tried to pull herself out of the dark currents. It was easier to slip back into unconsciousness than to face the raw agony that grabbed her chest.

Someone kept talking to her, a quiet voice calling her name, trying to draw her to the light. Hands pulled at her—sometimes hurting her, other times soothing.

Vaguely she became conscious of the bed with cool sheets, and from time to time a light that moved in and out. A cool hand touched her cheek, and a woman's voice asked, "How are you, Katie?"

She opened her eyes slowly but closed them again against the bright light. It was a woman's face, someone she'd met before. "Where—where am I?" she asked, her voice rusty.

"You've been very ill, Katie. Do you remember me? Lola Winslow?"

Katie forced her eyelids open and she nodded. "Yes. You came to see me at the saloon."

"That was a long time ago, wasn't it?" Lola said. "Are you hungry?"

"Yes, a little."

"Good! I'm tired of ladling soup down your throat! I'll go get something solid." She left the room for the small kitchen where

Barney was washing dishes. "She's awake."

"Thank God!" Barney murmured. His eyes were deeply circled, as were those of his mother. They had maintained around-the-clock watches with the sick girl, and the strain showed.

"I'll cook some eggs, something soft," she said. They spoke little as Lola prepared the food. It had been Barney's idea to have his mother care for Katie, and she had not left the mission since Katie had come a week ago. Barney and his mother had grown very close, sitting at Katie's bedside for long hours in the stillness of the night. Barney had never had anyone to talk to, so he shared freely about the past. She learned much about him during those times—how sensitive he was, how honest.

Lola finished cooking the eggs and put the food on a tray. "Here, Barney," she said, "you take it in. I need to go home. My husband's probably ready to divorce me!"

"But you can't go!" Barney exclaimed, apprehensive. "Who'll take care of Katie?"

"You can do it. And Mrs. Taylor will be in to cook. She'll help."

Barney tried to argue, but Lola simply left him talking, so he had no choice but to take the food down the hall. He tapped on the door, and when a voice said "Come in," he opened it and entered.

Katie looked like a child, so fragile. She stared at him, her eyes large because of her emaciated condition. "Where's your mother?" she asked.

"She had to go home," he replied, adding quickly to cover up his discomfort, "but she said you're hungry. That's a good sign. Try some of these eggs and hot milk." He helped her to a sitting position before handing her the plate of scrambled eggs and the fork. She could not hold the milk, so he set the glass on the side table and sat in the chair beside the bed as she began to eat.

Katie *was* hungry, she realized, and it seemed as if she couldn't eat fast enough. Barney cautioned her to slow down or she'd choke. He offered the milk, which she drank thirstily.

When she had finished the eggs and milk, she lay back and smiled. "That was so good!"

Barney put the plate and the glass on the table. "Do you feel better?" he asked, leaning forward.

Katie touched her cheek. "Yes. What happened? Did you bring me here? I remember seeing you on the street, but I can't remember much of anything else."

"I was looking for you," Barney said. He took a deep breath and spoke with a rush lest he lose courage. "Katie, maybe you don't know about it, but I've had a big change. Not long ago I got saved." He paused and saw that she was watching him carefully—and somewhat suspiciously. "I know that sounds funny, but it's made me a lot different. I'm not a fighter anymore. I spend all my time trying to serve God. Well, the thing is, I've felt so bad about the way I treated you. . . ."

Katie listened as he related how he had hit bottom, and how he'd blamed her for his being sent to prison. He described his conversion, and finally how God spoke to him about beating her in the street.

"I—I was drunk, Katie," he said haltingly, twisting his hands together nervously. "It was like a demon from hell was in me! I know it's a lot to ask . . . but, I'm asking you to forgive me."

He dropped his head and waited, unable to say more.

Katie had hated him for what he did to her, but now that he had told her about himself and the change in his life, and was so obviously sorry, she could forgive. "I forgive you, Barney."

At her words, hope sprang up in his heart. "You *do*? You *really* do, Katie?"

"Yes," she said. "After all, if you hadn't found me and brought me here, I'd probably have died. You saved my life—you and your mother."

"Oh, Mother did most of it," he protested at once. Then he took a deep breath and said, "You know, Katie, I feel as if I've been carrying a big rock on my back—and now it's gone!"

Katie was getting sleepy, but she nodded. "I feel the same way, Barney." Her eyes began to close and she murmured, "Thank you, Barney . . ."

She dropped off, and Barney left the room. For the rest of the day he went about whistling and singing, returning often to check his patient. That night in the packed service, he sang with all his might.

Awful grinned at him. "You've come out from it, dear boy.

You was pretty worried about our lassie upstairs."

The following day Katie got out of bed for a short while to enjoy the sunshine by the window, but most of the week was spent sleeping. Awful would come and sit with her, sharing much about the Rescue Mission. As the days went by, she was impressed by the joy she saw in Gardner and Barney, though neither one pressured her in any way. When she was well enough to go downstairs, she listened to the singing and the preaching, wondering what it all meant.

Lola visited twice, doing most of the talking at first; but as Katie grew more confident, she began to relate her personal tragedy. The heart-rending revelation touched Lola's heart so deeply that she loved the girl like a daughter—something Katie needed and absorbed hungrily.

Each day she grew stronger and was able to stay up longer. One of those days, when Awful visited her, she said, "I've got to leave here."

"And go where, Katie?"

She had no answer. Just the thought of going back to the dark room and the dreary work of the cafe depressed her. "I don't know," she sighed.

"I've got an idea," Gardner said. "There's a nice room next door. Why don't you live there? You can help out here at the mission."

"But . . . I can't do that!"

"Why not, dearie?"

"Because—well, you must know. You know what I've been." Katie's face flamed as she referred to her past, and she turned away from Gardner.

Her feeling of shame was not lost to Awful, but he went on as though she as a person was what mattered, not what she had done. "We want you to stay. The room's already paid for, though I'm bound not to say who paid it. You can eat with Barney and me and help around here with the cleanin' and a little cookin'. Will you have a go at it, Katie dear?"

Katie nodded, her eyes moist.

Later, Gardner told Lola, "It wuz a kind thing, rentin' that room for Katie. She had tears in her eyes when I asked if she would stay. I'm thinkin' it won't be long before she's brought to the Good Lord!"

Lola reported to Mark what she'd done and he approved. When they went to services two nights later, they saw Katie sitting at the back of the room, wearing a lovely dress. "Why, she looks so pretty!" Mark said in surprise. "You'd never guess what a life she's had!"

Andy was there that night. Now that he was out of seminary, he came often and had even preached several times at Gardner's invitation. He sat close to the front, for that night he had brought a visiting missionary from Africa—Reverend Stanley Beecham. Beecham was a native of Wales and had come to America as part of a speaking tour while he was on furlough. He had so stirred the students at the seminary that Andy had insisted Gardner have the man speak at the mission.

After the congregation had sung a few songs, Gardner introduced the visitor. Reverend Beecham showed no hesitancy as he began. Unlike some pastors who didn't know how to address the motley gathering at the Rescue Mission, he knew exactly what to say.

"I bring you greetings from darkest Africa," he said in his clipped British voice. "A few weeks ago I was preaching to cannibals in Liberia. I intend to preach the same message tonight. There is but one gospel. It does not change from country to country, nor from century to century. And what is this glorious gospel that can take the vilest of sinners and make them pure? It is clearly set forth in First Corinthians, chapter fifteen. Paul says in verse one: 'I declare unto you the gospel.' And what was that gospel? He tells us plainly in verses three and four: 'For I delivered unto you first of all that which I also received, how that Christ died for our sins according to the scriptures; and that he was buried, and that he rose again the third day.'"

Beecham's eyes burned as he looked up from his Bible, his voice holding every hearer with anticipation. "Christ died, Christ was buried, Christ rose again. *That* is the gospel! Anything more than that is false doctrine!" He flipped through the Bible, from Genesis to Revelation. His passion was obvious and his knowledge of the Word of God was awesome. He led his hearers down a logical road, yet with such emotion that there was no escape.

"It is Jesus Christ and life, or it is hell forever," he declared bluntly.

Then he said, "But what shall you do *after* you are saved by the blood of Jesus? Shall you go on merely eating and drinking, living your lives as you please? No! For the Lord Jesus gave us a stirring challenge when He left this earth. You will find it in Matthew, chapter twenty-eight, verses nineteen and twenty: 'Go you therefore, and teach all nations, baptizing them in the name of the Father, and of the Son, and of the Holy Ghost: teaching them to observe all things whatsoever I have commanded you: and, lo, I am with you alway, even unto the end of the world. Amen.' "

For the next half hour, Beecham gave a graphic picture of Africa, pointing out the hardships, the dangers that awaited any man who set foot on it. He did not minimize the problems—on the contrary, he emphasized them. Finally he paused and looked over the ragged men before him. His voice was quiet as he concluded his message.

"Some of you need to come and receive the Lord Jesus as your Savior. He will save you if you will repent and ask Him for His salvation. There may be a few of you—perhaps only one—whom God has selected for a special service. I do not encourage you to come, but if God is dealing with your heart to follow Jesus to the foreign field, let me say that there is no life better spent than as a missionary for Jesus."

Beecham stepped back, and soon the altar was filled.

While Barney and others went to pray with the seekers, Beecham remained on the platform, standing erect, still as a statue, his head bowed. Barney had been tremendously moved by the message, and as he looked up he saw Beecham lift his head, then fix his eyes on someone at the back of the room. He suddenly called out, "Jesus Christ is calling you, young woman! Will you come to Him?"

Barney turned to look and saw Katie walking slowly down the aisle, her face pale and wet with tears. The missionary moved toward her, saying, "Let us pray together."

Barney lifted his head from where he was praying and met his mother's eyes. Lola was weeping, and she came to kneel with Barney.

They heard Beecham pray briefly, then counsel Katie. Soon her sobs could be heard, and after a time she cried, "Oh, Jesus! Jesus!" and continued weeping.

Barney and his mother stood up. The room seemed charged with the glory of God. They watched as Beecham put his hands on Katie's head and looked straight up, his eyes wide open. He held that position as if he were listening to someone. Then he dropped his eyes to Katie. "My daughter," he said slowly, "you are now a handmaiden of the Lord." Katie's shoulders shook as she cried. After another pause, Beecham spoke quietly: "You will serve Me far from your native land. Many dark-skinned people will call you blessed, for you will lead them from the darkness of sin to the Light of the world!"

A cloud of silence hung over the room. Only Katie's sobs sifted into the stillness. Then Beecham gazed around slowly, seeming to search for something. Finally he said, "This young woman is not the only servant of God who will go from this place to the foreign field. The Lord this day is raising up a company who will take the gospel across the sea. And Jesus will be with you always, even unto the end of the world!"

CHAPTER TWELVE

THE COMPANY

★ ★ ★ ★

By August the heat baked the streets of New York. There seemed to be no letup from the blazing sun, and the workers at the Rescue Mission sweltered under it.

But the spiritual temperature was no less hot, for as Awful Gardner put it, "There's no such thing as a cup of tea or a Christian who's *too* hot!"

The newspapers had played up the mission for a time, but as the novelty of the "aristocracy" working with slum people grew to be old news, the reporters left for more fertile ground. This was a relief to the leadership, for the crowds that came to satisfy their curiosity took up space the desperate could use.

But if the mission prospered beyond his wildest dreams, Gardner was baffled by something he couldn't put his finger on. He spoke of it to Barney early one afternoon while they were sitting in the backyard in the shadow of the building away from the blistering sun.

"It's wonderful, laddie, how so many have found the Lord Jesus. But I've been a bit confused lately."

Barney was lying on his back, a hat over his face. He pulled it free and sat up. "What's wrong, Awful?"

"Well, I can't rightly say that something's *wrong*." Gardner drew his words out. The perplexed look on his face reflected his uncertainty. "But it seems to me that there's a kind of—oh, I don't know! It just seems we're all sort of waitin' for somethin' to happen. And I haven't the foggiest what the blazes we're waitin' for!"

Barney nodded. "I think I've felt it, too, Awful. It's like we're all waiting for some sort of *sign*." He laughed ruefully and got to his feet. "Maybe we're all crazy. Here the mission is going fine and we're sitting around wondering what's *wrong*. We ought to be thanking God for all the blessings that've come to us."

"Aye, lad, you're right, I suppose," Awful sighed. "Well, let's go help with the cookin'. With Mrs. Davis out, we've all got to pitch in." They walked inside and found Katie peeling potatoes. "Now, Katie," Awful said, "you've been at it all day in this hot kitchen. Let Barney and me take over."

Katie smiled. She was dressed in a simple white dress with a yellow trim around the collar, and despite the heat of the kitchen, she still managed to look neat. She had literally bloomed after her sickness, and from the night of her conversion, she'd plunged into the work with a zeal that exceeded them all. "All right. You can finish peeling the potatoes, Awful. And Barney, if you'll help with the stew, I think I can manage the rest."

As the three worked together, Barney stole a look at her from time to time, marveling at the change. It was not only outward, though she had regained the beauty he had seen in her the night at Antoine's, but she radiated a glow of happiness that communicated itself to everyone she met. The rough men who came to the mission treated her as if she were a princess. And the women, most of them prostitutes, could not believe the love she expressed toward them.

As Barney chopped carrots into a bowl, he thought of what Gardner had said, and mentioned it to Katie. She listened to him, then said, "There *is* something, and I think I know what it is."

"What is it?" Barney asked, holding the knife in midair.

"Do you remember what Reverend Beecham said the night I was converted? He said that some would be called out of this place to serve Jesus overseas." Katie had been stirring dough in a large bowl, but she paused for a moment. "Barney, I have no idea how I could ever do such a thing—but I *know* that I will do it someday. And I think what we all feel is God working to get a company ready to go to Africa."

Barney's mouth dropped open. "But, that's—that's almost impossible!"

"With God, *nothing* is impossible," Katie affirmed, slapping the dough to punctuate her declaration.

Barney was itching to know what was on her mind. "Yes? Go on."

"Barney," she said, her voice so low he had to lean forward to hear, "have you ever felt that God was calling *you* to go as a missionary?"

Her words struck him like a rock. He was so still she knew she had touched a raw nerve. "Barney!" she cried, her eyes bright as she regarded him. "You *have* felt like that, haven't you? Oh, I'm so glad!"

"Now—now, just a minute, Katie!" Barney protested. "Don't be rushing me!" He was agitated, and glanced over to see if Awful could hear, but he had stepped out. "Well, I *have* been thinking about it, but I don't know if God is calling me. Maybe I just *want* to go." His dark eyes gleamed. "That would be some life, wouldn't it, Katie? I've thought about it ever since Reverend Beecham was here."

"Barney, if *you* would go, I wouldn't be afraid of anything!"

He laughed. "Well, I can't go to Africa just to keep you from being afraid, Katie Sullivan!" Then he sobered. "I can't see how it could happen, though. I wouldn't know how to go about it. It would take a lot of money and we'd have to learn the language. And I don't know how to be a missionary."

"I don't either, but I'm going to learn," Katie said. Then she laughed at herself. "But before I go to Africa, I've got to get this supper cooked."

That was the beginning for Barney. The idea never left his mind. And he was not alone. Reverend Beecham had made his mark on the mission, and the group of young people talked about him and about Africa constantly. When Beecham sent a letter telling of his return to Africa and asking for those who felt God calling to write him, they were overjoyed.

But it was three weeks before Barney came to a firm decision. He went to see his parents to share his dream. "I wanted to tell you first," he said simply. "God has called me to go to Africa."

Mark and Lola were speechless. They had been so happy with the change in Barney that it never occurred to them that he would make such a decision. Finally Mark found his voice. "Son, are you *sure* about this? I know Reverend Beecham made a tremendous impression on you, but that's not the same as actually going."

"Why, Barney," Lola added, "you can't think what you're saying! God is blessing your work at the mission. Your father and I are ready to expand it, and we thought you would want to be in charge."

"Well, Mother," Barney said, "it's not so much what *I* want. I've prayed about this for weeks. I've tried to get out of it, but God won't take no for an answer."

They talked for a long time, but nothing his parents said could shake his intention. "I love you both, and if I could, I'd do as you ask. But I've found God, and I've got to do what He says."

He left the house feeling very low, for he could see that they were upset. But he squared his shoulders and went back to the mission. When he got there, the young people were discussing some projects with Awful and Katie, so he took the plunge.

"I've got something to tell you," he said, and saw Katie's eyes open wide. "You all remember what Reverend Beecham said about some being called out of this place for service in Africa? Well—God's called me, and I'm going!"

Katie let out a squeal and ran to him, throwing her arms around him. "Oh, Barney! I'm *so* glad! Now I won't have to go alone!"

One of the young men, Slim Ranken, said with a slow grin, "I guess this is the day for announcements. I was going to tell you all later, but I'm in the same shape as Barney. God's called me to go to Africa, too."

"And me, too!" Irene Bailey, a young woman who had been saved out of terrible sin, piped up. "Isn't it wonderful?"

Tobe DeLaughter and Del Saunders, both smiling from ear to ear, confessed that they, too, had received the call. "We told each other a week ago, but we thought we were both crazy!" Tobe said with a wry grin. "Now we're all crazy, I guess."

Gardner was delighted and began to laugh. He laughed so

hard they all wondered what was so funny.

Gardner finally got his breath. "I guess I'm the crazy one," he admitted, a twinkle in his eye. "I wrote to Reverend Beecham three days after he left here. I told 'im God was callin' me, and I'd jump on a boat the minute he told me to. And what's more, I got a letter back just a week ago."

"What did it say?" Barney said.

"I leave for Liberia in December!" Awful shouted. "Ain't that lovely! Me, a missionary!"

Gardner's news shocked them all, for up until he spoke, going to Africa was just an *idea*, but Awful was actually *going* to Africa! They all burst forth with questions. Finally Barney raised his hand. "Quiet! We've got to make plans." He turned to Awful. "I'm going to write today. What's his address?"

"Write for all of us, Barney," Slim Ranken suggested. "Tell him the Company is ready!"

★ ★ ★ ★

The next two months were the most hectic—and the happiest—Barney had ever known. From dawn to midnight he hurried from one task to another, for the leadership of what the newspapers called "The Water Street Company" had somehow fallen to him. No one ever elected him, but Gardner was busy training those who would operate the Rescue Mission after the group left for Africa. The others just seemed to assume that Barney was in charge, so he found himself as active as a man could be.

He stayed in constant contact with Reverend Beecham, trying his best to carry out all the instructions the missionary sent. It was a complicated business, involving lots of red tape—passports, finances, supplies to be taken on the ship.

The first major obstacle proved to be the matter of identity. Barney had asked several denominations to sponsor the Company, but they all said the same thing: "You'll have to go to our schools and prepare yourselves for the mission field."

But the tickets for the Company were already purchased, and Beecham was laying the groundwork for their arrival in January or February. For several weeks things were rather grim. Where was the support for the group to come from? Barney said little, and prayed much. The others assumed that somehow *he* would come up with a solution, but when November loomed ahead and they still had no support, slivers of doubt began to filter into Barney's mind.

He didn't voice his thoughts to the others, but began to fast and pray in earnest. One night the Lord came to him, and Barney felt a peace he had never known. He went about his work with a smile, and when someone asked about finances, he would reply, "God is faithful."

He found out *how* faithful one Friday evening when he took time to visit his parents. He still felt guilty about leaving them, and tried to see them as often as he could. They had a good dinner, and afterward the three sat on the porch together.

The sky was clear, and as they looked up, Mark mused, "I wonder what the sky looks like from Africa? Not like this, I guess."

"You'll have to come and pay us a visit, Dad," Barney said.

"We may do that." Mark was silent; then he turned to face his son. "Barney, your mother and I haven't been too supportive of your calling. I apologize for that. I'm so blasted selfish I just want to keep you with me."

"Both of us have been selfish, Barney," his mother said. She looked very young in the moonlight, and her eyes were glistening. "But we're so proud of you! So very proud!"

"That's—that's so good to hear!" Barney said. His heart was full, now that he had their consent, and he said tightly, "I love you both very much."

They sat there quietly, all of them thinking of the long road they had traveled to reach the point where they now stood. "I was talking to a few of my friends last week," Mark said, breaking the silence. "You've heard of some of them, I suppose. We got to talking about missions." Mark grinned in the dim light. "Well, I had to brag a little on you and the Company. Getting senile, I suppose! Anyway, one thing led to another, and it turned out pretty well."

"Oh, tell him, Mark!" Lola urged when he paused.

"Some of us organized a nonprofit organization. I got the Union Pacific to ante up, and when the collection was taken, it turned out that we had enough to finance a mission to Africa. Guess which mission we picked?"

"Dad!" Barney stared at his father. "I can't believe it!"

"The money's in government bonds," Mark went on, enjoying his moment. "The interest will be paid monthly, so if you'll just let me have your address, you won't need to worry about cash."

Barney's throat tightened with emotion. "God is good!" he said. "I've been praying for support—but I never *dreamed* it would come from you!"

"Oh, Barney!" Lola cried. "It's so hard to give you up!"

Barney tried to comfort her. "Well, Mother," he said, "you'll still have Andy around."

But he was mistaken, as they all learned three days later.

Barney had asked the Company to meet every evening after services to pray for the mission work, and it had become a rich time for them. On Tuesday night, Andy came to the service, and afterward asked Barney, "Could I talk to you?"

"Well, those of us who are leaving for Africa have a little prayer meeting in a few minutes. Can it wait?"

"May I join you?" Andy had a mysterious smile on his lips.

After the group had spent some time in prayer, Barney said, "Let's just thank God for all He's done for us."

Expressions of gratefulness for God's leading and provision were offered spontaneously. Andy, too, uttered his thanks to the Lord, then said aloud, "I've something to say to all of you." Questioning eyes focused on him. "I've been very unhappy the past few months," he confessed. "God has been dealing with me, and it's been quite difficult. I've watched you all carefully. And to be truthful, I couldn't convince myself your plan was of God. It seemed so reckless!" His eyes met those of Barney's.

"But," he blurted out, "I've *got* to go to Africa with you. God has left me no choice!"

The news startled and excited everyone and they jubilantly gathered around him. "Well, we'll have one real, live preacher in the group!" Tobe DeLaughter laughed. "The rest of us are all amateurs!"

"No, I'm the newest member," Andy protested. "Besides, the minute we step off the boat in Africa, we're *all* greenhorns!" He grinned at Barney. "Well, Bishop, what do I do first?"

Barney laughed. "First, you start work! We've got a million things to do and little time left!"

In the next few days Andy was very visible. Somehow without anything being said, the leadership of the group passed from Barney to him. It was a subtle matter, and only Katie commented on it.

"Barney," she said one evening after service, "I don't think it's fair.'"

"What's that?"

"The way Andy's taken over the Company."

Barney smiled at her. "He's good at organizing things, Katie. I'm not. We're lucky to have him."

Katie didn't argue, but later she brought up the matter to Gardner.

"Well, it's not been what I'd like," Gardner agreed. "Andy is a fine man. Got more education than the lot of us put together. But Barney wuz doin' quite well, I thought."

"When we get to Africa, I suppose Reverend Beecham will take over," Katie said.

"I suppose—but it's a big place, Africa. I'm thinkin' we'll all have to walk a little taller to match up to it."

Nothing more was said, and the weeks seemed to fly by. All of a sudden Christmas was upon them. A huge party was held at the Rescue Mission, with every square inch packed. During the evening Gardner introduced the new leadership to carry on the mission, special prayer surrounded them, and the mission leaders in turn prayed for the group going to Africa. It was a joyous occasion.

That night just before they went to sleep, Awful said to Barney, "It's been a grand time, ain't it, Barney? Who'd have thought when we wuz in Sing Sing that me and you would ever be goin' to Africa?"

"I'm a little scared, to tell the truth," Barney replied.

"And why not? But the Good Lord will never forsake us!"

Two weeks later they were standing at the rail of the S.S. *Caledonia*, Barney between Katie and Andy, waving goodbye to the ones who had come to see them off.

"Goodbye, Mom! Goodbye, Dad!" Barney called at the top

of his voice, his eyes fixed on them as the ship slowly left the dock.

As the faces faded from sight, Katie said, "It's sad, leaving people, isn't it, Barney?"

He looked down at Katie, who had tears in her eyes. "Yes," he replied, "but we'll see them again."

Barney was excited about the future. The huge bulk of Africa lay ahead, and his heart swelled at the thought of what God was going to do through the Company in that great continent, of the teeming millions who would hear the gospel for the first time.

"God won't let us down, Katie! Didn't He promise, 'I am with you, even to the end of the earth'?"

PART THREE

THE PIONEERS

★ ★ ★ ★

January 1898–October 1898

CHAPTER THIRTEEN

Across the Atlantic

★ ★ ★ ★

The first day of 1898 swept in like a lion. The *Caledonia* had plowed through bad weather almost since leaving New York, but as the first pale gleam of sunlight came from the east, all Barney could see was heavy rolling seas. He had come up early to spend some time alone on deck, but the ship rolled under the heavy seas so badly that he could do little but hang on to the rail. Finally he gave it up and went below.

He shared a small cabin with Awful. Barney smiled at the slumbering Australian, peacefully asleep in his narrow bunk. Winslow well knew that most of the others were probably not so much at ease. He sat down on his bunk and read the Psalms for an hour until Awful awakened.

"Well, it's 1898, dear boy," he said cheerfully, rolling out of his bunk and assembling his shaving gear. "Think of it! A whole year to serve the Lord Jesus!" He shaved with clean, swift strokes, talking constantly, dressed, and said, "Let's go have us a little service, lad. Nothin' like a rousin' service before breakfast!"

They made their way down the narrow corridor. The *Caledonia* was primarily a cargo ship refitted to carry about twenty passengers, with a room, fifteen feet wide and twenty feet long, assigned as the recreation room. It held a few chairs, a couple of tables, and a worn collection of games—checkers, darts, cards. It was the best place, or perhaps the *only* place, to have their services, and most of the passengers spent the majority of their time there. The tiny cabins were too much like coffins to appeal to most of them.

They found Andy and Del Saunders already there, arguing over the book of Genesis. "Happy New Year," Andy grinned. "You two sleep any last night?"

"Why not?" Awful asked with some surprise.

"The way this old ship rolled, I thought I'd have to tie myself in," Del grumbled. He was a short, strong-looking fellow with blue eyes, red hair and freckles to go with it. "I didn't sleep a wink!"

"You slept like a rock! I heard you!" Andy countered with a grin. "You're the world's worst hypochondriac, Del. Always got some new disease."

It was true enough. Though Del was probably the healthiest person on board, he complained constantly about his health. "I was too sick to open my eyes, that's all," he said. "Where's the crop of newlyweds?"

Barney shook his head. "I hope they're not still sick. Not much of a honeymoon for them, is it?"

Slim Ranken had married a girl named Lily Jones, and she had been sick from the moment she stepped on board—even when the ship was docked and steady as a rock. Slim had spent most of the voyage holding her head and trying to comfort her.

The other couple was no better off, though it was Tobe DeLaughter who was seasick, and his bride, Pearl, who had to nurse him.

Barney had been uncertain about the quick marriages, but Beecham had approved. "The jungles of Liberia are the loneliest places on earth. A single man has a hard time. I wish *all* of your Company were married!"

Soon the four were joined by the others—except Lily Ranken. "She just can't make it," her tall, wiry husband said, scratching his rapidly receding hairline. He was close to being a genius in his field, they had soon discovered. His skill as a mechanic would come in handy in the jungle.

Andy began the service by saying, "It's the first day of the new year, and I'd like us to commit ourselves to God again. Let's read a few lines from the Psalms."

As the meeting progressed, Barney studied his fellow missionaries. *We're all tied together,* he thought. *When we get to Liberia, we'll only have each other.*

Andy Winslow. There was a man with confidence. The others might have fears or misgivings, but not Andy! He was the most intense of all, of quick intelligence, with a flair for leadership. Yes, he would make a good leader.

Slim Ranken. Barney was pleased that Slim was there. Lily might be a problem because of her fears and tendency to worry, but she would get over that.

Tobe DeLaughter. Tobe was twenty-five and of slight build. Though he was eager to plunge into the work and was absolutely dependable insofar as his powers allowed him to serve, his health might be a predicament. He suffered from a severe form of respiratory ailment, and Liberia was known to be hard on the healthiest individuals.

Pearl DeLaughter. Of all the missionaries, Pearl was the one Barney understood least. She was a tall, attractive woman of twenty-five, with curly black hair. She could have married well, having come from a rather well-to-do family in Chicago, of whom she said little. Why she had chosen Tobe, no one could figure out. Pearl had wandered into the Rescue Mission one evening, drunk, and Katie had prayed with her. She had given her life to the Lord, but kept a wall around her none could penetrate.

She caught Barney watching her, and smiled slightly, then turned back to listen to Andy.

Irene Bailey. Short, blond, with blue eyes and a forward manner, she had been successful working with the common women who came to the mission. She had led a rough life, and made no secret of it. She was a pretty tough lady. She might not be quite as spiritual as some, but she didn't seem to be afraid of anything.

Katie Sullivan. In spite of the rough sea voyage, Katie's face shone with fresh color. And there was an expectant air about her, one that did not require great events or high drama; the little things drew her attention. Barney had noticed her intense pleasure at the first bud on a tree, or the flight of a gull over the sea.

She was a mixture of gentleness and strength, Barney thought. The gentleness was in her soft blue eyes, her voice, and her quick sympathy for others. But beneath that softness lurked an unexpected core of strength. He had seen it exposed a few times, when the soft lips would grow tense and the mild eyes would lose their serenity. Her strength came through in difficult situations as she relied on the Lord. Katie's excitement in her new life in the Lord was infectious. She would be a strong member of the Company.

Awful Gardner. The Australian, wise, cheerful of spirit and bold in courage, was the forerunner, the pioneer, the father of their group. Had it not been for his love for God and others, his inspiration and persistence, none of them would be here, on their way to Africa as missionaries.

Bringing his thoughts back to Andy, Barney listened as his brother expounded the Word. He had much knowledge and zeal. But Barney wished Andy would take Gardner's wisdom into consideration. Andy liked Gardner, but paid no heed to the few mild suggestions that had come from him. But then, Andy seldom paid attention to suggestions. He was like a powerful locomotive, pounding down a single track with one hand on the throttle. *Oh, Lord,* Barney prayed. *Guard and direct us in this momentous undertaking, for apart from you we can do nothing!*

Finally the service was over, and they went to the mess hall for breakfast. They joined the officers of the ship and the other passengers, though the latter were conspicuous by their absence. The rolling seas and heavy weather did not create hearty appetites for most landsmen.

Barney sat next to the first mate, Gerald Sipes, a large man, with heavy muscles and great physical strength. He appeared to be about forty years of age. The officer was not thrilled at having the missionaries on board, and he wasted no time in venting his displeasure. His disgust took the form of a string of sarcastic remarks directed at the Christian religion.

"Well, gentleman, we'll have to watch our manners," he said as soon as Barney sat down. Sipes' eyes pulled down in a squint. "The saints have gathered."

"Good morning, mate," Gardner said. He was seated across from Sipes. "Did you ask the blessing yet, Mr. Sipes, or shall I do it?"

Laughter erupted from the sailors, and the captain said with a slight smile, "Mr. Sipes did forget to pronounce grace this morning. Perhaps you'd better remedy his oversight, Mr. Gardner." Captain James Seale, a native of Maine, was not a religious man, but was interested in philosophy. He had spent several evenings talking with Andy, the sole member of the team who could debate him in this area.

Gardner responded, "That I will, Captain." He bowed his head, thanked God for the food, then asked Him for better weather and to bless the members of the crew and the officers.

The prayer was hardly finished before Sipes jumped in. "So you think you can talk God into changing the weather, do you, Gardner?"

"Right-O!" Gardner nodded as he piled his plate high with food. "A sea-faring man like yourself can appreciate the tale of how the Lord Jesus handled storms." Without missing a bite, Gardner quoted the passage: "And when he was entered into a ship, his disciples followed him. And, behold, there arose a great tempest in the sea, insomuch that the ship was covered with the waves: but he was asleep. And his disciples came to him, and awoke him, saying, Lord, save us: we perish. And he saith unto them, Why are ye fearful, O ye of little faith? Then he arose, and rebuked the winds and the sea; and there was a great calm. But the men marvelled, saying, What manner of man is this, that even the winds and the sea obey him!"

Gardner nodded at the mate with a smile. "Now, that's what I've always liked about Jesus. He always knew what to do."

The captain considered Gardner thoughtfully. "And do you believe that actually happened, Reverend Gardner?"

"No fear!" Gardner exclaimed. "It's in the Bible!"

Sipes growled, "The Bible! Nothing but a book of fables!"

Andy jumped in. "Did you ever make a study of fables, Mr. Sipes?"

"Study fables? Of course not!"

"Then how do you know the Bible consists of fables if you don't know what they're like?"

"You don't think the stories in the Gospels are a little like fables, Reverend Winslow?" Captain Seale asked.

"Not a bit! Take the story of the woman taken in adultery.

When they brought her to Jesus and accused her, what did He do?"

The captain answered promptly, "He stooped down and began to write in the dust."

"You know your Bible, Captain!" Andy said warmly. "Well, that simple action of a man writing in the dust with his finger— you cannot find anything compared to it in any fables that I know. I've read fables most of my life, and there's nothing remotely like the account in the Bible."

"That's interesting," Captain Seale said. He considered the missionaries carefully, then asked, "But do you really believe that Jesus spoke to the storm, and that at His word it grew calm?"

"Yes, I do," Andy nodded. "The scripture says in John that all things were made by Him, by Jesus, that is. If He made them, He can command them. You command this ship, Captain. With one word you can send it wherever you wish. I think that Jesus Christ has that power over all nature."

Sipes swallowed a huge bite. "Than why don't you ask Him to make this storm we're in give up?"

"Because God knows what He's doing," Andy said easily. "It's not for me to give Him orders."

The meal went on slowly, and Barney listened as Andy handled the questions, some of them sarcastic and some genuine. He caught Katie's eye and winked at her, for he knew she was grateful, as he was, that Andy was there. *I'd sound like a fool if I tried to answer Sipes!*

But after dinner there was a different contest with Sipes. The burly officer had thrown barbed comments during the entire evening meal, and finally he'd said, "The thing that makes me sick is what a bunch of weaklings you Christians are!"

"Well, some of us are pretty feeble," Gardner admitted. "But so are folks who don't know God."

As the meal had progressed, Barney's mind drifted to future plans and wasn't paying much heed to Sipes. But he looked up when Sipes said contemptuously, "Look at you! I could wipe the deck with one swipe of you all."

"Mr. Sipes is quite a pugilist," Captain Seale said. "It's his strong right arm that keeps the crew obedient, I suspect."

The second mate, a dusky-faced fellow named Davis, asked,

"Are you having the bouts tonight, Sipes?"

"Yes, we are. We're—"

"What's this, Mr. Sipes?" Awful interrupted.

"The crew likes to have some boxing matches from time to time," the captain said. "Some of them are quite good, aren't they, Mr. Sipes?"

"Fair, just fair," Sipes admitted reluctantly. Then his eyes gleamed. "Now, why don't one of you fine young men join us? I'd be glad to go a few rounds with one or two of you."

"You'd kill them, Sipes," Davis grinned.

"Not if the Lord blessed Sipes' opponent," Gardner insisted. "Think of David. He had no trouble with the best heavyweight in the world because the Lord wuz with 'im."

Sipes stared at him. "Another fairy tale!"

"You don't really believe what you're saying, do you, Reverend Gardner?" Captain Seale asked. "It's not even reasonable that the average man can stand up to a trained boxer like Sipes."

"I think it might happen, Captain."

The captain turned his gray eyes on Andy. "Surely *you* don't agree?"

Andy had seen where Gardner was headed, and he turned his head and looked down the table, giving Barney a slight wink. "Why, certainly I do!"

"Then let's have a man from among you!" Sipes cried out. "If he beats me, I'll come to your blasted church every Sunday until we make port."

"I might even make the same promise, Mr. Winslow," Captain Seale added, a look of humor in his eyes. "As a matter of fact, I think I can speak for all the officers and the crew. If your man is able to stay with Mr. Sipes for—oh, say four rounds— why, you can count on all of us to be at the services. Right, men?"

The other officers had seen Sipes, and they agreed—with some laughter. Then one of the passengers said, "I can't speak for the rest of the travelers, but I'd make the same promise." Several people, taken by the challenge, called out their willingness.

Andy said, "Of course, as ministers we're opposed to fighting—"

"I knew it!" Sipes shot back. "Not a backbone in the crowd!"

"However—" Andy lifted his voice. "I think we all have enjoyed sport at one time or another. For the sake of sportsmanship, I think we might allow one of our number to go a few rounds with Mr. Sipes. Let's see, who shall it be?"

He pretended to look the men over, as though trying to make a choice.

"Barney!" Katie said, "you'd be willing to accommodate Mr. Sipes, wouldn't you?"

Barney looked at Gardner, who nodded. "Well, I couldn't do it without warning Mr. Sipes."

"Warning me?" Sipes demanded.

"Why, yes," Barney shrugged. "You see, actually, I did a little boxing when I was younger."

Laughter circled the table, and Captain Seale said, "I really can't permit this to go on. I wouldn't want you to get hurt, young man, and that's what would happen."

"I see it as a test of faith, Captain," Andy insisted. "We believe that God is able to take care of Barney. You don't think so. I think we are bound in this case to cast ourselves out on faith."

"Let them fight!" someone cried.

Obviously captivated by the challenge, Captain Seale said, "Very well, but I will referee the fight myself." He gave the first mate a stern look. "It's to be a boxing match, Mr. Sipes. Nothing else."

"Right, Captain!" he replied, but when the captain looked away, Sipes winked at Davis. "Well, I'd better go get myself prepared. If I've got to go into the ring with a wildcat like that young fellow, it's going to take all I've got!"

"The match will be at eight tomorrow night in the main cargo hold," Captain Seale announced as he got up. "I expect it will be an interesting evening."

Word of the match spread like fire through the ship. Crew and passengers alike talked of little else that day, and Davis said to the captain, "I've never seen so much excitement, Captain. We'd better lay-to until the match is over. I don't think we can get enough men to operate the ship!"

"It won't take long, Mr. Davis."

"You're right about that, sir!" Davis laughed. "I just hope Sipes doesn't hurt the fellow. That wouldn't look good."

"I'll stop it immediately if it gets bad." Then he smiled. "What if the minister wins?"

"Can't happen!"

"I suppose not. But if such a miracle does take place, we'll all get more preaching than we've had in our entire lives."

"You'd go to the services?"

"Yes, and so would you!"

"Aye, sir—but it won't come to that!"

Barney was amused at the way the other missionaries were so protective of him. "They act like there's been a death in the family," he said to Katie as they held to the rail and watched the gray swells rock the ship.

"I know I suggested you, but we're all afraid you'll get hurt." Her eyes reflected her concern. "I don't think you ought to do it."

"I'm not sure about it myself."

"So you *are* nervous!"

"About getting hurt? Not a bit."

"But he's so big—that old Sipes!"

"And slow," Barney shrugged. "If he were twenty pounds lighter and in good shape, I'd be a little worried. But he's gone to fat and can't move fast. All I have to do is stay away from him for four rounds."

Katie was not convinced. "Then what *does* bother you about the match?"

"Oh, I just think it's a cheap thing to do," Barney said slowly. "It's a trick. A sort of practical joke on people."

"I—never thought of it like that."

"These men are lost, most of them," Barney said. "And how's Sipes going to feel when he can't beat me? That's all he's got— his strength. Do you think he'll want to hear the gospel after he's been beaten?"

Katie stared over the rail, thinking hard. Finally she said quietly, "Well, Barney, both of us had to get whipped before we'd listen to God. Maybe that's what it's all about. Maybe Mr. Sipes needs to learn he *can* be beaten."

Her comment provoked interest, and he asked, "Do you think so, Katie? I'd just about made up my mind to call it off."

"Everyone would call you a coward, you know."

Barney laughed and turned to look at the waves. The wind was cold, but he loved the clean smell of the sea. "One thing about doing time in Sing Sing, Katie, it sort of takes the edge off remarks people make. After that hell, who cares what people say?"

Andy came up on deck to stand beside them. "Barney," he said, "do you think you can stay away from him for four rounds?"

"Sure."

"You're taking this pretty lightly!" he said, irritated. "Don't you realize how important it is?"

"It's just a boxing match, Andy," Barney shrugged. "And I wish we hadn't gotten into it."

"Barney's not sure it's right, Andy," Katie added. "He thinks it might even do harm."

"Barney!" Andy argued. "It *is* right! It's a glorious chance to prove to some sinners that Christians aren't a lot of weaklings! And remember, if you can do it, we'll have them listening to the gospel every service. You see how important that is, I hope?"

Barney hesitated. He had never been able to argue with Andy. Now he felt the same pressure, and it bothered him. But he gave in. "If you and Awful think I ought to do it, I will."

"Why, you know Awful! He's in his element! You just do your part, and I'll preach some sermons to those men that will burn their hides!" Andy beamed as he hurried off.

Katie said, "I'm not sure Andy is the right one to preach to the crew, Barney."

"He's the best preacher."

"I don't know that," she said stubbornly.

"I think *you* ought to preach," Barney suggested.

"Don't be silly!"

"Well, you'll be giving the people in Liberia the gospel, won't you? So why not get a little practice." The idea tickled him. "Yes, that's the way it will be."

"Andy would never permit it," Katie protested. "Besides, I'd be too scared."

"Don't worry about Andy," Barney said. "You just get a good sermon ready."

"Barney, don't get hurt." Her voice was laced with concern.

The wind whipping her hair and the cold sea spray giving her cheeks a rosy flush was a lovely sight, but went unnoticed by Barney. "You didn't come all this way to get beat up in this old ship!"

★ ★ ★ ★

At eight o'clock the hold was almost full. During matches every passenger and crew member possible would come to the match. Lighted lanterns hung above the makeshift ring. Unlike those in a real ring, the ropes were made of manila instead of the softer material.

Tonight the missionaries were added to the regular attenders. They were grouped together on one side, facing the crew on the other, with passengers mingled among the spectators. Captain Seale lifted his hand for silence, then announced, "There will be four matches this evening, but the first match will be the most interesting. We have at one hundred and seventy-one pounds, Reverend Barney Winslow. His opponent, at two hundred and six pounds, First Officer Melvin Sipes."

Barney came to the ropes wearing a suit coat over his shoulders and a pair of worn trousers that he'd cut short.

Sipes had a coat slung over his shoulders, covering his trousers. When the two men tossed their coats aside, a murmur rose from the crowd. Sipes' bulk was awesome—thick muscles in the arms and shoulders that rippled as he moved. He had a thick paunch, but it looked hard and firm.

Barney appeared slender and fragile next to his contender. He himself knew he was in better shape than he'd been since he had fought regularly. He'd run for miles every day and was feeling stronger than ever. It had been part of his training to get ready for the mission field.

Captain Seale gave his instructions, warning the fighters about low blows and instructing them to step back at once in case of a knockdown. As he spoke, Barney paid little attention. He let his eyes rove over the crowd and was amused to see the alarm and fear in the eyes of his friends. None of them knew how fit he was, and how that skill always won in the ring. He saw the hunger for violence in Sipes' face, and then the captain said, "Shake hands and come out fighting!"

They touched gloves and retreated to wait for the bell.

"I hope the dear boy don't hurt the poor lad," Awful said as Andy joined him.

The bell rang and the match began. Barney had known the burly officer would charge like a mad bull, and was prepared for it. He simply picked a wild right off with his left glove and stepped aside, sending Sipes into the ropes. He jumped back and came at Barney again, angered at his failure to connect. But again he was unable to lay a glove on the smaller man. He was throwing tremendous punches, but they were slow, making Barney almost laugh as he evaded some and picked others off.

Katie watched with bated breath. It looked as if Sipes were overpowering Barney. She cringed as the officer threw blow after blow, any one of which would have destroyed Barney. But as the round ended and the two men retreated to their respective places, she noticed Sipes was heaving, while Barney was breathing normally.

Andy desperately wanted his brother to win, so he cautioned Barney to stay away from Sipes. This instruction amused Awful because he knew what Barney was doing.

The bell rang, and this time Sipes was more careful. He had fought many times, usually overcoming his opponent by brute force, but this match was different. In the first round he discovered that the preacher was tricky.

Barney perceived Sipes' strategy and waited for the left punch. It was a good one, good enough for the amateurs Sipes dominated. But compared with the swift, crisp blows Barney had seen from expert boxers, it was but a puff. Bat simply moved his head, and as the arm lunged past, Barney landed two sharp blows with his left to the officer's cheek, followed by a hard right to the body.

Cries of surprise filled the air. Was it possible that a preacher could possess such skill? A red welt stood out on Sipes' face, and the man knew he had been beaten but refused to concede defeat. Throwing lefts and rights from all angles, he tried to smash his opponent, only to have him skillfully avoid every punch.

Captain Seale had seen many fights, and he knew that Barney could have sent crushing blows to Sipes' face and body. The big man was slow; Barney moved like lightning!

But Barney made no effort to hurt Sipes. When the bell rang, he went to his place and stood against the ropes. Sipes, on the other hand, was gasping for breath but refused to give in when his coach demanded, "Stop fooling with this guy! What's wrong with you?"

"He—some kind of—dancin' master! But I'll get him—this round!"

Sipes was crafty, and though his plan was illegal, he was going to do it to save his pride. In the next round, he suddenly threw his arms around Barney and drove him to the ropes. Holding him there with one vise-like armhold, he sent crushing blows to Barney's kidneys and then to the nape of his neck. It was like getting hit by an axe handle, and Barney tried to break free.

The captain tried to pull Sipes from Barney, but the man hung on and continued to batter Barney.

"Stop it, Sipes! That's illegal. Let him go!" the captain yelled, getting a good hold around the waist and jerking him away.

Barney's head was swimming, his eyes wouldn't focus. But he had no time to recuperate, for Sipes broke free from Captain Seale and lunged at Bat again, smashing a right to his head that sent him to the floor.

"Foul blow!" the captain shouted and would have stopped the fight, but Barney got to his feet.

"Are you all right?" Seale asked.

Barney felt dizzy but he nodded, and the captain stepped back. This time Winslow reverted to his old skill, acting from pure instinct. As Sipes roared in, Barney stood flat-footed and drove his fist at the officer's unguarded chin. The blow stopped him dead in his tracks, and he dropped his hands. Barney could have sent a killing punch in, but his head had cleared, so he simply waited until Sipes regained his senses.

Every spectator recognized Sipes' helplessness and knew Barney could have half killed the man if he had wanted to. But he chose not to. As the fight went on, Barney moved around the ring, and Sipes followed, trying a jab here and there. By the time the round ended, Sipes could hardly breathe or hold his hands up. Barney had clearly won, and the captain raised Bat's gloved hand in a symbol of victory.

The missionaries, as well as a few of the spectators, cheered wildly. Andy was elated and was already preparing his sermon in his mind.

Captain Seale raised his hand for silence and said with a slight smile, "I will see all of you at services this Sabbath day according to the terms of the match."

"Hey, Captain, you don't really mean that!" one man groaned, followed by a mixture of laughs and groans from the others.

Barney's voice broke through as he called, "Captain, may I have a word?"

"Why, of course!"

The crowd grew quiet as the champion raised his hand. "I'd like to release all of you from the promise you made about this match," he said.

Andy stared in unbelief; the captain's eyes glinted with interest.

"This was not a fair match, and I am sorry to have taken part in it. You see, I was a good boxer for some years. It's like you officers. You can run the ship because you're professionals. That's how I won the fight—I'm a professional boxer." Then Barney turned and walked over to Sipes.

"Mr. Sipes, it was not a fair match, and I apologize."

Dumbfounded, Sipes gazed at him wide-eyed, then at the crew, who waited for the usual stream of curses.

But Sipes' face split in a grin and he said, "Well, blast my pants! You're a cool one!" He stuck out his hand, saying, "I ain't no welcher! I said I'd be at church—and at church I'll be!"

"So will the rest of us," Captain Seale echoed, his steely eyes sweeping his crew and officers.

Later, Captain Seale said to Andy, "It was the best thing that could have happened to you people. We would have come—but a congregation by force isn't worth much, is it?"

"No, it isn't," Andy agreed, adding with a smile, "That brother of mine! He's supposed to be a little slow! Imagine his thinking of such a thing! And it was so right!"

"You may know your philosophy, Andrew, but that young man knows people!"

CHAPTER FOURTEEN

WELCOME TO AFRICA!

★ ★ ★ ★

The S.S. *Caledonia* docked at Liverpool, and after a ten-day layover, proceeded on its journey to Africa. The bad weather that had plagued them on the first leg of their journey now gave way to milder, warmer winds, and the ancient ship nosed steadily through the gray waters.

Lily Ranken and Tobe DeLaughter had finally recovered from their seasickness, and the voyage became almost like a pleasure cruise.

But Awful Gardner knew better and was fully aware that difficult days lay ahead. Though he said little to the others, he often spoke of this to Barney. His premonitions were confirmed late one Sunday afternoon ten days after leaving Liverpool. Barney and he were having coffee with Captain Seale in the dining room when the subject came up. "Well, now," Gardner said, "these are fine days for all of us, Captain." He sipped his coffee, his face thoughtful, adding, "I'm thinking, though, we'll look back on this time as the golden days once we're into the country."

Captain Seale stirred his coffee slowly, put the spoon down, and after sipping the hot brew, remarked, "You're right, and I'm worried about your young people—about all of you, as a matter of fact."

Barney raised his eyebrows in surprise. "Why, we'll be all right, Captain."

Seale gave him a steady look. "You're all babes in the woods, Reverend," he said. "I know a little about the place you're going to. Do you know what it's called?"

"Liberia, of course."

"It's called 'The White Man's Grave' by many," Seale said grimly. "I've taken many passengers there. Some of them were missionaries like yourselves. And I've hauled many of the survivors back to the States."

"It's a rough country," Gardner agreed. "We'll have to toughen up."

"Not a matter of that," Seale insisted. "Some of the people I took back to America were fit enough, but no man's tougher than malaria. Everyone gets it, and I understand that a man never gets over it. Three years ago I put a lovely family off in Monrovia, parents and three children. Methodist missionaries. They were a picture-book family, all strong and healthy. Eight months later I took the man and one son back to England. They were living skeletons. The mother and the other two children died within six months."

The three men sat silently, thinking of the dark mass of land that lay beyond the ship's prow. There was something ominous about it, the vast distances, the unknown rivers, and the wild animals—not to mention the savage qualities of some of its people.

"'Course, the Good Lord has promised to be with us all the way," Awful remarked. A smile lifted the corners of his lips, and he gave a gentle jibe at the captain. "I wish the voyage were a little longer. We'd have your whole blinkin' crew converted, Captain!"

A fleeting smile crossed Seale's face. "You have me there, Reverend Gardner." Several of the crew had given their hearts to the Lord in the Sunday services, and the officers had noted that their work had been affected for the better. "Wish the whole bunch would get converted," Sipes had said. He himself had mellowed, and spent considerable time with Gardner and Barney.

Katie came into the dining room, and the three men rose. "I

have to get back to the bridge," Captain Seale said. "We'll make port in a week, so you'd best enjoy yourself. It's going to be a hard life." He tipped his hat to Katie, smiled, and added, "I understand you'll be the speaker for the service this evening. I'll look forward to hearing you."

"Splendid chap." Gardner nodded toward the retreating officer as they all sat down. "Andy's got hopes for him, but he's a hard case."

"Oh no!" Katie protested. "He's not at all like some of the others, Awful."

"That's true. However, he'd be a sight more likely to get saved if he wuz," Gardner retorted. "Ain't you noticed that none of the educated ones have found the Lord? Or only one, anyways. The captain thinks too much, that's his trouble. Wants to figure everything out."

"I agree," Barney nodded. "Andy talks philosophy with him all the time, but he needs to know he's a sinner. He's such a decent man he doesn't see his need of God."

"And that stoker who got saved last Sunday, he didn't have no doubts about what *he* was, did he, now?" Gardner said. "A regular drunk and everything else. And when he heard that Jesus Christ could take all that out of 'im, why he come runnin' to get saved!"

"We'll just have to pray that the gospel will get through to Captain Seale," Katie said.

Gardner stood up. "Well, I'm goin' to find that young engineer and give him a dose of Romans. The Spirit's been convictin' him, and I want to water the seed a little."

"Got a good sermon for us tonight?" Barney asked after Gardner left. He had pressured Andy into asking Katie to speak, and had been surprised at his brother's reluctance. Andy felt that with so few services left, *he* should do all the preaching.

"Oh, Barney, I can't do it!" Katie almost wailed. She bit her lower lip, turned her eyes on him, and pleaded, "*You* preach tonight!"

"Not a chance!" he laughed.

"Some of the people on the ship don't even believe in lady preachers," Katie argued.

"Give 'em a good dose of fire and brimstone," Barney teased.

"And you'll—" He stopped when he saw Pearl DeLaughter enter.

"Hello, Pearl," he said, pulling out a chair for her. "Can I get you some coffee?"

"That would be nice."

After Barney left for the galley, Pearl said, "You and Barney are getting quite close, I see."

Katie's cheeks turned pink. "Well," she laughed, "he saved my life, so I think I'll always be in his debt."

"He's not as good-looking as Andy, is he?"

"Not many men are."

"That's right. Are you interested in him?"

Katie had recognized from the first that Pearl was rather blunt, and that she took a great interest in the single members of the group. "I'm interested in being a good missionary right now. How's Tobe?"

"Oh, he's fine," Pearl said absently.

"I've worried a little about him," Katie frowned. "I hope he doesn't have any of those attacks he had in New York."

"I don't expect—oh, here's Barney."

"Sugar and cream. That right?" he said as he placed the coffee before her.

"Just right. Thank you, Barney." She smiled at him warmly. "You'll spoil me." She sipped the coffee as she studied him over her coffee cup. "I've been talking with Katie about you. We've decided that you're not nearly as eligible as Andy."

Barney grinned. "Aside from the fact that he's better looking and smarter and knows how to make women happy, I don't see why you should even voice such a thing. And remember, if a girl gets a fellow like that, some hussy is likely to run off with him. A girl wouldn't have to worry about that if she got me."

Pearl and Katie both laughed, and he grinned broadly. "Well, some girl might run off with me, too—but who would care? So you can see, there are advantages to a low down sort of fellow like me."

"Oh, Barney, don't talk nonsense!" Katie admonished. "Look how you and Awful got the Rescue Mission started. Why, Andy could *never* have begun a work in the fourth ward with the down-and-outers!"

"No," Barney said thoughtfully, "he hadn't been in Sing Sing.

That's another advantage I have over him—being a jailbird."

"You're a tough brute, Barney," she commented, taking in his broken nose and muscular frame. The expression in her eyes was difficult to discern, for she had a way of scrutinizing and weighing people. "You'll probably be carrying the whole lot of us on your back after the first week on the field."

"Not me. That'll be Andy. Or Awful, maybe." He got to his feet. "See you later. I'm going for a nap."

Pearl turned to Katie as Barney walked away. "You know what I think? You better get him, Katie. He's not handsome, but he'd be caring and loving, one who would protect a woman."

"Oh, Pearl, I'm not going to *get* anybody!" Katie exclaimed.

"If you don't, I expect Irene will. A man needs a woman, and you and Irene are the only choices. And you know Irene—she's pretty and knows how to please a man."

There was an implied criticism in her words, but Katie ignored the remark. "I've got to go work on my sermon for tonight," she said. "Pray for me, Pearl. Or better still, why don't *you* take the service?"

"No, it's you they need to hear," Pearl said languidly. She continued sipping her coffee after Katie left, then got up and joined two officers at the rail who were taking a sighting. "Is that Africa, in that direction?" she asked playfully.

Back in the cabin, Katie labored over her sermon, staying secluded most of the day. Fortunately, Irene hated the cabin, which the two shared, and was there only when asleep. The thought of preaching to the passengers and crew had been troublesome, and when Katie eventually joined the others for dinner, she still felt restless in her spirit.

She sat next to Del Saunders, saying little and eating less. His conversation seemed to be occupied with his lack of appetite, yet he devoured his food like a shark. *What a motley group we are*, she thought. *How will we ever exist?* Her mind returned to the message she was to give. She prayed much, half listening as Andy expounded around the table.

"I've been reading about Liberia," he said. "The place has a very odd history. The name Liberia means 'free,' taken from the fact that it was settled by freed slaves. An organization called the American Colonization Society put the first group of freed slaves in the country in 1822. This society started the town of Monrovia, naming it after the President of the United States, James Monroe. He'd led the move to empower the U.S. Navy to board slave ships and release the slaves in Monrovia."

"I never heard of slaves starting a country," Irene spoke up.

"Well, it was pretty grim," Andy said slowly. "Hunger and disease hit them hard, but gradually their numbers increased, and our government recognized the Liberian independence in 1882. It's still sparsely populated."

"What about mission work?" Del Saunders asked. "Will we find any of that?"

Andy hesitated, then said, "You already heard what they call the country—'The White Man's Grave.' The name came partly from the high death rate of missionaries. Of seventy-nine missionaries sent to Liberia by the Church Missionary Society of London before 1830, forty-four died of fever during their first year of service."

"My word!" Awful gasped. "It ain't no bloomin' health resort, is it, now!"

The dark, foreboding information was anything but promising—some members paled at the prospect ahead, others accepted it as a challenge, seeing God's hand of direction and provision.

That evening more people than usual attended the service. "I think they've come to hear me because I'm a woman," she whispered to Barney. "I feel like a freak!"

But when she faced the audience, the apprehension left and her voice was firm. She shared frankly about her life of sin, of how she had sunk to the lowest levels of society. As she bared her heart before them, she had no conception of the impression her words made on the crew and the passengers.

"But the Lord didn't forget me," she said warmly, her eyes flashing. "He died for me, and when I needed Him the most, He sent one of His servants to me. He doesn't want me to mention it, but if it hadn't been for Barney Winslow and the faithful workers of the Rescue Mission, I would still be lost, without hope, and away from God."

She concluded with a pleading that all her hearers look to Jesus for salvation. In response, two members of the crew came forward. Barney and Awful knelt with the men, praying with the two and showing them the way. The reality of their experience of receiving Jesus as Savior showed in their faces and caused much rejoicing among them.

Afterward, Captain Seale said quietly, "I appreciated your sermon." There was an expression of pain in his eyes, and he added, "I have a daughter who's living a terrible life. Would you pray for her?"

"Yes, of course," Katie responded, adding, "I've been praying for you, Captain Seale. I believe God is dealing with your heart, too. Do you think He wants to give your daughter a Christian father?"

He dropped his head, trying to hide the strong emotions stirring beneath his even demeanor. Katie waited for a moment. Then sensing the prompting of the Holy Spirit, she said, "When God is dealing with you, it's not a good idea to ignore Him. Would you let me pray for you, Captain?"

When he lifted his head, she saw the tears in his eyes. He said nothing but nodded assent. Katie prayed a simple prayer for his daughter, and when she ended, she asked, "Would you ask the Lord Jesus to come into your heart? That's all one can do." She urged him quietly. Finally he closed his eyes and his lips moved. Katie prayed, and when she finished, he lifted his head, and she saw that something had happened to him.

"I . . . I feel much better," he said, his voice filled with wonder. "Is this what you called 'being saved'?"

"Yes!" Katie said joyfully. "You asked Him to come into your life, didn't you? Well, Jesus always comes when we ask. Now, could I give you a suggestion?"

"What is it?"

"Don't keep what's happened to yourself. Jesus said we were to confess Him before men. It may be a little difficult for you at first, but it will make you a stronger Christian. As you do, you'll experience the reality of His love for you, and the desire to tell others will grow. Will you do that?"

Captain Seale seemed uncomfortable, but the shining face of the young woman before him gave him courage. "Yes, I will. As a matter of fact, I think right now would be the best time. I might lose my nerve later on."

"May I tell the others the good news?" she asked, and when he nodded, to his astonishment she called out loudly, "Everybody! Let me have your attention!"

"You going to preach again, lady?" First Mate Sipes called out with a grin. He had enjoyed her sermon tremendously and would have listened to her again with pleasure.

"No, Mr. Sipes, I am not—but we have wonderful news for you." She paused, tears running down her cheeks.

The others stopped what they were doing, wondering what she was going to tell them. "It always makes me cry when someone comes to the Lord Jesus." She brushed the tears away with her hand and looked straight at Seale. "Captain Seale wants to say something. Right, Captain?"

Seale was basically a private person, and when he found himself the target of every eye, he flushed and stammered. But gathering courage, he said firmly, "For a long time I've been interested in Jesus Christ, but a few moments ago, I discovered that—that He's not just a person from ancient history but He's alive! I've received Him into my life and I intend to follow Him with all my heart."

The room broke out into cries of joy—mostly from the missionaries, of course. But the captain's fellow officers were dumbfounded. Though they admired Captain Seale, knowing him as a fine seaman and an educated man, his sudden announcement came like a clap of thunder.

Sipes waited until the others had moved away before he approached Seale with a trace of uncertainty. "Well, Captain," he mumbled, "I'm glad for you. Hope it lasts." He looked at the missionaries and added in a subdued tone, "They ain't like what I always thought Christians was like. Sort of makes a fellow think, Captain, when he meets up with the real thing, don't it, now?"

"Yes, Mr. Sipes," Captain Seale agreed. His eyes rested on Katie Sullivan. "It gives me a start, thinking that fine young woman, and the rest of them, may all be in a shallow grave in six months' time."

Sipes stared at him. "Aw, Captain, don't talk like that!"

"I don't like to, but you know what that country's like." Then he looked at Sipes and added, "I don't think I would put off making a decision too long, Melvin. We never know what's around the corner, do we?"

As Captain Seale left, Sipes murmured, "Now he's preachin' at me! Wasn't enough that the rest of 'em were at me; now I'll get it from my own captain. Might as well give up and become a bloomin' Christian and be done with it!"

★ ★ ★ ★

"Katie! Come up on deck. We're here!"

Katie leaped off her bunk and joined the others who had heard Irene's cry. They elbowed their way, falling over one another as they excitedly scrambled up the ladder to the deck.

A stiff wind was scouring the sea, lifting the waves into whitecaps. The blazing sun on the ocean so blinded Katie that she stumbled to the rail. "Where? Where is it?" she asked, blinking against the midday light.

"Over there, see?"

Shading her eyes, she was just able to make out a low-lying shadow, merely a smudge on the distant horizon. The jubilation they all felt at arriving at their destination can be experienced only by those who have left all to follow a dream—and then to see it just ahead, to be tasted, to be tested, to be fulfilled. None could envisage the heartache, the agony, the frustration, the questions that would assault them. For now it was enough to know they had reached Liberia.

"I wonder when we'll get off the ship?" Slim Ranken voiced. "We'd better go start packing."

But there was no hurry, for by the time the ship dropped anchor, it was almost dark. Captain Seale announced at supper, "Well, this is almost our last meal together. You'll disembark early in the morning."

"What's the date?" Tobe asked.

"February the second," Captain Seale supplied. "We've made fair time." Then he added, "It's been a voyage none of the crew will ever forget." He had been faithful to his conversion, encouraging the men to attend services, and had plunged into a study of the Bible that was an example to those who had become Christians.

That night a rough tropical storm caught up with them, and

when they gathered on deck after breakfast, the sky was black, and a driving rain was falling. "The ship can't enter the harbor in this weather," Captain Seale told them. "You can either wait until it clears, or we can put you ashore in surfboats."

"Oh, let's go now!" Andy said, and the others agreed. One of the *Caledonia* crewmen rowed to shore, and after a while a boat flying the Liberian flag pulled alongside. Two Liberian officials for customs and immigration climbed the rope ladder to the deck. After considerable red tape, the missionaries were all cleared for landing.

The rain was still falling and the waves were breaking against the ship.

"Be a bit wet. Better wait until tomorrow," First Officer Sipes suggested.

But Andy wouldn't hear of it. "If we can't stand a little wet, how can we think of going where the going is really rough?" he said.

"Very well," Sipes nodded. "We'll have to use mammy chairs."

Mammy chairs proved to be a square box with board seats facing each other. The captain assisted Katie into the chair, and as he stepped back, he said quietly to her alone, "I'll pray for you, Katie. And I'll always be grateful for your kindness."

Katie smiled. "I'm so thankful I had the opportunity to become acquainted with you and to see what the Lord has done in your life. Write me about your daughter, will you?"

Then the chair was hoisted into the air by the ship's crane and swung over the side. The wind tossed it back and forth as it descended, striking the waiting surfboat repeatedly before steadying.

It was a tricky matter getting out of the mammy chair into the rocky surfboat, but Katie held on to her suitcase and made a jump. She fell headlong, dropping her bag and sprawling on top of two of the black oarsmen. They picked her up as though it were a routine occurrence and seated her securely.

"You be okay, Mammy. Bestman not let you fall!" one of the men assured her, his white teeth gleaming against his ebony skin.

It was Katie's first contact with one of the people she'd seen in her dreams. The raised tribal markings across the cheeks of the tall well-built man lifted as he spoke, and his smile and genuine air of open honesty put her at ease immediately.

"Thank you, Bestman," Katie said. "My name is Sullivan."

"Yes, Mammy," he grinned, then turned to catch Lily Ranken as she came tumbling into the boat, screaming with fear.

They were all finally aboard, and the commander of the small craft cried, *Kwiali! Kwiali!* All the rowers bent to their oars, moving in perfect harmony as they guided the surfboat toward the shore. When they were almost at the dock, Katie turned and looked at the S.S. *Caledonia*.

"Makes you a little sad to leave it, doesn't it, Katie?"

She turned to see Barney close to her. "Yes, in a way."

"Well," he smiled, "you got your first fruit as a missionary. Captain Seale, I mean."

Katie nodded, then turned her eyes to the shore. "It's going to be hard isn't it, Barney?"

He nodded slowly. The rain gathered on his face and ran down in streams. "Yes, but the Lord promised to be with us always. That's what we need to remember and remind each other when it gets hard."

The boat had now reached the dock, and Bestman helped Katie out of the unsteady craft, saying, "Be watchful, Mammy!"

"Thank you, Bestman," she said, smiling, then stepped out on the continent of Africa.

CHAPTER FIFTEEN

SERVICES

★ ★ ★ ★

Stanley Beecham was not at the dock as expected when the missionaries landed. This initial introduction to a strange land left the group feeling perplexed as they waited at the offices of the steamship line. Shortly, however, a short rotund man wearing a raincoat and hat breezed in. "Sorry I'm late," he said. "I'm Myron Hansen. Reverend Beecham told me to be on the lookout for you. Welcome to Monrovia!"

"Will Reverend Beecham be along soon?" Andy asked.

"No. He had to make a trip into the back country," Hansen replied. "But we've arranged places for your stay at our mission station. Let's be on our way; then when we get settled, we'll get on with the introductions."

He led the group to the two carriages, where a couple of dark-skinned drivers loaded the luggage as the newcomers climbed in. Andy jumped into the carriage with Reverend Hansen, hoping to ask questions, but the man gave him no opportunity.

"I'm the director of Monrovia City Mission," he said. "My family and I have been here only six years, and I'm happy to report that the work is thriving! You'll soon have a chance to see for yourselves."

He kept up a rapid-fire commentary on the sights they passed, the current events of the country, the condition of politics, and a great many other subjects until an hour later they passed through two large gates of the mission.

"Ah, here we are!" Hansen announced. "Let me show you to your quarters, and when you're settled, perhaps you'll join my family for lunch?"

"Of course, sir," Andy smiled.

"This is our dormitory," the portly missionary explained as they entered the mud construction, "but the Bible school isn't in session now." He assigned the rooms, saying, "If you need anything, one of the servants will be nearby, so you have only to ask. We'll expect you about eleven-thirty."

As the director hurried off, Andy inspected the room he and Barney would share. The walls were plastered on the inside and painted white. The accommodations seemed more than adequate, the furniture handmade, apparently of local material. As the men checked further they discovered a shower house two doors down, which could be approached through a canopy of palm leaves.

"This is pretty nice, Barney," Andy commented as they returned to their room and began to strip off their soaked clothing. "Beecham mentioned there was a large work in Monrovia, but I wasn't expecting the red-carpet treatment."

Barney nodded. "Good thing Reverend Hansen showed up. I haven't the foggiest idea of what to do next."

"Beecham said in his last letter that we'd work that out when we got here," Andy explained.

"I can hardly wait."

Down the hall the rest of the Company were getting settled in their quarters—Katie and Irene in one room, and the others in various accommodations.

"Better enjoy that shower," Katie said to Irene as they showered and changed to dry clothing. "It may be the last one we have."

"Sure is great after the trip over. Wonder if the rest are settled in." Irene finished dressing and opened the door. "Oh," she said, surprised to see a black girl nearby, "were you waiting for something?"

"No, ma'am. I am to help you. Is there anything you need?"

"Could we have some fresh water?" Irene requested, and

when the girl left, Irene turned to Katie. "Servants and all. I didn't know missionaries in Africa had it so good."

"I think this must be unusual," Katie said thoughtfully. "From what little we heard from Reverend Beecham, it's pretty rough once you get away from the larger cities and into the bush."

The Company was ready long before lunch and talked constantly, relieved to be away from the confines of the ship. Finally Andy said, "Well, I think we might as well go for our lunch." He asked one of the servants for directions to the dining area and was told, "I will take you."

He led them across an open compound to a large two-story structure built of stone. He pulled a rope hanging beside the door, setting off a bell inside the house. Immediately the door opened and Reverend Hansen greeted them. "Come in! Come in! We've been waiting for you!"

They were escorted to a huge room, furnished much like an American home, with beams across the ceiling and mounted heads of antelope, kudu, black leopard, and a nubian lion on the walls.

Standing next to a slim fair-haired attractive woman, Mr. Hansen said, "Let me introduce you to my wife, Emily, and my daughter, Dorothy." The daughter, about twenty-three, was the image of her mother. She acknowledged the introduction and then quietly studied the group.

"Suppose you introduce your fellow missionaries, Mr. Winslow?"

After the formalities were completed, Reverend Hansen said, "Now I propose we move to the dining room."

They were seated at a large table made out of a single slab of dark wood. Del Saunders and the two married couples sat at Hansen's left, with Barney, Irene, Gardner and Dorothy Hansen facing them, and Mrs. Hansen at the other end.

A silver tureen graced the center of the table, with matching bowls in front of each guest. "Suppose we have the blessing now," Reverend Hansen suggested, "so the soup won't get cold." He stood to his feet, and the others followed suit. The blessing was long and eloquent. *The soup could be frozen by the time he's finished prayin'*, Awful thought, shuffling his feet. "Blimey!" he said later to Barney, "I thought he'd never get the bloomin' prayer out of the way!"

"I think you'll like this soup," Hansen said as the white-coated male servants began filling the bowls. "It is sea turtle, fresh from the ocean just yesterday. And our cook is superb!"

After the monotonous shipboard diet, the missionaries found the soup and the food that followed delicious. They had a taste of native African game, including antelope steaks and a sampling of elephant meat—"just for the experience," Mr. Hansen smiled.

Despite his rather affected ways, Reverend Hansen was sharp and intelligent; and before the meal was half finished, he had learned all their names. As the meal progressed, he drew from his guests much of their life circumstances. Slim Ranken's expertise as a mechanic seemed to please Hansen, and Katie's role as a former entertainer in a saloon fascinated him, but shocked his wife and interested his daughter.

Katie caught Barney's eye and realized he, too, wondered what kind of man Reverend Hansen was.

Mrs. Hansen said little, but Dorothy perked up at the mention of Barney's exploits as a boxer. "Were you the champion?" she asked.

"Bless you, no, Miss Hansen!" Barney smiled. "Just run of the mill."

Andy, however, launched into the account of Sipes and Barney's match. He told it well, making it a humorous affair.

"I know the man!" Reverend Hansen exclaimed. "He was locked up for drunkenness two years ago."

"But it turned out well," Awful interjected. "The whole bloomin' crew was comin' to services after that, and the officers, too."

"Not Captain Seale?" Mrs. Hansen asked.

"Oh, that's the best of it all!" Gardner grinned. "Our little evangelist, Miss Sullivan, the one who's blushin' like a rose right now, why, she won the captain's heart—to the Lord, that is!"

"That's extraordinary!" Hansen replied, his eyes wide. "His ship stops here on every voyage, and he's been our guest many times. Such a fine fellow—but not religious."

"Well, he is now!" Del Saunders laughed. "He's even handing out Bibles to his crew!"

"I'm impressed," Mrs. Hansen murmured, staring at Katie.

"We've witnessed to Captain Seale, but he's always been so reserved."

"I suspect it was his concern for his daughter that broke him down," Katie offered.

"What's wrong with his daughter?" Dorothy asked.

"I don't really know the circumstances," Katie replied. "He was worried about her, and I suggested that if he knew the Lord, he'd be able to help her more."

Hansen nodded with satisfaction, saying heartily, "Now *that's* the way to deal with people! Use your head a little bit, find out what's going on inside; then you can get them where you want them!"

His view on evangelism bothered both Katie and Barney, but only Winslow spoke up. "That would be pretty hard to do with the natives in the bush, wouldn't it, Reverend Hansen?"

Mr. Hansen took a sip of coffee, thought about the question, then nodded. "You have a point, Barney—may we use first names? Ah, thank you. Well, we come to a matter that is a little touchy in missionary circles."

"Touchy? In what way, sir?" Andy asked.

"The point is, we have a certain amount of money, a certain amount of time and manpower—and woman power, to be sure! But I have felt that we are to some extent wasting much of those items. Or to put it more charitably, I feel that I have found a more efficient way to invest them."

"I'd like to hear it, sir," Andy said eagerly. "Anything you can tell us that will be of help, we'll appreciate it."

"Myron—" Mrs. Hansen broke in tactfully. "Perhaps it would be best if we postpone any discussion of methods until our new friends have had time to settle in."

Embarrassed, Reverend Hansen flushed slightly and laughed. "You are right, as usual, my dear!" Smiling at his guests, he said, "It would be especially inappropriate for me to discuss the matter with you until Reverend Beecham returns. He and I have been carrying on a friendly 'war' about methods for some time. And since you are here under his authority, we'll wait until you are better able to make decisions."

"As you say, sir," Andy agreed. "But we are certainly in your debt for the hospitality you've given us. I think we'd still be sitting in that station soaking wet if you hadn't rescued us."

"It's good to have you here," Dorothy smiled. "You don't know now, but you soon will, how wonderful it is to have someone from home to talk with. I warn you, I intend to question you to death!"

"Oh, there'll be lots of time for fellowship," Hansen beamed. "But I intend to put you all to work."

"That's great!" Andy cried.

"Tomorrow we'll give you a tour of the city and show you what we're doing. There are meetings every day, so you'll be preaching often. We also have schools and a hospital of sorts; if you are interested, you can be of great help. At night, you can start learning the language. And if that doesn't keep you busy, I'll take you hunting in the bush. That's my hobby, you see."

Barney glanced at the heads mounted on the wall. "Those are fine trophies, but we want to work. That's why we came. Would it be possible to go out into the villages?"

"Certainly! Nothing could be easier, could it, my dear?" he said, turning to his wife.

"I'll have to watch my husband," Mrs. Hansen said. "He'll have you worked to the ground before Reverend Beecham gets back."

True to her prediction, the next week was so busy that the young people were exhausted. They had done everything Reverend Hansen had said, and more. On Sunday Andy preached in the morning to a huge crowd at the church, and was thrilled at the response. That night, Gardner spoke with even greater results.

Dorothy sat in front with her mother during both services. After Andy's message, she said, "You're a wonderful preacher, Mr. Winslow. My father will probably be very jealous and refuse to let you do it again."

"Not true at all, Miss Hansen!" Andy protested. "This is a wonderful church, and the work here is splendid! You must be very proud of your father."

"I am, but we sometimes disagree."

What an attractive woman, he thought, then brought his mind back to the present. "Disagree how?"

"I'm afraid you'll dislike me if I tell you."

"No chance of that, I'm sure!"

"You promise?" She gave him a captivating smile. "I must confess I'm *very* ambitious. I want to see the work grow fast, but my father is rather slow."

"I'm afraid you and I are much alike," Andy grinned. "Your father will watch me like a hawk if he finds out we're both too impulsive."

"We won't tell him then. It'll be our secret."

"It's not very nice," Andy said, a humorous light in his eyes. "Here I am abusing the hospitality of my host!"

"It's for his own good, and he'll love it when it happens."

"Exactly what sort of attack are you launching, Miss Hansen?"

"Call me Dorothy," she smiled. "Nothing very original. You've seen the work in Monrovia? My father has the right idea, but your Reverend Beecham doesn't agree."

"Beecham? What's wrong with his ideas?"

"You'll soon find out, I'm afraid," she said. "Reverend Beecham doesn't think missionary work done outside the deep bush is worth much. As a matter of fact, he's not certain that my family and I are really missionaries at all."

"That's ridiculous! The work in this city is splendid!"

Dorothy smiled, her brown eyes wide with admiration. "I'm glad *you* think so, for *he* doesn't. That's what my father wanted to tell you the first night you all came to dinner. The two almost came to blows about it—father wanting to center the work in the cities and large villages and Reverend Beecham demanding that we all go to the interior."

Andy had guessed some of this, but he hadn't known the two men were so deeply divided. He shook his head. "We came under Beecham's invitation, so we'll have to wait until he comes. But I agree with you and your father, more or less."

"I knew you would!" Dorothy exclaimed. "I know Reverend Beecham will want you all to go to the interior, but I was hoping you could persuade him to let some of your people stay here. There's *so* much to do!"

"I'll see what I can do, Dorothy." His eyes lit up and he added, "I came to Africa to do my best for God. I want to serve Him as well as I can!"

"You're the leader," she said. "They'll do what you say."

"Not Barney or Gardner!" he laughed. "Those two are stubborn as mules!"

He was right—and discovered just how stubborn three days later. Stanley Beecham returned early in the morning, and after greeting them, said, "Well, vacation's over. I expect Brother Hansen's shown you the easy side of Africa. Now I'm going to show you the other side. Be ready to leave in an hour—and wear your roughest clothes!"

They all scrambled to get ready and were waiting in the compound when he appeared, seated on a large wagon pulled by four oxen. "Ladies in, gentlemen walk," he said with a smile. The women got into the wagon, and the driver called to the oxen and touched them with a long thin cane pole. They lurched forward, and soon were at the outskirts of Monrovia. The road turned into a narrow mud path, and after being jolted severely, Katie jumped to the ground, saying, "I'd rather walk."

They followed the narrow road for two hours, and then Beecham called for a rest. "Get out and walk around, but watch out for snakes."

Petrified, Lily Ranken clutched Slim's arm. "I'd die if I even *saw* one!"

"No, you won't die from *seeing* one," Beecham said cheerfully. "Most of them are harmless. But if it's an extremely long bright green snake, don't argue, just run."

"What sort of a snake is it?" Slim asked.

"It's a green mamba, but the natives call it a 'five-stepper' because if one of them bites you, you have about five steps to get help. After that, it's too late."

"I got bit by a rattler once," Del Saunders said. "He was a big one, too. But I didn't die."

"The rattler's poison works on the blood," Beecham explained. "The mamba's venom works on the nerves. It paralyzes a man so he can't breathe."

The warning was taken seriously, and they kept their eyes peeled to the ground, but no snakes were seen. The walking just about did them in, though. The long voyage and the ministry under Hansen had sapped their strength, and it was necessary to call a halt several times before they reached their destination.

"Here come your hosts," Beecham called out. "We'll be dining with them tonight. Before they get here, let me warn you, it's important that you eat what they set before you. I've brought along some very pungent hot sauce. If the food looks suspicious, I just douse it until all I can taste is the fire of the sauce."

Like all the others, Katie eagerly waited for the natives to come. "These people are from the Pahn tribe," Beecham explained as four men appeared. Katie gasped. Except for a small loin cloth made from bark, the natives were naked. She had known that this was common in Africa, but the stark reality of their nakedness struck her with the realization she was now, indeed, in an alien world. She noted that Lily Ranken had the same reaction, but Pearl and Irene seemed undaunted.

Reverend Beecham extended his hand palm up as he spoke to the men. One of them, with short legs and a face marked with tribal scars, responded.

"This is Chief Mawali," Beecham said.

Chief Mawali made a speech, which Beecham interpreted as a welcome. Then he and his headmen turned and led the missionaries to the village.

None of the fledgling missionaries ever forgot their introduction to that tiny African village. Katie had seen pictures of African chieftains, but they were of the Zulu and Masai tribes, big noble-looking men.

The village was far worse than any of them had imagined!

As soon as they were about fifty yards from the scraggly thatched huts, which composed the village, the stench assaulted their nostrils like a hammer. The smell of woodsmoke and sweating bodies mingled in one nauseating fetid malodor. The putrid smell of ulcerated bodies and human waste formed a miasma that caused the blood to drain from several faces.

At first Katie thought she would pass out. She tried holding her breath, but that lasted only so long. As they entered the village, they formed two lines. Some of the women, she saw, were dressed in even less than the men.

Chief Mawali led them to an open spot, evidently the place where meetings were held, and then began another long speech. As he spoke, with Beecham interpreting, Katie discovered that little by little she was becoming immune to the stench. *I suppose if you live with it long enough, you don't even notice it*, she thought.

Chief Mawali finished his speech, and Beecham said, "It's time for the service."

There was no instrument, no trained musicians, but there was plenty of rhythm and enthusiasm in the congregation. Katie and the others thought they recognized several of the songs, but weren't sure because of the heavy African flavor.

The song service went on for at least an hour. "Time may mean something to you," Beecham had warned them, "but it doesn't to the Pahn people. They don't have watches, and they don't have anything else to do. I've seen them sing for as long as four hours at a stretch."

Perhaps he took pity on the visitors, whose legs were beginning to tremble, for after an hour Beecham said something to the chief, then turned to Barney. "All right, brother, preach!"

Barney stared at him, not believing what he had heard! "But—I don't have a sermon!"

Beecham's blue eyes glinted with humor. "You just tell them about Jesus. I'll supply any necessary homiletics and theology."

Hesitantly Barney stepped forward and pulled his Bible out. He managed to preach for ten minutes, with long pauses after sentences so Beecham could translate. Barney made up his mind right then that he'd learn the language or die!

Finally he stopped, and all the people shouted.

"What did they say?" Barney asked nervously.

"They want more preaching. They say you are a good preacher."

Barney shook his head. "I don't believe that!"

"Well, I took out all the things that would offend and put in what made them happy. But you did fine, my boy!"

After the meeting they partook of the meal, an event the missionaries approached with some trepidation as they sat down with the chief and a few of the men. According to custom, the women were not invited to eat with the men.

As the food was served on wooden slabs, Beecham tried to create a climate of trust. "You'll like this—it's fried banana."

Various provisions were passed around, which Beecham would identify—except one. They all watched as he liberally sprinkled that item with the hot sauce he carried, then passed it to the missionaries.

The others were reluctant to eat the food, but Awful said, "Well, the Lord says in His book, if you eat any deadly thing, it won't harm you—so here goes!" He took a bite, chewed it, and said, "Not too bad. I've eaten worse in some dives in New York City."

The rest of them managed to eat a few bites, which brought Beecham's approval: "Good show!"

When they finished the meal, they said their goodbyes to the people. The Pahns crowded around, some of them reaching out to touch the visitors. A young woman, about sixteen, reached out timidly to touch Katie's blond hair, then drew back.

"How do you say 'sister' in Pahn?" Katie asked Beecham.

He told her, and she smiled at the girl and put her hand out, saying, "Cetay."

The maiden's face lit up in a smile and she took Katie's hand, repeating "Cetay! Cetay!" many times.

When they arrived at their wagon again for the long trip home, Barney said to Katie, "That was fine, the way you called her 'sister.' "

"You did well too, Barney, but I feel so helpless."

"I know what you mean, Katie." He smiled at her, noting the lines of fatigue around her eyes. "But we're in Africa, and that's what counts."

"Yes, that's what counts," she smiled. "But I wonder what it was we ate."

"I don't want to know!" he laughed. "Though I guess we'd better have a big supply of Beecham's hot sauce before we leave for the interior. I've got a gut feeling we're going to see more of their 'delicacies'!"

CHAPTER SIXTEEN

THE COMPANY DECIDES

★ ★ ★ ★

"Do you know the most difficult problem missionaries en-
counter in Africa?"

Stanley Beecham was looking out the window of his hotel
room, idly watching the flow of black humanity below on the
sun-dried walkways. Along with Andy, Barney and Gardner, he
had just returned from the government office, where he had
filled out more papers—an endless task, it seemed.

"I suppose disease," Andy replied. He was sitting on the
Englishman's bed looking at a map of the country.

"Or maybe the wild animals," Barney added.

"Neither." Beecham turned and regarded the three men seriously. "The most crucial problem missionaries face is . . . other
missionaries."

"Oh, come now, Beecham!" Andy protested. "I can't believe
that!"

"I can," Awful Gardner said. "And I think we've already seen
a bit of it."

A fleeting smile touched Beecham's lips. He was somewhat
reserved, a manner from his younger years as a British officer.
But beneath his stolid exterior was a streak of passion he could
not always conceal—like now.

"Blast it all!" he burst out angrily. "I wish you'd never *heard* of Reverend Myron Hansen!"

His impetuous outburst startled the men, Beecham saw, and he toned down. "Well, now—I don't suppose I mean that literally."

"I'd think," Andy said thoughtfully, "since we're all here for the same reason, and since we're more or less a little band of brothers surrounded by those who don't understand us, we ought to be very close to one another."

"Basically, of course, that's true," Beecham nodded. He stood erect, like a soldier, trying to convince the newcomers of the problems they would face—which he had learned the hard way over the years. Now he wished to prepare them as well as possible.

"All missionaries are strong-willed people," he continued, choosing his words carefully. "If they weren't, they'd never get to the mission field. It takes great determination. So what do we have when they meet fellow workers on the field? People who are accustomed to fighting for what they think is right. And when you have that attitude in a group, what will naturally occur?"

"A blow-up," Awful nodded wisely. "Couldn't be no other way!"

"Exactly!" Beecham exclaimed. "We all want the same thing, to see the gospel proclaimed and the kingdom grow. To see souls saved. But we sometimes don't agree on the most effective way to pursue these goals—and there it is."

Andy thought of the talks he'd had with Dorothy and her father and said frankly, "This is what's happened between you and Reverend Hansen, I take it."

"Right! Myron has done a great work in Monrovia. I praise God for it, and pray that it will grow mightily. But we'll never win Africa for Jesus by staying in the cities and large villages."

"But it's necessary to have a base, isn't it?" Andy insisted. "A foundation to consolidate the rest of the work?"

"Ah, you've been listening to Myron—or perhaps his lovely daughter?"

Andy flushed. The missionary had touched a sore spot. "Well, yes, I have." He became defensive, unable to hide the stubbornness in his face. "I'm not saying we shouldn't go into the interior. On the contrary, we must. But we ought to plan carefully. If we rush off into the bush without being prepared, without support, we may not make it."

Beecham clamped his lips tightly, fearing to express his strong feelings. He had gone to tremendous effort to bring these missionaries to Africa and didn't want his project derailed by anyone. He had already made plans to place the new recruits in strategic locations in the interior—and now there was a strong possibility Hansen had convinced them to remain in the cities.

Breaking the long silence, he said slowly, "I can't argue with you about that. I'll only say that Reverend Hansen has been in this city for several years—and not once has he attempted to send the gospel to the tribes living in the interior. Well, that's between him and God. But God has told me to carry the Word to those who've never heard the name of Jesus—and that means getting to them."

"I'm with you there!" Gardner said.

Beecham looked toward Barney and saw that the young man was having a struggle. *Hates to go against his brother*, Beecham surmised. But he was a wise man, and knew when to push ahead and when to pause and give people time to think.

"Look, you must decide this among yourselves," he said. "Pray about it, seek God—but there's little time to waste. I'd like to get started this week, to get you all in place. I'll make the preparations, and you can let me know your decision as soon as you make it."

The three men left the hotel and made their way back to the mission compound. Gardner spoke easily of the matter of getting ready to leave, but Andy said little. It had been obvious to Barney that his brother had come to agree with some of Hansen's methods that he'd been advocating to the group. And the young woman, Dorothy, had spent much time with Andy, the two of them going all over the city, working in the various outreaches of the City Mission.

When they reached the compound, Andy said, "We'd better meet tonight and have this thing out."

"Have what out, lad?" Gardner asked. His sharp eyes rested on Andy, and he added, "My mind's made up."

"Well, mine *isn't!*" Andy snapped. "And some of the others aren't absolutely sure either."

Awful gave him a steady look. "We were sure when we left America, Andy. It's this easy livin' that's got you confused. God didn't call me to Africa to eat off silver plates and have servants wait on me hand and foot."

"That's not fair!" Andy spewed. "You're not looking at this thing right. Go pray about it. I'll tell the others, and we'll discuss it tonight," he said and stalked off.

"You know, dear boy," Awful said to Barney, "sometimes when a man is determined to get his way and is trying to persuade others to follow—he'll say, 'Go pray about it.' But he doesn't really mean that. What he means is, 'I'm bound and determined, and you're a fool if you disagree with me!' "

Barney smiled briefly, but said, "I'm worried, Awful. This could split the Company."

"Aye, that it could. Some are waverin' right now. I'd be surprised if Lily goes to rough it in the bush, and Slim won't go without her."

"Yes. She's already talking about a nice house here in Monrovia."

"And I suppose that young lady Dorothy has helped her find one?"

"I suppose so."

"That young woman's got wiles like a serpent!"

"Awful, don't say that! She loves the Lord well enough."

"Aye, but she's leadin' that brother of yours around as if he had a ring in his nose! Andy's easily impressed, lad. He sees all their big doings—the schools, the hospital, the big church—and he's seen how it is in the small villages. He's a man who likes big things, dear boy, and that girl's at his elbow tellin' him that he's just the man to lead the whole show!"

Barney looked at Gardner with apprehension. The Australian was confirming what Winslow himself had noticed—and feared. Now he said, "I don't know how we can do anything about it, Awful."

Gardner had come to know Barney well and perceived the root of his problem. "Dear boy, I think you're goin' to have to do something that will be very difficult. I know how much you look up to your brother, but you may have to stand against him."

"I—I can't do that!"

"You never have, have you, lad? All your life you've stepped back and accepted whatever Andy said."

"He's so much more able than I am, Awful, that's all."

"No, that's not all, Barney!" Awful objected. "This isn't a matter of bein' smart or able. It's a matter of followin' the will of God, and in my judgment, you're closer to God than Andy."

"That's not so, Awful!"

"It is. But you can't see it. The only way a person can get close to God is to get broken. You've been through a lot, lad, and Andy hasn't—not yet. He's such an able man, with great gifts and talents. And he makes some decisions based on his natural ability, not on what God wants. He doesn't do it on purpose, not at all. He just hasn't learned to wait on God."

Barney shook his head dejectedly. "I think his mind's made up, Awful. And I can't do anything."

"You can if you stand up for what God's put in your heart, lad! Tonight in the meetin', Andy's goin' to do all he can to convince the others that we ought to stay here in the city. Well, you've just got to go against that idea. You've got to make them listen to you."

All afternoon Barney wrestled with Gardner's advice. He was certain that Awful's suggestion was impossible. Never had he won any contest when Andy was involved. How could he win now? Barney's mind was in turmoil and he stayed in his room, praying and reading his Bible. He didn't go to supper, and as the time for the meeting drew near, he felt deeply depressed.

It was nearly seven when Andy came to the room. "Come on, Barney. It's time for the meeting."

Barney followed him across the open compound to the schoolroom where the others were waiting. He took a seat, but Andy remained on his feet, taking charge as usual. "Well, this shouldn't take too long, I think," he said. "You all know the decision we have to make, and I'm sure most of you have prayed through. Let me explain the options again before we vote."

Andy was fair enough in his presentation, Barney thought. The way he put it, it wasn't a question of whether or not they should take the gospel inland, but *when* that should be done. He sketched a beautiful picture of how the interior could be evangelized *after* the base had been built in the city. While that was being done, he said, they could plan crusades to take the gospel to the more backward places.

He was an eloquent speaker, and when he had finished, Barney could see that some of those present were convinced. Slim and Lily Ranken showed approval of everything Andy said, as did Tobe and Pearl. That left Del Saunders and Irene Bailey, both independent thinkers, Katie, and Gardner. He, of course, was not impressed by Andy's proposal and gave Barney a penetrating glance.

"Let's have a little discussion before we vote," Andy suggested. "I think we need to move as a unit. So I'm willing to do whatever the group votes." *He's confident of the outcome, so there's no problem for him to say that,* Barney thought.

"It's the best thing, of course, to stay here. I think we can see the advantages of it," Lily said, bubbling over with praise for the work the City Mission was doing. "It's a mercy that God has led us to this place!" she concluded.

Slim, Barney noticed, seemed impartial. "I suppose there are many here who need the gospel" was all he said when Andy pressed him for an opinion.

Pearl spoke next. "It's fever season in the interior. If we waited, it would be better. You'd get sick the first thing, Tobe."

"I'll be all right, Pearl," he said. "I think we ought to stay with Beecham."

Irene Bailey and Del Saunders said little, a clear indication they were on the fence.

"I'm for the interior." Katie spoke with such determination that Andy didn't even try to dissuade her.

He calculated rapidly in his mind. He knew he and the Rankens would vote for the city. And, of course, Katie and Awful would vote for the interior. He was practically certain Barney would vote with them. *That's three for and three against,* he thought. The others were undecided, but he felt fairly certain Pearl would vote with the city faction, and without a doubt she would get Tobe to vote her way. *I think I can count on them—that's five for the city and three for the interior,* he decided. *If either Irene or Del vote with us, that'll be it!*

"Well, let's take a vote," he said quickly. "How many are for staying in the city?" He raised his own hand, and saw at a glance that the Rankens and the DeLaughters raised theirs too. Del and Irene looked confused. "Well, now," Andy said hurriedly, "it seems as if we've got a stalemate—five to five. Let's discuss it a little further."

He was certain he could change Irene and Del's votes, and had just started going over the advantages of staying in the city when Barney stood up.

"I'd like to speak, Andy," he said.

He's joining us! Andy gloated. Barney had always followed his lead, and now he was coming around! "Of course, Barney," he said. "Speak right up."

Barney faced the group as if he were in a boxing match. Pale and with clenched fists, he spoke slowly, as always. Only Awful knew how torturous it was for the lad to take this stand.

"In New York," he began, "there were lots of churches where people could go hear the gospel. But those who lived in the slums would never go near a church. That's why Awful started the Rescue Mission. It was a place where those who were lost could go—people who didn't have any other way to hear the gospel. Do you remember how they came? How they got saved?"

Katie listened as Barney told of the difficulties, how hard the work was. It all came back to her—the agonies and the joys. Barney may not have been as eloquent as Andy, but the passion of his heart was written on his face, and she found herself weeping.

"The way I see it," he concluded, "things are about the same here. There are churches in town for those who want them. But how are the natives out in the bush going to hear about Jesus? They won't—not unless someone goes to them with the gospel." He paused and said in a determined voice, "I don't want to see the Company broken up. We've come a long way together. I think God raised us up for this time and place. But whatever the rest of you decide to do, I know *I've* got to go to the lost in the villages—even if nobody else will!"

Andy was alarmed. He could see the effect of Barney's words on the group, and knew he had to find some way to diffuse that influence. "We'll pray about this and meet again tomorrow—"

"No, let's vote now!" Katie stood to her feet, her tear-stained face filled with determination. Andy was the self-appointed leader, but she impulsively drove in her stake. "All who vote for going to the interior, stand up!"

Gardner popped up like a cork. Del and Irene followed. Tobe glanced at Pearl, then rose. She smiled and joined him.

Ranken's eyes swept around the room as he made up his mind. "Honey, I'm sorry, but we're going in with the Company." Though Lily began to cry, she was forced to stand with him.

"That's nine out of ten," Katie said. "What about you, Andy?"

Sick with disappointment, he forced a grin. "Well, I see I'm outvoted—but I'll go along with the group." His words were lost in the joyous cry that filled the air. *We'll see*, he thought. *Some of them will be glad to come back after a month without a shower!*

The Hansens were crushed at the news, but Dorothy voiced their thoughts: "It's just a matter of time, Andy. New missionaries are the same. They have this romantic idea about Africa, going to the heathen in a sun helmet. Grass huts and cannibals being saved. But after a few months, the 'glamour' wears off. Most of them come back to us or return to America."

"You'll just have to be patient, Andy," her father agreed. "Just wait a bit, and we'll have you and your friends here in Monrovia where things are *really* happening!"

★　★　★　★

The sun shone like a benediction on the group waiting to board the surfboats. Stanley Beecham had been delighted at the news that all ten missionaries had decided to go to the interior. "We'll leave tomorrow," he said. "Garroway will be our first stop. From there we'll pair off to different stations. Since Garroway is about thirty miles up the coast, it'll be quicker to go by surfboat than overland."

One of the natives loading the baggage was Bestman, who had helped Katie when she'd left the ship. Surprised to see him, she said, "Why, Bestman, how good to see you again."

"Yes, Mammy. You be careful. Not fall down again." His white teeth flashed as he smiled.

When it was time to board the surfboats, the boatmen hoisted sails on both vessels and the group stepped in. The boats moved along the coast, sometimes driven at such a rapid pace it seemed they would be dashed to pieces on the rocks. Other times the waters would be so calm the oarsmen could frequently take a nap while they waited for the wind to become more favorable. This irritated Andy, who wanted to push on.

Beecham noticed Andy's impatience and smiled. "Might as well throw that watch away, my boy. These people keep a different time."

Andy's response was only a grimace.

The rocky ride made a few of them seasick, including Katie. "Don't *you* feel a little sick?" she asked Barney, seeing his concern.

"Nope. I heard once that only idiots are immune to seasickness. Guess I'm safe."

The long trip was trying—the scorching sun and wind left them sunburned, weather-beaten, and exhausted. It was a relief when the prow of the boat finally hit the beach at one-thirty the next morning.

Katie peered through the black darkness, seeing only shadows. The boatmen shouted and the shadows on shore moved. Soon there was a scramble as debarking began. Perplexed as to what to do, Katie waited.

"Mammy, you ready to go now?" a voice beside her said.

"Yes, I'm ready," she replied, recognizing Bestman.

He took her hand and guided her to the prow of the boat. "Now, you stand still, Mammy," he said, and she heard him step into the water. "Mammy, you come."

"How can I get to the shore?"

"Mammy, I go carry you."

He picked her up like a child and sloshed through the surf to the shore and set her down on a rock.

"You all right now, Mammy?"

"Yes, Bestman. I'm fine."

He carried the other women across the rough waters as well, and soon the entire group was together. The cool wind whipped around them, moaning eerily. It made the goose bumps rise on Katie's arms. Though she was eager for the challenge ahead, this depressing introduction to the wild, unknown world was unnerving.

"Come along." Beecham's voice was a welcome intrusion to Katie's thought. "The station's not far from here."

Beecham set out at a brisk pace through the darkness. The others followed, blindly trusting their leader. Shortly they saw the welcome gleam of a lighted window. "That's it," Beecham said cheerfully.

At the house they were met by a small native couple speaking a strange language, their white teeth prominent against the ebony skin.

"Gwani. These people are starved. They would like some food as soon as possible."

The servants' winning smiles won Katie's heart. As they scurried around preparing the meal, Beecham helped the missionaries get settled. The women were assigned to the only bedroom in the house.

As they stepped into the room, Lily screeched, "It's a SNAKE!"

"Oh, come on, Lily," Katie said. "It was only a lizard. You ought to be glad it *wasn't* a snake!"

"It went right across my foot! Oh, I should have stayed in the city! I'm not sure I'll make it!"

"You will, Lily—just give yourself a chance. Remember why we came."

Katie kept encouraging the others as they grabbed their bags and changed into dry clothing. When the call for supper came, they were all ready.

The table had room only for the women, so the others sat on their haunches. After the blessing, everyone dived into the rice and beans, hungrily scraping the morsels off tin plates.

While they ate, Beecham gave them a rundown on his plans. "I think we'll rest up for two days here and sort of get used to the surroundings before we go to our various stations."

"Where are they?" Del asked with his mouth full.

Beecham put his plate down and walked over to a map of Liberia tacked on the wall. "This is Rhodilly," he said, pointing to the area. "The work has been growing steadily. That's where the DeLaughters will be stationed. And this is Newaka, a good location with a nice house. The Rankens will serve there."

"See, Lily," Slim said, nodding at her. "We've got the pick of all the stations." He didn't know that it was on Lily's account they had been assigned there. Beecham had confided to Barney and Gardner that Lily would never survive anywhere else.

"This is Gropaka—your station, Barney and Gardner," Beecham went on. "This will be a pioneer work for you since the place has been empty the last few years. A young couple by the name of Tinner died not too long after they arrived." He paused and said, "You'll find their graves there."

"They *died*? From what?" Pearl asked incredulously.

"I'll tell you about that later." From Beecham's sad expression, it was evidently a tragic event. He continued pointing to the other locations. "This is your station, Del and Andy, at Chodi. It's got a good start, but needs lots of care."

"What about Katie and me?" Irene piped up.

"Right here. Maoli is the name of the village. It has a house of sorts, native style. But you two are tough," he smiled.

"Now let's get some rest. It's been a rough day, I know, and there'll be time to make plans tomorrow. I'll go with the Rankens to Newaka, and the rest of you will have guides."

Most of them slept poorly, thinking of the difficulties lying ahead. Once Barney thought he heard something moving outside the house, but he wasn't sure. Finally he dropped off to sleep in spite of Awful's loud snoring. At some point during the night he dreamed he was surrounded by a fierce tribe of natives who were screaming for his death. Startled awake he shoved his blanket off, then realized he'd had a nightmare.

"Go to sleep, Winslow," he chided himself. "You're getting to be an old woman—and not even far from the coast yet!"

CHAPTER SEVENTEEN

BESTMAN

★ ★ ★ ★

"I go with you, Mammy."

Katie stared at the tall young African who greeted her when she came out of the house at dawn on Friday morning. She had spoken to him several times during the past two days, finding him to be highly intelligent and a devoted Christian.

"Why, Bestman, the surfboats left last night," she said. "I thought you went back to Monrovia."

"No. I go with you to Pahn people."

He was determined, but Katie was not certain she had the authority to allow him to accompany her. "I'll have to talk to Reverend Beecham, Bestman. Why do you want to go? You know we can't pay you?"

Bestman nodded vigorously. "Jesus wake Bestman up last night. Say, 'You go with Mammy to village.'" His white teeth gleamed and he added, "We do plenty preaching. Beside, if Bestman go, Pahn people no eat Mammy."

Shocked, Katie couldn't believe what she had heard. She asked carefully, "Bestman, I am a stranger in your country. Will you help me learn the ways of your people?"

"Oh yes, Mammy!"

"Before I came to your land, I heard how Pahn ate somebody. Is it true that Pahn eat people?"

He didn't answer, just studied her face. She understood his silence, for cannibalism, once widespread, had been outlawed. She went on. "We came to help Pahn people. I only want to know how your people are. Maybe I don't hear the truth. Is it true? Pahn eat people?"

When he saw that she meant well, he grunted, "Yes, we eat somebody."

"You, Bestman, you ate somebody?"

"I eat plenty people."

"Who did you eat?" Katie asked.

"When we got war, we catch somebody from other side. We chop him."

"What means *chop*?"

He nodded solemnly. "Chop—eat. All same."

Katie smiled at him. "Someday, maybe, I will make you mad. Will you eat me?"

"Oh no, Mammy!" Bestman exclaimed, shaking his head vigorously. "You be white man!"

It was no time to take up the moral question of cannibalism, Katie knew. She went directly to Reverend Beecham, where he was helping the Rankens load their supplies. "Bestman wants to go with Irene and me. Will that be all right?"

"My word, yes!" Beecham exclaimed. "That is a bit of good fortune for you, Katie! He's a Pahn himself, of course, and with him to vouch for you, you won't have to put in a worrisome time gaining the confidence of the people. And it solves your interpreting problem. Not to mention the fact that you'll have a trusty servant right from the beginning. Usually you have to run through half a dozen lazy ones to get someone who'll do."

"Oh, I'm glad!" Katie said. "I'm going to tell him." She ran back and told Bestman that he could go, and then went to find Irene. "God is with us," she said brightly. "Bestman is going to help us."

Irene smiled. "That's good. We'll need a man around the place, won't we?"

All day they worked on preparations, though Beecham had done much of it beforehand. Supper was a fun time—rice and beans, of course, which seemed to be the staple of the country—and everyone seemed in high spirits. There was a great deal of bantering and laughter, but Andy did not enter into it as usual, Katie noticed.

"I think Andy's unhappy," she murmured to Barney.

"I suppose so. He thinks we're making a big mistake, you know. After you all went to bed last night, he talked to us men, trying to change our minds."

"But you didn't, did you?"

"Oh no," he smiled. "Andy will come around." Then he switched to another subject. "Say, I heard about your good luck—getting Bestman to go with you. That's wonderful!"

"He volunteered. He says Jesus came to him in a dream and told him to go with us."

"I wish I could get directions that easily!"

"So do I," she said. "I have to wait and wait—and even then sometimes I just have to give up and do what seems best."

Later as the group sat around, talking about the venture, Katie mentioned Bestman's dream to them.

"Probably just wanted to go back to his people," Pearl said.

"Not necessarily," Beecham countered. "It might be well for you to listen carefully when one of your flock gives you some word. All these people are spiritual, you know."

"Spiritual?"

"You mean they're saved?" Tobe asked.

"No, certainly not," Beecham answered. "These people don't think of the spirit world as we do. Most of us are very unaware of the spiritual world when we're lost—or even after we are saved. Ask the average American if he believes in evil spirits, and he'll think you're daft. But you ask an American Indian, and he'll know what you're talking about. The Indians are like the Africans, like any primitive people. They *know* there's a world that can't be seen."

"Isn't most of that superstition?"

"Some, of course. But from now on you're going to see things you've never encountered in America. There are witch doctors not a mile from this spot who can do things no ordinary man can. I've seen them put a curse on a man who was as healthy as any of us—yet forty-eight hours later the man died for no apparent reason."

"But that's just because they're so afraid, isn't it?" Andy demanded. "You tell a man he's sick often enough, and he'll more than likely *get* sick. It's the power of suggestion."

Beecham smiled grimly. "You'll get rid of that idea fast enough, Andy! There's plenty of superstition, God knows! But to the African, he's living with a world inhabited by spirits— good and bad. Powerful spirits! Nobody just *dies.* They believe some spirit was responsible. You'll be exposed to the 'avenger of blood,' I promise you."

"What's that?" Gardner inquired.

"When someone dies, the witch doctor goes through his incantations. He'll assign the responsibility for the death to someone in the village. Then the person is ferreted out and given the 'sass-wood test.' That consists of forcing the accused to drink the poison brew. If he vomits it up, he's innocent. If he dies, he is guilty of bewitching the one who died."

"How awful!" Irene gasped. "Can't we stop it?"

"Be careful how you go about interfering in the lives of these people," Beecham said clearly. "In the first place, there *are* evils spirits, and the only way to fight them is in the name of Jesus. Demon-possessed people are very common, and more than one missionary has been harmed by trying to deal with them. There's no other way than the biblical way, which is to command the spirits to come out in the name of Jesus."

"What if they don't?" Barney asked quickly.

"Then command them again! There are those who come out only by prayer and fasting. But be cautious about the customs. You won't like some of them, but don't rush in like a bull in a china shop, trying to right all the wrongs you see. It's common for these people to sell their children, especially their daughters. We all hate it, but it's been going on for hundreds of years. Someday it will change, but for the present we have to be careful to preach the gospel, heal the sick, cast out demons, and most of all—love the people. If you do *that*," Beecham said emphatically, "then no matter how many mistakes you make in other ways, you'll please God and win the people to Him."

For a long time Beecham talked about the work. Finally he said, "Well, you'll have to learn as you go. Now, I want you all to kneel. I'm going to lay hands on each of you. You'll need the power of God on your life, and I'm going to pray that you have it!"

It was a scene none of them ever forgot. Beecham prayed for Andy first, putting his hands on Winslow's head. It was a powerful prayer, claiming the power of God and asking God's protection over him. Then he began to bind evil spirits that would destroy the work. "I bind you in the name of Jesus Christ of Nazareth! Satan, you are defeated! You were crushed at the cross; and by the blood of Jesus, I command you to leave this young man alone!"

He prayed long and powerfully over each of them. Several times he would pause, wait for a time, then would have a word of encouragement or warning for the individual. When he came to Katie, he prayed a long time for her safety, then said, "You will be surrounded, my daughter, by the powers of darkness. The enemy will come against you with awesome power. You will face death itself. But greater is He that is in you than he who is in the world. When your spirit is being torn apart, remember my promise, you will cast out demons, and if you drink any deadly thing, it will not harm you. And you will see the power of Almighty God!"

It was late by the time he had finished praying for the entire group. Grateful for what the Lord had done, Beecham said, "Praise God for all He has revealed to us. When you face adversity, remember God's special word to you. He will not fail, for all the elements of your times are in His hands. Stand fast in the trying hour. His name and His blood are more powerful than the strongest force against you. Now, sleep well. We may never meet again in this world, for we are pledging our heads to heaven, as the old Puritan once said. But if you hear that Stanley Beecham is dead, remember, I will be in the presence of the King!"

★ ★ ★ ★

At dawn the next day the group separated, each pair heading in different directions. They were sober and a little frightened.

Gardner sensed their apprehension and called out, "Cheerio! Let's give the devil a hard time!"

Maoli, the station where Irene and Katie were to serve, was on the same route as Gropaka, where Barney and Gardner were going. It was thirty-five miles away, a two-day walk through the jungle. That meant the men would be with them all the way on the overland trail. Their little party set out, and for the first ten miles the trail was broad and easy. But that afternoon, they hit the heavier jungle, and traveling became difficult.

The trail narrowed the deeper they got into the forest, making it necessary to form a single line. Even then the vines and creepers were so enmeshed a native had to cut the way clear with a long knife. Not only was the path narrow, it was very crooked, as the Africans always detoured around fallen trees and branches instead of cutting them out of the way. The party wound around in such a serpentine fashion that at times it was difficult for Katie to tell if the songs of the marchers came from in front or behind.

By three o'clock Katie and Irene were staggering with exhaustion. Bestman saw it and cried out, "What we go do for Mammy?" He halted the caravan and soon had fashioned two makeshift hammocks, using canvas and clothesline rope from the missionaries' supply. Bamboo poles were added at each end. "We go carry Mammy now," he announced.

Katie awkwardly got into the hammock, and two natives picked up the ends and balanced them on their heads, using a rolled circle of grass for padding. "We go now!" Bestman shouted. Both hammocks were picked up, and Katie found herself suspended in the air. It was a strange sensation, swaying gently as the caravan moved through the dense jungle. She could see nothing, though she was too tired to care and soon dozed off.

She awakened when she heard Bestman call out something in his own language, and then the hammock was gently lowered. Getting out, she smiled at the two bearers, saying, "Madalla, Madalla!" which meant "Thank you."

Camp was struck beside a small stream, and the natives soon had a fire going. Overtaken by weariness, Barney and Gardner just sat with their backs to a tree.

"I thought I wuz in pretty good shape," Barney murmured ruefully. "I'm just a baby!"

"Those skinny fellas carried the women half the bloomin' day!" Awful shook his head. "They may have to carry *me* tomorrow!"

Bestman had disappeared, but the sound of a rifle indicated

why. Soon he returned with meat for supper. "Very fine!" he grinned, holding up the game.

Katie squinted, then covered her mouth. Monkey!

The other missionaries saw it at the same time. Irene gasped. Leaning toward Katie, she whispered, "We can't eat *that*, Katie!"

But Katie said boldly, "I hope we brought plenty of Reverend Beecham's hot sauce!"

Actually the meat was not too bad. Their cook made up a stew of rice and fish, and threw the monkey in for good measure. Katie took the bowl that Bestman handed her and glanced at Barney. A humorous thought struck her. "This is all your fault, Barney Winslow! You're the one responsible for making me come to Africa to eat monkey meat!"

The other three laughed, the natives joining them, though they didn't have the slightest idea what was so funny.

Barney took a bite, chewed it, and smacked his lips. "You know, this isn't too bad!"

Gardner agreed. "I knew a fella once from Arizona. Ate snakes, he did! And there wuz a Frenchmen who come to the mission, claimed he ate snails back in France." He shuddered. "Snakes and snails! I'd rather have good old monkey stew!"

By the time the meal was over, the sunlight had faded, and the darkness closed in. The natives huddled together for a time, the flickering firelight casting shadows on their ebony faces. One of them began to sing a slow, rhythmic chant, which the others echoed at intervals.

Katie and Irene sat close to the fire listening to the serenade, but after a while the bugs became too much, and the ladies climbed under their mosquito netting and lay down on a blanket, using the other for cover. The ground was hard, but they lost no time falling asleep.

The next day was even more tiring, but by sundown they reached a small collection of huts, and Bestman announced, "We here, Mammy."

Suddenly, a group of warriors armed with cutlasses, spears, bows and arrows, and cudgels appeared and surrounded them.

When they recognized Bestman, they lowered their weapons and smiled. A long conversation followed. Bestman, Katie discovered later, told them, "We come peacefully. We mean no harm!"

"Good thing he's here," Gardner said. "They look like a lynch mob, don't they?"

When the conference was over, the visitors were led into the village, and one of the warriors armed with an ancient rifle directed them to a thatched hut.

"Chief Teo say this your house," Bestman said.

It was only a single room, apparently abandoned for some time. But Katie smiled at Chief Teo, saying, "Thank you, Chief Teo. May the Lord of heaven bless you and your house."

Bestman translated, and the chief, a regal-looking man with teeth filed to fine points, grinned and made another speech. Bestman interpreted. "Chief Teo wants to know which of these two white men your husband."

Katie flushed, saying quickly, "Neither of them! Tell him that Irene and I aren't married."

The chief listened to Bestman, then shook his head. "That is bad thing," Bestman translated. "Chief say no good to waste two women!"

Gardner was amused by the exchange, but Katie was mortified. Barney saw her discomfort and came to the rescue. "We can't go on to Gropaka tonight. See if you can find a place for the two of us, Bestman."

Later that night, they once again ate rice. When a meat stew was passed around, all four missionaries added some fiery hot sauce to it. The chief asked for a sample, but spat it out on the ground.

"I think this stew has palm butter in it," Gardner commented. "Most of the natives use it as a gravy or sauce."

"Is this monkey meat?" Irene asked. "It doesn't taste exactly like it."

She asked Bestman, and he shook his head. "Oh no! This is rat stew, Mammy—very good!" A common dish for the Africans, they learned later.

They soon told Bestman they had eaten too much of Chief Teo's good food and couldn't eat any more. Bestman translated well without insulting the chief, but Katie felt her stomach churning for some time.

After the meal, the four went with Bestman to make what improvements they could on the house the women would be living in. Working by the light of one of the lanterns they had brought, and with some help from Bestman, they managed to rig two cots out of poles. They had brought plenty of rope, which they used to support the mattresses of stuffed grass.

Gardner looked at Barney and Katie's efforts. "You two go get some more grass. Neither of you can tie a decent knot."

"I'm not going out in the dark!" Irene cried, alarmed.

"Barney and I will get the grass," Katie said. "You can stay here and help Awful."

Barney lit the extra lantern, picked up the mattress covers, and the two went outside. The earth around the hut was trampled flat, but as they explored a little farther, they found a plentiful supply of long grass at the edge of the woods. They began pulling it and stuffing it into the ticking, and soon had two fat mattresses.

"They look like sausages," Katie laughed.

"Better than sleeping on the ground," Barney grinned. He looked up at the sky and added, "That's the same moon we have back home, but it looks larger here."

Katie nodded. "It does look big. And look at the stars!" The sky was spangled with countless points of light, some of them glittering like silver fire. "When I see the stars, I always think of what God said to Abraham," she mused. "That he'd have more descendants than all the stars he could see."

"God gave him a big promise. We are part of that promise, part of his covenant, Awful told me, and can expect the Lord to do big things for us here."

"He will," Katie said, thinking of Beecham's prayers for all of them.

Barney gazed at the panoply of the heavens, remembering how his father had wondered what the sky would look like in Africa.

"The stars look so close. I wish I knew enough constellations to write my father about them," he said. "Somehow it looks bigger here than at home."

As they stood in the small clearing, caressed by the warm wind, they breathed in the fragrance of the forest. Many of the odors were alien to Katie and Barney—the smell of ancient dark earth, the endless variety of trees, the rotting leaves, the compost that was made and remade endlessly as the trees grew to dizzying heights that cut out the light of the sun, then fell to become part of the black earth. In time those trunks would be reduced to dust through the work of worms and a thousand species of insects.

The sounds were as strange as the odors of the jungle. In addition to the faint drone of human voices, Barney could hear the animal life roaming the trackless woods. A sharp chattering sound came at regular intervals. A faint scream from far away scored the night, and then a hoarse grunting not too far from where he and Katie stood.

Barney sighed. "We're a long way from home, Katie."

"No, we're *really* at home now, Barney!"

He smiled at her. *She is lovely*, he thought. The moonlight made a silver corona around her head, framing her face. Her eyes sparkled from the soft light of the full moon.

"I'm glad you said that. I've been standing here feeling like some sort of out-of-place fellow. But you're right, Katie. This *is* our home now."

Her comment had drawn them closer somehow, and each of them felt better knowing they were not alone.

Suddenly a fierce scream rent the air, and Katie cried in fear as she grabbed Barney.

Barney instinctively wrapped his arms around her, hunching his shoulders to protect her from the sharp claws he fully expected to slice into his back. They stood there, nerves shrieking with shock. Then the scream faded into silence.

Barney felt Katie's body shaking as he held her. They were both too numb to speak. Finally Katie raised her eyes to his. Her lips trembled as she said, "I—I guess it's gone!"

Barney nodded and was about to release her when he was struck by the beauty of the woman he held in his arms. Her face was only inches away. Impulsively he lowered his lips to hers.

Katie had grabbed him out of sheer reflex, but as she felt his lips on hers, a sense of need rushed in. She had stood alone for so long, had been lonely for so long, that now she simply accepted his kiss and gently returned the pressure of her own. She had not realized her deep desire for someone to share with, for her call to Africa had obliterated everything else—including her need as a woman.

Then his arms tightened around her, and she gasped and pulled away. He released her and she stepped back, confused and afraid. Not afraid of him, but of herself, of the sudden streak of passion that had gripped her.

Barney sensed the emotional turmoil and was himself surprised at what had happened. "I'm sorry, Katie," he whispered. "I guess I just wanted to let you know—" He broke off and tried again, "I guess we were both frightened out of our wits. When I get scared like that, I just—I grab the first thing I see."

"Me, too, Barney," Katie murmured. Then with a burst of nervous energy, she picked up the mattress, saying brightly, "We'd better get back before that thing really comes to get us!"

Neither of them referred to the event, but the next day when Gardner and Barney said goodbye to the women, he could tell that Katie was not as open as she had been. *I've disappointed her*, he thought. *Why did I ever do a thing like that?*

"We'll come back in a month." Gardner's voice exuded excitement and cheer. "You ladies try not to get eaten by a lion or something."

Katie avoided Barney's eyes, her cheeks flushed.

Irene didn't miss a beat and after the men had left, asked, "Why'd you blush like that?"

"Oh, I'm just sorry to see them go, I guess," Katie said defensively. Then she forced herself to smile. "Well, we're here, Irene. Let's start being missionaries!"

CHAPTER EIGHTEEN

WITCH DOCTOR!

★ ★ ★ ★

"What day is it, Katie?"

Katie looked up from the notebook. "It's Thursday."

Irene stirred the beans in the cooking pot, put the lid on, then walked to the bench outside their house and sat down. "I mean what day of the month." She pulled her sun helmet off and wiped her brow with a limp handkerchief. "Every day's just like every other day here. I lose count."

"It's the twenty-fifth of August," Katie said after consulting a small calendar she had glued in the back of her notebook.

"We came on April fourth, so we've been on the station five months." She leaned her head back against the side of the house and closed her eyes. Fatigue had etched small lines on her forehead, and she had lost weight. Finally she said without opening her eyes, "It seems like a lot longer than that."

Katie nodded. "Yes, it does, Irene. Time's not the same here as it is back home."

She set the notebook aside, got up from the chair she'd brought outside, and walked to the gourd where they kept water. It was tepid and flat, and no matter how much she drank, she always seemed to be thirsty. She swallowed some more, then sought the shady side of the house.

The afternoon sun was a huge pale globe in the sky, throwing heat that would have turned her skin lobster red if she hadn't protected it. Shortly after arriving at the station, she had suffered a mild case of sunstroke because she'd forgotten her helmet.

Irene, too, had learned to be careful. She had visited a sick woman in a neighboring village, and discovered the next day that the African sun was not very kind to the white women as she removed layers of skin from her arms. The sun and the heat meant little to the Africans but was a constant enemy to the white missionaries.

"Time really *isn't* the same here, is it, Irene?" Katie said again. "I mean, the days go by, but there's nothing to really *mark* them, like at home. Here we just get up and cook early to avoid the heat, study the language, and visit the sick. But it's like being on a boat that goes down a river with trees on either side. Every day you go by more of the country, but the scenery doesn't change."

Irene opened her eyes. "I guess that's right. We never see anybody except the villagers. And they do pretty much the same thing all the time." She laughed. "You know, I thought our biggest problem would be wild animals or getting eaten by cannibals—but the deadliest is pure old *boredom*!"

They had seen no one except the natives of the village for three weeks. Gardner had come through in May, headed for the coast for supplies, but had pushed on after checking on their needs. On his return trip, he only stayed overnight.

Katie recalled their conversation. "Barney and me have been havin' a time of it," he said. "I took malaria, and after I got over it, Barney went down. Don't you ladies go off the station till you have your first round of malaria." When Irene had suggested they might not get it, he had said, "No hope of that, my dear. Everybody gets malaria. Just stay close to the station till you get well."

"How's Barney?" Katie had asked.

"He's a tough 'un, Barney is!" Gardner laughed. "Got all the natives talkin' about him. They ain't never seen many white men, see, and they ain't never seen one that could out-walk 'em. But Barney can! Oh, my word, he can! So they come up with a name for him—*Kwi Balee*. Means 'White Antelope.' Oh, he's got 'em thinkin' he's the big rooster, right enough. Made a few good shots with his rifle, bringin' down game, and they all say he can't miss, and he hits five monkeys with every shot!"

But aside from those two short visits, the women had only each other to talk to. The Pahn language was difficult for Irene to grasp and she would have given up but for Katie's prodding. From dawn till dusk they worked hard, going through their daily routine—housekeeping, cooking, washing, studying, teaching the children, ministering to the sick, and holding services. The deadly boredom of the "dailys" ate into their resistance and drained their strength.

Nothing had prepared them for this drastic change. The glamour of sacrificing all to bring the gospel to an unreached people on another continent had soon vanished.

Irene got up and checked the beans. "These are about done. Do we still have some of that meat Chief Tenki sent?"

"No, but let's finish what we got from Mutali. I still don't know what it is."

"It tastes like old rope," Irene grimaced. Then she brightened. "Let's go see Chief Tenki. I'll bet he'd give us something better than this."

Chief Tenki's tribe was located about fifteen miles from Maoli. Katie and Bestman had visited the chief, and to her delight had discovered that he was a Christian—a convert of one of the early missionaries who had died and was buried in his village. Tenki was a short muscular man of fifty, and could speak English fairly well. He had been delighted to see Katie, and had begged her to move to his village. When she had been unable to promise that, he had insisted she send another missionary as soon as possible.

"We have very bad witch doctor!" Tenki had said. "His name Maioni. Very bad man! Bring curse on many people here!"

His plea had disturbed Katie. *Could the open door to Chief Tenki's village be a call from God?* She shared it with Irene, who said, "As long as we stay together, it's all right with me." But Katie had been unable to arrive at a firm decision, so nothing had been done.

* * * *

Two days later, Katie was teaching hymns to the children—

her favorite activity—when Chief Mawali and Bestman came hurrying toward them, accompanied by a stranger. Both the chief and Bestman appeared very disturbed.

"What's wrong?" Katie jumped up.

"Bad thing!" Bestman said. "This man from Chief Tenki's village. Very bad thing!"

"Tell me, Bestman!"

"This man, he say Chief Tenki in bad trouble! He say chief die soon."

"Is he sick?" Katie asked with alarm.

"No! Witch doctor, he go kill chief! This man, he say Chief Tenki say Mammy come quick."

"I'll go at once!"

When Bestman interpreted, Chief Mawali shook his head, gesturing violently and speaking with great force.

"Chief Mawali say you no go, Mammy."

"Why not?"

"Witch doctor strong man—very strong! Chief, his brother, he die. Maioni, witch doctor, say Chief Tenki put evil eye on him. People lock up chief. Him die soon."

Katie set her jaw. "I'm going to Chief Tenki." She whirled and ran to her house, calling as she entered, "Irene, I've got to leave!"

She explained the situation while she packed, but Irene insisted on going along. "I don't like to be alone, Katie," she said.

"It won't be for long," Katie said. "One of us has to stay here." She didn't add that the trip was potentially dangerous, but said only, "I'll be back as soon as I can. You get all the Christians praying for me." With that she kissed Irene and ran out of the house. She found Bestman alone.

"Where's Chief Mawali?"

"Chief, he scared," Bestman nodded. "Nobody else go, Mammy."

"Will you take me to Chief Tenki, Bestman?"

The tall African nodded, surprised. "Bestman always go with Mammy."

"Bless you, Bestman," Katie smiled. "We go now!"

★ ★ ★ ★

As they walked into the cluster of thatched huts, an overwhelming oppression hit Katie. It was not doubt, or even fear. This was different.

The deeper she went into the village, the more suffocating the assault on her spirit became. She had never encountered such heaviness. Though the sun was overhead, there was a sense of darkness she knew was not physical. A strange silence hung over the village—no children laughing, no murmur of voices. Even the dogs were silent as she and Bestman walked slowly toward a large hut.

Katie could almost hear the palpitation of her heart. Her knees trembled, and she wanted to flee the miasma of fear and darkness that seemed to hover over the silent village.

When they neared the hut, Bestman whispered, barely able to speak, "Witch doctor, he come, Mammy."

What a heroic and courageous thing for Bestman to come, Katie thought. *He knows all about the fear, yet he came!*

Suddenly a grotesque figure burst from one of the huts. His long mop of hair, smeared with palm oil and cow dung, hung over a face deeply etched with tattoo scars. Almost naked except for the string of leopard's teeth around his neck, pouches of juju and fetish medicine hanging from his waist, and several white tails of bishop monkeys trailing behind him, the man was the strangest creature Katie had ever seen!

Her pulse throbbed in her ears, but by sheer iron will, Katie did not blink or show a sign of fear as the man came toward her, shrieking, his face contorted with rage. A line of men, armed with bows and arrows and ancient muskets, formed a circle around Katie, Bestman, and the witch doctor.

The witch doctor screamed and several times advanced to within a few feet of Katie, shaking bones in her face. She knew instinctively that he was trying to break her nerve, but she stood perfectly still, watching him without a word or sign of fear.

But there *was* fear—for evil, as palpable as black smoke, hung in the air! A sickening, filthy fear that gnawed at Katie's mind, seeking entrance—like a wild animal intent on killing the person inside a house. She could *smell* the evil! An odor of death and corruption filled her nostrils and throat.

Lord, I can't stand this! she cried out in her spirit. *You are master of this devilish thing. Give me your strength, Lord Jesus!*

As she prayed, the darkness that tried to smother her spirit lifted, and she spoke with authority. "I come in the name of Jesus Christ, the son of the Almighty God!"

At the name of Jesus, Maioni put his hands over his ears and ran around, howling like a dog.

Katie cried out again, "In the name of Jesus, Satan, I bind you and every demon in this place!"

As though driven by an unseen force, Maioni ran screaming out of the circle, knocking over some of the armed men in his mad dash to get away. The villagers stood stock-still, then turned to watch Katie with intense curiosity.

"Take me to your chief!" she commanded, and one of the men motioned her to follow him.

"Come with me, Bestman!" she urged.

When they drew near, the guide stopped and pointed to the house, saying something to Bestman.

"Come, Mammy!" Bestman said.

Inside, a fire had been kindled in the center of the mud floor, and the acrid smoke, pungent with a strange odor, made Katie's eyes water. Then she saw the piles of dried red peppers in the middle of the fire.

"Where is Chief Tenki?" she asked, her eyes smarting from the smoke.

"I get him, Mammy!" Bestman leaped to a ladder that led to an opening in the roof and disappeared. Soon he was back with the chief across his shoulders.

Katie gasped. "Bring him outside!"

Bestman obeyed and laid the chief down.

"Water!" Katie cried, and when no one moved, she stood to her feet and pointed to the native who had led them to the chief. "You! Get water now!"

The man stared at her, not moving, but when Bestman translated her words, the native's face filled with fear and he barked a command. Immediately a woman appeared with a jug of water.

Katie began bathing Chief Tenki's face with her wet handkerchief. "How long has he been up there?" she asked. Bestman inquired, and when he spoke, she echoed his words in astonishment.

"Three days!" She had grown nauseated and faint during the few minutes she had been in the lower part of the hut. What must Tenki have suffered in the torrid heat of that smoke-filled attic!

Katie had Bestman quench the fire in the chief's house, and as it grew darker, they moved him back inside. None of the villagers would help, of course; they were too frightened of Maioni. Only one person would enter the house, and that was Tenki's wife, Rineea, a short, plump woman. She was as terrified of the witch doctor as the rest, but chose to die with her husband if necessary.

Katie Sullivan was not a woman prone to anger, but for the next few hours as she and Bestman sat over the emaciated form of the chief, giving him small sips of water and bathing his shrunken form, a rage such as she had never known began to well up in her. It grew so intense she became frightened, and prayed, *Oh, dear Lord! Help me not to hate Maioni! You died for him; therefore he is precious in your sight! Help me to have compassion and love! Take away my anger and the hatred that I feel for him!*

As she prayed, she grew calm, but the anger was still there—this time at the forces of evil and superstition that bound the simple people, bringing death with it.

Bestman came close to her as she prayed, and when she looked at him, he said quietly, "Witch doctor come soon, Mammy."

"I know, Bestman," she answered. "But our God is stronger than the witch doctor."

Bestman studied her face carefully, his face breaking out in a smile as her words seemed to bring encouragement. He said no more, but all through that long night, Katie could hear him calling on God. She knew that Maioni would not give up. He had run away, but he would come back, fully intent on destroying them all, for only by doing that could he keep the people in fear and bondage.

And he did come, though it was not in the morning, but in that darkest part of the night—the hours just before dawn. Katie heard the sound of voices and looked over at Chief Tenki, who was now awake. "Chief, do you believe that Jesus is strong?"

"Yes," he said hoarsely. "He bring white woman to save me."

"Then we must go out and face the evil one. Help him, Bestman." Bestman stepped forward and assisted the chief to his feet. Katie stepped through the door and the two followed her. The night was dark, but burning torches threw flickering shards of light over the scene—more terrible than Katie could imagine!

By the light of the torches, she could see the armed warriors, their teeth filed to sharp points and the madness blazing in their eyes. They were inflamed with drink. *Maioni has seen to that!* she thought. They screamed, "Kill the white woman! Kill the white woman!" It was a deafening roar. Katie remained calm, drawing strength from the Holy Spirit as she stood with the two men. She watched the mob work itself into a frenzy, their bodies quivering from head to foot with almost uncontrollable rage.

Maioni was like a demented man, running up to shake his fist at Katie, then back to the maddened warriors. He was the personification of evil, and Katie knew he would not be satisfied with less than the death of all four of those who stood against him.

Finally Maioni held up his hand, and when he could be heard, cried out something.

Bestman said, "He say Tenki must drink poison cup."

Stanley Beecham's words flashed into her mind: "If they do not die, they are innocent. If they do die, they are guilty—but somehow they *all* die!"

Katie watched Maioni take a large wooden cup from a wrinkled old woman who leered demonically at the four who opposed them. The air was thick with the smell of evil. Katie's flesh crawled as she looked at the grotesque face of the witch doctor with the cup of poison in his hands. In the natural there was nothing that could stop what was happening.

Then she heard a voice, not with her ears but with her heart. It was Stanley Beecham, praying those special words over her before she left: *When your spirit is being torn apart, remember my promise, you will cast out demons, and if you drink any deadly thing, it will not harm you. And you will see the glory of Almighty God!*

Then the voice was gone, and all Katie could see was the leering face of Maioni, who was approaching with the poison cup. If Tenki refused to drink it, he would be speared on the spot—and the others with him, Katie sensed.

At that moment, she knew what she had to do, for something within her was saying, *Do not fear! You take the cup and drink it all, for I will manifest my power to these people.*

If Katie had paused to reason it out, she would never have done what she did—which was to step forward and hold her hands out, saying, "Give me the poison cup!"

Silence descended over the crowd. Maioni stared at her stupidly, but he did not resist when she reached out and took the cup. "Maioni," Katie said clearly, "are your gods strong enough to keep you from death?"

Bestman translated, and Maioni began to look furtively about the crowd. Every eye was riveted on him, but he could say only, "Tenki must drink!"

Katie held the cup high with both hands and cried out, "My God is strong! Your gods are weak!"

And then Katie lowered the cup—and drank the poison!

She felt nothing as she ingested the contents. It was as if someone else were performing the act and she were watching. Fear was gone! In its place was peace—a peace greater and sweeter than anything she had ever known.

There was not a sound, and she knew they were all waiting for her to fall down in convulsions. Beecham had told the missionaries that the poison was quick acting. But she felt no effects, and she began to speak to the crowd. A single doubt came to her, but she quickly prayed, *Lord, if I'm going to die, let me die giving the gospel to those who don't have it.*

"You have been in bondage to evil!" she cried out, and without being told, Bestman put her words into the Pahn language. "But the true God has sent me to tell you of Him. He is the God who made all things. He is the God who can do all things. You are all waiting to see me fall down and die. But God will not forsake me, for He wants you to know that He and only He is the true God!"

As she spoke the crowd stood still as statues, listening to her voice. For over an hour she gave them the gospel. At one point she saw Maioni creep to the edge of the crowd, and she cried out, "Maioni! Until you are ready to drink the poison cup, as I have, your power is broken. In the name of Jesus, I command you, evil spirits, depart!"

Once again, Maioni clapped his hands over his ears, and this time fell to the ground, writhing and screaming in torment. No one moved to touch him, and as Katie continued to cry out the name of Jesus and to command the demons to come out, he grew more violent.

Suddenly his body jerked, as if a giant had snapped his backbone, and he fell back on the earth, his mouth ringed with white froth.

"He dead!" Bestman said in shock. But when some of the men examined him, they shook their heads. He was alive but in a coma, and they carried him away.

A great weakness washed through Katie and she felt as if her legs would fold. Bestman grabbed her and led her away. Chief Tenki, weak as he was, was alert enough to use the occasion to reclaim his power. He began to speak as loudly as he could, and the villagers nodded excitedly as he assured them they didn't have to be afraid of Maioni any longer, that the true God was now in their village.

Bestman guided Katie to a cot inside the hut and bent over her. "Mammy, you be all right?"

The experience had drained her, but she managed to stay awake long enough to open her eyes, to smile at the dark face watching her anxiously.

"Yes, Bestman. God has been with me!"

And then she closed her eyes and slept like a child.

★ ★ ★ ★

The next two weeks were the happiest Katie had ever known. All that she had ever dreamed of accomplishing in Africa as a missionary was realized, for the Spirit of the Lord moved in a marvelous way.

The fall of Maioni was complete. Indeed, when he finally came out of the coma he had fallen into, he was not the same man! He seemed confused, and soon the villagers recognized that the evil witch doctor they had feared more than anything on earth was now an old man void of all power!

Katie visited with him many times and found him pathetic and eager to please. He asked her over and over to tell him the story of Jesus, and soon gave his heart to the Lord. This was the final breakthrough, and every afternoon when Katie preached, men and women turned to God. Chief Tenki rejoiced as a strong church was born; and when Katie finally announced that she was leaving, he almost wept. But she had no choice, for the rainy season had begun. Already the creeks and rivers were rising, and soon travel would be impossible.

"The church is strong," Katie assured him. "God is raising up wise elders from among the people. That is the way it should be. I will come back, and other missionaries, too; but now *you* should send Pahn missionaries to other tribes who do not know the truth."

That was a revelation to Tenki, and he nodded his head in agreement. "I will do," he said.

When Katie and Bestman were ready to return to Maoli, every member of Chief Tenki's tribe gathered, and there was a powerful final service.

As Katie walked with Bestman along the trail, she said, "Bestman, don't tell anyone about the poison cup."

"Why not, Mammy?"

Katie could not answer very well, but she tried. "I am afraid of it. God used it, but it could become a bad thing. People would want to see signs. They need Jesus, not signs." She had been troubled over her act, wondering if she had been presumptuous. But it was too late, so she determined never to speak of it again, and she never did. When a rumor would reach other people of what had happened, and she was asked about it, she would only say, "God always does miraculous things. He saved many in the village that time, and that is the miracle of all miracles!"

When they got back to Maoli, they were greeted by Chief Mawali, who, though he had heard about the miracle of the poison cup, was too concerned about Irene to ask. "Irene very sick," he said.

Alarmed, Katie rushed to her friend and found her desperately ill with malaria. When Irene saw Katie, she begged, "Take me to the coast! I'll die if I stay in this place."

"I'll take care of you, Irene," Katie said.

"No! Please, take me to the coast!" She begged so pitifully that Katie promised.

Katie sought out Bestman and said, "Go to Gropaka. Get one

of the other missionaries. Tell them we need help right away."

Bestman departed at once, and Katie took care of Irene the best she could. The rains began to fall harder, and Chief Mawali told her that it was unlikely any of the men would make it back from Gropaka. As the days passed and the downpour continued, she knew that even if Barney or Awful did come, it would be impossible to get Irene to the coast. The fear that death had been waiting and now would take Irene tormented Katie.

It was harder and harder for Katie to keep her spirits up. One morning, after she had prayed almost all night, she was slumped across the table, groggy and sick with fear.

"Katie! Are you awake!"

It was Barney's voice! Katie leaped up and opened the door. He came in dripping and with an anxious look on his face. But as soon as he saw her, he smiled. "Thank God!" he cried with joy.

She grabbed his shoulders and held on to him, unable to believe he had come. "Barney." Her lips trembled as she choked out the words. "She's going to die. We can't get her to the coast in this weather!"

Barney gave her a quick hug, and stepped over to look down at Irene.

"Maybe *we* can't, Katie," he said, smiling, "but *Jesus* can!"

CHAPTER NINETEEN

THE WALLS COME TUMBLING DOWN

★ ★ ★ ★

Katie rose at dawn and looked out the window. She could barely see the huts close to hers. The rain was still coming down, making the outside look like a world under water. All night she had slept fitfully, rising several times to try to get Irene to drink, then going to God in prayer.

She turned at a slight moan from Irene, who was thrashing feebly. Katie took a cloth, wet it in the tepid water and wiped the patient's face, then put her arm behind her and raised her enough to give her a sip of water. "I know you don't feel like it, but you need to drink more," she urged, but Irene shook her head from side to side. Malaria had taken such a toll on her that her eyes were sunken and her lips drawn tightly together.

At a knock on the door, Katie lowered Irene to the bed, then went to answer. "Come in, Barney," she said.

"How is she?"

"Worse, I think."

Barney himself had slept little, and the strain showed in the lines around his mouth. "A messenger came from Rhodilly about two hours ago. Bad news. Both the DeLaughters are down with malaria. Tobe is very ill, and Pearl wants you to come and help."

Shaking her head, Katie tried to think. The lack of sleep and the strain of the past hours had numbed her mind. "Can we get through to Rhodilly? The river's up, isn't it?"

"Yes, it is. But I think we've got to try it. Or maybe I should go alone, Katie." He glanced toward the still form on the cot, then shook his head doubtfully. "It's going to be close. Be better if you and Irene stayed—"

"No," a hoarse whisper broke in. Irene had wakened enough to hear the conversation. "I'll die—if you—leave me here, Barney. Take me with you," she begged.

Barney weighed the options. He was not afraid for himself, but the burden of two women, one of them critically ill—could they make it? He lifted his head, his dark eyes intent and his mouth set in a stubborn expression. "We'll leave in an hour. Try to eat something."

"All right," Katie said. She would not have forced herself on him, but was happy at the decision. "We'll need a few strong hammock men to carry Irene."

"I'll go see Bestman. He'll help."

Katie quickly fixed tea and broth for Irene, who forced some of it down. Working feverishly, she gathered the things they would need, then wrapped blankets around Irene. In this cold, soaking rain—with a desperately ill woman—it would take a miracle, Katie knew. *Oh, God, help!* she prayed. By the time Barney came, they were ready.

Barney walked over to Irene and said, "Time to go. We've got a long way ahead of us, but our God will help. Let's pray." Katie came close, and the three asked for safety. Then Barney picked Irene up and carried her out to the hammock. The four bearers lifted it up, and he said to Bestman, "You lead the way."

"Yes, Kwi Balee!"

Katie fell in behind the hammock, with Bestman and Barney ahead. The rain had turned the path into a quagmire, so going was tough, and with each step the mud oozed to their ankles. For two hours they plodded along. By then Katie was soaked— as well as everyone else. The rain ran down her face in rivulets into her sopping clothing; she was tired, and wished they would rest.

As though Barney had read her thoughts, he declared a halt,

and they rested for thirty minutes under the shelter of some trees. Allowing no more time Barney said, "All right, we'd better get moving." His voice sounded strange, and when Katie looked at him, she saw that his face was pale.

"Are you all right, Barney?" she asked.

"Yes," he said shortly, but she noticed his hands were shaking.

Katie had to force herself to stand up. They moved forward, but soon the hammock bearers were slipping and sliding as the ground grew more treacherous. The men were taxed to the limit of their strength, and it was necessary to stop every thirty minutes to let them rest.

Shortly before noon Bestman called a halt. The path had disappeared into what looked like a river or swamp. Katie stared at it, her legs trembling with exhaustion, but said nothing. It seemed impossible, and then Bestman pulled a hatchet from his belt and gave orders to his helpers.

"Katie," Barney said, "you rest with Irene," then moved to help with the construction of a raft.

Katie knew he was exhausted, and asked again if he was all right, but he didn't answer, so she turned to Irene and held her, trying to force some heat into her. Her eyes were closed, her breathing faint and irregular, and she mumbled as though confused. *Oh, God,* Katie prayed again, *please help!*

In a short while the men had built a raft of green logs tied with vines. It looked precarious, but it would have to work—hopefully.

"Let me have her," Barney said. He picked Irene up and placed her on the raft. "All right, let's go. Katie, hang on to me."

The raft sank almost out of sight in the brown waters as the men shoved it forward. One of the bearers carried the hammock, while Barney and Bestman helped the others maneuver the clumsy craft through the waist-deep water.

Katie clung to Barney's belt, floundering along in the water that rose almost breast high on her. At one point she nearly slipped under. Barney grabbed her, put his arm around her, and half dragged her along in the wake of the raft.

When it seemed that Katie could go no farther, Bestman called out, "Come on, Mammy! We be dry now!"

Relieved, Katie saw that the water gave way to land, and soon they were walking along a trail. It was muddy and hard going, but not so strenuous as wading in the swamp. Finally it grew darker and Barney said, "We'll have to rest until morning, Bestman. Let's take what cover we can find."

An hour later they found shelter under the trees. Bestman gathered punk—light, dry sections from inside a stump—and with Barney's matches wrapped in oilcloth, they got a fire started. The men rigged up a framework of saplings for Irene, and covered it with leaves; then Katie removed Irene's clothes, dried them by the fire, and dressed her again. By then Bestman brought the stew he had made. Like one used to long treks, he had packed provisions and a tin pot for cooking.

"Thank you, Bestman," Katie said. She tried to get Irene to eat, but she was having chills and shaking so terribly that she refused. Katie ate a small portion of the stew, then dried her own clothes and returned to sit beside Irene.

Barney joined her, nodded at Irene, and said, "She's in God's hands."

"I know," Katie replied, "but it is hard to understand."

"God is still sovereign," Barney assured her. "We can do only so much. He asks us to trust Him no matter what happens— trust, love, and follow Him with all our hearts."

Outside the frail tent, the men were eating and talking quietly before they rolled up and went to sleep. As the hours passed, Barney and Katie, too, were swallowed up in sleep.

Much later, Katie awoke with a start. It was Irene! Filled with fear, Katie shook Barney, and they bent over Irene. She was speaking incoherently, her face contorted, and her chest heaving as she gasped for air.

"What's happening?" Katie asked in alarm.

"I think she's going, Katie," Barney said.

"No!" Katie protested, taking Irene in her arms protectively. Like a mother she held the emaciated form of her co-worker, and with her eyes closed, whispered, "You can't die, Irene!"

After a few moments, Irene drew back and opened her eyes. They were clear as crystal! She stared at Katie, then shifted her eyes to Barney, and back to Katie, running her tongue across her dry lips. "Katie—you have been so good to me!"

"Irene—you'll be all right!" Katie choked out.

"No, dear," Irene whispered. "You and Barney must go on for Jesus. But He's calling me to come to Him." She smiled. "I thought it would be—be terrible to die," she murmured, taking Katie's and Barney's hands. "But it's like—it's like going home!"

Blinded by tears, Katie clung to Irene's hand, unable to say anything. Had it not been for Barney's arm supporting her, she would have fallen.

"You've been the faithful handmaiden of the Lord, Irene." Barney's voice was steady. "You're going now to be with Him who loved you and died for you."

"Yes!" she said. Her eyes turned upward and she gasped. It was faint but they heard her whisper, "I am coming—precious Lord!"

Then she took one deep breath—and her body slowly relaxed. Katie released her friend and sobbed with a grief that flooded her—sharp and painful as anything Katie Sullivan had ever known. Soon that passed and gave way to a peace that was another new experience.

She drew away from Barney and arranged Irene's hands and smoothed her hair. Her eyes were soft and more beautiful than anything Barney had ever seen.

"We'll take her to Rhodilly for burial," Katie said.

"All right, Katie."

They sat until dawn, both falling asleep from sheer exhaustion, but when Katie awakened, she cried in alarm, "Barney, you're ill!"

He was slumped over, his body shaking uncontrollably. He lifted his head.

"Barney, you've got malaria!" she said. "We can't go on!"

"We can't stay here," he whispered. "I can make it."

Bestman awakened and hurriedly got everyone moving. The hammock bearers sang as they moved through the jungle. After a while Barney began to stagger, and Katie called to Bestman, "He can't walk, Bestman."

"I see, Mammy. We carry Kwi Balee."

They reached Rhodilly at noon and were met by a native who spoke rapidly to Bestman. Bestman conveyed the solemn news to Katie. "He say, man he die. Woman very sick."

"Take me to her," Katie said. "But first, we must find a place for Barney." After Barney was settled, she went to Pearl.

Bending over the sick woman she asked, "Pearl? Can you hear me?"

Pearl opened her eyes and in a few seconds recognized her. "Katie!" she whispered, reaching out for her hand. As Katie held the thin hands, Pearl cried brokenly, "Tobe died—last night."

"Yes. He's with Jesus now, Pearl."

"I'm going to die, too," Pearl said. The tears rolled down her cheeks.

"No, you *won't* die!" Katie said emphatically. She began to pray for her, and finally Pearl whispered, "I'm glad—you came. I was so afraid."

"I'll be right here, Pearl," Katie promised. "Try to sleep now."

Pearl spent a peaceful night and seemed much better when she awakened. It was the encouragement both of them needed. However, Barney's condition had worsened.

That morning Katie had to conduct the funeral service for Irene. She was the only white person among the black Christians and felt very alone. In the short while she'd been in Africa, Katie had been faced with so many difficult situations, and she began to wonder if this was the normal life of a missionary. In the cold and dismal rain falling on the dreary setting, Katie read the verses from First Corinthians:

"Behold, I shew you a mystery; we shall not all sleep, but we shall all be changed, in a moment, in the twinkling of an eye, at the last trump: for the trumpet shall sound, and the dead shall be raised incorruptible, and we shall be changed.

"For this corruptible must put on incorruption, and this mortal must put on immortality. . . . Death is swallowed up in victory. O death, where is thy sting? O grave, where is thy victory?

"The sting of death is sin; and the strength of sin is the law. But thanks be to God, which giveth us the victory through our Lord Jesus Christ."

Throughout the simple service, she was conscious of God's peace. Afterward, she lingered at the graveside, her thoughts going back to the Rescue Mission, of Irene as she had laughed and sung with joy at the services. Finally she turned away from the spot and went back to Pearl.

When Katie told her that Barney had malaria, she wanted to leave immediately. "Katie, this place is deadly. Take us to the coast!"

Katie contemplated the possibility for a moment. "All right. I'll see what I can do. If possible, we'll leave in the morning."

She talked to Bestman, who said he'd get some men to carry the sick. Next she stopped to see Barney. "I'm taking you and Pearl to the coast in the morning," she said. "This place is rampant with malaria."

Barney was too sick to argue, and nodded. "I'd feel better about Pearl."

"I'd feel better about *both* of you." Katie reached out and put her hand on his forehead.

Her hand felt cool, and he managed a smile. "Nothing a woman likes more than having a sick man on her hands."

"It's my turn," she said gently. "Remember how you and your mother took care of me at the mission? So don't fuss. I've talked to Bestman, he's got the bearers, and they're working on the hammocks. You'll have to ride in one, you know."

As planned, they left the village at dawn, and it proved to be an easy journey, considering the circumstances. The rain had stopped, and the sun even gave off a few feeble rays. Bestman had persuaded a large number of bearers to make the trip, so by alternating, they could march all day with only short periods of rest.

Barney was delirious most of the time, but Pearl seemed to improve. Katie kept a close watch on both of them, but she was relieved when they reached the station at Garroway. She was surprised to find that Stanley Beecham was there to greet them.

"Well, we'll take care of the sick," Beecham said. "What about Irene?"

"She died on the way here," Katie said simply.

"That's too bad!" Beecham shook his head. "She was a fine girl! Very fine!" He stood there silently, then asked, "Did you know that Lily Ranken died two weeks ago?"

Katie stared at him. "I hadn't heard. What about her husband Slim?"

"He's well enough—except he blames himself for Lily's death."

"And Andy and Del?"

"They had malaria, too, but are well now." Beecham hesitated before saying, "They're in Monrovia."

"Monrovia? Why are they there? For supplies?"

Beecham shook his head. There was sadness in his eyes, and he said quietly, "No, Katie. They've gone to work with the Hansens." He saw how hard the news hit her, and said, "Come along. We'll talk about it later."

They did talk, and she discovered that the men had left the station two months earlier and had been working with the City Mission ever since.

"I think they were planning to visit all of you, to try to persuade you to return to the city," Beecham said. "Now they'll probably be more insistent."

"It will be hard on Barney. He hates to go against his brother."

Pearl recuperated quickly, but Barney was still very ill when Andy and Reverend Hansen and his daughter Dorothy arrived. They were all saddened to hear about Irene—and concerned for Barney. "We've got to get him to the hospital in Monrovia," Andy insisted.

Beecham thought it would be better to let him recover where he was, but Andy refused to take no for an answer. "You and Pearl had better come, too, Katie," he said.

Katie nodded. "Yes, I'll help take care of him."

"Oh, he'll have plenty of nurses in the hospital," Dorothy interjected quickly.

Dorothy was right, Katie discovered later when they admitted Barney to the hospital in Monrovia. The trip was made without any difficulty, and soon Barney was receiving expert nursing care. Katie visited him often, but spent much time walking along the shore, thinking of Irene a great deal, and of Tobe DeLaughter.

Barney grew better, but it was several weeks before he could get out of bed. He had little appetite and seemed confused.

Katie was concerned about that, but Reverend Hansen commented, "Common enough with this sort of thing. He needs lots of rest, that's all. We'll bring him to the house here until he has recovered."

As the weeks went by, Katie felt the need to go back to her station, but wanted to wait until Barney was well enough to return to Gropaka. Both she and Barney were staying with the Hansens, and she had waited for Barney to talk about returning, but he said little. Perhaps he was still exhausted, she decided.

It was on a Friday afternoon that Andy came by to talk with Barney. He had made short visits, but this time, Katie saw, he was determined about something. She had learned to recognize that element in Andy's character. Dorothy was with him, and she, too, looked solemn.

"Barney, we need to talk," Andy said. "Do you feel up to it?"

"Why, I guess so, Andy." Barney's face was thin. The fever had planed him down, leaving the ridges of his jaws sharp and his eyes more deep-set than usual. "What's the matter?"

Andy reached over and put his hand on his brother's shoulder. "Do you remember when you all voted to go to the interior, and I was against it?"

"Yes, I remember."

"We were ten when we came. Now Lily and Irene are gone. I doubt if Pearl or Slim will go back into the interior. Del feels that God wants him to work in the City Mission with the Hansens."

"What about you, Andy?" Barney asked quietly.

"Didn't Reverend Beecham tell you what I've decided?" Andy demanded.

"No."

The news made Andy slightly uncomfortable. "Well," he said, "I'm going back home. Somebody needs to be there raising support for the work here, and I can do it." He went on hurriedly. "Can't you see that it was a *mistake* to go off into the interior?"

"Andy," Katie broke in, "I don't agree."

"Katie, wouldn't you like to have Irene alive and well?"

Katie studied him. "All of us are expendable. If we spend our lives seeking a safe place, the gospel will never be preached to the world!"

Ignoring Katie, he turned back to Barney, earnestly trying to reason with him. For a long time he expounded on the practicality of working in a safe environment. There was no question as to his sincerity; he believed every word he was saying and spoke so eloquently that neither Barney nor Katie could counter his logic.

Finally Andy said, "Barney, you and Katie will have to look at this thing realistically." Then he paused and spread his hands wide, saying, "Only you two and Gardner are still determined to go on in the interior." He came and put his hand on Barney's shoulder, and there was real affection in his eyes as he added, "Barney, I love you too much to see you throw yourself away. You've come too far for that! I'm asking you, come with us! We've tried it your way; now you try it our way. That's fair, isn't it?"

Barney sat with his head down. It was a difficult time, for he could remember so many times as boys when Andy had swayed him to do things. Everything he said now sounded so *right*. But what about his call from God? After a while he lifted his eyes to Andy and said, "I'll have to pray about it."

"Of course!" Andy nodded. "Naturally, you will. And you must do the same, Katie." Then he skillfully turned the conversation to the things that had been happening in Monrovia, "big things that were going to make the world take note."

★ ★ ★ ★

Barney slept fitfully that night, his mind going in circles as he tried to arrive at the right decision. What did God want? Was Andy right again?

The next morning Andy was there early and said in front of the others, "Well, Barney, will you give me a chance to show you what can be done? And remember, I went with you when I thought it was a mistake."

Barney had made up his mind. He nodded slowly, and the words came painfully. "Yes, Andy. I've been wrong so much, I'm afraid to trust myself."

Andy beamed. "Praise the Lord! You'll see! You'll see, Barney! It's going to be great!"

★ ★ ★ ★

Katie slipped away without a word while the others were talking. She walked along the beach a great deal before returning to her room. That night at supper she noted that Barney was very quiet, and noted also that Dorothy was sitting beside him, talking animatedly. Later, she again went for a walk, and as she headed back she saw him coming out of the building.

"Barney?"

He stopped, surprised to see her. "Katie—" he began, then could say no more.

Katie walked over and stood by his side, waiting for him to continue. A night bird cried in the darkness, the echo fading as silence washed back over the land.

Barney sighed. "Katie," he said again, "I wish . . . Oh, what's the use. I'm not really sure of anything anymore. What will *you* do?"

"Me? I'm going back," she replied unhesitatingly. Her voice was firm and void of any doubt. "If I didn't go back, it would mean Pearl and Lily died for nothing."

"I never thought of it like that." Barney's face lost some of the tension. Turning his head, he smiled at her. "You're a strong woman, Katie Sullivan."

"Maybe I'm just stubborn," she replied. "My mother always said I was."

He nodded absently and looked up at the sky. "Dad wondered if the skies looked different over here. I guess they do in a way—but life goes on here just like at home."

Katie impulsively put her hand on his arm. "Barney, be sure about your decision before you do this."

He looked at her, his eyes tired. "I can't seem to do anything right, Katie."

"Not true! That's not true!" she insisted.

"Yes, it is." Barney's eyes mirrored something she couldn't understand. "Remember the old nursery rhyme 'London Bridge Is Falling Down'? Well, that's what it's like to me, Katie." He looked up at the sky again, let out a slow sigh, and said under his breath, "Everything is falling down." Then he turned and walked away.

Katie's heart ached for him, but she could do nothing. Beecham had told them about missionaries who performed well at first—then gave way under pressure. But she never thought Barney Winslow would be one of them.

With sad resignation she walked back to the beach. For a long time she listened to the waves washing in and out, throwing stones up on the beach. *We can be just like those waves*, she thought, *tossed about by doubt and fear when everything is coming apart. But, Lord, aren't you enough? Can't you energize and create within us the power and desire to do what you want—for your satisfaction, delight and pleasure, not ours? I've seen you work. Oh, Jesus, make my heart like your heart in this situation.* As she stood quietly waiting, her mind was triggered by the memory of Irene and the muddy grave in the jungle, and she lifted her head and walked back to her room. At dawn the next day she left Monrovia without saying goodbye. By the time the sun was high, she was pushing steadily through the jungle with Bestman at her side, headed back to Maoli and her people.

PART FOUR

THE OVERCOMERS

★ ★ ★ ★

January 1899–January 1900

CHAPTER TWENTY

WINSLOW'S COUNSELING SERVICE

★ ★ ★ ★

Dorothy Hansen stretched lazily, took a sip of tea, and looked toward Barney at the window of the City Mission office. He had been gazing for some time at the busy vendors in the courtyard below. His healthy, strong tanned face was a handsome contrast to the stark white of his shirt and trousers. Studying his profile, she thought, *He's not as handsome as Andy, but good-looking in a rugged way. And somehow he grows on people.*

When he had come to work with the City Mission four months earlier, she had not been overly impressed. Of course, at that time she had eyes only for Andy. Though Dorothy was not open with others, to herself she could admit her capriciousness. *It didn't take me long to trade one Winslow in for another!* she laughed to herself. *This one's not as flashy, but Andy will never settle for anything less than big time. But Barney will stay, and he's coming around much faster than I thought. He never mentions going back to the interior.*

"The meetings were fine, weren't they, Barney?" she said, speaking to him, more to gain his attention than anything else.

"Yes, they were," he replied. "I only wish they could have gone on longer."

The last service of the Bible convention had been held the previous evening, with national pastors from all over Liberia attending. It had been a stirring time, seeing so many coming to know the Lord and for the pastors to return to their ministries with new inspiration as God touched their hearts.

Dorothy sipped her tea and went on. "I haven't seen much of you. You really threw yourself into the meetings." She smiled, adding, "I think you must know every one of our pastors by name. And they all know you. How do you get so close to them, Barney? Nobody else has managed to become so well known so fast."

"I don't know, Dorothy," he shrugged. "I just like to be with them."

She knew that was true. Her father had said, "Barney Winslow has what most white men never have—a real gift for getting to the hearts of the African people. Most of us try too hard, but he doesn't have to. They're a discerning people, Dorothy. They *know* when somebody really likes them, just as they sense when someone feels superior."

The conversation had both disturbed and pleased Dorothy. She was disturbed because she knew she had never possessed the love for people she saw in Barney, but pleased that he was becoming known all over the country as a coming leader in the world of African missions.

"Let's take a few days off for a steamer trip," she suggested. "Meetings are good, but draining."

Barney shook his head. "No time for vacations, I'm afraid. Have you forgotten we're starting the new school for the Kru tribe?" The Kru people lived on the coast, and Barney had responded with alacrity when an opportunity had come to expand the City Mission in that area.

"Oh, we can throw ourselves into that when we get back. And we'll do better if we start in fresh." She came over to stand beside him, fresh and pretty. "Please, Barney." She smiled and tugged playfully at his arm. "Let's just take a couple of days."

"I don't know," he said, hesitating, then nodded. "Maybe you're right. On second thought, it's a good idea. We could catch the banana boat and go down as far as Tannmouth. I've wanted to visit the pastor there. I hear he's doing a fine job."

"Of course, Barney," she agreed, smiling at him radiantly. *That might be your idea,* she thought. *I'll just have to get your mind off work and onto other things, though.* "I'm going to tell Daddy and Mother."

"Sure. They'll probably want to come along," Barney nodded.

"Maybe," she replied, but she knew they wouldn't. With a contented look on her face, she went to her father's office.

"Hello, Daddy," she said, giving him a kiss on the cheek.

He looked up with surprise. "Well, what makes you so demonstrative, Dorothy?"

She pushed his hair back from his forehead, saying innocently, "Why, Daddy, you act as though I never paid you any attention!"

"You do when you want something," Hansen grinned. He knew this daughter of his well, and leaned back in his chair to consider her. "What's in that pretty head of yours?"

"Oh, nothing," she went on airily. "I've just been talking to Barney and he wants to go on a trip down the coast for a few days. I thought I might go with him."

"Oh?" He eyed her suspiciously. "Does he think it's his idea?"

Dorothy laughed. "I guess so. But he's worked too hard. He needs a vacation."

Hansen sobered. "You're right about that. Ever since he started working here he's gone night and day. We make a pair, I suppose. He works too hard—and I don't work enough!"

"I thought you would approve," Dorothy said demurely.

"Why, you never gave my approval a thought!" Shaking his head, he said rather strictly, "You've managed to manipulate *me* for so long, I suppose you're bored with it. Now you're out to run Barney Winslow's life."

"Oh, I'm not trying to run anybody's life, Daddy!"

"Dorothy, you do it all the time." Hansen paused for a moment. "You never were able to control Andy as you do Barney— but I suppose you realize that."

"Oh, don't be silly, Daddy!"

"I'm not silly—and I'm not blind. Neither is your mother. It's a good thing young Winslow is. Are you really interested in him?" her father demanded.

"He's . . . different."

"Yes, he is. But the question is, do you *want* somebody as different as he?"

Dorothy had asked herself that same question often enough, but the answer had not been easy. "Well, Daddy, the supply of eligible men isn't very plentiful out here," she said candidly. "Barney is stronger than most men, but he needs a push."

Hansen grinned. "Well, you're good at that, you know. And since he's rid himself of those ideas of the interior, I think he'll go far."

"You wouldn't mind having him for a son-in-law, I take it?" Dorothy asked quizzically. Despite her father's rather foppish appearance, she knew he was clever and shrewd.

"Not a bit—now that he's got his head out of the clouds. But you might want to look around a bit. There's the Ranken fellow. He'll marry again. And don't forget Del Saunders."

Dorothy shrugged lightly, tossing off the suggestion. "Not for me," she said and left the room, saying, "I'm going shopping. I don't have a thing to wear for a river cruise."

Shopping for clothes was one thing, while actually taking the holiday was another, she found. Barney had agreed, but he had thrown himself into the work of the mission with full vigor, making it impossible to simply walk off. Substitutes had to be found, and when that was done, they learned that the next boat wouldn't depart until the middle of September. Dorothy worked feverishly to find another ship, but failed.

For the next few weeks, Barney moved around the city, preaching and being available for any ministry needed. He was restless, and only by working long hours could he sleep well. He said once to Dorothy, "It's odd, how I slept so well in the jungle, lying on the ground with a million bugs trying to eat me alive. And now with a nice bed in a good room, I toss and turn half the night."

He enjoyed most of the work he did, for there were great needs in the city. A real hunger for the gospel message among the people existed, and many were saved as a result of his labors. But he dreaded the long hours he spent in the office. Myron Hansen was careful not to overburden him, yet warned, "It's not glamorous, Barney, but if nobody tended to the office details, the work would never get done in the back streets."

Barney did his best, yet no matter how busy he kept himself, he thought much of his time in Gropaka. He missed the life, and he missed Awful Gardner. He had missed the man's cheerful spirit, missed hearing him say every morning, "Well, dear boy, what can we do for Jesus today?" He had not realized until he left the interior how much he had enjoyed the long talks the two had daily, mostly on Bible themes, but on other subjects as well.

One late Tuesday afternoon in early September, after visiting the very poor in the heart of the worst sections of Monrovia, he was returning to his room, thinking all the way about Awful. Again that sense of loneliness pressed in on him. Once he paused and looked in the direction of Gropaka, then kicked a loose stone with a rare exhibit of frustration.

"Getting to be a spoiled brat!" he chided himself, and picked up the pace. When he entered the compound, he was surprised to find Del Saunders waiting.

"Barney!" Del's fair skin was sunburned, as always, and his blue eyes sparkled as he rushed over to give Barney a hearty blow on the back. "About time you got here," he said. "I was ready to come look you up!"

"When did you get in, Del?" Barney asked with a grin. Saunders had been a disappointment to Andy and the Rankens, for after two months of working with the City Mission, he had left to go back to Chodi. Barney missed the cheerful redhead and their many talks. They had much in common, and enjoyed each other's company.

"About ten o'clock," Del answered. "Came in for some supplies and a little wise counsel."

"I can get you the supplies, Del, and maybe both of us can find some wise counsel."

Del gave him a quick glance. "I think the kind of counsel I need, *you* can give."

"Well, I do all my heavy counseling over a steak," Barney smiled. Come along." As he led the way to his room, he asked, "Have you seen the Hansens yet?"

"Just Dorothy. Her folks are gone, you know."

Barney and Del foraged in the larder until they found some fresh beef steaks, which they gave to the cook to grill.

Del had not changed, Barney discovered as they dined. He

was still a hypochondriac—eating like a starving field hand, enjoying every bite, yet complaining about his delicate stomach. "I've got to get something for this stomach problem, Barney," he said between mouthfuls. "It's just awful."

"It must be," Barney nodded with a straight face. "Doesn't it bother you to eat huge meals?"

Del looked at the havoc he had wrought on the large amount of food and shook his head sadly. "Doesn't seem to matter. Large or small, it gives me trouble. And I've been having awful cramps, too." He went on for some time, listing his symptoms.

Barney did not allow himself to smile, though Del's imaginary illnesses amused him. Del Saunders was tough and muscular, could work almost any man to death, and, aside from the inevitable bouts with malaria, was never ill—except in his mind, of course. Barney could not understand the paradox, but medical complaints were so common with Del that they were part of his very makeup.

When the meal was finished and both men had discussed their individual mission work, Barney said, "I guess it's counseling time, Del. Dr. Barney Winslow, expert advisor. All cures guaranteed. We never close."

Del swiveled the coffee around in his cup nervously. "Well, Barney," he said slowly, "I guess maybe you can guess what I gotta talk about."

"Not really." Barney was puzzled. Del was one of the most outgoing men he had ever known, yet now he seemed to be embarrassed. "You having some sort of trouble, Del?"

"Well, not *trouble*, Barney, so much as a *problem*." Del twisted in his chair and finally blurted out, "Blast it all! The thing is, Barney, I've got a woman problem!"

Barney was appalled. *Had Del gotten involved with a native?*

"I want to get married, Barney," he rushed on.

A wave of relief swept over Barney. "You have a girl back home, Del?"

"Oh, I've had a few girlfriends, I guess, but none of them would do for the life out here." Del got up and paced the floor restlessly, then slumped in his chair. "Well, you can see where I'm headed, can't you?"

"I guess you'll have to spell it out for me, Del."

"I thought you might have noticed," Del said. His cheerful grin was gone, and he added, "I want to marry Katie."

A sliver of shock surged through Barney. "Marry Katie?"

"Well, sure!" The homely freckled face of Saunders was puzzled. "Didn't you know I've always liked Katie?"

Barney thought back, and he did remember that Del had been drawn to Katie, even during their days at the Rescue Mission. "All of us like Katie," he hedged quickly.

"Oh, it's more than that with me, Barney!"

"Marriage is a serious thing, Del. Maybe you're just lonesome."

"Lord knows I'm lonesome enough," Del laughed ruefully. "It wasn't so bad at first. Andy and I were together and everything was new. I didn't have *time* to be lonesome. But it's different now. I'm all alone, and I'm just not the kind of fellow to enjoy my own society, Barney."

Barney knew that for the truth. Del was outgoing, always with other people; and the long, lonely days at the station would be worse for him than for others.

"Have you told Katie?" he asked finally.

"Haven't told anybody except you, Barney." Del managed a grin. "I guess this is where you start earning your money as a counselor. What do you think?"

"About you getting married?"

"Heck, no! I *know* about that!"

"What then?"

"Why, about Katie, of course! Will she have me?"

Barney felt uncomfortable and said slowly, "Why, Del, you can't expect me to tell you that. You'll have to ask her."

"Confound it, Barney! That's the part I've come to you for!"

Barney's forehead furrowed. "I don't know what you're getting at, Del," he said, perplexed. "You've decided to get married already, haven't you? You're not asking me what to do about *that*?"

"That's exactly what I'm asking!"

Barney felt a streak of irritation rising, and said sharply, "Del, you ought to know better. What you're saying is that you've already decided to get married, and now you're shopping around for a wife. You don't get a wife like you would a suit of clothes—shop around until you find one you like!"

Del flushed angrily. "Blast it, Barney, it's not like that! It's not like that at all! I told you, I want Katie!"

"You said no such thing!" Barney snapped. "You said you *liked* her. That's not enough to marry on, Del."

Del stared at Barney, who was obviously upset, but then he shook his head, saying apologetically, "I guess I didn't put the thing right, Barney. Always was hard for me to say things about—well, about love, you know? Other guys can say things like that, but I never could. Dunno why, but it comes hard for me."

Barney sat quietly, disturbed. He didn't know how to analyze the emotions that had suddenly swept him when Del announced his problem, but he was agitated and it took an effort to keep his face and voice even.

"Del, do you love Katie?"

"Well, I *need* her, Barney!"

"Not the same thing at all!"

Del nodded slowly. "Guess you're right, Barney, but it's part of love, isn't it? I mean, we're both out here to serve God. A man needs a wife, and a woman needs a husband. Beecham's always said that he wished all of us were married. So I've been thinking about it for weeks, Barney, and now I've got to find out." Then he looked up and met Winslow's eyes. "So, what I want from you is . . . a little help."

"Help to do what?"

Del looked more embarrassed than ever. "Barney, I was lying to you about those girlfriends of mine back home. I never had a girlfriend. Not a real one. Don't know anything about women. So what I'm asking you to do is—well, sort of give me a hand."

"Give you a hand doing *what*, Del?" he asked, puzzled.

"Why, help me court Katie, of course!" He saw Barney's face change, and began to speak rapidly. "Barney, you *got* to do it! I mean, you and Katie are real close, always have been. Everybody knows that! So what you can do is talk me up to her, you know?"

"Del, that's crazy!" Barney protested. "Katie knows you. I can't promote you as if you were a new brand of soap!"

"Sure you can! Well, not like *soap*, of course—but she listens to you, Barney. She's told me lots of times how she admires you. So if you could sort of give her a good word on me, why, she'd listen to you!"

"Del—!"

"And that's not all, Barney," Del interrupted. "You know how to court a girl. So you can teach me. I ain't got the slightest idea of how to go about it—especially out here in Africa!"

"Del, I'm no expert on women! As a matter of fact, I'm not good with them at all."

"Oh, that's not so! Everybody knows how you've been courtin' Dorothy Hansen, Barney."

"Where did you hear such nonsense?" Barney snapped. "Dorothy and I work together, that's all!"

Del shook his head. "She likes you. Pearl said so, and Dorothy's a sharp young lady."

"Pearl is mistaken," Barney said stiffly.

"But Dorothy told me herself that the two of you are going off on a cruise."

Barney flushed. He was confused and wanted to end the conversation, so he said, "You need to talk to Stanley Beecham about this, Del. He'll give you some good advice."

"You really think so, Barney?"

"Why, of course!"

Del laughed, his face bright with relief. "That's great, Barney—because I did go talk to him, and he told me to come to you. As a matter of fact, it was *his* idea that you could help me with Katie!"

Barney felt as though he had stepped directly into a steel trap! He tried to think, but nothing came. After a while he said, "Beecham is a man of wisdom, Del, but I'm not sure he's right about this."

"Barney, I need help," Del persisted quietly. "Some men can make it alone, like Stanley. Others of us need companionship. So, I'm asking you right out, will you give me a hand with this?"

Barney swallowed hard. There didn't seem to be any way out.

He sighed. "All right, Del. I can't promise anything, and you'll probably be sorry you ever asked me—but I'll do what I can."

Del leaped up and pounded Barney's shoulders. "Oh, thank you! I *knew* you could do it!"

A deep unrest rose in Winslow's mind. Somehow, what Del was doing could not be right. But Barney'd said he'd do it. He was caught.

Del stepped back, his face shining. "I'm going to see if I can get two tickets on that boat you and Dorothy are going on, Barney. That way Katie and I can be alone."

He rushed out, and though Barney knew the ticket office would be closed, he didn't mention it. For a long time he sat staring at the wall. Then he snorted: "Barney Winslow's Counseling Service! What a joke!"

CHAPTER TWENTY-ONE

ANOTHER VOYAGE

★ ★ ★ ★

The *Falcon* made no pretensions to grandeur. She was merely an ancient cargo ship that had been owned and sold so many times that not even Captain Borg had any idea of her origin. Unlike most ships of her class, she did have several cabins available for passengers. None of them were ornate, and the passengers were expected to stay out of the way of the crew as they worked the ship.

Captain Borg looked down at the quay with a pair of cautious gray eyes, and muttered to the tall sailor standing with him at the rail, "There they come, Bjelland. When they get on board, get the ship underway."

"Aye, sir." Norman Bjelland was a typical Norwegian—fair hair and blue eyes. "I hope they don't give us any problems. That last bunch drove me crazy."

Captain Borg winced at the thought, but said, "This bunch won't be wild. They're all missionaries. Probably try to save all us heathens, but being preached at isn't as bad as having a chair bent over your head, is it, Norman?"

Bjelland touched the fresh scar over his left eyebrow and grinned. "I'll get them settled down, Captain." He went to greet the passengers at the gangplank. "Welcome aboard the *Falcon*. I'm the first officer, Lieutenant Bjelland."

"Thank you, Lieutenant. I'm Barney Winslow. Let me introduce you to our group."

As Barney named off the other two men, then the three women, Bjelland noted that they were all young—and all three women were attractive. *Have to warn the crew against getting familiar with them*, he thought, but said only, "I'm happy to meet you all. You'll meet the captain and the other officers at dinner tonight, but let me take you to your cabins." He hesitated, then added, "We have only four cabins. How would you like to share them?"

Dorothy broke in, "I'll take one of the singles, Lieutenant Bjelland.—That'll give you and Pearl some time together, won't it, Katie?"

"That will be fine!" Pearl said as Katie nodded.

"Why don't you and I bunk together, Barney?" Del suggested quickly. "Slim couldn't stand my snoring anyway!"

"Okay by me," Ranken nodded.

The first officer continued. "You know this is a working ship, of course, so you'll have to entertain yourselves. Let me show you the facility for recreation." He took them to a room sparsely furnished with a few tables and chairs. "This is it, I'm afraid. Not too plush."

Pearl smiled. "It *is* after a hut with mud floor and no screens, Lieutenant. We'll like it."

Bjelland looked at her, then at the others with fresh respect. "I'm glad you see it that way. Let me know if you need anything. Dinner will be served at seven."

He showed them to their rooms, and Katie headed straight for the narrow beds. "Not bad, Pearl," she said. "As you said, after a mud hut, it looks like a palace."

Pearl looked out the porthole. "I think we're moving, Katie. Feel the engines?" She watched for a while as the *Falcon* slowly left the harbor.

"I don't think we were supposed to be on this trip, Katie."

Katie looked up with surprise. "What makes you think that, Pearl? I understood Barney wanted us to get together. Sort of a gathering of the Company."

"That's what it turned into," Pearl smiled. "But I got it out of Del—the original idea."

"The original idea?"

"Yes. The way Del told it, he came in from his station for supplies and found out that Barney and Dorothy were taking a cruise. Sort of a vacation." Pearl ran her hand through her black curly hair, an amused light in her eyes. "Del invited himself, and then Barney got the idea of getting all of us together for a re-union. Which isn't what Miss Hansen had on her mind, I'm pretty sure!"

Katie put the last of her things in the small chest, shut the drawer, then sat down on the bed and considered what Pearl had just said. She had merely gotten a message that she was needed if she could get free. She mentioned this to Pearl, adding, "I don't think I would have come if I'd known that."

"*I* would!" Pearl said emphatically. "The last few weeks have been pretty hard." She stared down at her hands, saying quietly, "I miss Tobe a lot, Katie. More than I thought I would."

Katie had known that there had been some difficulty between Tobe and Pearl, but neither of them had ever spoken of it. She said, "He was such a fine man, Pearl. So dedicated!"

"Yes, I see that now. I—I wish I'd showed a little more—"Tears flooded Pearl's eyes, and she quickly dashed them away. "You see? I get all weepy over things. I thought it would be good for me to be with people again."

"It *is*! And we're going to have a fine time."

A mischievous expression came to Pearl's face. "I can't help but be glad that we interfered with Dorothy's scheme. She's pretty clever, but I understand, I think."

"Understand what, Pearl?"

"Why, she needs a husband!"

Katie smiled. "Well, so do I."

"Oh, nonsense, Katie! It's not the same thing at all." Pearl thought for a moment, then said positively, "She was going to get Andy, but he had the sense to leave. Now she's settled on Barney."

"I'm sure Barney will have something to say about that, Pearl." Katie was not at all certain Pearl's calculations were right, but she did remember how Dorothy had seemed to be very close to Andy.

"Barney's a sitting duck, Katie!" Pearl said. "He's a sweet fellow, but he can't say no to anyone. Isn't that obvious? He doesn't want to be here in Monrovia; he wants to be out in the bush. But he couldn't say no to Andy. And you watch what I say, sooner or later Dorothy will have a wedding ring out of him!"

Katie jumped to her feet. "Oh, Pearl, let them do what they please. Come on, let's go on deck."

Pearl said no more, for she could see that the conversation displeased Katie.

The two found Del and Slim standing up in the bow, watching the waves break as the *Falcon* pushed through them.

"This sea air is wonderful!" Ranken called out as Katie and Pearl approached. "It's so fresh!" They all stood at the rail drinking in the tangy breeze. It was hot on deck, but not like the steaming heat of the jungle; and after the smell of an African village, the fresh air was as intoxicating as wine.

"I'm glad Barney thought of this trip," Ranken commented. "I've been dying to see all of you. I get so lonesome sometimes, I catch myself talking to myself!"

"I'm worse than that, Slim!" Pearl said. "I even *answer* myself!"

Ranken looked at her, nodded slowly. "I guess it's worse on you and me, Pearl. We've lost something that can't be replaced." Then he shook his head disparagingly. "Well, this is no wake! Let me tell you about my latest blunder."

He plunged into a long story of how he had tried to accomplish something that failed miserably, and had the others rolling in laughter. When he and Pearl left the bow to go stand on the fantail, Katie said, "They've had it worse than any of us, Del. We've all been lonely. I've missed Irene and you've missed Andy—but to lose your husband or wife, that has to be terrible!"

Del smiled at Katie, admiring the color in her cheeks and the sunlight on her blond hair. She was fresh and fair in his eyes, but he could not tell her this. "That's right, Katie."

She waited for him to go on, but when he stopped, she said, "Tell me about the work in Chodi, Del. Is it going well?" She listened as he spoke, little knowing that it was not the mission work he wanted to discuss. When he finally paused, she said, "I was very happy when I heard about your decision—to leave the city and go back to Chodi."

"You were?" Del brightened. "It's been good—but it does get lonesome."

"I get lonesome, too," Katie admitted.

Del could have spoken to his advantage, but unsure of the right words, he missed the opportunity. Soon she went below, and Del groaned at his stupidity. He was glad to have been with her, but angry that he had not seized his chance to tell her how he felt. With chagrin, he went to find Barney but found him in deep conversation with Dorothy, so he went to his room to plot his strategy.

At dinner there were only four officers present: Captain Borg, Lieutenant Bjelland, Carlin, the chief engineer, a short, husky man, and Drake, the second officer, quite the opposite of Carlin.

"A little crowded," Captain Borg said as they all sat down. "But all the better for good fellowship." The food was brought in, and Borg nodded at Barney. "I suppose you are in the custom of saying grace, Reverend Winslow?"

"I'm afraid so, Captain," Barney smiled. "However, I'm known as a man with a quick prayer."

"Good!" the chief engineer laughed. "Get on with it, Reverend!"

Barney lived up to his boast, and in a few seconds they were eating, and conversation began to flow smoothly.

"Tell me about your voyage from America," the captain said. And when he heard they had sailed with Captain Seale, he nodded. "Fine sailor! Known him for many years."

"Have you seen him lately, Captain?" Katie asked.

"No, not for a couple of years."

"He's not the same man," Katie went on, and when Borg inquired how Seale had changed, Katie told how he had become a Christian.

Captain Borg thought about what she said, then nodded. "I'm not surprised. Seale's always been interested in that sort of thing."

"His first mate, a man called Sipes, got the same thing," Del grinned.

"Sipes got religion?" Lieutenant Bjelland lifted his eyebrows. "I find that hard to believe! Fellow was nothing but a bruiser!"

"Barney Winslow had a hand in his conversion," Slim Ranken

smiled. He told them the story of the bout with Sipes.

"You're Bat Winslow?" Drake, the second officer, exclaimed, his eyes wide. "Why, I saw you fight Kid Nelson in Troy!"

Barney shook his head. "Ancient history, Mr. Drake," he said. "I'm fighting worse than Kid Nelson now."

The officers were interested, and for a long time they all lingered over the meal as the missionaries told of their work. Finally the captain rose, saying, "This has been quite pleasant. We'll look forward to more of your experiences, won't we, gentlemen?"

The other officers nodded, and the company broke up. "Let's go to the recreation room," Slim Ranken suggested. "I'd like us to have all the fellowship we can on this cruise."

For the next hour they talked about old times. When it came to memories of those who had died—Tobe, Irene, and Lily—they didn't linger on the topic since it was too painful.

"Wish Awful were here," Barney said wistfully. "I miss that fellow!"

"Tell us again about how he witnessed to you in prison," Katie said. "I never get tired of hearing about that."

Dorothy had been left out—mostly because they had spoken of mutual experiences. Now she said with an edge of sharpness, "I don't think Barney likes to be reminded of that time, Katie."

"Why, of course, Dorothy. I'm sorry," Katie said.

But Barney only smiled. "Don't worry, Dorothy. That time was bad, but I can see now that it was God dealing with me. If I hadn't gone there, I'd probably have gone completely bad. But it was in Sing Sing that I first got a touch from God through Awful." He didn't speak further of his days in prison, and they all understood he was deferring to Dorothy.

"Speaking of Awful," Pearl said, "he's going through a rough time. Reverend Beecham came by two weeks ago on his way from Gropaka, and he said that Awful was having a lot of sickness."

Barney bit his lip, but said nothing.

"I'll go see him when we get back," Del offered. He turned to Katie. "Maybe you'd like to make the trip, too. It's not very far from your station."

"Yes, I'd like to go, Del."

It was Dorothy who made the first move to leave. "I think I'll stroll around the deck before I turn in."

Barney got up, saying, "It's getting late. I'll go with you, Dorothy."

"That was pretty boring for you," Barney said as they walked around the deck. "Nothing worse than listening to people talk about old times that you didn't have a part in."

"It's nice for all of you," Dorothy replied. She was wearing a green silk dress that shimmered in the silver moon as she moved. "I *am* jealous, though."

He stopped abruptly. "Jealous? Of who?"

"Not who," she smiled. "I'm jealous of the experiences you all share. It's silly, but I wish I could be part of it."

She was looking up at him, her hair ruffled by the breeze and her large eyes wide. "But we'll have experiences of our own to remember, won't we, Barney?"

"Sure," he nodded, uncertain as to how to answer. The faint throbbing of the engines and the hissing of the sea as the ship moved along in the moonlight made him feel light and free. "You know," he said, "you're looking wonderful, Dorothy."

"Why, thank you, Barney!" She laughed softly and reached out to touch his cheek. "I'll have to mark this in my date book. It's an event."

"An event?"

"Yes," she said with a curving smile. "It's the first time you ever said a personal thing to me. I've been wondering if you ever would. I've begun to think you look at me as if I were a piece of the furniture!"

"Oh no!" he protested. He hesitated, then said, "You've been good for me, Dorothy. When I was sick—and afterward, too—I felt pretty low. It seemed as if all I came to Africa for had fallen through. And then you came along and talked to me, cheered me up. It—it's meant a lot to me."

Dorothy waited, her heart racing, but when he made no move, she said, "You've been good for me, too, Barney. I've felt so—so *right* when you've been with me!"

At that moment the ship changed course, and the slight tilt of the deck threw her off balance. She fell against him with a small cry, and he instinctively put his arms around her. As she looked up, she closed her eyes and felt the warmth of his lips on hers. It was not a long kiss, but enough for Barney to feel her response. She drew back and said, "That was sweet, Barney! Good-night!"

She gingerly tripped off the deck, her willowy shape disappearing around the corner as Barney watched, a dazed expression on his face. *Why did I do that?* he asked himself, solemnly turning back to the rail to stare vacantly at the wake made by the ship. Below, the water glittered in the moonlight. Above, a scattering of tattered clouds drifted across the sky. He gazed up at the fluffy cotton balls advancing toward the moon, the tendrils draping the crescent so that the brilliance of its face dimmed. With a sigh, he left, and when Del came to bed, Barney feigned sleep.

The next morning Del was impatiently waiting for Barney to wake up. "Barney, have you talked to Katie—about me, I mean?"

Barney pried his eyes open and tried to focus on Del. His voice was thick with sleep as he grunted, "No, Del, I haven't." He lurched to his feet, gulped down some water, then filled the basin and started working up a lather. He shaved carefully, paying little heed as Del talked steadily, mostly about Katie.

When he was finished, he dressed, and only then did he ask, "Have you said anything to her?"

"Well, not really," Del admitted. "I'm working up to it, though. We had a great talk on deck yesterday."

"Did you tell her how you feel?"

"Barney, I just can't seem to work up to it!" Del's face was filled with despair. "But if I knew that she had some sort of warning—why, I could do it."

"Warning? What kind of warning?" Barney asked as they left the cabin and headed for the dining room.

"I mean, if you'd sort of *talk* to her, Barney. Kind of let her know how much I think of her." Del reached out and pulled Barney to a stop as they approached the dining room. "Do that for me, Barney, will you?"

Barney took a deep breath and released it. "All right, Del. I'll try. But it sounds stupid to me. A girl wants to hear that kind of thing from the man who loves her—not a messenger boy."

★ ★ ★ ★

All day long Barney mulled over the chore Del had forced on him. The ship docked at noon to take on supplies, and everyone went ashore to see the town and visit the open markets. That night after supper, Dorothy asked Barney to help her go over some plans she had for a mission project with the lepers, and he agreed.

It was late when they put away the papers, and he walked her to her state room. Instead of going in, she paused. "It's so good to have someone to work with on these things, Barney!" Then seemingly on impulse, she reached up and pulled his head down, kissing him lightly.

Just as she did so, Katie emerged from her cabin, and when she saw them kiss, she whirled and strode away. "I guess we shocked Katie," Dorothy said. "Good-night, Barney."

"Good-night, Dorothy," he said.

He hurried up to the deck and caught up with Katie just as she reached the rail.

"Katie," he said, "I've been wanting to talk to you."

She looked at him, then turned her face away. "About what?"

Her voice was sharp, and he considered postponing the talk, but there were few times as private as the present, so he leaned over beside her. "We haven't had much time to talk, have we?"

"No, Barney."

Her spare reply was not encouraging, and he floundered. For a time he told her of the work he was doing, and in turn asked her about hers in Maoli. But there was an uneasiness in the conversation.

Finally he plunged in. "I guess it's been hard for you since Irene went home."

"Yes. She was a great comfort to me."

"Sure. A person needs somebody. I mean, it's no good being alone all the time, is it?"

"It's very difficult, but the Lord is with us."

"That's true, but like Stanley's always said, two are better than one." He felt like a man walking over broken glass. *Got to do it now or else*, he thought. "Katie, you and I have been real close, and we've gone through a lot together."

Her eyes focused on him, and her lips softened as she

thought of earlier days. "Yes, Barney," she said. "I think of those days all the time."

"Well, so do I. And I worry about you, Katie."

"You do? I didn't know that."

He licked his lips, trying to find the right way to say what he had to. She was very beautiful as she stood there. He had always been aware of her beauty, but never had he seen her looking so soft and vulnerable. It made him nervous, somehow, but he straightened up and said as firmly as he could, "Yes, Katie, I *do* worry about you. I think about you all alone at the station. It's bad enough when you've got help, but you don't have anyone." He hesitated, then said, "And I think you need someone, Katie."

"You do, Barney?" Her eyes were wide and her lips slightly parted. She seemed to be totally immersed in his gaze, waiting for something.

"Y-yes, I do," he stammered. His voice was unsteady because he suddenly thought of the night in the village when he had kissed her. The moonlight had been shining that night, just like it was now, shedding silver rays over her. He was annoyed to discover that his hands were unsteady and he could not get his mind on Del's problem.

"What are you thinking of, Barney?" Katie whispered.

"Well—Katie—I was just wondering—"

"Yes? What is it, Barney? You can tell me."

"Well . . . have you ever thought of marrying?"

Katie stood transfixed, in mute silence. After a while, she nodded. "Yes, I have thought of it."

She looked up at him, her eyes luminous and her expression sweet and expectant.

"Well," Barney blurted out, "had you ever thought of marrying Del?" She stood so rigid he thought she had not understood him, so he said hurriedly, "He—he really thinks the world of you, Katie. And he's such a fine man! He'd make a wonderful husband!"

She dropped her head, refusing to look at him. "Is that what you came to talk to me about?" she asked quietly.

"Well—Del asked me to talk to you—"

With a jerk Katie lifted her head. She had tears in her eyes, and his heart sank. But she dashed them away and in a voice filled with anger cried out, "Do you think I'm so anxious to get married that I'll take anyone, Barney Winslow?"

"Oh, no—" he stammered, surprised at the anger he saw in her.

"You're worried about *me*? Well, why don't you worry about yourself?" she spewed. "Poor Katie doesn't have a husband, so Good Old Barney has to find her one!" She stamped on the deck, jolting Barney at the sound. But she wasn't finished.

"You're so busy with your matrimonial agency you don't even *know* what's happening to you!"

"Happening to me? What—"

Katie shook her head, her eyes bright and her voice sharp. "You were quite a man when you came here. Kwi Balee, the white antelope! But what are you now? You're a lap dog for that woman!"

If Katie had not been humiliated, she would never have said such things, but now the dam had broken, and for five minutes she stood there shaking her finger in Barney Winslow's face, telling him what a poor imitation of a missionary he was. She ended by saying, "You're a straw man, Barney Winslow! When Dorothy pulls your little chain, you start barking the tune she wants to hear."

She was weeping now, but didn't know it. As the tears ran down her face, she doubled up her fist and struck him in the chest. "You're worried about *me*? Don't bother! Worry about yourself! You've sold out, Barney! Sold out to a woman! All God did for you—and you gave it up!"

Then she whirled and ran off, leaving Barney alone on the deck.

He had taken terrible blows in the ring—but never one like this. Paralyzed by the verbal onslaught, he looked at her retreating figure in unbelief. Her words echoed in his ears: *All God did for you—and you gave it up.*

All night he walked the deck, searching for peace. Yet when dawn began to fire the eastern sky, Barney was still walking—still without peace. *What can I tell Del?* he thought. But another question plagued him more: *How did I get to this place in my life?* A depressing silence mocked him. There was no answer—not then or in the following days.

CHAPTER TWENTY-TWO

"I'VE GOT TO GO!"

★ ★ ★ ★

The *Falcon* moved slowly, touching several ports, then headed back up the coast toward Monrovia. On their final evening, Captain Borg threw a farewell party for the passengers. The dining room was decorated with flowers Borg had managed to purchase at their last port of call.

"Oh, how beautiful, Captain!" Pearl cried. "I never knew captains were so romantic!"

"Say, this is all right!" Slim Ranken said, joining Pearl and the captain. "Just like Del Monico!" he exclaimed, admiring the flowers and the white tablecloths. He guided Pearl to her seat and took the place next to her. "I hope the food is as good as the decorations," he grinned.

When Katie arrived, she went immediately to an empty place between Pearl and Del. What a lovely sight she was in a blue dress that perfectly reflected the color of her eyes. Avoiding any eye contact with Barney, she unfolded her napkin, smiled at the captain, and directed her conversation at Lieutenant Bjelland, who sat across from her. The young officer was flattered, and wondered how such an attractive young woman could bury herself in the depths of Africa.

The food was good and the entertainment amusing. Four of the crew had formed a quartet and made up in enthusiasm what they lacked in skill. Dorothy sat between Barney and the captain, and, true to her provocative personality, completely charmed Borg.

At the end of the meal, Captain Borg rose and acknowledged the joy of having such a wonderful group of passengers and invited them to make other voyages on the *Falcon*. "In all my years at sea," he said, "I've never had such a delightful experience."

Ranken spoke on behalf of the passengers, and seemed happy and far more relaxed than at any time since his wife had died. When he came to the end of his speech, he hesitated, giving Pearl a questioning look, then went on. "This has been a good voyage in many ways, but it will be more special to me than to any of you." Smiling at Pearl, he continued. "Let me share with you that Pearl and I have become engaged to be married."

There was a short burst of applause and a rush to congratulate the couple.

"I'm so happy for you, Pearl!" Katie whispered. "You two will have a wonderful life!"

When everyone was seated again, Captain Borg brought out a bottle of wine to toast the engaged pair. To look at Borg's beaming face, one would have thought he was responsible for the happy event.

Later, back in their cabin, Pearl grew quiet, and after they were lying in their beds waiting for sleep, she said, "I feel very strange about this, Katie. Somehow—it seems too soon."

Katie rolled over, propped her head on her hand, and said cheerfully, "No, it's not too soon." She smiled, realizing Pearl needed encouragement. "You and Slim love and need each other. And I think Tobe and Lily would be happier about it than any of us."

"Oh, Katie, do you? I've been so miserable!" Pearl sniffled into her handkerchief. "I know what people will say. I can hear it now: 'Well, he needed a wife and she needed a husband.' But it's more than that, Katie!"

"I'm sure it is," Katie assured. "You and Slim are right for each other and, I believe, in the center of God's will." She continued to reassure her, Pearl's tension lessening as she listened. "Don't pay any attention to what anyone says. It doesn't matter what they think as long as you know God's leading. After all, a man and a woman—a husband and wife—have their own life. And nobody can take that away. At least," she said very softly, "that's what I've always hoped marriage would be like."

"You're so good with people, Katie!" Pearl said. "You always know just what to say to those who are hurting." She hesitated for a moment, aware she was touching a sensitive area. "I wish I could comfort you. I know you've been hurt in some way."

"I'm all right, Pearl. Or I will be when I get back to my station."

Pearl had not been ignorant of the little drama aboard ship. She had discerned that something, or someone, had driven a wedge between Barney and Katie, but she couldn't mention it. She reached over and touched Katie's arm. "It's going to be fine. You'll see."

The next day when they debarked from the ship, the Hansens were at the dock to meet Dorothy. They were surprised but pleased at Slim and Pearl's engagement and insisted that the wedding be held in the Hansens' church.

"When will the wedding be?" Mrs. Hansen asked.

"Not soon enough for me," Slim smiled. "Will a week be too soon, Pearl?"

"Oh no. That's not very long—but I'll love it!" Pearl turned to Katie. "You'll stay and help me, won't you?"

Katie wanted nothing more than to escape back to her station, but she agreed. "Of course, Pearl."

The week flew by. Katie offered to make the wedding gown, but since she was not an accomplished seamstress, she sought the aid of one of the local women. Whenever Katie was free, Del didn't miss an opportunity to find a way to make his speech—without success . . . again and again!

Katie saw little of Barney, for he submerged himself in the mission work, driving himself so hard that Myron Hansen cautioned him. "My boy, your zeal is commendable, but you can't last at such a pace! You must learn to be more moderate!"

Dorothy, always ready to wield her charm, intervened. "Barney," she said sweetly, "Pearl and Slim have felt bad that they've seen so little of you. Couldn't you leave some of the work for a few days? It would mean so much to them."

"All right, I'll try."

True to his word, Barney attended the festivities the latter part of the week. He saw Katie often, and though they carried on an amiable conversation, underneath both could feel the discord. Outwardly, it was as if they had made an agreement: "All right, we had a terrible scene, but we're going to pretend that it never happened."

Only Pearl saw the strain in their relationship. She never spoke of it, however, but it grieved her.

Dorothy was exuberant. She had not enjoyed the cruise, but now she was caught up with plans to expand the mission and sought Barney's help in the minutest detail. Every day they worked on the project, often with her father and mother. Her manipulating, controlling spirit raised its ugly head whenever possible, expertly guiding the noose. "Barney," she would say, "this is bigger than Monrovia! We can use this as a model. The whole country is wide open, waiting for something like this. And we can do it, can't we? You and I?"

Barney always agreed, and at times he seemed to catch some of Dorothy's enthusiasm. He spoke of it to Del, and when Stanley Beecham arrived for the wedding, Barney went over the details with him. Beecham agreed that it was a noble idea and promised to help as he was able.

The wedding supper was held the night before the wedding. The only one absent was Awful Gardner. Barney kept his eyes peeled for the man's arrival, for he had sent a special letter by a fast runner, asking Awful to come. He knew Gardner was fond of both Ranken and Pearl, so he couldn't understand why the Australian had not come.

It was a lively party, lasting until ten o'clock. When it was over, Barney still waited for Awful. He walked around the grounds, checking the gate several times, but no Gardner. His absence made the darkness over the land even darker. At eleven o'clock Barney went to the kitchen, made a pot of tea—and waited.

He slumped in his chair and watched the pendulum on the large clock on the mantel tick the time away. His eyes were burning, his heart was heavy, and his thoughts a chaotic mixture of the mission, Dorothy, Awful, the interior, Katie—God. After a while, he grew sleepy and finally dozed off.

For an hour he slept, then awakened with a start at the sound of footsteps.

Katie had entered the kitchen, unaware that anyone was there. At the sight of Barney she wanted to flee, but it was too late.

"I didn't mean to disturb you," she said, awkwardly shifting from one foot to the other, not knowing what to say or do.

Barney felt equally ill at ease. "I've been hoping Awful would come," he said. He looked at the stove. "I made some tea if you'd like some."

"No, I just wanted some water." She walked over to the large barrel with fresh drinking water, drank a glass of it, and headed for the door. When she got there, she paused, then swung around to face him.

"I'm sorry for the way I spoke to you on the ship," she said evenly. "I had no business meddling in your private affairs."

Barney had thought of her words for days—even now he could quote them word for word. But he said only, "That's all right."

"No, it's *not* all right!" Katie shook her head, her back rigid. "No one has the right to speak to another as I spoke to you." She had thought many times of coming to him, of making an apology, but her nerve had failed. But now she had blundered into him, and she set her jaw, saying, "Who am I to tell you what God is doing in your life? I was so judgmental! And I ask you to forgive me."

Barney got to his feet, his face haggard. "Why, Katie, you have my forgiveness if you think you need it."

"Didn't the things I said hurt you?" she demanded.

"Maybe a little, but that didn't last long."

Katie took a deep breath. "Do you know *why* I lashed out at you like I did?"

"Why—you think I'm doing the wrong thing."

"I've always thought that, Barney," Katie said honestly. "But I never said a word to you, did I?"

"No. But I knew how you felt."

Katie nodded, and wished she'd never come to the kitchen. But she had to spill it all out—now. "I said all those things to you," she said quietly, "because I was angry and humiliated."

Barney looked into her eyes, trying to read her. "I knew that. I just didn't know why."

"You really *don't* know? Not even now?"

"No. I just knew you hated me."

"Oh, Barney!" Katie said, shaking her head. "You don't know *anything* about women, do you?"

"Obviously not," he replied soberly. "What made you so mad?"

She stared at him silently. "I was humiliated and angry because when you asked me if I'd ever thought of getting married—" She broke off, her face flushed and strained. "I thought you were going to ask me to marry *you*!"

"Marry *me*!" Barney's jaw fell in absolute shock. "Why, Katie, I'd never ask you to marry *me*!"

"Yes, Barney, I know that now," she said. "But I didn't then."

Befuddled, Barney burst out, "Why, Katie, you'd never marry a dolt like me!"

Katie studied him a moment. "Well," she said, "I never will now. I suppose you'll be marrying Dorothy."

"Why, we never talk about such things!"

The clock ticked loudly as they stared at each other, and then her face softened. "Barney, this will be the last time we'll see each other for a long time. I'm glad I was able to tell you how awful I've felt over the way I spoke to you. Good-night."

She turned to leave, and he sprang forth like a leopard to his prey. "Wait!" He grabbed her hand. "Katie—" He took a deep breath and expelled it slowly. "I've felt terrible since that night. I don't know what God wants of me, but I know what I want from you. I want what we used to have! We've been such great friends! Can't we be that again?"

Katie shook her head. "A man and a woman can be friends—but when you marry, things will be different. They have to be, Barney. Don't you see that?" Her voice was gentle. The confession seemed to have relieved a great pressure that had burdened her, and now she could say with a good spirit, "Let's have our memories, Barney, but let it end here. Goodbye, and God bless you!"

Then she was gone.

Barney wanted to run after her, but knew that would not do. He returned to the table and sat down, mulling over her strange confession. He had always been a simple man, singleminded. But the last months had been confusing, and he longed for the days when life was simple.

Life had been simple at the Rescue Mission—simple on the station at Gropaka. But since he had come to Monrovia, life had gotten so complex that he could not think clearly.

Finally he got up and walked around the compound, longing for Awful to come to rescue him. *I could talk to Awful,* he thought over and over. *He could tell me what's the matter with me! He always knew me better than anyone else.*

But Gardner didn't come—not that night and not for the wedding. Barney moved through the day, saying the right things, but his heart was like lead. The bride looked beautiful and so did Dorothy in her new dress designed just for the wedding. Barney joined in the laughter and rejoicing, but it was all superficial, and he was relieved when it was all over.

Two days after the Ranken wedding an exhausted runner came staggering through the gates of the mission compound. The word was relayed to Barney, and he rushed out to the well, where the dust-covered native was gulping down the water.

"Not so much!" Myron Hansen was warning him, then turned to the small crowd. "Bad news, I'm afraid."

"What is it?" Barney demanded.

"The situation at Gropaka—it's terrible. This runner says Gardner has been carrying on a feud with one of the Pahn tribes. Chief's name is Batoni."

"I know him," Barney said. "Know *about* him, that is. He's bad. What about Gardner?"

Hansen shook his head. "He's critically ill—or so this man says. The way he tells it, Batoni or one of his witch doctors has put a curse on poor Gardner. That sort of thing. But he's very ill, at any rate."

"I'll leave immediately," Barney said.

"That's not all," Hansen said reluctantly. "It seems that Batoni's tribe has kidnapped one of our people." He turned to Katie. "Your servant, Bestman. Batoni is going to kill him."

Katie's face became ashen. "I'm going to him."

"Neither of you must go!" Hansen cried in frustration. "It's politically explosive, don't you see? We can't afford to take part in these tribal wars, and that's what will happen if you go trying to get your servant back."

"Father's right," Dorothy said. "We must notify the authorities."

"Notify anybody you please," Barney said evenly. "I'm leaving in an hour."

That deadline was too ambitious, for it took until the next morning to get ready. Dorothy and her father argued against the journey most of the night, but Barney kept repeating, "I've got to go!"

Dorothy eventually gave up, dejected, but her father had discovered a new quality in Barney. "You've found out that there's some part of that young fellow you can't touch, daughter—and I like him the better for it!"

At dawn the party was ready to leave, including Del, when he heard the news. That made three—Barney, Katie, Del. After a quick breakfast they were off.

They took a surfboat to Carroway, and pushed on by foot toward Gropaka. They talked little, prayed much, and walked as fast as they could. As they trudged along all day, Katie recalled an earlier trip when she'd been forced to ride in a hammock most of the way.

The evening of October 15 found them a few hours from Gropaka. As they made camp, Barney said, "This may be our last night on earth, you know."

Del nodded. "Blessed are the dead who die in the Lord."

"No," Katie countered. "God will deliver us. He will deliver Awful and Bestman, too."

"Let's trust so," Barney said. They sat around the fire, praying and reading the Scriptures before settling down for the night. Exhausted from the whirlwind events, they slept, oblivious to the curious animals sniffing out these huge mounds of humanity. What would tomorrow bring? Life? Death?

CHAPTER TWENTY-THREE

THE JUJU HOUSE

★ ★ ★ ★

"Oh my, 'tis good to see you, dear boy!"

A wave of relief swept Barney when he entered the center of the village and found Awful sitting at the well instead of lying in bed, unconscious and burning with fever. The tension that had been building since word had come from Gropaka lifted, and Barney cried, "Awful! We heard you were dying!"

"No. I'm not plannin' on it!" he laughed, turning to greet the others. "Del, how fit you look! And Katie, how wonderful to see you!"

Katie took his hand, noting the bony surface—not strong and wiry as usual. "We were worried about you. The messenger said you were deathly ill."

"Oh, not as bad as all that!" But despite his protests, they could see he was not well. Though he had always been thin, now he was almost emaciated. He looked years older, his face was lined, and his eyes sunken into his skull. He moved slowly and carefully, like a very old man—or a very sick one—so unlike his vigorous self.

"Come along, now," he urged, "let's have a spot of tea." He hobbled through the village to the small house he and Barney had built.

Along the way the villagers called "Kwi Balee!" while reaching out for Barney's hand.

Perceptive as usual, Katie noticed that though the natives greeted him, they seemed frightened, so she asked quietly, "What's wrong with them, Barney? What are they afraid of?"

"I don't know, but something has happened. Let's wait till we talk with Awful."

Inside the house, Awful had already made up a pot of tea when the rest got there. Barney wasted no time. "Awful, what's happened? You've been very ill. Was it malaria? And what's wrong with the people? They're scared to death."

"Ah, now, one question at a time, laddie," Gardner said. He sipped his tea with a trembling hand, his eyes drooping drowsily. Finally he put his cup down and began to speak. "Well, now, I did have me quite a bad time a couple of weeks ago. Matter of fact, I'm still not too well."

It was the first time Barney had ever heard Awful utter a negative word, and he leaned forward. "Malaria?"

"Actually, it wasn't so much like that," Gardner replied slowly. "I didn't have no fever, or at least not so much. If it was just malaria, I wouldn't have thought much of it."

"What was it like, Awful?" Katie asked.

Gardner blinked his eyes several times, fighting sleep. "More of a—a spiritual thing, it was. Hard to describe, you know. Once I had a bad accident back home and was given large doses of laudanum. You know what that does to a chap! You get all groggy . . . can't sleep, yet not really awake either. That's sort of what it was like." He looked disturbed as he tried to recall the experience. He bit his lower lip. "It was like that—only worse."

"The runner said Chief Batoni had put a curse on you. Is that true?" Del asked.

"I'm not sayin' that ain't so, lad." Awful drawled out his words. "We've all seen things out here that nobody would believe on Water Street. And Batoni would do me in if he could, you can believe!"

"What's been the trouble with Batoni?" Barney pressed.

"It's the juju, I suppose. Since you left it's been pretty lively."

The Pahn people, like many tribes in Africa, believed strongly in fetishes, a type of idol worship. They wore fetishes around their necks or about the waists, and often hung the charms above the doorways of their huts. Special celebrations, directed by the local witch doctor, were held in honor of the large fetish. On moonlit nights the people would sometimes sing and dance all night, accompanied by the beating of drums.

Most of the people were very superstitious. By wearing fetishes on their bodies, they believed they could be protected from wild animals and hostile tribes. They thought the fetishes would keep sickness away and assure long life. Even babies and little children would be decked with charms hung about their necks.

"You and me have been tryin' to get our people to get rid of them things ever since we came to Gropaka," Awful said to Barney. "So, about a month ago, I decided to meet the thing head-on. I wanted to show the people that the Lord Jesus is the true God, and I kept askin' the Lord to help me."

"It's the same in my village," Katie said. "They're afraid to get rid of the fetishes because the witch doctors tell them they'll die if they do."

"So they do," Gardner nodded. "Well, it happened this way. I called a meetin' with Chief Lodi and his head men, and I said, 'Chief, it ain't right to have that big heathen shrine in the same village with a Christian mission station.' And I told him he ought to get rid of the big juju house."

Barney remembered the juju house. It was built in the form of an arch made of wooden poles and thatched with grass. On each side of the structure was a bench made of bamboo poles; and on one seat sat an image of a man made with goat's hair, shells and mud. On the opposite side were two earthen jars that served as beehives. The bees belonged to the fetish and were considered sacred.

"What did Lodi say?" Barney asked.

"Well, he made quite a speech, lad," Awful nodded emphatically. "I was wishin' you wuz there while he was talkin'. He said he'd heard both of us preach that our God could do anything— open the eyes of the blind, cleanse lepers, even raise the dead. Then he said, 'You want us to give up our old gods. First, we want to see your God do these things.' Quite a speech," Awful smiled. "And when he was through I didn't have the foggiest idea of what to do."

"We've all heard that sort of thing in one fashion or another," Del nodded. "I never know what to say. It wouldn't be right to get into any sort of competition, would it? Beg God to do miracles just to satisfy the people?"

"That didn't even work for Moses," Katie added. "And when the Israelites saw God destroy Egypt, when they went through the Red Sea on dry land—even that didn't make them strong believers. They just went on complaining."

"Right-O!" Awful nodded. "Exactly my thought. But at the same time, Lodi had a point. Jesus *did* perform miracles, and we've all seen God do the impossible, haven't we, now?"

"Wish I'd been here with you, Awful," Barney said quietly. "Though I don't know what I could have done. What happened next?"

"I done a lot of prayin', but for a few days it seemed like nothin' wuz goin' to change. Then Chief Batoni comes in with some of his witch doctors."

"Is he as wicked as they say, Awful?" Katie asked. "I've heard he practices human sacrifice."

"He's deep into witchcraft himself," Gardner nodded. His voice was getting scratchy, so he took a sip of tea. "And his tribe *is* powerful, much more warlike than Lodi's people. All the local tribes are scared of him, so when he come to Gropaka, it just about put poor Chief Lodi under!"

"We heard what Batoni did to the village over near the coast," Del said. "When they crossed him, he took his band and massacred the whole village."

"Yes, he done that, and he's lookin' for an excuse to take over this village," Awful nodded. "He hates Christians particularly bad, he does. When I went to the meetin' he wuz havin' with Lodi, I thought he'd do me in right then! He jumped up, pulled out his knife and made a run at me, yellin' and screamin' like they do. Well, I just said, 'Jesus, take care of your old servant,' and he finally cooled down. But he kept threatenin' Lodi, tellin' him if he didn't run me out of the village, he'd have bad luck."

"What did Lodi say?" Barney asked.

"Oh, he tried to straddle the fence," Awful shrugged. "He's a good man, but scared stiff of Batoni. The argument went on for hours, with Batoni sayin' I had to go and Lodi tryin' to find a way to let me stay." Gardner grimaced as if recalling that dreadful scene.

He shook his head, a look of amazement on his face. "Well, while the two chiefs were debatin' the thing, we heard the death wail. Went through me like a knife, it did, just like it always does! Well, somebody come and told Lodi his favorite wife Laota had just died."

"Poor woman!" Barney murmured. "She was a leper. Nothing but a skeleton! I've prayed for her many times, but she just got worse."

"Yes, she was a good woman, but sufferin' a lot." He sighed and went on. "We all got up and went to Lodi's hut, even Batoni. I hated to go! You know how I always detested the way these people treat their dead!"

The tribe did not bury their dead. Instead, they carried the corpses to a fetish grove and left them for the hyenas, jackals, and vultures to devour. Consequently, every village that practiced this type of rite reeked with the sickening smell of decaying human flesh. But the people clung to their custom.

Awful continued. "There wuz a lot of women at Lodi's house, cryin' and wailin', and there wuz Lodi's wife, all laid out on a trash heap, wasted to mere skin and bone. But then I noticed something." Gardner's eyes grew bright. "I saw her muscles were twitchin', so I says to Lodi, 'She ain't dead, Chief. I seen her move.' "

"But Lodi said, 'That's nothing. It will stop soon.' "

"I looked at the woman, and suddenly I thought I could hear God speakin' to my heart and He was sayin', 'I'm goin' to show my power to these people. Pray for this woman.' You can imagine what I thought! The whole thing was so impossible!"

Katie remembered when she had faced the witch doctor with the cup of poison. She leaned forward. "What did you do?"

"Do, lass? There was nothin' for it but to trust God! So I said to the chief, 'God is able to raise your wife.' Well, that set off something I can tell you! Batoni laughed at me, the poor chief was dumbstruck, but I was in too far to back out. So I put my hands on the woman and began to pray. I mean *pray.* If ever this old man prayed a fervent prayer, that was it! I can't say how long, but it was a long, long time. I more or less lost track of time, because when I came to myself, it was dusk. Most of the people were gone. Only Chief Lodi and a few faithful ones still there."

Gardner stopped, seemingly overcome. When he lifted his head, tears filled his eyes. "The woman's body began to jerk in hard spasms, and then her eyes opened and she spoke to her husband! Oh, there wuz rejoicin', I tell you!"

"What did Batoni and his witch doctors say to that?" Barney asked.

"Well, he'd gone back to his village, but when he heard about it, he scoffed and said the woman wuzn't really dead. He'd *have* to say that, of course!"

"Is she well, the chief's wife?" Del inquired.

"Yes, she's gettin' better all the time, muscles fillin' out, walkin' stronger, even leprosy disappearin'." Gardner seemed to be tired, but his eyes were bright. "It's been a great thing for the village. Everyone knew she was dyin', and now she goes about tellin' the people about the miracle, how Jesus raised her from the dead.' He frowned, adding, "Of course, the trouble with Batoni started when I asked the chief to get rid of the juju house, which he did."

"I noticed it was gone," Barney said. "That thing was a monument to Satan! I'm glad he got rid of it."

"Yes, but Batoni wuzn't," Gardner told them. "They say when he heard about it, he swore that he'd kill me. Then when I got sick right after that, everyone thought his curse wuz workin' on me."

"You had a hard time of it," Katie said sympathetically. "But what about Bestman? We heard that he'd been kidnapped by Batoni."

"I'm afraid that's true," Gardner nodded. "He heard about the miracle God did and came down to see the chief's wife. He's a relative of hers, you know. Well, he went wild for joy, my word, he did! But the next day he was gone. I asked around and found out that he'd left to go preach the Good News. But he went straight to Batoni's village, and that old pirate locked 'im up."

"We heard that Batoni was going to kill him," Katie said. "We've got to do something!"

"Yes, we do indeed, lass." He had a determined look in his

eyes as he spoke. "I would have gone to get him before this, but I'm too weak. And these people are still terrified of what will happen to them if they cross Batoni."

"I'll go first thing in the morning," Barney said grimly. "We can't let him stay in the hands of Batoni."

"Ah, that's my dear boy!" Awful smiled. "I've been prayin' that the Good Lord would help me get to that village, and He's sent you."

"You're in *no* condition to make that trip, Awful!" Del protested.

"I've got four good men who've agreed to carry me." Awful looked at him defiantly. "I was goin' to start in the mornin' by myself anyway. But now you can come along with me."

The argument was sharp, but brief. Nothing would dissuade Gardner. "You'd be better off prayin' than arguin' with me." A humorous light touched his eyes. "God may answer your prayers to save Bestman, but I'll never let you change *my* mind!"

"You are a rebel!" Barney smiled. The sight of Awful, sick as he was, brought a sense of joy to him, and he hugged the thin man, his friend. "I'd lock you up, but you'd probably pick the locks!"

Awful looked Barney straight in the eyes. "I've missed you, dear boy—indeed, I have!"

Barney's eyes burned, and he turned his head away. "Katie, I'll get you a place to sleep. Del, you can stay with Awful and me."

Barney took Katie to a hut where a middle-aged woman was cooking over an open fire, and called, "Laota!"

Overjoyed to see Barney, she dropped her stick and grabbed his hands as he came near. She talked so fast Katie couldn't understand a word.

"Katie, this is Chief Lodi's wife. You'll stay with her tonight."

Katie fixed her eyes on Laota and stammered, "I—I thank God that He touched you, sister."

Bobbing her head and smiling broadly, Laota chattered on.

"She'll talk you to death, Katie," Barney smiled. To Laota he said, "I'm so happy God has made you well."

Tears ran down her cheeks, and she said in broken English, "God Him good. Bring back Laota from dark place!"

She beckoned to Katie. "Come. I show you bed."

Turning to leave, Barney said, "I'm going back to talk with Awful, Katie. He really looks weak."

"I'll go with you, Barney," she insisted. She took Laota's hands in hers. "I will come later," she promised.

Katie and Barney started toward the mission house, waving to the smiling faces along the way. "You'll never change his mind," Katie said soberly. "He's very stubborn."

"I don't want you to go to Batoni's village, Katie," Barney said abruptly. "It's too dangerous."

"Oh yes?" Katie set her jaw adamantly. "I'm just as stubborn as you are, Barney. What did you say over and over to Dorothy when she begged you not to come here? *I've got to go!* Wasn't that it?"

By now the morning sun was steaming hot and Barney suggested, "Let's sit in the shade for a while." It was really an excuse to give him time to answer Katie's probing argument. "That sun's burning me up," he went on. "Haven't been in the bush for a while." They dropped down on a fallen log beneath a spreading tree.

Katie knew Barney was troubled. And she guessed it was mostly about her safety, so she said, "Barney, if you clutter up your mind with worries about me, you won't be able to pray. Right now we all need to be seeking God. It's going to be dangerous, of course, but what isn't dangerous in this place? Why, I'm more afraid of malaria than I am of that old witch doctor of a chief!"

As she spoke, he watched the animated movements of her face. Her skin had sunburned deeply from the intense heat. Beads of perspiration gathered on her upper lip and over the fine fatigue lines etched on the edges of her mouth. *She's very attractive, in spite of the harsh climate*, Barney thought.

He dropped his eyes, lest she read his mind. "You're right, I suppose. But we are in a tough situation for sure. There're no policemen out here, Katie. Batoni is like all these warlike chiefs, as unstable as gun powder. One spark and they blow up. He could have a fit of anger and kill all of us. It's happened before out here."

"We knew coming here wouldn't be easy, didn't we? Remember how we used to talk about it at the mission?"

"I remember."

Barney's eyes were half shut against the brilliance of the sun. His sweat-soaked shirt clung to his body, the swelling muscles of his chest and shoulders clearly outlined. He was strong physically, Katie knew, but in the craggy planes of his face and the steady light of his brown eyes, there was another kind of strength. That was what had drawn her to him in the early days, and she realized it was still there. He had lost his way, but underneath he had not changed. This thought made her smile.

"What makes you smile?"

"Oh, I'm just thankful that I'm here," she said quickly, hiding the undercurrent of emotion. "God's been good to me. I was so lost, and He brought me out of the pit. All of this—" She waved at the primitive village—stench, poverty, clutter. "Why, it's not as bad as New York, Barney. It's a little dirtier, maybe, but the people long for God. I think our people have too much. They have so many *things*, they crowd God out of their lives. These people don't have anything, so Jesus can find a place in them. They make room for Him."

"That's the way I've always thought about it," Barney replied. "Andy, he's able to see the big picture. He can think of the entire continent of Africa, but all I can think of is Bestman or maybe Laota." He laughed shortly, ashamed at his lack of vision.

But Katie said cautiously, "That's the way Andy is." She wanted to add, *And Dorothy too.* But she was too wise for that. Instead, she said, "Do you have any plan? About getting Bestman away from Batoni, I mean?"

"Not even a part of one! How about you?"

"My mind's a blank!" she confessed. Then the humor of the situation struck her. "Here we go—one woman, three men, one so sick he has to be carried. And we're going to march into the village where the most wicked chief in Africa wants to kill all Christians!" She laughed aloud and shook her hair free, letting it cascade down her back.

He watched her for a moment, grinning. "You're good for a man, Katie Sullivan! Most women would be nagging to take them back to safety. That's what I saw in you back in New York."

She flushed at his praise, and jumped to her feet. "Come on," she commanded. "I want to see what's left of the juju house."

He led the way to the charred remains of the structure. In no time they were joined at the site by the children of the village.

"Kwi Balee, you remember honey?" One of the young boys spoke up.

"The honey in the juju house that was here?" Barney asked.

"Yes! When chief burn juju house down, bees, they leave. I wait. When fire go, I eat honey."

"Was it good?" Barney smiled.

"Very good! Some peoples say, 'You die!' But me, I sing song you teach." He opened his mouth wide and sang, "Oh, there's honey in the rock! There's honey in the rock!" Then he grinned widely. "Very good honey, Kwi Balee!"

"Good for you, Luke!" Barney laughed, patting him on the head.

"He's a fine boy, Luke," Barney said as he and Katie continued toward the mission house. "I baptized him last year."

"These people love you, Barney," Katie said soberly.

Her comment triggered something deep within him and he whirled around, his eyes sweeping over the village. "I *miss* this place, Katie!" The words burst out like a gusher. "I wish—" He stopped and his shoulders slumped. "But a man can't be every-where."

"God only wants us in one place."

God only wants us in one place. The phrase echoed in his mind as they walked along slowly. He kept his head down until finally he nodded and lifted his eyes to hers. "And all we have to do is find that *one* place."

She didn't answer, for by then they were at their destination.

"Hey," Del cried as the two entered, "this is the best rat stew I've ever tasted. Better sit down before it's all gone."

The thought turned her stomach, but she took a chair across from Barney and cautiously tasted the helping Del dished up for her. Surprised, she said, "It *is* good!"

"You've come a long way, Katie Sullivan," Awful smiled. "I remember when you had to douse rat soup with Stanley Bee-cham's hot sauce to get even one mouthful down."

Katie nodded. "I guess we've all come a long way, Awful. But we've got a ways to go yet."

They spent the day quietly, mostly in prayer. Barney implored, "Lord, you know how unable I am. But *you* are able, so no matter what it costs me, let us bring Bestman back with us." Awful had a difficult time, dropping off to sleep, then awakening just as abruptly.

That night after Katie had gone to Chief Lodi's house and Awful was asleep, Del said, "Barney, remember when I asked you to help me with Katie?"

"Sure do." Barney turned to look ruefully at his friend. "I made hash out of it, didn't I?"

Del's honest face broke into a grin. "Well, you didn't have much to work with. Anyway, thanks for trying."

"Want me to try again?" Barney asked carefully.

"Nope."

The blanket statement of resignation took Barney off guard. "What's happened to you, Del?"

Saunders ducked his head, then lifted it again. "Why, I found out three things. One, I'm not in love with Katie. She's a great girl, but not for me. Two, she's not in love with me. So you can take down your sign as a marriage broker, Winslow!"

Barney smiled with relief. "Guess you know best, Del. But what's the third thing?"

A strange expression flashed across his face. "Well, Barney, that third thing, I'm going to let *you* find out for yourself."

CHAPTER TWENTY-FOUR

POWERS OF DARKNESS

★ ★ ★ ★

Batoni's village was only fifteen miles from Gropaka, but the pathway was steep, winding through a series of serrated mountain ranges and crossing two swift rivers. The rivers were down, so the small party forded them with no difficulty. But the porters carrying Gardner were slowed by the dense undergrowth. At times they had to get on their hands and knees to plow through the mass of vines; and late that afternoon, Barney decided to make camp beside a small river. As the porters built a fire, Barney took his shotgun and headed for the riverbank.

Del looked down the river where Barney had disappeared, then at Katie resting nearby. "Katie, did you know I asked Barney to help me court you?" He'd made up his mind to confess the affair to her on the trip, and took the first chance.

His bluntness amused Katie. She studied his open features, and said, "He asked me to marry you, Del. Why didn't you ask me yourself?"

"Aw, Katie, I don't know!" Del pulled up a handful of grass and threw it down with a sudden gesture. He grinned, his red hair standing out against the green wall of the jungle. "It was a crazy idea I had. I've always liked you, and I was lonesome."

"That's the way I've felt about you, Del," she replied gently. "I've been a little lonesome myself." Then she asked curiously,

"Why'd you ask Barney to do your courting?"

Surprised at the question, his brow furrowed. "Why, you and him are so close, Katie. It made sense to me at the time." With a sly smile, he added, "But now I know better. The thing I don't understand is why he keeps hanging around Dorothy Hansen."

"She's an attractive woman, Del. It's natural that Barney would be drawn to her. And," she continued, though the subject made her uncomfortable, "it looks like he just might marry her. Slim and Pearl are married. That leaves you and me as the only single ones left, Del." She laughed shortly. "Maybe I *ought* to marry you!"

Alarmed, Del protested, "No, Katie, that won't work!"

Surprised at the sheer dismay on his face, she laughed. "Oh, don't worry, Del," she said, putting her hand on his arm. "I'm not going to chase you down and make you marry me." But she was curious. "You *did* want to marry me. What changed your mind?"

"Like I told Barney last night," Del replied, "I found out three things, Katie. You don't love me and I don't love you."

"That's two. What's the third?"

"That's for you and Barney to find out," he said enigmatically. Suddenly the sound of two explosions broke the silence that followed his answer, and he added, "I bet he got something. He never misses. Except with women," he added with a broad grin.

The sage comment was lost to the wind as the expert hunter returned with two fat waterfowl, which the natives roasted hurriedly. The missionaries sat around the fire, eating and discussing the next day's activity.

"Awful, what's your plan?" Barney asked. "I hope you've got one, because I haven't."

Gardner looked worse than he had before the journey. But his eyes were alert, and he said cheerfully, "My plan? Why, it's to rescue Bestman and bring 'im back!"

"That's a good *overall* plan, Awful," Barney agreed. "But I'd like to hear a few of the details."

"Haven't got none!" Gardner stared into the fire, watching

the dancing flames. "Most of the time when we make plans, we make 'em up and ask God to join us as we carry 'em out. We don't stop to think that God's got a plan already made. Now, what I'm tryin' to do is find out what *His* plan is—and get in on it. Because His don't fail like mine!"

Barney poked a burning log with a stick, sending a myriad of blazing sparks swirling into the air. The jungle was rank around them, and the raw odor of a thousand miles of trees was wafted on the slight breeze.

"Seems like most of us have trouble finding out what God's plans are, Awful. He doesn't always publish them in the morning paper."

"That's right enough," Gardner answered. "There's a little gem of a verse in the book of Deuteronomy, lad. It's the last verse of chapter twenty-nine. It says, 'The secret things belong unto the Lord our God: but those things which are revealed belong to us and to our children forever, that we may do all the words of the law.' "

Katie broke in. "Strange you should mention that verse, Awful. It's become one of my favorites."

"I don't get it," Del said, puzzled. "What *secret* things?"

"Anything that God, for His own purposes, doesn't want us to know," Awful replied. "Sometimes God has a plan, but it's so different than anything we could think of, we'd never follow it."

"Like what?" Barney asked. He had long ago discovered that the uneducated Australian heard from God and was able to get things from the Bible that most people missed completely.

Awful thought for a moment, then said, "Remember when Lazarus wuz sick? Mary and Martha sent for Jesus. Well, *their* plan wuz for Jesus to come runnin' and heal their brother. Nothin' wrong with that! I'd do the same thing. But God had somethin' else on His mind. Jesus said, 'This sickness is not unto death, but for the glory of God.' And so He stayed where He wuz—and let His friend Lazarus die."

"Pretty hard on Lazarus," Del observed.

"Aye, we'd think so," Awful agreed. "And hard on the sisters, too. So the first thing they say to Him wuz what?"

" 'If you'd been here our brother wouldn't have died,' " Katie answered. "Just about what I'd have said."

"Most of us would," Awful nodded. "But God had a 'secret' He didn't let the others in on. He intended to demonstrate His power by raisin' Lazarus from the dead. And He did just that."

Barney mulled over that for a few minutes. "So we don't need to be making God's plans for Him? That what you're saying?"

"No, it's not *that* simple, I'm thinkin'. Proverbs twenty-five has another little gem. It says, 'It is the glory of God to conceal a thing: but the honor of kings is to search out a matter.' "

"It sounds as if God likes to hide things," Katie spoke up.

"So He does," Gardner agreed. "And He likes for us to look for them. Don't ask me why, though. The apostle Paul called such things 'mysteries.' "

The walls of the jungle seemed to move closer to them, listening and watching as they huddled around the fire, each lost in thought. Barney gazed into the flames, remembering the way God had worked in his life. He raised his head, voicing his opinion. "I've discovered that God won't be backed into a corner. Sometimes we just have to wait. I guess that's what we'll do tomorrow, Awful. Just go in and see what God's plan is."

"A little bit scary," Del observed.

"Walking by faith is always an awesome thing, lad!" Awful said, his words fading away as he succumbed to the ever-present drowsiness.

★ ★ ★ ★

The next morning as they approached the collection of thatched huts on the outskirts of Batoni's village, they were confronted by a band of warriors armed with knives, spears, rusty guns and clubs. The leader, dressed in trousers and an ancient derby on his head, looked like a gladiator in western dress.

"That's Batoni," Awful whispered. He had insisted on leaving the porters behind and walking the last mile. Now, facing the invincible opponent, Gardner knew his frail frame could have been slain by a breath from the warrior's nostrils.

Batoni carried himself like a king, his bright intelligent eyes spewing out defiance. He advanced within ten feet of the four missionaries, paused, and threw his head up with an imperial gesture.

"Jesus men go away!" he cried, his command echoed by a rumble of voices from the other warriors. Two witch doctors were positioned directly behind Batoni, and at his side stood a young boy about sixteen, carrying a long spear with a wicked-looking spearhead. He took a stance like Batoni and appeared to be his son.

"Chief, we have come for our friend," Gardner said. He stood straight in the sunlight, his voice growing stronger as he spoke. "You give us our man, and we go away."

Batoni reached over and snatched the spear from the boy beside him and brandished it over his head. "White man go away!" he cried. The warriors picked up the cry and stomped the ground with one foot, making a booming sound. They held their weapons high and screamed again and again, "White man go away!"

Katie glanced at Barney and Del. Neither one seemed ruffled. Her own nerves were tightly strung, but she kept her face calm.

Finding it impossible to make himself heard over the tumult, Gardner simply fixed his gaze on Chief Batoni until the chief lifted his hand, quieting the natives. Then Gardner said, "We need a place to camp, Chief Batoni. When you are ready, we will talk."

Batoni glared, his eyes boring into Awful. Finally he nodded. One of the witch doctors came close and whispered in his ear, but he shook the man off and turned to his son. "Take them to old hut," he commanded, then whirled and stalked away.

The warriors made a path as the boy marched toward the huts, followed by the missionaries.

"That wuz pretty close, dear boy!" Awful said with relief. "I wuz afraid they'd cut us down without waitin' to talk."

"You handled it well," Del replied, brushing his sweaty

brow with his arm. "What now?"

"We wait until the meeting," Gardner replied. "They won't miss a chance like this! But it probably won't be until tomorrow, or maybe even a week."

"A week!" Katie gasped.

"Yes. That chief is pretty tough. He knows how to break a man's nerve. So our job is to just enjoy ourselves until he gets tired of tryin' to break us down."

The boy stopped just outside a hut with a peaked thatched roof. "You sleep here," he said and stood aside, watching them carefully.

Barney remained outside. "You speak good English. Where did you learn white man's talk?"

"Missionary teached me."

"Is he around here now?" Barney looked at him with surprise.

"No. We chop him."

The boy gazed at him insolently, proud of having eaten a missionary—although Barney suspected the chief's son was boasting about his part in the event.

"Did he teach you about God, this missionary?"

The boy hesitated, then shook his head and slapped his chest. "Bendi no listen to white man talk!"

He was the image of his father and was no doubt a pretty tough specimen, Barney noted. Young African males grew up quickly, and in a hard school. Bendi's teeth were already filed to a point, and his chest was ridged with an elaborate set of tribal markings—a very painful procedure—and he spoke to the boy with respect. "Did white man tell you about Jesus, Bendi?"

Bendi seemed to shrink from answering, but said, "No. We chop him!"

"Oh, Katie," Barney said as she came out of the hut, "this is Bendi, son of Chief Batoni. Bendi, this is Katie. She comes from far over the big water. She is a servant of Jesus, of the God who made everything."

Bendi fixed his eyes boldly on Katie. His eyes revealed nothing as he spoke. "Soon you get food."

"Pretty hard nut, Bendi is," Barney said as he watched the boy stride away. "But he's heard the gospel. I'm sure of it."

"We'll have to work on that, but right now I wish I could see Bestman," Katie responded.

"Better not try it. Remember what Awful said last night?"

"Yes. He has a wonderful gift of bringing the Scriptures to life, doesn't he?" She thought about it, then said, "It's like he said, Barney. I'd like to get busy and *do* something! But it might be God's plan to let Bestman stay a prisoner for a while—just like Jesus let Lazarus actually die so that He could show the glory of His—"

"Barney!" Del rushed out. "Awful just collapsed!"

They dashed inside and over to Gardner's limp form. He was lying on a bamboo bed, his face ashen and his breathing labored.

"No fever," Barney said, touching the man's forehead. He leaned forward and called, "Awful! Awful! Are you all right?"

Fear rippled through Katie—not fear of bodily harm, but the presence of evil. "It's not a natural sickness," she whispered. "This is evil. You can *feel* the powers of darkness!"

Barney and Del both agreed, for it was obvious that Gardner had been stricken down, not by malaria or sleeping sickness, but by a sinister force hovering over them.

Barney peered outside. "They're all gathered outside," he said quietly.

"Like a bunch of vultures!" Del muttered, as he, too, checked the situation. "I feel sick myself," he said, showing his trembling hands to Katie and Barney. "I didn't think anything could do that to me!" he exclaimed, shocked.

Even Katie was affected—a filthy fear that crept into her mind, so obscene that it shamed her in an inexplicable way beyond her conception. Like Del, she began to tremble, her legs grew weak, her mouth became parched.

Barney watched his friends, his senses reeling in confusion as he found himself unable to combat a force that threatened to destroy him. In the ring he'd learned to face physical destruction, to control all fear. But this fear was foreign to anything he'd encountered. It was much stronger and seemed to settle on his mind like a heavy fog, making him want to flee for his life. *Get out of here!* the voice screamed at him. *You can't help him—save yourself!*

Suddenly from deep within him rose a supernatural strength and he cried out in a hoarse voice, "I rebuke you, spirits of darkness! Satan—you were defeated at the cross of Jesus! By His blood and in the name of Jesus Christ, I *command* you to leave this place, you foul spirits. . . !"

As Barney continued to call on the name of the Lord, Katie could sense an awesome battle in the unseen world. It was as if two armies met in a tremendous clash of arms. She had been caught once in a violent thunderstorm, and the lightning bolts had filled the skies like huge tracks of silver fire as they reached down to smash the earth. She had been rocked with the violence of sound and fire that broke over her. She recalled the battle against the witch doctor and the power of the name of Jesus as the chief was delivered from the death clutch on his life. Now she fell to her knees and cried out the name of Jesus Christ over and over.

As Barney, Del and Katie battled, they felt the darksome power begin to wane. Slowly it left the room like a sullen wave withdrawing from the beach to find its place in the depths of a deadly abode. Katie sat motionless, her lips moving silently, tears coursing down her face.

"Thank you, Jesus!"

Katie's head jerked up as she recognized the voice. Awful! He was sitting up, his eyes clear, and a victory smile on his face. "Bless the Lord! We gave the devil a lickin' that time, didn't we?" he exclaimed.

Katie scrambled to her feet and almost fell before Barney caught her. His own face was drained and pale, but he cried with joy, "Yes, Awful, I think the Lord Jesus won that one!"

Del moved from where he had been leaning against the wall, his face tense and drawn. "That was terrible!" he said hoarsely. "I couldn't do a thing except call out to God!"

"Ah, well," Gardner nodded, "that's all we're told to do, isn't it, now? 'In my name you'll cast out demons.' Remember?"

"Do you think it'll happen again?" Katie asked.

"Maybe. But we've got the name of Jesus, lass," Gardner said. "Let's check on Batoni. He and his friends expect me to be dead." He got to his feet and walked to the door and peered out. "Come along. Let's go out and let them see what the Lord Jesus can do for His servants!"

He walked out the door, the others right behind. Batoni, his headmen, and the two witch doctors had their backs to the missionaries. "Hello, Chief Batoni!" Gardner cried out.

A muted cry rose from the crowd as they whirled in unbelief, eyes like saucers.

"I see you're all meetin'," Gardner went on. "Shall I tell you about Jesus? How He is stronger than all your gods?"

Batoni's haughty expression did not change. Instead, he wheeled away, his entourage at his heels.

"*That* got to him!" Gardner said gleefully. "The blighter didn't show it, but he lost this time. He expected me to be dead."

They stayed close to the hut assigned to them, reveling in the joyous presence of the Lord, the wonder of His name, the assurance that His Word was as true that day as when Jesus walked on earth—and they could trust Him to be all He said He would be.

Two hours later the chief's son brought some palm nuts and rice. As he set the food before them, Bendi kept glancing sideways at Gardner, a mixture of unbelief, fear, and awe in his eyes. The older man was not dead!

Barney noted Bendi's expression. He winked at Awful and nodded slightly toward Bendi. "How do you feel, Reverend Gardner?"

Awful responded by throwing his arms out and crying, "Good! I feel wonderful! The Lord Jesus makes it a good place!"

Bendi stood stock-still, watching the drama before him.

Katie perceived the men's intent and said brightly, "Yes! The old gods are weak. They cannot stand against the great God!"

None of them spoke directly to the boy, but declared to one

another the goodness of God, thanking Him over and over. Bendi moved slowly toward the door, delaying his going, then slipped out.

"Well," Barney smiled, "he was a congregation of one, but he got a good gospel sermon."

"Batoni is very proud of his son," Awful nodded. "And the lad is smart. He don't let on, but he wuz the best student in the school Brother Milum had here when the lad wuz just a boy. Milum stuck it out till he wuz near eighty, Beecham told me. Had a good church, but when he died, the witch doctors moved in, and they got their hooks into Batoni."

The day passed slowly, with no word from Batoni. That night they slept fitfully, awaking once when it seemed that Gardner was having the same symptoms again. Immediately they took authority over the forces of darkness, and soon Awful was resting peacefully.

As dawn broke over the village, the visitors emerged from their lodging. People were moving around, the women cooking and the men gathering in small groups, talking.

Bendi approached the missionaries with some more rice and a portion of meat. "Goat meat, very good!"

"Will you join us, Bendi?" Barney asked on impulse. "We have something you might like to try."

Bendi shook his head, but Awful urged, "Come now, just have a bite!"

The boy looked hard at the item Barney had pulled from his pocket, then took it cautiously. "It's candy," Barney explained. "See if you like it. We will eat the food you've brought."

They pretended not to notice Bendi as they ate and talked with one another instead of directly to the boy. Katie watched him put the candy in his mouth, taste it, and his eyes light up with surprise. It was hard candy and he ate the entire stick as he listened to their conversation.

"What?" Barney said in surprise. "All gone? I think I might have a bit more here somewhere." He found another stick and gave it to him.

This time the boy stuck it in his mouth without hesitation, his face blissful.

Awful wasn't hungry, so he pulled his old black Bible out, saying, "Well, let's have a little Bible for breakfast, eh?" He read the story of David and Goliath, turning it into a rousing adventure that riveted the boy's attention.

"So this giant, who wuz about as big as an elephant, and had a spear the size of a tree, come at David and said, 'I'm goin' to kill you and feed you to the vultures!' But David, who wuzn't much older, I guess, than—oh, than Bendi here—he said, 'Goliath, my God is stronger than your gods. I've only got a little slingshot, but today God has given you into my hand!' "

Then Gardner acted out the fight. "And David ran right at that giant, and he took his sling and threw the rock—and it hit that old giant Goliath right between the eyes! Bam! Down he went, dead—and David took the giant's own sword and cut off his head!"

Gardner saw the boy's eyes widen in surprise. "David had a big God, didn't he, Bendi?" Awful said.

Bendi stared in wonder. "This god of David, he is strong. What is he called?"

"He's got many names, Bendi," Gardner replied. "But the name I like best is *Jesus*. It means 'one who saves.' "

The lad studied the old man carefully, thinking hard. Then he said, "I go now!"

Gardner watched the boy as he dashed away. "He's thinkin' it over, he is. It's hard for these folks to give up their old gods."

"It would be hard for Bendi if he became a Christian, wouldn't it?" Katie said thoughtfully.

"Hard! I expect that father of his would feed him to the wolves!"

Time dragged on and after the third night, Awful said, "He's tryin' to wear us down!"

"Well, he's doing a pretty good job!" Del complained. "We haven't gotten even a glimpse of Bestman—and we can't stay in this hole forever!"

However, just after midday the next day, the missionaries got their call. But it was not what they expected. They were sitting outside the hut when Chief Batoni strode through the village toward them, with Bendi at his side and a long spear in his hand. He marched straight up to them. "You come!"

Startled, Gardner asked, "Is it a meetin' of the elders, Chief Batoni?"

The proud features of the chief did not change, but Katie thought she saw a sardonic light in his deep-set black eyes.

"Not meeting," he said. Then he smiled slightly. "You come hunt lion with Batoni."

The four missionaries could not have been more shocked if he had announced they were going to play chess!

"I tell about David and how he kill giant," Bendi said.

Batoni nodded. "Bad lion, kill many my peoples. You come. We let you show us how strong your god is." He stood there, amused at their confusion, then demanded, "You come? Kill lion?"

Barney got to his feet. "We come, Chief Batoni."

The chief fixed his gaze on Barney. "Pahn people no use rifle gun for lion. Use this." He handed Barney the spear. "Come. You show Pahn people how strong is Jesus God."

Surprise flickered in the chief's eyes as Barney took up the challenge. "Let's go find the bad lion. My God will slay him."

CHAPTER TWENTY-FIVE

"GOOD-NIGHT, DEAR BOY!"

★ ★ ★ ★

The long line of Pahn tribesmen marched through the forest. Barney had been fascinated by the initiation rites of the tribes, and none was more dramatic than the killing of a lion with just a spear. He knew that among the Masai tribes, only men who had performed this feat were permitted to wear the headdress made of the lion's skin.

The lion was usually found in the plains, Barney knew, but part of the Pahn territory was dense jungle, and he had once seen a pride of them at a distance. What would he do at such a disadvantage? It was one thing to face a mighty foe with a rifle or a shotgun, as he had done successfully many times, but to fight a *lion* with a *spear*—that was different! Sometimes a full-grown lion weighed up to five hundred pounds, to say nothing of the razor-sharp claws and massive jaws that could crush the bones of a zebra as if they were dust. Barney envisioned those deadly weapons sinking into human flesh—his flesh!

He glanced down at the eight-foot spear in his hand. He understood that it was thrust into the chest as the beast charged, never thrown at him.

And *he* was supposed to kill it with a single thrust? Barney had heard that these tribesmen spent years developing the skill and strength just for the opportunity of killing a lion. He had practically no chance—in the natural, at least.

Batoni and his warriors kept a close watch on him, he saw. *Expect me to run like a rabbit*, he thought. He smiled grimly. *Which is exactly what I'd like to do!*

By noon the country flattened out, the tall trees of the rain forest giving way to scrub brush.

"Halt!" Batoni called. He searched the horizon, then divided the men into small parties and waved them off, leaving the chief, his son, and Barney.

"Lion, him there!" Batoni stated, waving his spear toward a low-lying hill with a flattened top. "You go with us?"

Barney nodded. "I go."

Batoni scrutinized the white man, amazed that the missionary would come this far. "You never use spear?" he asked.

"No. Only rifle, Chief."

"Lion—bad! Strong and fast."

Barney looked at the spear, then at Batoni. "Some of your finest men have been killed hunting lions, is that not so?"

"Plenty men killed. Lion strong!"

"We both know that if your men, who know how to hunt with a spear, have been killed, I don't have much chance."

"You go back?" Batoni demanded at once.

"No. I go with you to kill lion."

Bendi was listening to the conversation closely. He had a spear of his own, and looked at the white man with keen interest.

Barney noted this and asked, "What about your son, Batoni?"

"Is his first hunt." Batoni felt he had to explain, so he added, "My son watch his father kill lion. Learn how. Like I learn from my father."

Barney smiled. "I didn't learn from my father. Will you show me how?"

Batoni blinked his eyes, surprise registering in his face at Barney's response. Unknown to Winslow, this chief respected little—except courage. He was a warrior, and the code of the hunt was pride. A man who could not hunt was no man in his sight! But he was in a bad position, for his prestige had been damaged by the fact that despite the spells he and the witch doctors had made, the old missionary hadn't died. And now, this young one was set to prove that his God was able to keep him from the lion's jaws.

The chief was a savage man of war and led a wicked life, but he couldn't help admiring the white man he had hated. He nodded. "You watch Batoni kill lion."

"All right. I will watch the chief."

Batoni nodded and moved across the ground noiselessly, which Barney could not do, no matter how hard he tried. The country looked flat, but it was very rough. The three had to scramble down into gullies, sometimes six feet deep, then claw their way up the other side. Barney kept up, and he saw that both father and son were surprised at the white man's agility.

When they reached a long line of bushes, no more than three feet high, bordering the plain, Batoni stopped. A brook flowed beneath the weeds and across the dry plain. Even as they stood there, a herd of antelope lowered their heads to drink, and farther down a pack of wild dogs fought over the remains of a carcass.

"Lion—him hunt here!" Batoni whispered. "We wait—be still!"

The sweat collected in Barney's helmet as the blazing sun beat down upon them. He held the spear tightly at first, but after a while his hand cramped and he was forced to loosen his grip.

The brook was a magnet, drawing all sorts of animals and birds. The sides of it were lined with white bones, no doubt victims of the lions' jaws. Scanning the distance, Barney thought he saw a movement along the edges of the scrub, perhaps other hunters. He lowered his eyes to the brook again but was arrested by another stirring in the brush.

Batoni slowly raised his arm. "Lion!" he whispered.

At first Barney could see nothing. Then he saw her! The female lion was creeping out of the bush, moving stealthily, freezing from time to time. Barney held his breath as he watched, mesmerized.

Batoni moved forward, his motion pure grace. Holding his spear lightly in his right hand, he crept toward the lioness. At once she turned, then broke into a charge. Over the ground she leapt, fast as a gazelle toward the enemy who lifted his spear with both hands and waited. Barney could see his face—alert, pleased, fearless.

The lioness flew through the air with great leaps, then rose, claws outstretched, straight toward the waiting Batoni! The chief drove his spear into the center of her throat and fell backward himself by the power of the animal's lunge. Huge spurts of blood gushed from her neck, but she caught Batoni with one ripping motion of her claws even as she dropped to the ground, kicked and lay motionless.

It happened with such lightning speed that Barney had not moved, but a cry behind him made him freeze.

"Lion!" Bendi cried.

A huge lion raced across the plain. Barney could not believe his eyes. Batoni was struggling to his feet, but his leg was torn so badly that it gave way, sending him sprawling—right in the path of the charging beast!

Bendi raced toward the lion just as Barney went into motion. Gripping the spear, he sped toward the boy. *I can never make it!* screamed in his mind. Batoni shouted as he tried to get to his feet.

Barney lunged forward with strength he didn't know he had. He saw the lion come to the end of his charge and launch himself at Bendi, who stood with his spear grasped with both hands. He drove the spear into the lion's chest, but missed the center. The point ripped a gash that only infuriated the beast as he leaped toward the boy again.

Winslow's vision narrowed to the lion and Bendi. The lion, thrown off by the spear wound, missed the boy with his full weight, but one slashing blow of his talons caught the lad in the shoulder, tossing him aside like a rag doll; and before Bendi could recover, the lion was on him! The boy dug his hands into the lion's cheeks, trying to evade the jaws from crushing him.

With a cry Barney hurled himself forward, screaming, "Jesus—help me!" He thrust the spear into the lion's body with all his strength.

The spear lodged in the beast's shoulder, and with a thunderous roar, the animal whirled, leaving Bendi on the ground, bloody but alive.

The lion bit at the spear and rolled over in pain, releasing the weapon. It had not been a deadly wound, but the pain enraged the lion. He bounded to his feet, saw the boy struggling, and once again lunged toward him.

At that moment Barney lost all sense of reason and launched himself at the lion, landing on his back. He whipped his right arm around the neck of the lion and grabbed the wrist with his left hand, simultaneously wrapping his legs about the body of the animal to a viselike grip.

But he was not prepared for the raging power of the lion! Great muscles hard as steel coiled as the lion thrashed wildly from side to side, trying to shake off his attacker. Barney felt the awesome power of the huge cat and knew that no man could ever match such strength! He put every ounce of power he had into his arms, knowing that if he let go, he would be torn to ribbons.

He had little hope, but he clutched the lion like death as the wounded beast clawed and roared, rolling on the ground with rage as he tried to get at the hunter. Then he reared, Barney's weight as nothing, and threw himself over backward, almost crushing Barney. Somehow he held on as he cried again, "God! God! Help!"

Suddenly the lion coughed, a raw, hoarse sound, and staggered to his feet. Barney felt the deep chest swelling and knew that the loss of air was weakening the animal.

Over and over words penetrated Winslow's mind: *Hang on! Hang on! Don't let go! Don't let go!*

Then the animal's hindquarters gave way and he sprawled on his side, choked to death. Still Barney clung like a leech, forcing every bit of strength he had left into his right arm.

Even as he felt something touch his face, he hung on.

"Lion dead," a voice said.

Barney felt hands pulling him free. He could not see because of the blood running into his eyes from a deep cut a jagged rock had made as he landed beneath the lion. A hand wiped the blood away. It was Chief Batoni!

Barney tried to get up. His legs wouldn't hold him. His arms were useless. "I can't move my legs and arms!" he whispered.

"Do not move," the chief said. "Lie still." He had managed to hobble over to Barney and his word was a command.

"What about Bendi?"

"I am here."

Barney turned to see Bendi squatting beside him. "Are you all right?"

"Yes." Bendi's shoulder was slashed with four long bloody gashes, plus other wounds, but he ignored them. "You kill without spear!" he whispered. "Your God is the real God!"

By now Barney could move his left arm and wiped his eyes. "Help me up," he said. Strong arms assisted him, and though his legs were weak and trembling, he could stand.

He looked down at the body of the huge lion, beautiful even in death, and then he looked up.

The hunters had formed a ring around him, their eyes fixed on his face, but saying nothing.

"You are my brother now," Batoni said evenly. He motioned to one of his men. A warrior walked over with a knife. Batoni held his arm out and made a cut. As the blood welled out, he looked at Barney. "Will you be brothers with Pahn people?"

Barney nodded and put his arm out. After the cut he felt the pressure of the chief's arm against his own.

They both gazed at the joining of blood—a black arm and a white arm. Batoni broke the solemn moment. "We are of same blood now. Never will my people harm you."

"And my people will do nothing but good to you, Chief Batoni," Barney replied, joy rising within him. He knew that when he was an old, old man, he would still see this scene as clearly as he did now—the black faces, the dead lion, the black arm of the African chieftain next to the white man's.

★　★　★　★

"They're back!" Del cried as he stuck his head in the doorway. "They've just come into the village."

"Is—is he all right, Del?" Katie asked, dropping the damp cloth she was using to bathe Awful's face.

"I don't know. Let's go see."

Katie took one look at Gardner, then followed Del outside. It was getting close to noon, and she had not slept. Awful's illness and fear for Barney had kept her awake.

"Look! There he is!"

"I see him!" she said.

Barney had a handkerchief tied around his head, but as soon

as he caught sight of them, he hurried over.

"Are you all right?" Katie asked.

"Sure. Lost some hide, but nothing serious."

"What's wrong with Batoni?" Del asked.

"He got mauled by a lion," Barney replied. "Bendi got some bad slashes too, but they'll both be all right."

"We expected you back yesterday," Katie said. "I've been worried sick."

"We had to patch the chief up. His leg's pretty badly torn, so we had to make a hammock to carry him."

"I'm glad you're back," she said simply.

Del was more direct. "Did you kill a lion?"

Barney laughed. "In a manner of speaking, I did. And it's going to make a big difference around here, I think."

"Tell us about the lion," Del insisted.

"Not now."

But that night at the celebration, Batoni told the story. Awful was feeling better and sat with Barney as the chief related the event—twice, in his own language and then in broken English. In the manner of natural story-tellers, he threw in some embellishments, which made Del stare at Barney in awe!

Bendi, too, gave his version, looking at Barney with hero worship.

"It's all hot air," Barney whispered to Katie. "All I did was choke a dying lion to death."

"I'm sure there was more to it than that," she said softly. "In a few years you'll be a legend around the Pahn people."

"Good night! I hope not!" he exclaimed. "Look! the chief's going to make another speech. Hope it's short."

"Now," Batoni said, "I will say more. First, here, my brother, is your man."

"Bestman!" Katie cried as he appeared.

He grinned from ear to ear. "I be fine, Mammy!" he insisted. "I come to preach Jesus to Pahns."

He took his seat with the others to listen to the chief.

"Lion Killer is my brother," Chief Batoni said. "He save my life and the life of my son. Pahn people now his people. We no do him bad." He added, "You leave missionary in my village. Preach Jesus. Maybe you stay, Lion Killer?"

"You will have a missionary, Chief," Barney said. "Maybe me. Maybe this one," he said, nodding at Katie.

Then Batoni looked at Awful and smiled, showing his filed teeth. "You strong man. Any other man die from curses we put on you. Maybe you stay with Pahn people?"

"No, Chief," Awful replied, smiling at him. "It's for these young ones. I must go home soon."

Startled, Barney glanced quickly at Awful.

★ ★ ★ ★

The next morning the missionaries left the village. It was a triumphant departure, with the entire village calling out, "Lion Killer! Lion Killer!"

"If any of you call me that after we get back, I'll drown —Awful!" he cried mid-sentence as he saw his friend staggering.

He called the porters, and they lifted Gardner into the hammock.

"What's wrong with him, Katie?" Barney asked, worried.

"He's been sick since you left. I don't know what happened."

"I don't like it," he replied.

The party made its way back to Gropaka, camping at the same spot on the river on their way in. The next morning they arrived at the station.

Though all were exhausted from the past day's traumatic events, none was as bad as Awful, who was nearly unconscious as they put him to bed. "I don't like it," Barney said again, his lips tight. "It's not malaria—and it's not that awful thing we fought against in Batoni's village. What's the matter with him, Katie?"

"Barney, I don't think he's sick at all," she said, looking at Gardner's face. "I think he's just reached the end of his tether."

Her lips were compressed as she tried to conceal the fatigue that pulled at her.

Barney denied her words with a vigorous shaking of his head. "He just needs rest," he protested. "I'll take care of him."

But the next day, even Barney saw that Gardner was worse. He slept, but it was not a natural sleep. When he awakened, his mind was not clear. He recognized Barney, but he thought they were back in prison. "Don't worry, dear boy," he whispered, smiling up at Barney. "God will get you out of this place."

His appetite failed, and they all knew it was a matter of time. Barney never left his side, often falling asleep in his chair, but waking instantly whenever his friend moved. Sometimes Awful would look at them, and his mind would be as clear as ever. Once he said, "Dear boy, I'm weary. It's good to go home."

The end came at dawn, with Katie and Barney at his side. Awful had not awakened since the previous afternoon, when Del had left for his own station.

Katie thought their friend would die without awakening. But just as the sun came up over the hills, he opened his eyes.

"Ah, dear boy," he whispered. "What a time we've had with the Lord Jesus! Haven't we, now?"

"Yes! It's been good, Awful!" Barney said, trying to hide his grief. He choked and added, "But you're the one who brought me to it! It was always you!"

Awful took Barney's hand, then reached for Katie's and placed it on Barney's. "God be with you both—and make you to . . ." His voice faded, and they thought he was gone. But he opened his eyes and looked at them with such love that they both wept.

"I'll tell the Lord Jesus . . ." he whispered faintly, so faintly that they had to lean forward to catch his last words: ". . . how much you love Him—and how much—you need each other." He was slipping away fast but rallied enough to say, as he had a thousand times to Barney, "Good-night, dear boy! It's good to serve Jesus, ain't it, now?"

Then he closed his eyes . . . and was gone.

CHAPTER TWENTY-SIX

THE THIRD THING

★　★　★　★

Lola's eyebrows narrowed as she addressed Myron Hansen, trying to hide her displeasure. "Reverend Hansen, I don't think this is fair to Barney."

"Not fair?" Hansen echoed her words. "I'm afraid I don't understand, Mrs. Winslow. Why, this is just what the boy needs!"

Mark Winslow followed the sweep of the preacher's fat hand, but agreed with Lola. "I think it will just embarrass him."

The three were standing in the banquet room of the Nelson Hotel, which was packed with guests. It was a glittering exhibition—just what Reverend Hansen loved and could promote. The moment he heard about Barney's exploit, the idea of a banquet in his honor was spawned. Of course, it wouldn't hurt the mission either, Hansen had to admit with some satisfaction, for the news of the lion adventure had hit the papers—first in Liberia, then other news services by cable.

★　★　★　★

When Mark and Lola and Andy had learned about Barney's killing a lion with his bare hands, thus saving the life of a cannibal chief and converting the entire tribe, they were thrilled.

Andy had been ecstatic and could hardly wait to leave for Liberia. He wanted to make sure Barney received the recognition he deserved—in the eyes of Andy at least! But Mark and Lola had been convinced that too much was being made of it.

Andy overruled all protests from Lola and Mark. He had launched a triumphant campaign in the States, which had raised enormous sums, and then set sail for Africa with his parents.

They had docked on December 22, and on that same day, Reverend Hansen and Andy plunged into a furious round of activity. "Dad," Andy insisted, "you and Mother have to understand that publicity will bring in hundreds of thousands of dollars for missions! Barney is big news! I intend to take him back with me, and we'll hit every large church in the country!"

Barney had not even returned to Monrovia since the incident, but Hansen had sent a party to get him. He would arrive on Christmas, according to the plan created by the Hansens and Andy. And he would find himself the guest of honor at the biggest party ever given in the history of missions!

Mark and Lola had given up the struggle. "Let him do what he wants," Mark said. "Soon as this nonsense is out of the way, we can see the real work over here."

★　★　★　★

As he looked over the crowd, Mark felt he had been wrong. "I should have put a stop to this, Lola," he said. "I don't care what Andy says; it's too much—like a carnival! Barney will *hate* it!"

"You're probably right, but it's too late to change it, dear." Lola was wearing a black dress, and she looked more beautiful than she had twenty-five years ago. Only a single white streak marked her hair, and that made her even more attractive.

"What time will he be here?" she asked for the umpteenth time.

"Exactly at seven o'clock—and it's nearly that now. Andy went to meet him. He's got some scheme to keep Barney in the dark about this extravaganza." He glowered as he stared around the room. "I hate surprise parties! They're for fools!"

"Hush, dear!" Lola said quickly, pressing his arm. He had the same strength and drive he had when she first met him in Texas. "They'll hear you. Come on, let's go sit down."

She led the way to the large raised table, and had just been seated when a man rushed over to Reverend Hansen.

"He's coming!" Hansen called out. "When you get my signal, we'll give him a real City Mission ovation!"

Everyone rose and waited silently. The door opened, and Andy marched in with Barney at his side. He held up his free hand in a gesture of triumph. "And here he is, the Lion Killer himself!"

Hansen began to clap, and then the entire room exploded with cheers and applause.

Lola saw the shock mirrored in her son's face, and murmured, "Mark, I hate this! Look how embarrassed Barney is!"

Andy gripped his brother's arm so tightly he couldn't escape—which was his first impulse. He had heard nothing about the stir his work with Chief Batoni had made. "What is all this, Andy?" he demanded, confused and heartsick.

"It's all for you, Barney!" Andy smiled. "Look over there."

Barney followed his gesture. *Mom and Dad!* "Andy, why didn't you *tell* me they were here?"

"Part of the surprise, old boy! This is *your* night. Come along!"

He propelled him forward for a way until Barney pulled his arm free and asked, "Andy, where are Katie and the others?" But Andy acted as if he didn't hear.

"Here he is!" Andy announced to his parents.

Mark grinned and grabbed his son in a tight embrace, then pulled back, his hands on Barney's shoulders. "Well, son," he said, looking into his eyes, "you've gotten to be a real publicity hound, I see!"

His father was joking, Barney saw, so he mustered a smile. "Would you like my autograph?" he asked. He gave his mother a hug, and when he kissed her, tears filled her eyes.

"You look tired," she said with concern.

Her mothering remark restored some of Barney's good humor, but he felt very uncomfortable. Just then he heard Andy introduce him as the guest of honor, "the greatest missionary on the continent!"

"What nonsense!" Barney sputtered. Since becoming a Christian he disliked such ostentatious displays. *Lord*, he prayed, *I need more grace now than when I faced Batoni.*

After Reverend Hansen asked the longest blessing Barney had heard, they sat down to partake of the luscious food. But before Andy took his place next to his parents, near the Hansens, Barney called, "Katie, you and the others come over here!"

Katie cringed and wanted to hide, but Del grinned. "Come on, the Lion Killer has spoken."

Del led the way from where he, Katie, and Slim and Pearl Ranken had been seated in back of the room. When the four reached the front table, Barney asked the waiters to get more chairs and place settings, then said to the guests at the table, "How about we crowd up a little?"

"Good for you, Barney!" Lola whispered.

He smiled, thankful for the courage to do what was right. The meal was excellent, the speeches eloquent—especially Andy's. He did a masterful job, interjecting wit and a detailed account of Barney's exploits, making him look like a saint! Finally he introduced the honored guest with a flair.

The crowd rose and applauded as Barney got to his feet. When the people were seated again, a hush fell.

"My brother Andy has told you how wonderful I am," Barney said with a straight face. "So I don't have to go into that. But he did leave out a few details, which might interest you." He saw Andy's face stiffen, and was amused. "For example, he left out the fact that I served time in Sing Sing for armed robbery." A muted rumble swept over the room, furtive glances flitted from one to another, and Andy's face grew red instead of white.

"I also flunked out of school and became a prize-fighter for a time." He looked over his audience, pleased that many evidenced discomfort, others anticipation. "But I want to set one thing straight. I am not the greatest missionary on this continent. Not even the greatest in this *room!*"

He paused for a moment. "You've heard that I killed a lion. Well, that sort of thing makes headlines, but it doesn't make great missionaries. Tonight, I had no knowledge about this banquet. If I had, I'd probably be running right now. But I'm here, and you're all interested in missions. So I'm going to tell you about some *real* missionaries!"

For the next hour he told them about the mission field, the men and women who worked, died, and were buried there. He was not eloquent, but he spoke from firsthand experience, and his words drew vivid pictures of what it was like. Many of his hearers *were* missionaries, and their heads nodded in agreement. "That's right! That's the way it was," they would whisper to those nearby.

Much of his speech centered around Awful Gardner, beginning with their first meeting—in prison. Barney made the Rescue Mission come alive for the audience; and the Rankens, Del, and Katie wept as he told of the hundreds who came to Jesus under the influence of Gardner. Then he told of the heroic struggle Awful had endured in Africa, of his witness to Chief Batoni. "It wasn't the killing of a lion that made the difference. It was the faithful witness of that man of God."

He concluded by telling about Awful's death. When he finished, there was not a dry eye in the house. "God bless all of you for coming," he said. "But I want you to forget *me.* Remember those who've found lonely graves out there. And let's bind ourselves together to get the gospel of Jesus Christ to every soul possible who hasn't heard the Good News!"

He bowed his head and prayed a fervent prayer for the lost tribes and the missionaries who would go to them. Then he raised his head. "Forgive me if I don't stay to talk, but my parents are here."

Somehow he maneuvered his family and friends out of the banquet room into a side room, shutting the door firmly. With a deep sigh of relief, he said, "Lock the door, Del." But he was too late, for the Hansens had found them—followed by a corps of reporters.

"Let's meet for breakfast," Lola suggested.

"All right," Barney replied.

"I don't care if you don't like me to say it," she whispered in his ears. "But I was proud of you tonight! I'll see you tomorrow. Good-night."

Lola and Mark left Barney to the fate of the reporters—and Hansens—and went to their room. "Oh, Mark!" she cried. "I'm so happy!"

"Me, too, but poor Barney. Wait till he finds out what Andy's got planned for him!"

Sure enough, the next day when Andy brought the subject up at breakfast, Barney set his jaw stubbornly.

"No, Andy, I'm *not* making any tour in America to raise support for missions!"

Mark let Andy argue for fifteen minutes before he interrupted. "Andy, can't you see it's useless? You're wasting your time."

Andy slumped down, defeated. "Well," he asked, "what *are* you going to do, Barney?"

"I'm going back to preach to that old cannibal, Chief Batoni."

"I give up!" Andy groaned. "Brother, you just have no *vision* at all!"

"Andy!" Lola remonstrated. "You have no right to say that. Barney doesn't have *your* vision, but he's caught God's vision, His heart, for reaching those who may never hear the gospel. Already I have seen a tremendous growth in Barney's spiritual life." She paused, then went on. "I only wish I were younger. I'd go in a minute, with Mark, of course." She smiled, softening her words to Andy.

Andy nodded toward Barney. "Sorry for my outburst. Guess we see things differently. It's just that I was looking forward to your working with me."

"I appreciate that, and I want you to know how good it feels to have a family. But I *have* to do what God has called me to do, no matter what the cost."

They dispersed then with a promise to meet at Mark and Lola's hotel for supper.

All the original missionaries from the Rescue Mission had been invited. No banquet could compare with the rich time they had sharing God's dealing in their individual lives.

Del, they discovered, was going to marry a young woman from Oklahoma.

"I didn't know you were courting a girl from there, Del," Katie said in surprise.

"Oh, I've never met her," Del said. "But we've been writing. She's on her way here to be a missionary, right here in Liberia."

"When did you propose?" Barney asked.

"Well . . . I . . . I haven't actually done that, but it's just a matter of time!"

"Same old Del," they laughed. "Slow and easygoing!"

The Rankens were opening up a new station, and it was easy to see that they were happy in their marriage.

"What about you, Katie?" Barney asked.

"Oh, I'm going back to start a school for Chief Batoni."

Barney stared at her. "Why, that's where *I'm* going!" he said. And he smiled broadly. "Won't it be wonderful, working together again!"

But it was not as simple as that. In the afternoon of the last day of the year, Katie was asked to meet with Reverend Hansen. When she arrived, she discovered Barney had also been invited. "What's it about?" she asked. But Barney was in the dark as well.

The door opened, and Hansen walked in with Stanley Beecham. He was very glad to see them both, but said little.

Reverend Hansen began the discussion. "Well, now, we seem to have a problem here," he said. "A personal problem, I suppose you might call it."

He seemed a little flustered, so Beecham took over in his evenly clipped British manner. "Myron and I seldom agree, but in this one instance I feel he is right. The two of you can't go to the same village. It would create problems all the way around."

"But I've already promised to start a school there! I can't go back on my word!" Katie protested, her face flushed.

"And I promised Chief Batoni to be his missionary," Barney added. "We've got to move quickly! This tribe is ripe for the gospel, and you know how those witch doctors can move in!"

There was a lively discussion for half an hour, and the longer it went on, the more determined each participant became.

By now Katie was almost in tears, but Barney remained undaunted. God had handled more difficult situations than this. There had to be a way.

"Of course, there is *one* solution . . ." Hansen left the sentence hanging.

Katie looked at him, perplexed, but Barney's face lit up.

"Why, of course!" he said, turning to Katie. "What do you think? I mean, if we were married, there'd be no problem, would there?"

Beecham added a word of encouragement. "It would work out very well indeed, in my opinion."

The three men waited.

Katie slowly got to her feet, her face pale, her eyes enormous. She glared at Barney, and with contempt dripping from her voice, said, "You've been around the villages too long. They *buy* a wife when they need someone to work, don't they?" She whirled and raced out of the room, leaving Barney with his face flaming.

"Ahem," Beecham said, clearing his throat. "Your idea didn't go over too well, Myron."

Hansen shrugged. "Guess you two will have to decide, Barney. Let us know who goes, who stays."

Barney's heart was heavy. *Who goes, who stays* echoed in his mind as the door closed behind the two men. *What a mess!* he thought and walked blindly out, pacing the street for several hours. When darkness fell, he returned to the mission station, still with no answer. For a long time he sat mulling over the predicament.

Suddenly like a bolt of lightning it hit him. "What a fool I am!"

He jumped from his chair and marched straight to Katie's room and knocked on the door.

No answer. He knocked again.

"Who's there?"

"It's me, Barney."

"Go away!"

"Open the door, Katie. I've got to talk to you!"

"No! Do you know what time it is?" she demanded, clutching her robe about her.

"I don't care. Open the door or I'll kick it down!"

He's drunk! They mustn't find him like that! she thought. She slipped the bolt and opened the door.

He stood there for a moment, then said, "Let me come in. I've got to talk to you."

"But—it's two o'clock in the morning! You *can't* come into my room at this hour!"

"Then you'll Have to come out!"

"I *can't*—" Katie gasped, and stopped. He didn't *seem* drunk. The moonlight coming through the window into the hall was bright enough to see his face. And his voice was clear.

"Katie, all that talk with Beecham and Hansen, it was wrong!"

"I don't *want* to talk about it, Barney!" she said sharply.

He gazed at her silently. Her eyes sparkled with agitation. How lovely she looked in the moonlight! Finally he said, "Do you remember the time I kissed you on the ship?"

"No!" She shook her head angrily, refusing to admit she remembered. "What do you *want* with me, Barney. I can't stand out here all night!"

"I want to marry you," he said softly.

"So you can go to Batoni's village?"

"No," he said, his eyes never leaving her face.

He made her so angry! "What do you mean *no*? Can't you say *something*?"

"Katie, I want to marry you—because I love you."

Struck silent by his words, her mouth dropped open.

Wasting no more time, he pulled Katie into his arms and pressed his lips to hers. "I've loved you for a long time," he whispered as he kissed her again, gently. "I'm just slow. You *know* that, Katie."

Katie's limbs almost gave way under the emotional stress. Then she threw her arms around his neck and drew his head down. She kissed him slowly, cherishing the moment. When she raised her head, she murmured, "You know what?"

"What?"

She smiled through her tears. "I'll expect a little more courting than this, Barney Winslow!"

"Oh, Katie! Katie! I love you so!" He pulled her close again, burying his face in her hair, so fragrant, fresh, clean. "I'll bring you flowers every day! I'll bring a band at night and serenade you! You'll get sick of the sight of me!"

She laughed deep within her as she looked into his eyes. "I've loved you for so long! Now I'll *really* have you!"

"Katie! You've always had me! I was just too dumb to realize it." He smiled. "I just thought of something Del said. He found out three things: one, he didn't love you; two, you didn't love him."

"He told me that too, but wouldn't say what the third thing was."

"I think I know." He cradled her in his arms and murmured against her cheek, "That you and I love each other!"

"And always will, Barney!" she said with her heart in her eyes.

"Always . . . By the way, do you know what day this is?"

"Why, it's Tuesday morning."

"No, it's the morning of a new century."

"That's right—it's the first day of the year."

"First day of the century," he smiled. "January 1, 1900." He stood there silently, then said, "It's going to be a different kind of world, Katie. I've been thinking about what it'll be like. And I've wondered what my ancestors would have thought of it."

"I don't guess they'd recognize it. Things change so fast."

"The first Winslow wouldn't. His name was Gilbert. He came over on the *Mayflower* in 1620."

Barney grinned. "If you think *I* was a prodigal, you'll have to hear about *him*. He fought duels with a sword, was a spy. But he got saved and became a great preacher."

"He sounds very romantic, Barney."

"Oh, all Winslow men are incurably romantic!" he said. "Let me prove it!"

A few moments passed, and then he laughed. "You see?"

Katie's eyes mirrored the happiness bursting within her. "A new century, and the House of Winslow will be a part of it! I want to have ten children and live to see all of them grow up to become preachers!"

"Whoa!" Barney cried. "One step at a time! But God's brought the Winslows through the last two hundred years, so I expect He'll have some use for us—whatever happens!"

The stars twinkled through the window as the prodigal and his love held each other. Soon the sun would lift itself in the east and shine on the first day of the new century, and the new century would begin.